SWORD OF CALEDOR

A TYRION & TECLIS NOVEL

More William King from Black Library

• TYRION & TECLIS •

Book 1: BLOOD OF AENARION
Book 2: SWORD OF CALEDOR
Book 3: BANE OF MALEKITH (December 2013)

• GOTREK & FELIX •

GOTREK & FELIX: THE FIRST OMNIBUS
(Contains books 1-3 in the series: *Trollslayer,
Skavenslayer* and *Daemonslayer*)

GOTREK & FELIX: THE SECOND OMNIBUS
(Contains books 4-6 in the series: *Dragonslayer,
Beastslayer* and *Vampireslayer*)

GOTREK & FELIX: THE THIRD OMNIBUS
With Nathan Long
(Contains books 7-9 in the series: *Giantslayer,
Orcslayer* and *Manslayer*)

• SPACE WOLF •

SPACE WOLF: THE FIRST OMNIBUS
(Contains books 1-3 in the series: *Space Wolf,
Ragnar's Claw* and *Grey Hunter*)

SPACE WOLF: THE SECOND OMNIBUS
With Lee Lightner
(Contains books 4-6 in the series: *Wolfblade,
Sons of Fenris* and *Wolf's Honour*)

• THE MACHARIAN CRUSADE •

Book 1: ANGEL OF FIRE
Book 2: FIST OF DEMETRIUS (May 2013)
Book 3: FALL OF MACHARIUS (2014)

More High Elf action from Black Library

• TIME OF LEGENDS •

By Gav Thorpe

THE SUNDERING
(Contains the novels *Malekith, Shadow King*
and *Caledor*)

AENARION
A Time of Legends audio drama

A WARHAMMER NOVEL

SWORD OF CALEDOR

A TYRION & TECLIS NOVEL

WILLIAM KING

BLACK LIBRARY

For my sons, Daniel and William.

A BLACK LIBRARY PUBLICATION
First published in Great Britain in 2012 by
Black Library,
Games Workshop Ltd.,
Willow Road,
Nottingham,
NG7 2WS, UK

10 9 8 7 6 5 4 3 2 1

Cover illustration by Raymond Swanland.
Icon by Nuala Kennedy.

A CIP record for this book
is available from the British Library.

UK ISBN 13: 978 1 84970 261 4
US ISBN 13: 978 1 84970 262 1

See Black Library on the internet at
www.blacklibrary.com

Find out more about Games Workshop
and the world of Warhammer at
www.games-workshop.com

Printed and bound by CPI Group (UK) Ltd, Croydon, CR0 4YY.

THIS IS A dark age, a bloody age, an age of daemons and of sorcery. It is an age of battle and death, and of the world's ending. Amidst all of the fire, flame and fury it is a time, too, of mighty heroes, of bold deeds and great courage.

THESE ARE BLEAK times. Across the length and breadth of the Old World, from the heartlands of the human Empire and the knightly palaces of Bretonnia to ice-bound Kislev in the far north, come rumblings of war. In the towering Worlds Edge Mountains, the orc tribes are gathering for another assault. Bandits and renegades harry the wild southern lands of the Border Princes. There are rumours of rat-things, the skaven, emerging from the sewers and swamps across the land. And from the northern wildernesses there is the ever-present threat of Chaos, of daemons and beastmen corrupted by the foul powers of the Dark Gods.

AN ANCIENT AND proud race, the high elves hail from Ulthuan, a mystical island of rolling plains, rugged mountains and glittering cities. Ruled over by the noble Phoenix King, Finubar, and the Everqueen, Alarielle, Ulthuan is a land steeped in magic, renowned for its mages and fraught with blighted history. Great seafarers, artisans and warriors, the high elves protect their ancestral homeland from enemies near and far. None more so than from their wicked kin, the dark elves, against whom they are locked in a bitter war that has lasted for centuries.

PROLOGUE

MORATHI, QUEEN OF the elves of Naggaroth, watched the tidal wave of flesh thunder towards her. Hundreds of thousands of feral warriors emerged out of the grim, grey wasteland, mounted on horses, drawn on chariots, carried by monsters, borne by their own booted feet. Enormous plumes of contaminated dust rose in their wake. Savage, sinister chants boomed out, audible even over the thunder of hooves and the turning of iron-bound wheels.

The onrushing horde bore the marks of Chaos on their skin: the stigmata of mutation, the tattooed runes of evil magic. The banners of the Dark Gods fluttered in the chill wind that blew out from the uttermost north.

Morathi moistened her lips with her tongue. Her spell of far-seeing allowed her to make out the smallest details if she focussed on them: the rings that pierced warped flesh, the blood that caked the spikes of black armour, the unholy fanaticism that glittered in every eye.

How many times had she seen their like before, she wondered?

How often had she encountered the followers of the Dark Gods since that first time more than six thousand years before? Her own legion trembled. They feared for their lives and rightly so. Compared to these deadly newcomers they were a flock of lambs in the path of a pack of wolves.

She strode to the front of her force and stood beneath her unfurled banner. She raised one delicate and lovely fist in the air. Her musicians struck up. Trumpets sounded. Braziers were lit. Narcotic incense drifted on the wind.

Her followers slowly deployed in the cold desert, a carnival procession in the midst of a slag-strewn wasteland. There were thousands of them, selected for their beauty and their erotic skills and their ability to endure the caresses of even the most repellent with a smile. Hers was not an army that could conquer anyone in battle nor was it expected to. Her son had legions of warriors who could kill and slaughter. This army would triumph in another way.

It was just as well she was not expecting these pampered pets to fight, she thought. Most of these beautiful girls and boys could not hold a blade properly. Their talents ran in other directions, just as hers did. The difference between her and them was that she could do battle if she needed to and would if the necessity arose.

She had fought beside Aenarion in the days of her youth, killing daemons, slaughtering the enemies of her people with wild abandon. She had cast spells and brewed poisons and worked out battle strategies for his armies. She had used her gift of visions to grant the elves victories innumerable.

The so-called high elves had forgotten that now, preferring to cast her as the villain in the simple-minded morality plays they so enjoyed since her son had sundered the realm. They had no idea what it had cost to win those battles back when all thought the world was ending, or the price she had paid for victory.

Still, she felt no need to crow about those millennia-gone triumphs. She preferred to live in the moment. All across the world, she was known, feared and desired. Her reach was long, longer even than her son's and quite as strong in its way.

Malekith would learn to appreciate her again. He always did. At the moment, he was going through one of his independent phases, but he would learn soon enough that his followers were unreliable. At the end of the day, they were elven nobles and one of the things that made them so was the secret belief that they owed allegiance to none but themselves, and that no one was better or cleverer or stronger than they.

It was ironic. Out of the whole self-satisfied race, only one really had been so unique, and Aenarion had not needed to prove it or boast about it. He had been respected, loved and feared as their son tried so hard to be and never would.

Poor Aenarion. He would have been more than seven thousand years old today if he had lived, but he had turned down the immortality she had offered him to walk his own fatal path. It was one of those things that had made her hate him as well as love him.

She glanced at the dreary land around her once again and the huge army of deformed barbarians moving towards her. She would need to act soon but she felt a strange lassitude. She let her thoughts drift back to her first husband. She could still picture him all too easily, tall and mighty, with his strange, sad eyes and that terrible blade glowing on his hip.

Better to be ashes than dust he always said, and yet in the end there had been no hero's pyre for him. He had walked into the fire and it had rejected him. Now his bones were dust that mingled with that of the millions his sword had killed. No one even knew where he had fallen in the end. She had looked many times and she had never found him.

They said that Tethlis the Slayer had found his broken armour but there had been nothing in it. She could not believe that he had rotted away. She did not like to think about it either. She preferred to remember him as he had been, brutal and beautiful and burning like the sun. There had never been another elf like him and she did not know whether that made her sad or grateful.

Poor Malekith, she thought. Her son had tried so hard to be like his lost father but he had never managed it. Malekith had his own cold genius, and he could make himself feared but never loved. He was stronger in some ways than Aenarion and certainly cleverer, but he lacked the fire that had made Aenarion what he was. He built empires as monuments to his desire to impress his absent father, a goal that defeated him even when he succeeded.

Aenarion was not there to be impressed and his achievements could not be matched. Malekith did not even understand why. Aenarion was safely dead. The elves could project onto him their own idealised image of themselves and there was no awkward living being to contradict them with his inconvenient goals and desires.

She sometimes wondered whether that was his appeal to her too. Their love, if love it had been, had not had time to grow stale, for her to learn to hate and despise him. She pushed that thought aside, not wanting to consider it.

No, Aenarion was the one the elves would always remember, their first Phoenix King, the warrior demigod who had saved them from certain doom.

Except, of course, that he had not.

He won every battle and yet he would still have lost that ancient war, had it not been for his so-called friend, the Archmage Caledor Dragontamer. Caledor had been the architect of the spell that had finally driven the daemons away and stabilised Ulthuan, keeping its quake-ravaged lands from sinking below the sea.

The elves choose to remember only the great battle and the heroism of Aenarion as he fought to protect you during those final hours, but it was you that saved the world, wasn't it Caledor? You built the spell that drained magic from the world and sent the daemons back to hell.

The Chaos army had noticed her now, as she had intended that they do. Even at this range, she could hear the bellowed threats and promises. They were so lacking in originality that she could not even muster any contempt. The worshippers of the Dark Gods were ultimately so banal that she struggled to keep her attention focused.

It seemed to be a day to remember ancient times so she gave in to the desire. She thought about Caledor. With his gaunt features, his high balding forehead so unusual in an elf, his eyes cold and blue as a glacier in the Mountains of Frost, the master wizard had been as memorable as Aenarion. Perhaps he would have been a better tool than Aenarion. But no – he was too cold to be manipulated and far too clever, and she could not have loved him as she had loved Aenarion. Caledor was no hero.

And yet in his calm, calculating way he had been as terrifyingly brave as her husband. In the end, he and his fellow archmages had laid down their lives to make their great spell work, knowing that it would bring them only death and worse. Their ghosts were trapped to this day, frozen in the eternal amber of the moment they had died by the power of the spell they had woven.

Are you out there now, old ghost? Can you see me? Do you understand what I do and do you shiver at the thought? For millennia you have woven and re-woven your ancient fraying spell, and for millennia I have tried to unravel it. The day is fast approaching when I will succeed and this world will change forever.

She felt her age sometimes. She had lived long enough to see the shape of continents change, to watch the great rivers of ice advance and retreat, grinding mountains down as they went. She had watched nations rise and fall. There had been times when she had given them a push. It kept her amused.

She was perhaps the oldest living being in the world. Only the gods were older and they did not dwell in this place as she did and were not bound to it as she was.

All of those around her were moving shadows, alive for a few flickering moments and then gone. How many were there now who remembered the days of ancient glory? Herself, her son, a few daemons and the mad ghosts who guarded creation from destruction and rebirth.

It was a shadow-play but it afforded her some entertainment as she waited for the end of the world. She still pursued her pleasures as relentlessly as her son pursued his dreams of empire.

It had all seemed so different when she was young. Then the world had been bright. The shadow of Chaos had not yet fallen on the land. The elves had been at peace. It had been disgustingly boring but she was too stupid and naive to know it.

Or at least she had been until the visions came.

They had been her gift from her eleventh year, tormenting her with glimpses of the apocalypse to come. She had seen the dark, daemon-haunted future and no one had believed her. She was a prophetess whose gift it was to see and yet not be heard. Or so it had seemed back then.

The elves had not believed her visions of destruction because they could not believe her. Their lives had been so sheltered during the long golden reign of the first Everqueen that they had no idea of just how dreadful the world could be.

She had told them and they had not listened, simply because they were incapable of understanding. They were cattle grazing in summer fields, unwilling to believe in slaughterhouses because they had not yet been inside of one. The sun was shining, the grass was tender, and their alien masters looked after them and fed them well.

Long before the other elves had learned what the world was really like, she had known. She had seen the coming bloodbath and she had tried to warn them.

And no one had believed her.

Sometimes that thought could still outrage her. Mostly now it just amused her.

She had tried everything to get their attention. She had prophesied, she had seduced, she had used her great beauty to get the attention of princes, of the Everqueen herself. No one had taken her warnings seriously, because they had not wanted to. Their world was golden and it was ending and they had wilfully blinded themselves to its coming destruction. They had been taken by surprise when the daemons of Chaos came and the Old Ones had fled or been destroyed.

None of the people who had refused to believe her were alive now and she was. She would live forever and she would remake this world in her own image. The day would soon be here when she was a goddess and these barbarians would help her bring that dawn.

The huge metallic arm of a daemon-forged siege engine sent an enormous boulder arcing towards her. The rock hit the ground a hundred strides ahead of where she stood, bounced forward and came to rest not too far from her feet. It was close enough so that she could see the cursed runes scratched on it. Behind her, her legion moaned with anticipatory terror. She knew they only stood their ground because she did.

They were among those who worshipped her and adored her as something like divine. But that was not what she wanted. She did not wish merely for the empty gratification of her ego, although she enjoyed it. She desired the real, actual power of a god and she knew how to get it. All she had to do was destroy Caledor's masterwork, the Vortex.

Her visions had shown her that too. In the beginning, the knowledge had horrified her. She had thought that daemons sent them. She thought what she saw was evil beyond imagining, but over the long lonely years she had come to see the power of the daemons as well as their horror. She had realised that they too could be manipulated and used and bound to her will.

Knowing the end was coming, she had prepared for it. She had sought out all manner of forbidden knowledge. She had made pacts with the enemies of her people while the sun still shone and the invasion was merely the tiniest cloud on the horizon. If her folk would not help themselves, the best she could do was ensure her own survival.

It was strange how in all of those tormenting visions she had never seen Aenarion. Perhaps if she had, things might have been different. She might have been different. But she had already walked a long way down a dark road when she met him and it was far too late to turn back, even if she had really wanted to.

He was famous then and mighty beyond all others, a grim, mortal god with haunted eyes. He had believed in her visions too. It was easy then, for they had all come true. And oddest of all, he had not wanted her. He did not abase himself before her beauty. He looked at her and saw just another elf woman.

His indifference had been a gauntlet thrown in her face, a challenge she could not back away from. She had set herself to win him, to woo him from his grief, to bring him over to her cause. And the oddest alchemy of all had been the trick fate had played on her. In pretending love, she had discovered the real thing. In trying to snare him, she had snared only herself.

She laughed at the irony of it. The sweet malice of her voice attracted the attention of her followers. She smiled at them, enjoying the fact that they did not understand, taking pleasure in their pleasure at the sight of her. They thought she was laughing at the oncoming horde, and it heartened them.

She had won Aenarion over in the end, but he had never loved her as she loved him. He was not capable of it. His dead Everqueen and his lost children filled his heart with gall. He was too lost in his own black grief and his dark desire for revenge. It had consumed him in the end. It had threatened to consume the world.

The barbarians laughed now too at the sight of the force they thought opposed them. Their laughter was bright, mad and cruel and it sounded so like the mirth that echoed through the towers of Naggarond that it was chilling. These humans had much in common with the elves of Naggaroth. Their Dark Gods had taught them well.

Briefly she considered the fact that she might die here, that her visions might be wrong, that the lords of Chaos might for their own reasons have decided to stamp on her face and end her immortal existence.

Part of her would honestly have welcomed it. She was sometimes weary unto death of the ways of this world, and longed to see what might wait on the other side of death's dark doorway. Unfortunately, she had a good idea of what waited for her and those like her. In the endless night of the Realm of Chaos, the daemon lords lusted to devour the souls of her people. She would make a particularly tasty morsel for them, a soul fattened on millennia of sin. No, she was not keen to undergo that ultimate experience just yet.

She called for her mount. It was led to her by nervous grooms, a coal-black, burning-eyed hell-steed with enormous folded wings. Mist emerged from its nostrils, suggestive of the poisonous gas vented by the chasms of this unwelcoming place. It greeted her, eyes blazing with lust and hatred and a curious, twisted love. She stroked its cheek and it whinnied with pleasure from the spells woven into her hands. She vaulted onto its back and rode towards the Chaos horde, her mount becoming airborne after a dozen strides.

She heard her own followers gasp in wonder and fear. Perhaps they thought she was abandoning them to their fate and, for a moment, her malicious elven mind considered it, but she was too wise to do so merely to gratify a whim of the moment. Instead she soared above the oncoming tide of warriors, allowing them to view her half-naked form and luxuriate in the aura of unbridled, wanton lust that she projected. Ancient spells amplified the effects of her matchless beauty. All who looked on her groaned with desire.

She landed her steed defiantly in front of the chieftains of the horde, touching her heels to its flanks so that it reared and whinnied. A dozen brutal faces inspected her, a dozen muscular, mutated bodies stiffened with lust.

She paused for a moment to let them examine her as she

examined them. They were powerful but primitive and they were already responding, although they did not know it, to the ancient sorceries surrounding her. She smiled at them and they smiled back and licked their lips, and she knew that in that moment, she had them in the palm of her hand.

She dismounted, showing no fear, and strode towards them, and they waited expectantly to hear what she had to say, as they would have if a messenger from their Dark Gods had descended in their midst. It was a role she was perfectly suited to play. She carried herself with the imperiousness of one who had ruled for nearly seven millennia and who expected homage as her right.

She had much to offer them, and they to offer her, and she was sure that a pact could be made with them. She would divert them from their drift southward into the lands of Men and offer them a much more tempting prize, the island-continent of Ulthuan. Her son saw it as part of a plan to put him back on his rightful throne, which it was, but she had reasons of her own as well.

The end of time was coming. She would begin the unmaking of the world soon, as a necessary prelude to its reshaping. The time of her ascension was close. Soon the daemons would return and the time of mortals would be at an end. New gods would be born. She intended to make sure that she was one of them.

IN A COLD cavern chamber beneath his freezing winter citadel, hidden even from the eyes of his mother's sorcerous spies, Malekith the Great, Witch King of Naggaroth, prepared to perform the ritual that would make him master of first a continent and then the world. Frozen spikes of ice sheathed the stalactites surrounding him. Their cold gave him some relief from the divine fires that burned eternally and agonisingly within his flesh.

The whimpering of terrified virgin slaves did not disturb him any more than the icy chill. He had long ago ceased to let trivial things interfere with his concentration. He was about to seize control of the destiny of millions and he would not allow himself to be distracted by the mewling of the worthless. By casting one monstrous spell and binding one dreadful being to his will, he would alter the fate of kingdoms.

A girl looked at him. Tears ran down her face. She was frightened and alone. Malekith knew that the appearance of his gigantic metal-sheathed figure terrified her. He spoke a spell of calming and the fear disappeared to be replaced by a numb smile.

Malekith felt no sympathy but he had no desire to be needlessly cruel either. He was not like his mother or those of his drugged, deranged, self-indulgent subjects who feasted on the pain of others. He was merely doing what was needed to ensure that right prevailed. He would take the throne of Ulthuan in accordance with his father's command and his own desires.

He raised one huge armoured hand before his face and studied it through the visor of his helmet. Hotek, that renegade priest of Vaul, had done his blasphemous work well. The ancient runes inscribed millennia ago in the aftermath of his greatest failure glowed with power. Caledor Dragontamer's jealous disciple had forged this armour in the wake of Malekith's attempt to pass through the Flame of Asuryan. Malekith had ordered him to wield the hammer despite the agony that had almost crippled him with every blow. It had kept him alive ever since.

He told himself he barely felt the pain any more. It was merely the reality in which he lived, as water was to a shark. There had been a time when his scorched flesh had both pained and humiliated him, a badge of the rejection of the gods who had refused to acknowledge him as great as his father, a symbol of his failure and weakness. Over the centuries the fire in his flesh had burned down and his own control had grown greater.

Even during the worst of times he had not let it stop him. He had learned from his mistakes. He had emerged from the period of agony and despair stronger than ever. The armour had hidden his scorched flesh from the view of his enemies and made him more potent than any living being before or since.

Before you can rule others, you must first rule yourself. That was the maxim he lived by.

He had lived for millennia and every passing year had added to his power and to his knowledge. He had studied his mother's secret grimoires until he was more proficient in sorcery than she. He had outlived the generals who had defeated him in the long gone ages of the world.

As ruthless with himself as with his subjects, he had learned from his errors and drawn strength from his mistakes. No one would ever or had ever beaten him the same way twice. He was still here when his ancient opponents were in their graves. Despite the pain, despite the losses, despite a black despair that would have driven lesser beings to seek eternal oblivion, he endured.

He had toppled kingdoms and reshaped the world. He had lived longer and done more than his father, Aenarion, ever had. He would yet re-unify the kingdom that the treachery of his enemies had denied him. One day soon, all elves would bend the knee before him and acknowledge the righteousness of his rule. Then he would lead them into a new age of glory. They would subjugate the kingdoms of men and throw back the powers of Chaos and a new golden age would begin. All of them would see that they had been wrong.

And it started now.

Glory would be purchased by the suffering of these few slaves. They ought to be grateful to him. Without him they would have lived out their meaningless, insect lives. At the cost of a few of the years that would have swiftly passed anyway, they were being allowed to participate in the creation of a new world order. He pushed the thoughts away. They smacked of needless self-justification, of moral weakness. He was who he was. What he did was right. He need justify himself to no one.

He studied his handiwork with some satisfaction. He had carved the altar to the ritual specifications with his own hands. For six years he had sanctified it with blood and souls. He had forged the black iron sacrificial knife, tempering the blade by passing it through the body of a still living hero six times. He had inscribed the symbols of Slaanesh and his six favoured princes over the period of six moons.

He had prepared the chains from an alloy of truesilver and black iron and inscribed them with runes older than the world. At their centre was a gem so potently ensorcelled that it could entrap the soul of a daemon prince. The finding of that gem and the binding spells it contained was an epic in itself which would one day be recounted across his empire.

Everything was ready. It was time to begin.

He spoke the words he had memorised from the great grimoire and gestured for the first of the slaves to advance to the altar. She tried to refuse but his will bound her to obey. Slowly, one step at a time, as if pulled by overwhelming magnetic force, she advanced up the basalt steps and bowed her head before the altar.

A slash of the knife opened her jugular. Blood spurted into the font. He threw the flopping carcass to one side and summoned the next with a gesture of his armoured hands. The whimpering went on but his will was strong. He would allow himself no weakness. One by one he sent their souls out into the void through the gap in reality his spell had created. They were his messengers to the dreadful being he intended to summon. Their very presence was part of the message.

As the ritual built to its climax, his words took on a strange sibilant resonance, as if they echoed through unseen chasms in the unhallowed places beyond. Somewhere far off, in a darkness so deep it could swallow worlds, something responded.

IN A PLACE that was not a place, in a time that lay outside time, N'Kari, Keeper of Secrets, great among daemons, felt the faint irritating tug of a summoning spell.

At first he ignored it. That a being should be foolish enough to draw his attention piqued his curiosity, but not very much. The

realms of mortals were full of those who sought to barter their
puny souls for the benefits they thought daemons could provide.
Sometimes, when he was bored, N'Kari allowed himself to be called
and then destroyed those who sought to bend him to their will.
Sometimes he granted their wishes and allowed them to destroy
themselves, just so he could have the amusement of watching.

There was something about the being making this summons
though – something that nagged at N'Kari's vast store of memories
and set them to swirling, the way a scent of some half-remembered
perfume makes an old rake remember the fleshpots of his youth.

Yes, something familiar indeed.

In this place that was not a place, in this time that was not a
time, N'Kari's mind worked in a different way than it would have
had he been bound to the chronal flow of mortal reality. He
remembered many things simultaneously, sometimes as vividly as
if he were actually experiencing them, sometimes as if they were
as remote as the birth of the universe. This summons triggered a
fugue of memories and images.

It reminded him of the mortal god Aenarion, and his descendants whom N'Kari had once tried so hard to kill. And there was
about it a faint, frightening taint of the Flame of Asuryan, the god-
thing that was numbered among N'Kari's greatest enemies.

N'Kari was curious now as he suspected he was intended to be.

More virgin souls were offered up to him, slain in exactly the
correct ritual manner to please him. It was nice that the proprieties
were being observed. Languidly, he extended a tentacle of thought
towards the gap in reality from which the summons had come. He
forced a small portion of his mighty essence through the portal,
and allowed it to take shape according to the whims and expecta-
tions of the summoner.

In that moment, mortal reality crashed in on him. He found
himself trapped within a sorcerer's circle in the dank underground
depths beneath some cold northern castle. An armoured figure as
monstrous as any daemon loomed before him.

He was pleased. This was going to prove more interesting than he had anticipated.

SLOWLY A SHAPE arose out of the pool of blood in the font of the altar. It was a beautiful woman made of congealed red plasma, snakes of hair swirling from her impossibly lovely head. She beckoned at Malekith in a lascivious, enticing way. Her hips swayed sinuously in a way that promised great pleasure.

The Witch King was not even tempted. The wards on his armour neutralised the potent spells of intoxication. His destroyed olfactory nerves were insensitive to the narcotic musk. Seeing that this strategy was not working, the daemon changed tactics and shape, becoming something monstrous and four-armed and clawed. The blood congealed and hardened into a glistening carapace. The hands extended into talons and claws. The skull became horse-like, the teeth great tusks and fangs.

This was more like its true shape, Malekith thought, if a greater daemon could be said to have any such thing.

'N'Kari, I name you and bind you,' Malekith said. He spoke the ancient words of the ritual. The daemon resisted them. It was enormously strong, far more powerful than anything he had ever bound before. For a moment, and a moment only, the possibility that he might have encountered something too powerful for even his mighty will to dominate entered Malekith's mind.

'It is not so simple, little mortal,' said the daemon in a voice at once beautiful and terrifying. 'I am no mere daemonling to be bound by a passing sorcerer.'

'And I am no mere mage, hell-spawn. I am Aenarion's heir and Witch King. And you will do my bidding.' The air between them crackled with the force of their conflict

'Aenarion. That is a name you should not have mentioned,' N'Kari said. 'You shall pay for your presumption.'

'I know you hate him and all his descendants, but I have summoned you to offer you a chance of vengeance.'

The daemon paused for a moment. 'Revenge I shall have. Starting with you.'

'That is not possible,' said Malekith, not letting any of the strain that he felt show in his voice. 'But I will let you drink the blood of those who humiliated you a century ago. I will let you have all of the others who claim descent from Aenarion.'

'I can take my own vengeance,' said N'Kari.

'No, you cannot,' said Malekith. 'I have wound you round with spells that prevent you from returning whence you came. And while this avatar is trapped here, you cannot bring another into this world. I can keep you here until the end of time if I so desire and vengeance will never be yours.'

The daemon raged against the ever-tightening web of spells constraining it but they held. N'Kari was trapped within. His appearance changed again, becoming that of a seductive female elf. Its voice was the very essence of reasonableness.

'State your terms,' it said.

N'KARI CONSIDERED THE Witch King. As mortals went, he was impressive. His massive armoured figure radiated power and not unjustified confidence. The spells he had woven were well-constructed, a trap that it might take N'Kari millennia to escape from.

He had already spent too much time in this pathetic place bound into the Vortex. In mortal form, ennui would press as heavily on him as any other resident of this time and space. He felt sure that he could free himself eventually, but it might be easier to appear to give the mortal what he wanted. He was also sure that, in the long run, he would find a way to turn the tables on the arrogant fool. He always did.

'State your terms,' N'Kari said. The Witch King laughed triumphantly. *Laugh away little mortal*, N'Kari thought. *I will have the last laugh.*

'Extend your arm,' said the Witch King. N'Kari complied. Perhaps his foe would be foolish enough to break the magic circle binding him… Bracelets and chains snapped into place. The most powerful binding spell N'Kari had ever experienced snapped into place with them.

'Now you truly are my servant,' said Malekith, unable to keep the satisfaction from his voice.

N'Kari wanted to howl with rage, but the spells binding him would not even allow him that.

THE DARK ELF assassin known as Urian Poisonblade and Prince Iltharis and dozens of other names looked across the carved table at the beautiful woman he was going to kill and smiled. She smiled back. Her glance moved from the table to the sleeping silks that filled the remainder of this small intimate tent. Outside throngs moved through the tent city that was the capital of the Everqueen. Inside spells kept all noise at bay. They could have been alone in the wild woods of Avelorn and not surrounded by her subjects.

It was a pity, he thought. She really was lovely and he liked her, and none of that emotion was caused by the aura of compulsive magic that surrounded her. It could not be. Centuries ago the Witch King of Naggaroth had wound him round with spells that made him immune to such sorceries.

As with Morathi, the Everqueen had great natural beauty and great natural charm and these were only amplified and enhanced by her magic, not a product of them. She was every bit as good-natured as she seemed and she looked genuinely interested in him as a person. Unlike some mighty personages he had encountered, she was not just acting the part.

If it had been up to him she could have lived out her natural span of days in peace. But, as always, it was not his decision, it was the Witch King's. He felt sure that he was only one small link in a very long chain of plans and conspiracies his master had woven.

Urian was only Malekith's tool in this matter as he was in so many others. Malekith had made him, had raised him up and could knock him down again. And if the woman sitting opposite him had been aware of his true history she would be calling for her guards right now.

Briefly he wondered why the Witch King was having the Everqueen killed now. She would simply be replaced by her daughter who was kept in a secure place far distant from the court, like all of an Everqueen's daughters. The elves had learned long ago from the loss of Aenarion's children by the first Everqueen. Never again would their royal family be assembled in one place, able to be killed in one fell swoop, or saved only by an accident so unlikely it smacked of divine intervention.

Doubtless timing had something to do with it. Or perhaps Malekith had found the Everqueen's daughter and other assassins were even now at work…

'You look very thoughtful, Prince Iltharis,' the Everqueen said, reaching out to touch his hand in a most intimate manner. 'Are you contemplating some deep matter of ancient history once again?'

Urian smiled. She thought of him only as a scholar and a formidable duellist, one of the many glittering talents who visited her court. He had made his reputation as a student of the history of the line of Aenarion, to which she was not the least ornament. It was a cover story that he had actually enjoyed living and which he was going to miss once he had shucked it off. That was assuming he was still alive after this evening, which was not exactly a certainty.

'As a matter of fact, I was, your serenity,' he said. It was true in a way too. The grudge Malekith bore against the Everqueen was a very ancient one. They were of the same family, and she had what Malekith had always desired, the love and respect of the elves of Ulthuan. It was as much for this as for political and strategic reasons she had to die. The envy and malice of his master were boundless when aroused, as Urian had more cause than almost anyone to understand.

'It is ever the problem with true scholars that they are so easily distracted. You were telling me of the time when you worked out the plans of the daemon N'Kari, who planned to exterminate all of the line of Aenarion, including myself, a century ago.'

'Mine was only a minor contribution. I saw the pattern in the apparently random destruction it had wrought, but it was mostly luck. I had talked with many of those who it killed, as part of my researches.'

'You are too modest, Prince Iltharis.'

'Alas, that is not something I have ever been much accused of your serenity. I doubt even my worst enemy would say that of me.'

She laughed, a silvery sound. He enjoyed it, as he always had. His pleasure was given a certain piquancy by the fact that he knew he would never hear the sound again after this evening.

'And how is your new work coming?' she asked.

'Slowly, as these things always do. I have a great deal of research to go through before I even commit pen to vellum. That is why I am here. To consult the scholars of your court.' He stroked her hand in return. 'As well as to enjoy the boon of your company, of course.'

Urian lived his cover to the fullest, even though he knew he would not have any use for it much longer. Several centuries of deception were coming to an end. He was almost sorry. Soon he would be leaving Ulthuan forever and returning in secret triumph to Naggaroth to claim the rewards of his long covert service to Malekith's interests.

It was strange – he was more at home now in the land of his enemies than he was in his ancestral home. He wondered what it would be like to go back to his estates finally and forever. Never to have to look upon this place again.

He knew he should be filled with nothing but contempt for the high elves, but he was not. He had found a great deal to respect in Ulthuan and over the long years, a great deal he would miss. Still his life was not his own. It never really had been since he entered Malekith's service. The Witch King had taken a pit fighter from an impoverished ancient line and made him into the deadliest assassin in the world. He really ought to be grateful for that, but he wasn't any more.

He leaned forward to pour more wine. As he did so, he allowed the powder he had palmed to drop from his hand. It was dragon-spike, a poison inevitably fatal to mages, its effects stronger the more magical power they possessed, and the Everqueen had a very great deal indeed. He would soon find out if the poison were potent enough to kill an avatar of godhead. According to legend it was, but legends were notoriously unreliable.

It would slow her breathing and destroy her nerves and stop her heart. It could be found only in the forbidden jungles of the lost continent of Lustria, and it had no effect whatsoever on those not possessed of magical power. Urian sipped his own wine. The taste was not in the slightest impaired.

The Everqueen's hand hovered over her own goblet. He wondered for a moment whether she had seen him, whether she suspected what was happening here. Part of him rather hoped that she did. He was surprised by that. He was not usually sympathetic to his victims. He kept the smile pinned to his face and waited to see what she would do.

She raised her glass to him, and then put it to her lips. 'Your health, Prince Iltharis. May you live a thousand years.'

'And you, your serenity.' The queen drank. Her eyes widened. The glass dropped from her hands.

Urian rose from the cushions on which he rested and shouted with genuine concern. 'Come quickly. Her serenity has been taken ill.'

Urian was possessed by a sudden sense that a war that would shatter the world had just begun and that he had played a vital part in starting it.

CHAPTER ONE

Tyrion sprang to one side as the stegadon erupted from the undergrowth. It was reptilian, far bigger than an elephant, with a parrot-like beak large enough to snap an elf in two. Horns long as lances protruded from the huge shield-like crest protecting its head. The thing was massive, even by the overgrown standards of wildlife in the sweltering Lustrian jungles.

It felt like facing an angry dragon. He heard bones snap and flesh pulp as one of the human porters was crushed under the stegadon's foreleg. The rest of the expedition scattered in panic, hoping to find safety in flight.

Tyrion knew he was very close to death. The hot, humid air carried the acrid, lizard stench of the beast. The ground vibrated beneath its monstrous tread. It bellowed deafeningly and it felt as if the wave of sound alone might knock him off his feet.

He drew his sword, feeling faintly ridiculous. Trying to tackle this huge creature with such a weapon was like trying to fight a bull with a pin. He could not win this battle on his own. He needed help.

'Hold your ground, men!' Tyrion shouted to the humans. 'Stand steady! Don't flee! If you get lost in the jungle, you will die!'

There was something about his voice that commanded obedience even in the most fearful. There always had been. Over the past century he had bestrode hundreds of battlefields and always inspired courage and respect in those around him. It was no different now.

Most of the warriors, the majority of them Norsemen from Skeggi, paused in their flight and drew their weapons. They considered cowardice a great shame. All it had taken was Tyrion standing his ground to remind them of their own honour. The huge blond warriors would not flee when a lone elf refused to.

The porters were less brave, being only thralls to the Norse. They were not looking for a heroic death. Even they wavered though.

Only Leiber, their guide, a shipwrecked sailor from the Old World, looked calm, and he was seeking cover in the trees above. Sensible man, Tyrion thought.

Tyrion's shout drew the attention of the beast. Its head swivelled to inspect the small creature that had the temerity to defy it. Its beady eyes glared at him with ferocious hatred. Its huge razor-edged beak snapped open and it lunged towards him with a speed that was utterly unexpected in a creature so huge.

Tyrion threw himself forward, rolling under the creature's front legs, passing through their mighty arch and coming out on the creature's side.

As soon as he did it he knew that he had made a mistake. His twin brother Teclis had been standing behind him. He now became the focus of the creature's attention, the target of its attack.

Although he was no longer a sickly cripple, Teclis did not share Tyrion's speed and strength. He could not get himself out of the way of the charging beast before it closed the distance between them. Instead he spread his arms wide, chanting ancient words and making mystical gestures. He was trying to cast a spell, but there would not be enough time for him to work his magic before the creature was upon him. Tyrion needed to get the stegadon's attention now if his brother was going to live.

He lashed out with his sword, aiming for the weak point where the leg joined the torso. The skin there was soft, not covered in armoured scales like the rest of the beast's body. Flesh parted and muscle gave way slightly. The beast let out a deafening pain-filled roar. Tyrion barely managed to get himself out of the way as the columnar leg swung his way.

The Norsemen had taken up their spears and axes and joined the fray. Hagar, a large maniac with a bristling red beard, threw himself at the monster, chanting the names of the old gods of the Norse. His axe smashed into the creature's beak, chipping part of it and drawing blood.

The stegadon turned on Hagar, jaws snapping shut around his torso, beak cleaving through his flesh. His shield buckled under the pressure. Bones cracked as Hagar's ribcage gave way. The man gave a final defiant roar that was transformed into an agonised death scream as his body was snapped in two.

Watching their friend die gave the rest of the Norsemen pause. The beast raced towards them, a loud hiss escaping from its nostrils. Its beak was painted red with Hagar's blood but its lust for death was not slaked. In an instant, many more of the Norsemen died beneath its clawed feet. Tyrion winced. They had lost more men and they were no closer to their goal. It seemed like this expedition was doomed.

A sweep of the stegadon's gigantic head tossed another Norseman high into the air. He crashed through the branches above him and returned to earth, falling face-down in the mulch of the jungle floor. His body writhed for a few seconds, his bones broken by the impact, and then turned to jelly as the beast trampled him.

That was too much for the thralls. They raced off into the surrounding forest. At least one of them encountered some other terror, for an agonised scream rang out. Tyrion had no idea what might have killed him – the jungle was so full of perils that it could have been almost anything: some giant man-eating plant, a huge vampire bat, a sabretooth jaguar as large as a horse. He had seen all of these things on his recent travels.

One or two of the humans had taken refuge in the branches of the trees. This gave Tyrion an idea. He clambered into the bole of one monstrous plant, reached up and grabbed a vine, then swung himself out over the monster, dropping onto its back. So enraged was the giant brute that it barely noticed this presence. He ran along its spine, thinking that he would cut the vertebrae in the neck.

As he reached the bone shield, he caught sight of Teclis out of the corner of his eye. An aura of flame surrounded his brother. He made a gesture and a jet of fire blasted towards the creature. The pyrotechnic wave expanded to fill Tyrion's field of vision.

The stegadon let out a screech of fear and pain. Tyrion ducked down behind the bone shield to get out of the way of the fiery blast. Even so he felt its scorching heat. The vines dangling from the trees above withered and died. The monstrous brute reared on its hind legs. The bone shield swung backwards and it seemed like it might come down and crush him against the flesh of the monster's back.

Tyrion let go, dropping to the ground. He tried to scramble clear but his booted foot slipped in the bloody mess of one of the human corpses. He fell sprawling as the maddened dinosaur reared and roared and whirled around, threatening to trample him underfoot.

Tyrion half-crawled, half-sprang out of harm's way. The beast crashed into a nearby tree, sending some of the hiding humans tumbling to the ground and to death beneath its paws. The tree broke in the middle and fell into the inferno that Teclis had conjured. Sap bubbled and burst into flames as its moist interior was exposed to the fire. The explosive firecracker sounds panicked the giant reptile even more.

The monster turned and glared at Tyrion. He was directly in the path of the creature's escape. For a moment he met its gaze and he saw the fury there. The creature pawed the ground like an angry bull preparing to charge. There was no way he could get out of its path in time. He had seen how fast the creature moved. The stegadon lowered its head and raced straight at him, an enormous engine of living death.

Tyrion smiled and stood unmoving, making himself the easiest target possible. The creature came straight at him, covering the ground with appalling speed. At the last possible moment Tyrion sprang, vaulting onto its long snout, stabbing it in the left eye with his sword, before leaping over the great bone shield that protected its neck, landing on its back, slashing the vertebrae and then rolling clear.

It did not fall to the ground as he had expected. It kept moving as if unaware that the connection between its brain and its body had been severed. He recalled something that Teclis had once told him – that according to natural philosophers these monstrous creatures had several brains, and they did not die easily.

This creature certainly seemed to be living proof of that. It kept moving, and he thought that for one horrible moment all he had succeeded in doing was attracting its attention and providing a focus for its anger. But this was not the case. Bleeding heavily from its wounds, its flesh scorched by Teclis's magic, the great beast blundered off into the woods, trying to escape the flames and the source of its agony, bellowing its rage and pain to the heavens.

Tyrion stood up, half expecting the creature to return. Teclis moved over to where he stood. 'Are you all right?' his brother asked.

'Never better,' Tyrion responded. 'But I don't think some of the people with us feel quite so good.'

Tyrion looked around: a score of the humans lay dead on the ground, some of them reduced to a bloody pulp, many of them whimpering in agony as they died. He was not sure it was a good idea to shout out to draw the attention of any of the survivors because it might also draw the attention of the great beast back to them.

On the other hand, he could not see what else to do; if he waited too long then all of the people with them would get lost in the woods and separated forever. They still had need of their porters and guides if they were to achieve the goal they had set out with when they started this expedition into the green hell of the Lustrian jungle.

In the end they only managed to find a few humans alive and capable of following them. Fortunately one of those was their guide, Leiber, the one man who claimed to know where the lost city of Zultec lay. They divided the remains of their supplies between them and then wearily trudged on, deeper into the deadly jungle.

GIANT PLANTS BLOCKED out the light. The air stank of perfume and rot. Brightly coloured birds shrieked amid the boles of the huge trees. Small scuttling things moved through the carpet of mulched plant life on the forest floor. The heat was sweltering. In the distance something huge and reptilian crashed through the undergrowth. Tyrion thought of the stegadon and slowed his pace accordingly. Reduced in numbers as their party was, it would be better to go around than encounter another of those great bad-tempered beasts.

He pushed an enormous cloying leaf to one side. It stuck to his skin. When he pulled his hand away from its sticky surface faint drops of red clung to his fingers. They were already disappearing from the surface of the leaf. He knew then that if he took his blade to the plant, blood would mingle with the gushing sap. Even the plants here were vampiric. Everything seemed to live to eat anything else that came within its grasp.

He glanced enviously at his twin. A faint aura of silvery light surrounded Teclis. He looked as cool as if he were out for a stroll along a windswept beach in Cothique during a day in early spring. His spells protected him from the heat and the jungle's claws.

Despite all the hardships they had encountered, Teclis looked confident and at ease. Over the past century, magic had filled out his scrawny form and removed the worst effects of the wasting ailments that had crippled him in childhood. The potions he mixed for himself kept him healthy and active. He would never be as tall or as muscular as Tyrion, but now he could go for leagues through the tropical heat and endure hardships that would have killed him only a century ago. The only sign of his many debilitating childhood illnesses was the faint limp with which he now walked and which no amount of alchemy seemed able to get rid of.

At this moment Tyrion very much envied his brother's magecraft. He was sweating heavily even though he had stripped off everything except the undergarments he needed to keep his light mail armour from chafing. His face and clothes were dirty and torn although not as much so as their human guide's.

Leiber looked like a lunatic: tall, emaciated, with madness glittering in his bright blue eyes. His long hair was thinning on top and drawn back in a dirty blond ponytail at the back. A moustache that reminded Tyrion of a rat's whiskers drooped down past his chin and gave his whole face a mournful air of defeat.

Leiber was originally from the Old World, a shipwrecked sailor from the human city of Marienburg, but he had spent much of his life looking for gold and treasure amid the ruins of the slann cities of the Lustrian continent. He claimed to know these jungles better than any man alive, although Tyrion was starting to think that perhaps this was not so great a feat as Leiber made out.

Very few humans lived long in Lustrian jungles. They came here seeking fortunes but what they mostly found was death. Already most of the company of men the twins had hired as porters or guards had died or vanished, some from mysterious fevers that not even Teclis's medicines could cure, some from the attacks of the giant jaguars common in this part of the jungle. This had only been the latest of the misfortunes to bedevil their expedition.

One man had died screaming when the larvae of a bloodwasp emerged from where he had been stung a few days before. The foul little maggots had eaten their way out through his entrails. Two thralls had been devoured when a skittering cloud of piranha lizards dropped from the branches above them. The flesh had been stripped from their bones in the seconds it had taken Teclis to cast the fiery spell that had turned their killers into shrivelled exploding corpses.

Others had simply deserted, vanishing in the night, never to return. Tyrion did not blame them for that under the circumstances.

Leiber had not vanished. He was just as obsessed with finding the city of Zultec as the twins were. Of course, he had his own reasons. For Tyrion and his brother, Zultec was the last known possible resting place of Sunfang, the mystical blade forged for their ancestor Aenarion by the archmage Caledor Dragontamer during the wars at the dawn ages of the world.

For Leiber, it represented a trove of gold and mystical secrets that he hoped would let him reclaim the ancestral lands he had lost back across the wide ocean. He claimed to have penetrated to the very heart of the city once and to have spent the past few years trying to find a way back.

Tyrion was not sure how much he trusted the man or the remainder of his companions. They were desperate rogues even by the standards of the rough crew you met in the makeshift human camps of the Lustrian coast. They had the look of casual killers. Most of them were descended from the same Norse folk that had raided the coasts of Ulthuan for centuries: big, wild-looking, blond men with braided hair and beards. Their eyes were the blue of painted Cathayan ceramics. Their manner was bluff and fierce. They swore by the names of strange Kurgan and Hung gods. These ominous deities reminded Tyrion of the Ruinous Powers of Chaos, and he would not have been surprised to find out that they were related.

All of the humans except Leiber glanced at the two elves as if considering murdering them for their gold and scampering back to the old, decaying port of Skeggi, the only real permanent settlement along the whole coast. No one there would ask them how they came by the money, or what had happened to those who had went off into the jungle with them. Skeggi was a city of pirates and robbers and mad dreamers.

Tyrion was not troubled. There were only five of the humans now and he could handle them himself even without the aid of Teclis's magic. Providing, of course, they did not cut his throat while he was sleeping. He smiled nonchalantly.

'You find something funny, sir elf,' said Leiber. His voice was a harsh croak well suited to his guttural native speech, so unlike the liquid tongue of the elves.

'No, Leiber, I am merely happy,' said Tyrion in Reikspiel, the common language the humans used. It was true too. There was something about this desperate venture that gladdened his heart. He was rarely happier than when off on some quest in the company of his wizard twin.

'You find all of these deaths cause for happiness? I had heard elves were cruel, my friend, but I had not thought to find you to be an example of that.'

'You are confusing us with our kinfolk, the druchii, whom you call dark elves. The deaths give me no happiness. It is the adventure I enjoy.'

He did not know if he could explain himself to Leiber or whether he should. At times like these, he felt as if he was living out one of the hero tales he and Teclis had loved when they were boys.

It seemed to him that their lives had turned out exactly the way they would have wished them too. He was a warrior who had fought in the service of the Phoenix King and made himself wealthy trading and raiding the coasts of Naggaroth. Teclis had served his apprenticeship in magic under Lady Malene in Lothern and was now a student at the White Tower of Hoeth in Saphery. He was the youngest Loremaster in generations. His twin was widely acknowledged as possibly the most brilliant wizard Ulthuan had produced since the time of Bel Hathor.

He was going to need to be. Both of them knew it was only a matter of time before the daemon N'Kari, the most ancient enemy of their family, returned and attempted to claim their souls. The Keeper of Secrets had very nearly succeeded in wiping out the entire blood line of Aenarion during his attack on Ulthuan a century ago. Only Teclis's invocation of the power of the Phoenix God Asuryan had defeated him and saved the twins' lives.

According to Teclis, at least a century would need to have passed before N'Kari could be summoned again, or could reform a body of his own will and emerge from the Chaos Wastes. That time had come and gone. If he wanted to, the Keeper of Secrets could return to this world.

Tyrion felt sure the daemon would not make the mistakes he had made during his last incursion either. Even for an entity as powerful as N'Kari, a direct attack on the shrine of Asuryan, mightiest of the elven gods, had been an act of self-destructive hubris.

The certainty of the daemon's return was one reason they were seeking Sunfang. A mighty weapon borne by the first Phoenix King, it should be capable of harming even a greater daemon and it would give Tyrion some chance of surviving an attack.

He smiled again somewhat ruefully. By some chance, he meant an infinitesimal chance. He had fought the daemon once and was a good enough warrior to know exactly how little hope he had of beating something like N'Kari, even with a magical weapon. Still, it was better than no chance at all.

'I wish he would stop smiling like that,' one of the humans muttered. 'It makes me nervous.'

Tyrion felt certain that most of the humans had no idea how well he understood their tongue, having learned it in the rougher quarters of Lothern during his long residence in the city. It was a small advantage but any advantage was to be cherished here.

'How much further?' he asked Leiber.

Leiber scratched his chin to make himself look more thoughtful. 'A few more leagues at most.'

'You've been saying that for some time now,' said Teclis. His ironic tone was understandable even to Leiber.

'Finding your way through this cursed jungle is not like sailing a ship, your honour,' said Leiber. 'I can't simply navigate by the stars. Things grow here. Landmarks get hidden. Rain washes away trails. It's guesswork at best.'

To be fair to Leiber, he had never lied about any of this, or made any bones about the difficulty of finding Zultec. He had been perfectly open about how hard it would be. He had merely claimed that given time they would find it, and he still seemed perfectly confident that it would prove to be the case.

'So your plan involves wandering randomly through the jungle until we stumble upon Zultec,' said Teclis. Tyrion gestured for him to stop provoking the human, but self-restraint did not suit his twin's temperament.

'No, your highness. We will continue to march westwards until we hit this stream here.' He produced his grubby tattered map from within his shirt and stabbed his finger at the blue line that marked the position of the watercourse. 'Then we will turn north until we stumble on the outskirts of the city.'

'Your confidence is awe-inspiring,' said Teclis.

'Look, your honour, you hired me because I had been to the city and could find my way back. You paid for the gear and the guards and the porters and I am grateful. If you want to turn back now, I can't say as I would blame you. It's been a hard road and no mistake. But we are so close now I can smell it. And I would advise you to stick with me for just a bit longer and we will reach our goal.'

It was an impressive speech, made more impressive by its delivery. There was a mad conviction in Leiber's eyes and his voice compelled belief. Tyrion believed him, as he had all along. He was sure his twin did too, but Teclis simply could not resist provoking the man.

'I am not sure I believe you have ever seen the city,' he said.

'I've seen it, your honour, and I almost died there when those scaly-skinned lizardmen attacked with their poison darts and their stone axes. I saw Argentes go into the central pyramid and never come out too. I was the only one of our party as did, and I only managed it by fleeing into the jungle and throwing away all my gear. It took me months to find my way back to Skeggi.'

'I am surprised your map is so accurate then,' said Teclis.

Leiber spat on the ground but he spoke with the air of a man who does not wish to provoke an argument, 'I am too, your honour. I did my best to remember landmarks and that stream stayed in my mind. I followed it all the way to the coast from that fork, and we can follow it back if you will stick with me.'

'We've stuck with you through the swamps and the pygmy attacks and the giant bats and the fevers. I see no reason to stop doing so now, when you say success is so near,' said Teclis.

'I am very grateful for that, your highness. Now, perhaps we can stop yakking and start walking. We need to get moving if we are ever going to find that treasure and Herr Argentes's sword that you have spent so long looking for.'

Somewhere far off, something roared. Tyrion wondered if it was coming their way. This did not sound as large as the stegadon, but there was something about the sound that suggested words or at least some form of communication. It was answered from across the jungle. He wondered if it had anything to do with their presence. He supposed he would find out soon enough.

CHAPTER TWO

THE RAIN PATTERED down lightly on the canopy of leaves, dripping down to turn the track to mud. The birds were subdued and the light was dim. In some ways it felt like they were walking under the greenish surface of the sea. Tyrion's legs were spattered with runny earth and it was work just to lift them from the sucking, squelching path.

Teclis pushed on through the jungle following Leiber. He had no trouble with the path. His feet seemed to float above it and he left only the faintest imprint in its surface. Such were the benefits of magic, Tyrion thought sourly. He walked beside his brother, ready to intervene if there was an attack. Teclis might be a powerful magician but his reflexes were nothing like as quick. *A dagger in the back kills the mightiest mage* was a proverb in which Tyrion had implicit faith.

He fought to contain his own excitement. After decades of searching it seemed like the end of their quest was finally in sight. They had finally tracked down Sunfang. Or rather his brother had.

Teclis had spent years in the library at Hoeth searching through collections of obscure manuscripts for some clues as to the whereabouts of Aenarion's lost blade, the legendary weapon forged for him by the Archmage Caledor amid the volcanic fires of Vaul's Anvil, a companion piece to the armour the mage had made for the first Phoenix King.

Aenarion had put the blade aside once he had taken up the Sword of Khaine and its burden of damnation and ultimate power. He had given it to Furion, one of his most trusted lieutenants who had in turn passed it on to his descendants.

The Witch King of Naggaroth, with his customary hunger for all the possessions of his father, had coveted the weapon. Furion's family had refused him it. Over the course of time, agents of the Witch King had made many attempts to acquire the blade, and always failed.

In the end, Nathanis, the last descendant of Furion had sailed for the Old World on a trading trip. He had arrived there but never returned with his ship. There were tales of an elven adventurer fighting in the lands of the Empire armed with a magical sword that shot bolts of flame. He had visited the fabled forest of the wood elves and fought alongside wardancers and backwoods archers, eventually making his way down to Tilea and the Border Princes and on to Estonia. The elf had died there but his sword had been taken up by a human, or so the tales told. It had passed from father to son down the fast, fleeting generations that humans experienced.

The power of the blade had made its possessors heroes and mighty champions among humans. It had not brought them luck though. Johan Argentes, the last bearer, had become a landless wandering mercenary.

Tyrion and his brother had spent years following this long trail across the Old World, retracing Argentes's steps, following up all rumours of his whereabouts. The trail had been lost when Argentes had set sail from Estalia aboard an explorer's ship bound for the uttermost west. Leiber had been the ship's captain. It had never returned to its home port and it seemed the trail was lost.

Pure chance had brought word of a shipwrecked captain called Leiber washed up in Skeggi. He had been spotted by a trading captain from House Emeraldsea who knew something of the twin's quest and remembered the name of the lost ship's master. It was a very long shot, but the twins had followed it up, taking passage on a trading clipper to the coast of Lustria. They had heard another rumour about a human with a fiery sword who had vanished into the interior, searching for the gold of the lost slann cities.

Eventually they had found Leiber who had witnessed Argentes's disappearance and been the only survivor, and who brought word of Argentes's loss, staggering out of the jungle half-mad with hunger, thirst and fever.

He had spent months making a map to Zultec and seeking to tempt accomplices with tales of a hoard of treasure big enough to fire the imagination of a hundred pirate kings.

Leiber had agreed to guide the two elves to Zultec in return for gold and their protection. The three of them had organised this expedition and followed the long trail that had led them to this accursed place.

So far, Leiber had proved to be a bold and reliable companion, but Tyrion was not sure of his friends.

Not that it mattered much at the moment; they were all in the same boat, outnumbered and far from home, seeking a ruined metropolis haunted by the last degenerate remains of the once mighty race of lizardmen who had built the place when the world was young.

Tyrion could not keep from grinning. He was hacking his way through the overgrown jungle in search of a lost alien city, where he hoped to find a legendary artefact from the dawn ages of his people.

'Why do you have that inane smirk on your face?' his twin asked.

'I was just thinking that this was exactly the sort of thing we used to talk about doing back in father's villa when we were boys.'

Teclis smiled back. It was a slow secret smile, a mere sliver like a quarter moon seen through cloud, but coming from him it was like a belly laugh from any other elf. 'We've come a long way from the mountains of Cothique, brother.'

'That is something of an understatement.'

'I like to keep in practice at that. A talent unused rusts.'

'Of course, I did not imagine the mosquitoes. I thought it would be vampires that tried to drink my blood and dragons that tried to bite me to death.'

'An old swamp witch back in Skeggi told me that the mosquitoes there once drained a baby of blood while it slept. She swore to me it was true. She had seen it with her own eyes. Of course, she also swore to me that the charms she was selling would make me irresistible to women and a mighty warrior.'

'Stranger things have happened.'

Teclis shrugged. 'There was no magic in them, brother. Even you could have seen that with your vision.'

'I have heard it said humans practise a different type of magic.'

'There is only one type of magic. There are different ways of using it, true enough, but all magic draws its power from the same place and all magical objects radiate a similar aura.'

'I'll take your word for it.'

'That would be an excellent idea. If you keep giving me advice about magic, I will have to start giving you my views on warfare and blade work.'

'Let's not stoop to absurdities,' said Tyrion. Leiber gave the sign that it was time to halt for food.

TYRION SLAPPED THE mosquito that had landed on the back of his hand. It exploded in a small burst of blood and flesh, leaving a faint blotch on his tanned skin.

'How do you do that?' Leiber asked. It continued to rain, not quite the usual monsoonal downpour that could turn tracks into streams, but a light drizzle that collected on the leaves and over-flowed in a million tiny random waterfalls.

They had paused to eat and their lack of motion seemed to be drawing the insects to them. The few remaining humans lay sprawled against the trunk of a huge tree chewing on strips of dried beef. Teclis prepared his drugs, mingling the contents of two silver flasks in an alembic he had produced from inside his pack.

'Do what?' Tyrion replied. He looked beyond Leiber into the shadow avenues made by the great trees. He was becoming uneasy and he was not sure why, although he knew enough to trust his instincts in this matter. They had kept him alive in many places where other elves had died.

'You always hit the buzzing little bastards. Does not matter how bad the light is, whenever one of them bites you, you kill it.'

'So?'

'You *always* kill them. Always. I have never seen you miss. I have never seen you even come close to missing or look like you are making any effort. Sometimes I never even notice the bloodsuckers until the bites swell and when I do try and hit them, the little swine are too fast for me. But they are never too fast for you.'

'That is because I am an elf and you are a human.' Even as he said it, Tyrion realised he was making a mistake. It was the sort of failure of diplomacy he would not normally have let happen. His only excuse was that he was tired and his mind had been on other things.

'And you think elves are better than humans?' There was an edge to Leiber's words that Tyrion could not miss. There had been a lot of deaths and a lot of fear lately and they still had not found what they were looking for. Such situations had a way of becoming slowly explosive. He knew this from bitter experience with his own kind. It seemed things were no different with humans. He tried to defuse the situation with a joke.

'Apparently we are when it comes to swatting mosquitoes.'

Leiber made a rueful grimace and took a pipe from out of the pouch on his waistband and then a flint. He walked over to Teclis's magically created fire and lit the tobacco that he had stuffed into the bowl of the pipe with a wooden spill. He continued to look into the distance for a long moment, puffing away and then letting the smoke billow out in two streams from his nostrils. Once he had done that he turned to look Tyrion in the eye and said, 'That is not what I meant and you know it.'

Tyrion felt his own temper rise in a way it would not normally have done. It was the heat and the humidity, he told himself, but there were other things involved as well. He was not used to being talked to this way by humans.

Did this man seriously think that there was any comparison between an elf and a human? Both races had a head and two arms and two legs. In some ways they looked quite similar. But elves lived longer, knew more, did not fall sick, and were not prey to the numerous superstitions that humans were. They were faster, more agile, more intelligent, more beautiful; superior in every possible way.

Leiber was less than a third of Tyrion's age but already he was starting to look decrepit. His skin was lined. Some of his teeth were missing. The way he squinted told Tyrion that his eyesight was not what it had once been. He looked like an elf might look after half a millennium had passed, and only if the elf were very unlucky.

Of course Tyrion thought he was better – he was just too polite to rub it in. Leiber seemed to be questioning his right to think that way which was, to say the least, impertinent of him.

For a moment Tyrion saw the relationship between all of his people and all of the humans reflected in the way that he thought about Leiber and Leiber thought about him. He wondered if it was worthwhile trying to put his own thoughts into words and explain them to the man, but he realised that it could do no good, could cause only friction. Leiber would simply take it as an insult. Perhaps he would be right to.

After all, the elves were a dying race and it looked like humans would inherit the world. Their civilisation was becoming more powerful by the year, spreading across the globe in an irresistible wave. Already there were probably more humans in the city of Lothern than there were elves, and Lothern was by far the most populous city in elvendom.

He told himself that the ability to breed quickly and irresponsibly was not exactly a sign that the humans were the equals of the elves. They could not create art the way the elves could. They did not know magic the way the elves did. They were not the intellectual equals of the people of Ulthuan.

But did that really matter in the eyes of the gods?

The elves were becoming extinct. The humans were not. Did that mean they were simply better adapted to living in this new and dreadful world? Did it mean that their gods were more powerful than the elven gods? Did it mean anything at all or was he simply speculating uselessly?

This was not really any of his business. He was a warrior not a philosopher. It was his duty to guard his people and he would do that to the best of his ability until the day that he died. He did not have any answers. He would need to leave that to people like his brother. And he was not sure that Teclis could get any better answers than he could himself.

'Do you think that we are better than you?' Tyrion asked, because he could not think of anything else to say.

'You are certainly better than we are at killing mosquitoes, your honour, that's for sure and I suspect that *you* are much better at killing almost anything. You have that look about you. And you're a damn sight prettier than I am, that's for sure. But I am not sure that you're a better man than me.'

'I am not a man at all,' said Tyrion.

'That's not what I meant. Are you braver than me? Are you morally superior? Or were you just born luckier? I sometimes think that the noble in the big castle on the hill is not a better man than the peasant he looks down on. He was just born into better circumstances – ones that ensured that he got better food, a better education and better training with weapons, as well as the weapons themselves.'

Tyrion could see that Leiber was talking about something he had given a lot of thought to. This was a matter that had deeply troubled the human for a long time. He was not really talking about the relationship between men and elves anymore – he was talking about the way humans lived, the way he himself had lived.

'Why do you ask me this?' Tyrion asked.

'Can you see what I'm saying, Prince Tyrion? Can you see what I'm getting at? In my life I have met a lot of noblemen and a lot of them have looked down on me. Argentes for one. And the truth of the matter is that he was not any cleverer than I was, nor any braver nor any better. In the end, he is dead and I am still here. Who is to say who the better man is now?'

Tyrion understood the point being made only too well. And perhaps Leiber was right to make it. Perhaps it was simply the fact that Tyrion had been born in a different place to a different people that made him feel superior.

'I am still an elf, and you're still human. It does not matter what either of us think about that, the world remains the same.'

'Does it though, Prince Tyrion? The world is changing. Who knows what the coming centuries will bring?'

'Most likely I will still be here to see. Will you?'

Leiber did not have an answer for that. Tyrion had not expected him to. Leiber took another puff on his pipe and regarded Tyrion balefully for a moment, then he smiled and laughed out loud.

'I should have known I could not get the better of an elf in an argument.'

TECLIS TOOK A moment away from concentrating on mixing his potions to listen to what his brother was talking about with Leiber. He needed to concentrate. Like his sight, his hearing was not good at the best of times, and the spell he used to keep the insects and the jungle heat and humidity at bay made it even worse. It flattened out all sound as if he had placed a layer of beeswax in his ears.

He could see that Tyrion was troubled by the human's words and was giving serious thought to the matter, but his brother was not capable of looking beyond the common prejudice against humans.

Tyrion really did believe himself to be superior to the human and had ample empirical evidence to back this up. By almost any measure, he could prove himself to be better than the man. He was even prepared to admit it to the human when pushed. What he did not see was the simple fact that he was judging the matter by standards set by himself and other elves.

Teclis added a pinch of saltpetre and powdered gryphon bone to the mix and smiled sourly. The potion smelled infernal but it was necessary for keeping his strength up and not just his strength. Without these medicines his sight and hearing would be even worse than they were now. He would be more or less blind and deaf as well as decrepit.

Of course, elves were better looking than humans by any standards. Of course, they were more knowledgeable about lore. Of course, elves were better at all the things that elves were good at than humans were. It was a competition in which all of the rules were made by the elves and all of them reflected to their own advantage.

No elf bothered to think that there might be things that humans knew that elves did not. No elf ever was prepared to admit that already the humans occupied and controlled a greater portion of the globe than the elves ever had and that this process was only likely to continue.

All of the elves imagined that just because they lived longer they enjoyed more favour in the eyes of the gods. Teclis felt sure that humans could judge this contest by their own standards and feel superior to elves if they really wanted to; it was just that so far they had not done so. They were still used to thinking of elves as the Elder Race. They were still dazzled by beauty and culture and magic. But that would not last.

One day, and that day could not be that far off, the humans would see beyond glamour and begin to judge the elves as they deserved to be judged. They would see that the elves were not really so much better than they were, after all.

They would see that the elves were split into two warring factions. They were, in their own way, just as divided as the human realms. Perhaps more so. He could not think of any human kingdoms that were involved in so bitter a fratricidal struggle as Ulthuan and Naggaroth. Or which had been fought for so long.

And the humans did not seem to suffer from the madness that plagued the elves: the strange obsessions, the lust for power, the furious desire to acquire knowledge and magical lore that the elves suffered from.

Of course, these things did affect humans, but not with the same intensity as they affected elves. Some of his own kindred would see that as proof of superiority. The elves felt things more keenly, appreciated things more and moved through the world with much more intensity than humans could.

Teclis was not at all sure that this did make them superior. It merely made them different. In fact, there were times when he believed that the excessive nature of their temperament was a definite disadvantage. They were capable of focusing on one thing exclusively to the point where they would miss other more important things.

He finished swirling his medicine and drank it down. It was bitter and the aftertaste tingled on his tongue. He braced himself for the dizziness he was going to feel as it first took effect.

He thought with some bitterness about his own father, lost in his obsessive pursuit of the secrets of the dragon armour of Aenarion. Prince Arathion had neglected his own children and his own estates and allowed the fortunes of his ancient family to fall into decline as he worked on his own personal obsessions. If Tyrion had not rescued the family finances with his ventures into piracy and trading, they would most likely be living in the gutter now or on the charity of their wealthy Emeraldsea relatives.

There had been times in his childhood when Teclis suspected he had almost died because his father was more interested in the secrets of ancient sorcery than he was in the well-being of his children. And yet, Teclis could not find it in himself to blame his father. He understood only too well the burning hunger that consumed him. He felt the same way about his own pursuit of magical knowledge.

Look at him now – he had followed the trail of an ancient arte-fact halfway round the world simply because it promised to reveal to him some secrets of how it had been created. He'd undergone a great deal of personal discomfort and boredom, and not a little danger, in pursuit of that knowledge and he'd done it without a second thought.

Of course, he had other reasons. He wanted to help his brother find a weapon that might help him survive when the daemon that pursued them caught up with them, as Teclis feared it inevitably would.

And he also thought that if he could locate the blade and pen-etrate its mysteries he might find something that would help his father with his own magical research. He should be the last one to blame elves for their obsession; he knew that only too well. But he could not help but feel that elves judged themselves too favour-ably and humans not favourably enough.

And even knowing this he could not help but look at Leiber and his brother and judge his own kin as the better of the two. He was not immune to the normal prejudices but, at least, he was aware of the fact that he suffered from them.

And he knew the dangers of concentrating too much on one thing, while ignoring his surroundings. Out there innumerable dangers lurked. They might not be as lucky as they had been this time when the next attack came.

Was it the effects of the medicine or was something disturbing those nearby bushes? Even as the thought occurred to him, a long-snouted, tooth-filled monstrous head emerged from the undergrowth.

'Watch out!' Leiber shouted. 'We've got company.'

They were under attack.

CHAPTER THREE

Wᴇᴛ ʟᴇᴀᴠᴇꜱ ꜱʟᴀᴘᴘᴇᴅ Tyrion in the face, obscuring his vision. Something heavy and scaly and rain-slick slammed into him. Its momentum bowled him over.

Instinctively, he let himself go with the flow of the motion. Landing on his back in the soggy mulch, he kept rolling and kicked out with his feet, pushing the thing off.

Fang-filled jaws snapped shut in front of his face. Something slammed into his leg with bruising force. He caught sight of something green and vaguely humanoid. He continued his roll and somersaulted upright.

On his feet now, blade in hand, Tyrion sought enemies.

His attacker disappeared into the undergrowth. It looked like a big humanoid lizard, running upright, balancing itself with its long tail. The head was something like that of a dragon, with enormous powerful jaws and massive teeth that looked easily capable of tearing flesh right to the bone.

It was one of the legendary servants of the slann. A warrior of some sort, although very primitively armed. In one scaly hand it clutched a stone axe tipped with coloured feathers. Only luck had stopped the thing from braining him. As he watched, the thing's skin changed colour, scaly patterns altering so that it blended in with its surroundings. That chameleon-like camouflage was what had allowed it to get so close.

Tyrion's heart beat faster. His breathing deepened. He had a sense that he was lucky to be alive. Judging from the crunching noises nearby some of his own people had not been so lucky.

He looked around to see how Teclis was doing.

The glow of a protective spell surrounded his brother. A group of the lizardmen circled him, snapping at him with their massive jaws and striking at him with their axes. His alchemical gear lay discarded at his feet. His fire was scattered. So far, Teclis's spells had warded off their blows but it was only a matter of time before they managed to do him some harm.

Tyrion sprang forward, lashing out with his sword. His first blow separated the head from one lizardman's body. His blade caught another in the chest. Greenish blood flowed and the air took on an odd coppery tang.

The lizardman shrieked, the sound of its voice like the hissing of a boiling kettle until the note went too high to be audible to his ears. Tyrion twisted his blade, turning it until it grated against rib. He leaned forward, hoping to hit the heart but not sure of the layout of the internal organs that a lizardman might possess.

Of one thing he was certain – he was causing his victim a great deal of pain, judging by the way it screeched. Its tail curled around, threatening to hit him with the force of a bludgeon. He leapt over the blow, even as two of the lizardman's companions closed in from either side.

Tyrion caught one in the throat with his sword, where the windpipe ought to be. Something crunched under the blow and the lizardman fell backwards, mouth open in a silent scream, no sound being emitted from its broken voice box, then the pommel of his blade connected with the snout of the other lizardman with sickening force. It too halted momentarily, stunned.

Tyrion split its skull with his sword and then wheeled to stab the other as it clutched at its slashed throat.

With the force of a striking thunderbolt he smashed into the melee, dancing through the swirl of combat with impossible grace. Every time he struck a lizardman fell. Within heartbeats he had turned the course of the battle and slaughtered half a dozen more of the cold-blooded ones. The rest of them fled off into the undergrowth, shrieking and bellowing like beasts.

Something flickered in the corner of his vision. A dart erupted from the bushes heading straight at him with eye-blurring velocity. He plucked it from the air, careful to avoid its sharpened obsidian point. He had no doubt that the black goo smeared on the blade was a deadly poison. He hurled the thing point first into the bushes from which it had come, but whatever had fired it was gone. The dart stuck quivering in the bole of a great tree.

Around him, the humans went around finishing off the wounded lizardmen, smashing their skulls or stabbing them through the eye or heart. They were brutal, driven by fear.

A lot of their cruelty came from that fear. Tyrion disliked this. He enjoyed violence but he had never understood this need to abuse defeated foes that many people had. He supposed one thing bred the other. Fear was parent to cruelty.

He looked over to make sure that Teclis was unharmed. The wizard stood there, glaring around him, looking for a target for his spells. The battle had been fought so quickly that he had had no chance to unleash his power.

Tyrion could tell that he was frustrated by that and he could understand why. His brother did not like to feel powerless in any situation – he had experienced too much of that in their youths.

'They are gone,' Tyrion said. 'For the moment.'

'How can you be certain of that?' Teclis asked.

'I can't,' said Tyrion. 'But normally when you kill things to the point where they run away, they don't come back quickly. Of course, with these slann creatures you can never be sure. They are too alien.'

'Those were skinks,' said Teclis. 'That's what they were called. According to the *Chronicles of Beltharius*, they are servants of the slann, not the slann themselves.'

'I'll take your word for that,' said Tyrion.

'You would do well to do so,' said Teclis. His brother sounded keen to assert himself, even if only by displaying superior knowledge. 'Beltharius is the only elf to have left any records of visiting an actual lizardman city, and he barely survived that.'

Beltharius was the captain of the explorers who had visited the Golden Pyramid of Pahuax back in the reign of Bel Shanaar. He had been one of the few to fight his way out of the city when the great toad-god that ruled it had turned nasty.

The tale was well known, but his brother had spent a great deal of time in the library at Hoeth, studying the actual journals Beltharius had kept. Before they had made this trip he had studied every scrap of information the elves had ever compiled about the jungles of Lustria and its inhabitants. With his usual thoroughness he had turned himself into an expert on the matter.

Tyrion glanced around to see how the humans were doing. One of them was on the ground, dead, his skull crushed by one of those stone axes. It had been left buried in his forehead.

'Bastards!' Leiber said. 'Those scaly bastards killed him. They killed Fritz.'

'These lands are sacred to them,' said Teclis.

Tyrion shook his head. This was not the sort of thing that Teclis ought to be saying to the humans right now. They were upset by the loss of their comrade and they were on edge, ready for violence. It would not take much to turn them against the elves, or cause a violent argument and Tyrion had no great wish to kill the humans and still less of a desire to be killed by them.

'We need to move on,' said Tyrion.

'We need to bury Fritz,' said Leiber.

'We could all die if we don't get out of this place,' said Tyrion. 'Those skinks will be back with friends soon, and there will be a lot more of them than us.'

Leiber looked as if he wanted to argue but he could see the sense of Tyrion's words. His companions looked torn between their anger and their fear. The way Fritz's dead eyes stared at the sky was a compelling argument for Tyrion's case. None of them wanted to end up that way. Heads nodded.

'Dead men spend no gold,' said Teclis sardonically. Tyrion could have cursed him. Now was not the time for his gallows humour, but that argument too held considerable force.

'All right, let's go get us some treasure,' said Leiber. There was a note of aggression in his voice that Tyrion did not like at all. It was possible that before too long it would not just be the skinks that would be numbered among their enemies.

THE RAIN POURED down, turning the track to flowing mud. It splattered off the leaves and splashed down from the giant trees in small waterfalls and the noise of it covered the normal small sounds of the surrounding woods.

Tyrion envied his brother's magic even more. His tunic was soaked. His hair was plastered against his skull. The insides of his boots squelched. The rain did not touch Teclis. It stopped a finger's breadth from his form, leaving him looking dry and calm.

Leiber spluttered and coughed as he led them along the track. Red mud stuck to his bare feet and made it look as if he was wearing a glistening set of magical stockings. The other humans tramped along with slumped shoulders and miserable expressions in their eyes. They looked as if they wanted to be anywhere but here.

The ruins emerged slowly from the jungle. At first Tyrion was not sure that they were not simply large outcroppings or hills. It took some effort to discern the shapes of the tumbled down buildings in the undergrowth, but if he looked closely, he could see lichen-blotched, time-eroded statues and the chipped remains of monstrous stone blocks partially buried in moss and peaty earth. Great trees had grown around them and sometimes through them, the power of their long slow growth tumbling even the heavy stonework.

'There must have been an earthquake here,' Tyrion said in elvish to Teclis. His twin looked thoughtful.

'Or monstrously powerful sorcery. They say the forces of Chaos struck these cities with mighty magics during the first incursion. For a long time, the slann and their lizardmen slaves bore the brunt of the Dark Gods' attacks.'

The ground squelched underfoot. It was as if they were moving through the limits of a great swamp.

'Flooded?' Tyrion asked.

Teclis nodded. 'Seems most likely.'

'Let's hope the whole city is not under water then.'

'It would not be the first slann city to be so.'

'You do not reassure me, brother.'

'We still have to find what we came here for,' said Teclis. 'We still need to find the sword.'

Tyrion sprang upwards and grabbed a vine. It was wet and slippery, but he was agile even by the standards of elves and he had soon pulled himself up into the lower branches of the trees. From there he used his dagger as a piton and climbed as high as he could go.

He was hoping for a good view of his surroundings, and even through the downpour he managed one. Although these trees were not as tall as some of the millennia old giants of the deep forest, they were still far taller than the mast of an ocean-going ship. What he saw was as awesome as it was disheartening.

They had found Zultec.

The old slann city stretched to the horizon. Less than a league away were a number of ziggurats, partially overgrown but the size of small hills. They had been hidden by the jungle until he climbed above it. He counted at least a score and gave up. He knew that there would most likely be smaller ruins hidden among the wreckage. They had found the city but it might take years to search it for what they sought, assuming it was even there. He scrambled back down the tree and told Teclis what he had seen. His brother smiled. He did not look at all put out by Tyrion's discovery.

'Zultec is not all that huge by the standards of slann temple cities,' he said. 'This was a mere satellite town of Pahuax according to Beltharius.'

'If this was a small town, their cities must be gigantic indeed,' said Tyrion.

'They are.'

'What now, brother?'

'You have shown what brawn and eyes can do here. I will show you the uses magic can be put to.'

'I would be grateful if you could,' Tyrion said. 'I do not fancy spending the rest of my life searching this place for Sunfang. There is a woman in Lothern I am anxious to get back to.'

'I am not so sure her husband will be that keen,' said Teclis.

Tyrion shrugged. One of the reasons they had set out on this quest was to let that particular scandal die down. Lady Valeria's husband was a powerful ally of House Emeraldsea and he doted on her the way she doted on Tyrion. A duel would not have done anyone any good. It would have damaged a powerful faction in politics.

The humans were looking at them again, wondering what they were saying. Tyrion turned to them and said, 'It is Zultec, no doubt about it. Unless there is another huge slann city we have not heard of hereabouts.'

He turned to Teclis and said in elvish, 'Sorry, I meant to say small slann village.'

'I told you we would find it, didn't I?' Despite the wet misery of the rain, and the sunken look of their surroundings, Leiber could not keep the triumph from his voice. He sounded like a man who had come close to realising a lifelong dream. Tyrion could not deny the human his moment of triumph.

'You were right, Leiber,' he said.

Leiber smiled again, showing his missing teeth and blackened stumps. 'We are all rich, lads,' he said. 'The slann gold is almost ours.'

There was nothing like the prospect of wealth for cheering humans up, Tyrion thought. Even soaked to the skin and swatting at mosquitoes, they looked happy at Leiber's announcement and ready to run off into the nearest ruins to seek for treasure. Tyrion could not really blame them. For the most part their lives were short and miserable and gold helped humans find comfort in their hovels.

'The really big pyramids start about half a league away,' Tyrion told them, to add to the good cheer.

'What about the monsters that attacked you the last time you were here?' Teclis asked, always ready to spread a little gloom when things started to get too light-hearted.

Leiber nodded at this. 'We should move slowly and cautiously and try not to raise any ruckus. Once we find the gold we'll make a grab for it and do a runner.'

'You are supposed to help us find what we are looking for. That's what you are getting paid for,' said Teclis.

'That's what I meant,' said Leiber. 'We're all looking for treasure.'

'We're looking for a very specific treasure,' said Tyrion. 'And we won't be leaving until we find it.'

'Argentes died here. His burning sword will be here still. You'll find it.'

'Let us hope so,' said Tyrion. 'And let us hope no lizardman has made off with it. That will make finding it a lot harder.'

That did not lighten the mood any either, Tyrion thought. Maybe he was acquiring some of Teclis's talent for depressing people. The humans looked at him as if he had just announced a plan to start cutting off their noses one at a time.

'You might never leave if the lizards find you,' said Leiber. It was a good point.

'We'll all do better if we stick together,' Teclis said.

'No lie there,' said Leiber. 'We could all leave our bones bleaching in this jungle if we are not careful.'

'Can you remember where Argentes fell?' Teclis asked. There was an urgency in his voice too now. He was excited by the fact they were close to their goal.

'It was a lot closer to the centre, I think, in a pyramid much bigger than these ones,' Leiber said.

'Then we'd better get moving.'

THEY MADE THEIR way through the streets of Zultec, pushing through the undergrowth and hacking their way through the bushes when they became too dense. All of them were nervous now as well as excited. All of them feared that death might spring upon them from the shadows at any time, and all of them held themselves ready to meet that threat. It would be a terrible thing to be slain so close to their goal.

Tyrion studied their surroundings. It would be an excellent setting for an ambush. The jungle and the ruins of ancient buildings provided so much cover. The sound of the rain would drown out any stealthy approach made by aggressors, aided and abetted by the natural noises of the jungle itself – the chattering of the monkeys, the screaming of the birds, the distant roar of the big predatory carnosaurs as they sought prey.

He did not like this place.

It had an atmosphere to it that made him uneasy and there were very few places in this world that had that effect on him. He was an elf; he was used to living in places that had an aura of antiquity. But they had been built by his own people.

This was more ancient than any place in Ulthuan and it had not been built by anything remotely like the elves. Minds, alien almost beyond his comprehension, had conceived the strange geometry of the architecture. He could look at structures created by humans and dwarfs and he could see that they were the product of a sensibility at least close to his own. Such was not the case here.

These buildings have been created by beings that thought in a very different way, according to a very different system. There was a pattern here but he could just not tell what it was. He doubted that he ever would be able to.

It had something to do with numbers. The builders had obviously been obsessed by them. If he counted the number of statues on the sides of each building, as he found himself unconsciously doing, he got the sense that they fitted into some numerical pattern, although he could not tell what that pattern was. He suspected it had something to do with basic mathematical formulae, but he could not tell what that formula was.

Perhaps Teclis could; he had a gift for solving such puzzles. His mind was more flexible. Perhaps he could gain some insight into the minds of the alien creatures who had built this place.

Looking at his brother, he was sure that Teclis was gnawing away at the problem. He had a look on his face that Tyrion recognised; he was confronted with something that he did not understand but he was determined to do so. If anyone could get to the bottom of this mystery, Teclis could. All it would take was time, and, being elves, they had plenty of that.

The humans' expressions were very revealing too. Leiber resembled a man on the verge of religious conversion. He was very close to achieving some long-held dream. He looked excited and intense. His gaze darted around their surroundings, seeming to take everything in, as if he wanted to memorise every single detail of every single building and every single object that they encountered.

The other men simply looked scared and greedy and torn between those two emotions. They too were excited to be here, but would have preferred to be somewhere else. They were dwarfed by the sheer scale of their surroundings, by these monumental, crumbling ruins emerging from the sticky humid jungle.

If he felt out of place here, Tyrion thought, what must these humans be thinking? Their civilisation was much younger than the elves and they believed the ancient slann to be daemons, in the same way that they believed almost every race but themselves to be daemons or descended from them. They thought that this was a place in which they could lose their souls if they died here. Maybe they were right. Who knew what was possible with the magic of the ancients?

Tyrion was astonished by their bravery. He never usually gave much thought to courage. He never really felt much fear himself, merely some prodding instinct which told him that his survival was in question and that he had better do something about it.

What must it be like to live with an emotion that could leave you paralysed at the moment of maximum danger?

He knew he was unusual even among elves for his inability to feel fear. Teclis certainly knew what it was and his friends back home in Ulthuan did too. He sometimes felt that there must be something missing in him, when he could not share in so common an emotion.

Perhaps it was all part of the curse of being descended from Aenarion. Perhaps this was the legacy that his great ancestor had passed on to him, like the killing rages that sometimes overwhelmed him in the heat of battle. It was said that Aenarion had felt no fear, that he had been willing to risk his life without a second thought on behalf of his people and his friends.

Tyrion pushed that thought to one side; he did not like to compare himself to Aenarion in any way. Too many other people were already doing that.

Everyone told him how much he looked like the great statue of Aenarion in Lothern harbour although he had never been able to see the resemblance himself. And back home in the city of Lothern and in other parts of the kingdoms, there were already those who compared him to the legendary Phoenix King.

That he and Teclis had defeated the Keeper of Secrets N'Kari had made him something of a celebrity among the elves. And certainly their deeds since they had overcome that potent daemon had won them a great deal of fame.

They had travelled to the four corners of the world while still very young, searching for Sunfang and ancient magical knowledge. Tyrion had already taken a distinguished part in several famous battles. He had raided the coasts of Naggaroth and sailed as far as the Citadel of the Dawn. He had been victorious in scores of duels and survived numerous attempts on his life. He was talked about in every corner of Ulthuan and many places beyond wherever elves gathered.

He had already heard himself mentioned as a potential candidate for the next Phoenix King even though Finubar's reign had only just begun less than two centuries ago. It was a truism of politics that the election of the next Phoenix King began with the coronation of the current one but it was one thing to listen to those platitudes, it was another thing entirely to find yourself the subject of one of them.

He smiled. Perhaps he was deceiving even himself. Perhaps he had believed them all along. Perhaps this was the reason why he was seeking Aenarion's sword. It would be another link in the chain that connected him with his ancestor in the public mind, and in politics that could be a very important thing indeed.

He admitted it. It was certainly possible that one of the reasons he was here was to advance his political career.

What young male did not dream of becoming Phoenix King?

In most of the cases it was an empty dream but Tyrion knew that this was not so for himself. He had the potential to be a candidate backed by one of the great merchant houses of Lothern. If he acquired sufficient acclaim from his adventures, that would count for a great deal with many others who had some say in the process of selection. After all, had not Finubar himself built his reputation on his deeds in the Old World?

He shook his head; it was funny how these ideas intruded into your mind in the strangest of places. Here he was in the ruins of an ancient city that had been destroyed while Lothern had been a collection of small wooden huts around an empty bay and he was thinking about the consequences of his actions here when he got back home.

He forced himself to concentrate on his surroundings. None of these speculations would matter if he was cut down by some monster's blade here in Zultec.

They passed on through the shadows of the titanic stone buildings, under the glare of massive stylised heads that looked as if they were modelled on some bizarre combination of human, daemon and toad. They moved along massive causeways which ran through gigantic ponds, in whose murky waters strange and frightening shapes swam.

A shadow fell upon them. Looking up Tyrion saw a monstrous bat-winged flying lizard pass overhead. It screeched once as if in warning and then soared off, rising on the thermals until it was merely a distant point that vanished into the clouds. Tyrion wondered why it had not attacked them. Perhaps it was not hungry. Or perhaps it was spying on them for the benefit of some unseen master.

'I see an opening here,' said Teclis, pointing to an entrance that had appeared in the side of a crumbling step pyramid they had just passed. 'Let us get out of the rain and I will try a divination.'

The humans looked worried, as if he had just announced he was going to summon a daemon. Tyrion hoped there was not going to be any trouble.

CHAPTER FOUR

WARM WATER TUMBLED down the sides of the ziggurat and poured over the lip of the entranceway. It ran down the back of Tyrion's neck and beneath his jerkin as he passed through. He cursed inwardly. It was difficult enough to maintain his gear in these tropical conditions, getting it wet was only going to make that harder.

Inside the gloomy chamber it smelled of mould and rotting leaves and ancient dampness. A snake slithered out of the light of Teclis's illumination spell. Tyrion reached up and touched the ceiling. It was low enough for him to do so easily.

The stone was chill and wet and blotched in places with some sort of fungal growth. This place had been built for a race shorter than humans or elves. He would have suspected dwarfs had something to do with its building if he had not known better. The stonework had some of the monumental quality he associated with the sons of Grungni. Massive blocks had been placed together with great cunning to make this structure.

It was the carvings in the stone that told a different tale. One look at them and anyone could see that this place had not been built by the dwarfs.

Pictograms had been chiselled into each stone block, depicting oddly square-looking humanoid lizards going about their incomprehensible business. They were of all different sizes. Some were obviously rulers, carried around on palanquins by ones who were obviously slaves.

'Fascinating,' Teclis said. For once there was no irony in his tone. He was genuinely interested in this alien artwork.

'I am just glad to be out of the rain,' Tyrion said. He spoke in the human tongue. Given their unease, he saw no reason for making the humans any more uncomfortable than they already were.

'Be grateful you are not in the Old World, yer honours,' said Leiber. 'It would be cold there as well and you would most likely take fever.' He paused for a moment and made a face at his own foolishness. 'Of course you would not. You are elves. You are immortal.'

'Not immortal,' said Teclis. His tone was sour. 'And some elves suffer from diseases.'

'I believe you, yer honour, but let's get on with finding this treasure of yours. None of us is getting any younger.'

Teclis nodded and gestured for the humans to stand back. All of them did so as quickly as they could and all of them wore the worried expressions of humans who knew they were about to be in the presence of sorcery.

Tyrion wondered whether his brother was making a mistake exposing the humans to his magic in this way. They were uneasy enough as it was from the constant expectation of attack. This might push them past the breaking point. He stared hard at Teclis but his brother was already in a world of his own, preparing. He had that inward look that he always wore when getting ready to cast a spell.

Tyrion came to a decision and shepherded the humans out of

the chamber and deeper into the pyramid. They looked at him with something between resentment and gratitude and then found their way into another cavernous chamber within the slann structure.

He told them to stay there before returning to where his brother was performing his magic so that he could stand guard. As always, he felt the need to do so. This time in particular, he had a sense of impending danger.

It was just this evil place, he told himself. That was all it was.

TECLIS BARELY NOTICED that Tyrion had entered the room. His mind had sunk into a trance and he was reaching out with his soul to touch the strange, alien realm from which magic flowed.

He would have liked to have inscribed a pentagram and a mystic circle and all of their associated runes on the floor, but it was too wet and damp for that. And, of course, he had already passed beyond the stage of needing such props in order to work magic. They would have made casting a spell easier but that was all.

He could achieve what was needed simply by uttering the proper incantations and making the correct gestures to bind the winds of magic to his will. Eventually, if he worked at it long enough and practised hard enough, he would be able to work the spell without even needing chants or hand movements.

He spoke the words of power and trailed his fingers through the moist air, flexing them in the way he had been taught by the Loremasters at Hoeth. As he did so sparks flared from his fingertips and his hands left trails of light behind them as they moved.

With those trails of light he sketched out the pentagram and the circle so that they shimmered around him. The mystical structure he had created sculpted the winds of magic around him, adding new layers to the spell, channelling the potent ambient energy. He shaped it with his hands and his voice like a potter shaping clay backing in Lothern. He built something that was like the eye of a daemon.

Once his tool was formed he closed his eyes. He could still see although he now saw from the point of view of the magical eye that he had created and he looked out upon a different world. It was no longer a place of light and darkness illuminated by the blaze of the Sun or the cold glimmer of the Moon. It was not a place where walls blocked vision. It was a place where he saw the patterns of magic, the souls of living things and the flows of magic itself. Stone did not block his sight but other things did – the remains of ancient spells of protection and warding, the static snowflakes created by the winds of magic themselves.

Looking around him he saw the golden glow of Tyrion's spirit. A little way beyond that he saw the flickering greed and hunger of the humans. All around him small pulses of light represented lizards and birds and stalking jaguars in search of prey.

Somewhere far off in the distance he felt the gigantic, terrifying presence of a monstrous alien intelligence, a thing half-asleep but still vaguely aware of what was going on around it. This would be one of the great slann lords of Hexoatl, slothfully vigilant, watching over its ancient ancestral lands even as it dreamed. He knew he had best do nothing to attract its attention and rouse it to full wakefulness. There was a power in the thing that was close to that of a god.

With an effort of will, he moved his magical eye and his point of view shifted, passing through walls as if they were not there and rising into the sky above the city. He could not move the eye too far from where he was without breaking the connection and ending the spell that he hoped would have leeway enough to get what he needed done. He raised the eye as far into the air as he could and looked down upon the city like a bird would have if it could see the flows of magic.

The city itself channelled magic in the same way as the spell he had created. He saw pulsing lines of light laid out beneath him. He was not sure what the purpose of this vast magical structure had been but he could see that, though it had been intended to fulfil some function, it was no longer capable of doing so.

Parts were dead. The pattern was incomplete. Something had gone wrong. He guessed that the whole city was like one huge rune and parts of that rune had been defaced by the destruction of buildings and the way the city had become overgrown by the jungle.

Whatever it had once been intended to do, the city was no longer capable of it. All that functioned now were the remnants of that vast spell. It still trapped power in pools and he dreaded to think what the effect of that could be. Perhaps it was what was responsible for the riot of growth here. Perhaps it had changed and altered the living things around it, making them angry mutants.

Fascinating as it all was, it was not part of his purpose here to study the magic of the Old Ones. He was looking for a specific object, one not made by the builders of the city but by an elf. It would have a very different magical signature that would stand out against this background like a gem on black velvet.

He made his point of view circle until he saw something that made him hopeful, a glittering pattern of light somewhere in the distance. He moved his magical eye as far in that direction as the tether of the spell would allow.

His heart began to race. He was looking at something that definitely had an aura. It could be only one thing. All they had to do was march in that direction until they found it and one of the greatest works of one of the greatest mages in history would be within their reach.

It was then that he noticed that they were not alone in the city, that other sentient beings were present and that those beings bore no resemblance to either elf or human, but were something monstrous, alien and savage. The servants of the slann were out there, and they were most likely looking for him and his brother.

And there was something else that worried him. All around the place where the elven magic flared there was the glow of other, darker, more sinister sorcery. One of the pools where the magic channelled by the city had collected, had curdled and congealed into something inexpressibly loathsome that made him want to shudder.

He summoned the spell back to him, and opened his eyes. Tyrion raised an eyebrow.

'I know where we must go,' said Teclis. 'Although there may be some slann in our way. And worse – Dark Magic too.'

'Oh good,' said Tyrion. 'We wouldn't want things to be too easy now, would we?'

AHEAD OF THEM, a monstrous ziggurat erupted out of the jungle. It was the largest they had so far seen and it was in somewhat better condition than the rest. It loomed over them like a mountain: gigantic, eternal, indestructible.

The rain had stopped, but water still dripped from the leaves as they pushed them aside. The moisture ran down the face of the humans like tears. Tyrion was soaked with rain as well as with sweat.

'This is the place. I remember it,' said Leiber. 'This is where Argentes vanished and where we were attacked as we waited for him.'

For once Teclis did not mock him. The other humans looked reluctant to continue. There was something about the sheer scale of the place that intimidated them. Leiber sounded angry when he spoke, as much with himself as with them. 'We've not got all day. There's treasure in there. Don't you want it?'

Up ahead, Tyrion could see that there had been hundreds of statues on every step of the ziggurat. Most of them were toppled over although he was not sure what had done it. It might have been an earthquake or a war or something else entirely, some magical disaster perhaps.

The main bulk of the structure was completely intact and that was hardly surprising. It was built of blocks of stone, each of which must have weighed tens of tons. The creation of this pyramid must have involved magic or the labour of tens of thousands of slaves.

He tried to imagine putting together this gigantic building in the sweltering heat of the tropical jungle. He tried to imagine it being built by the savage lizardmen who had attacked them earlier. It was difficult to believe that such creatures could have been capable of architecture on such a scale but he knew that such thoughts were deceptive. Once the slann had been the greatest of races, the master magicians of the world, the mightiest scholars, the chosen servants of the Old Ones, or so the most ancient legends claimed.

Look at them now, he thought – degenerate troglodytes barely capable of making stone tools. And yet this same people had once been masters of the world. It was alarming to consider that something similar might happen to his own people one day. Perhaps it had already started, this process of degeneration.

He thought about Lothern, with its empty palaces and its streets deserted by night. It was not so hard to imagine that one day it too would be overgrown and tumbled down, and that strangers might wander through the ruins overcome by a sense of melancholy and loss.

Perhaps one day, all that would be left would be the humans and their enemies, the beastmen of Chaos. Perhaps they would fight wars over the crumbled ruins of metropolises built by people who were by far their superiors. Perhaps all of this was merely a foretaste of the way the world would end.

They began to make their way up a massive staircase in the side of the ziggurat. There were both steps and ramps and it was easier to walk on the ramps because the steps had been placed at distances that were awkward for the human or elf stride.

Eventually they came to a massive arched opening and Teclis stopped, considering. After a moment he nodded and pointed through the archway.

'We go down here,' he said. All of them paused. The humans were plainly reluctant to go down into the darkness within the pyramid and Tyrion could not exactly blame them for that.

A strange smell of rot and decay, stronger even than that which brooded over the jungle, emerged from the entrance like the stinking breath of some undead giant. It felt like entering the mouth of a huge monster, a thing that might devour them. The ziggurat had an unearthly, evil, inhuman presence. It seemed to be waiting like some gigantic beast of prey.

'We have no light,' one of the men said. It should have sounded pathetic but it did not. They were all afraid and none of them wanted to admit it. They were close to their goal and Tyrion sensed that this in part was what caused their reluctance to proceed. They were as afraid of what they might find as they were of any guardians. They were afraid that they might be disappointed and that their golden dreams might turn out empty. It would be a brutal blow after all the hardships of getting here.

Teclis gestured. A ball of light sprang into being around his clenched hand. He flexed his fingers and the ball of light drifted away, floating around like a will-o'-the-wisp, illuminating the shadowy interior with a dim yet adequate light. He repeated the process until each of them had his own personal floating lantern. This display of magic made the humans even more uneasy. Tyrion could not see what else there was to be done under the circumstances though. It would take some time to collect the right sort of wood to make torches and it would be so wet that getting them lit would involve magic anyway.

'Ready?' Teclis asked.

'I am, brother,' said Tyrion. The humans nodded reluctantly but still did not move. They needed someone to give them a lead and it looked like he was elected for that duty. He shrugged and moved through the archway.

'These lights are going to make a stealthy approach impossible,' he said with a smile, hoping to lighten the situation.

'I think anything down there would know that we were here anyway. They could probably smell us. It is said that some of the skinks can track like dogs. They use their tongues instead of their noses but the results are the same,' said Teclis.

'One of the joys of travelling with you, brother,' said Tyrion, 'is that you're always so full of interesting facts.'

That got a feeble laugh from the humans and warily the party entered the pyramid and descended downwards into the darkness.

The ceilings in the corridors were so low that in some places Tyrion had to stoop. They were wider than he would have expected but lower. He suspected that it had something to do with the way that the lizardmen walked. They kept their heads much lower, even if their bodies would have been longer than those of a human or an elf lying stretched out on the ground.

'Which way?' Tyrion asked.

'Follow me,' said Teclis. Tyrion would have preferred to take the lead, but this seemed like a wise time to defer to his brother and his magic. He prepared himself to spring forward at the first sign of danger.

He sensed it would not be long before it showed itself.

CHAPTER FIVE

'WE NEED TO be careful here,' said Teclis in Reikspiel. 'This ziggurat was the central temple of Zultec. This means that we are moving into the heart of the most sacred area in the city.'

'Why is that important?' Leiber asked.

'Because they did not want infidels to come here into the most holy shrines. Before this city was abandoned I believe the slann laid spells here to prevent that from happening and there may well be physical traps too. And there is something else present, something I don't like at all.'

Tyrion could see that, if anything, the morale of the humans had dropped still lower. They had thought they merely had to fight the degenerate remains of an elder race. Now they were being told that they would have to face dangerous magic and deadly traps too.

'What are we talking about here?' Tyrion asked. He switched language to keep the humans from understanding the nature of the discussion that he was having with his brother. 'Daemons?

Fireballs? Strange runes that summon deadly clouds of poison?'

'It could be any of those,' Teclis said. 'There's something odd here. I think this whole city was built to be a sort of giant collector of magic and that this temple was its focal point.'

'And?'

'And I think something has tainted the power, made it corrupt. It may be why this place was abandoned.'

'I still don't see what kind of threat that might imply,' said Tyrion.

'Where magic flows strangely and is tainted by Chaos, there is the chance of all sorts of strange manifestations. Think of what happens in the Annulii, of all the monsters and mutations that emerge from those glittering mountains.'

'You are saying we might encounter something like that?'

'I am saying we might encounter things that are much worse.'

The humans were becoming restless because the two elves were spending so much time talking in their own tongue. They looked suspicious.

Teclis switched back to their language. 'I want you to all move very slowly and pay very close attention to what I say. If there is any inimical magic here I will see it and I will tell you what to do. I don't want anybody running ahead and setting off any traps. Is that clear?'

Tyrion did not think there was much chance of that. He was fairly sure that his brother's words were aimed at him. Teclis did not want him heroically striding into hidden dangers.

That was fine with him. He knew that his brother's magesight was much better than his own and that Teclis was far more likely to discover any subtle spells in operation in the area.

'Shall we go?' Tyrion asked. 'I am keen to see Sunfang.'

'Just make sure your enthusiasm is not the death of you,' Teclis said. 'I only have one brother and I am not keen to lose him.'

'I am not any keener to be lost,' said Tyrion. 'Let's go.'

The inside of the ziggurat was a huge maze, clearly designed, or so Tyrion thought, to confuse any intruder. Teclis did not seem troubled by the way the corridors fitted together though. He clearly saw a pattern to it and Tyrion asked what that was.

'It was built according to slann geomantic principles,' Teclis said. 'Most of the central chambers of slann temple cities are laid out according to the same pattern. I've seen the maps in the library at the great Tower of Hoeth.'

'So you're following the layout of a map that you can remember seeing once upon a time. You don't actually know whether this city is laid out according to the same principles?' Tyrion was speaking in elvish again. Just the fact that he was doing so was a cue to make the humans uneasy, but he could not help it. He thought they would be even more disturbed if they knew what he was actually talking about.

'I have not gone wrong yet, have I?'

'There is a first time for everything, brother.'

'I'm sure it will give you some satisfaction when it happens.' There was a brittle nervous edge to his brother's words that told Tyrion that his twin was not quite as confident as he liked to appear.

'It would give me no satisfaction whatsoever for you to be wrong. I very dearly want to find that sword. And I would like to have it soon.'

'Don't worry, we are very close indeed. I sense a powerful aura of magic just ahead of us. Be ready! If there are going to be any traps, they will be here.'

The corridor ended in a massive stone wall. It was etched with the strange pictoglyphs of the slann and even Tyrion could sense the magic in it. It was too heavy to be lifted by mere strength and too thick to be broken through even with a battering ram. It looked like they had come to a dead end.

'Whatever it is, it's beyond this wall,' Teclis said.

'I knew you were going to say that,' Tyrion said.

'You seem to be developing a gift for prophecy. Perhaps you

would care to use your powers of divination to reveal how we are going to get through this. No? Then pray have the good grace to remain silent while I work out a way of doing so.'

TECLIS PAUSED IN front of the wall. The mass of the thing, the sheer thickness of it, did not trouble him. What bothered him was the magic woven into it. Powerful spells converged here. Magic flowed all around him. It had a strange taint to it. Some kind of energy that he did not fully understand was part of it, along with the unmistakable spiritual taint of Chaos.

Something was being done to the winds of magic here. Some alien element was being added. He was not sure to what purpose but he was certain that it was happening.

He concentrated on seeing the whole thing with his magesight. His vision of what most elves would call reality receded. Now he was looking at the world painted in the bright, vivid colours of the winds of magic. He could see currents of power pulsing through the walls and knotting together like nests of writhing snakes. It seemed clear to him that one purpose of the spells here was to control this great doorway, for that was what the wall was. It was a doorway blocking the entrance to whatever chamber held Sunfang.

Argentes had somehow managed to penetrate into the heart of this pyramid. He had got past this barrier. Teclis doubted that he had done it by magic although he could not be sure. None of the information they had collected pointed to Argentes's party having a mage with them, but that did not mean it was not so. Leiber did not know everything and there were many reasons why a mage might have kept his gift to himself among humans, not the least being a wish to avoid a knife in the back.

He was speculating too much. There was most likely a much more simple explanation. Perhaps the sword bearer had entered the secret chamber by a different route and if they circled round this maze they would find a different method of entry. Or perhaps there was some secret passage through the walls that the sword bearer had known about but they did not. It was said that the temple cities of the slann were riddled with such things. Or maybe the doorway had closed as part of an elaborate trap.

He was wasting time. If the tunnels were there, he did not know how to access them. If the was another route in, it would take him a long time to find it. This door in front of him would provide a means of access and it was controlled by magic which was some-thing he did understand. All he had to do was work out the spell that would control it.

Magic was as much his gift as warfare was Tyrion's. Now was his time to shine. He still felt embarrassed and insecure about the way his brother had saved him during the attack by the skinks. He could have handled it if he had been given time. He could have blasted the lizardmen with his spells. But by the time his magic was ready, the skinks were already dead, killed by his brother's deadly blade.

Now they were confronted by a problem that could not be solved with a sword. He would find a way through this door using only his knowledge and his talents. And he'd better make a start soon or they would be here forever.

Once again he gave his full attention to the slann magic. He could see that untangling one knot of power would move the door. All he had to do was utter the words of an opening charm. What gave him pause was the web of magical energy that flowed out of that turnkey spell.

He was not sure what would happen if he did not neutralise those connections first. It might be that the whole complex of spells was completely harmless. Perhaps they fulfilled some ritual function. He doubted that was correct and he was not willing to take any chances with magic he understood so little.

He inspected the web of spells once again, concentrating not so much on their function as simply their place in the pattern. He wondered what would happen if he cut the connections.

Would it trigger something? Would some protective process react? Would guardians spring to life?

He did not know and he could not. The minds that had created this magic were too alien for him to understand. He was simply going to have to do what was necessary.

He hesitated for only a moment longer, knowing that he would gain nothing by waiting, but still reluctant to commit himself to an action that might have fatal consequences. Once again he found himself envying Tyrion. In moments like this he lacked his brother's decisiveness.

He cast his spell almost savagely. The door shook as if caught in an earthquake. The humans looked around in panic, ready to bolt. Another miscalculation, Teclis thought sourly. He should have warned them. Too late now anyway.

The doorway slid sideways, disappearing into a recess in the wall. It was an awesome feat by the builders, combining magic with engineering on a huge scale. What was revealed in the chamber beyond immediately stopped the humans from taking flight. Teclis heard Tyrion catch his breath and saw him begin to take a step forward.

In the distance lay bodies. Some magic had prevented them from decomposing although they did look desiccated. The corpses were human. In the hands of one was a naked blade which glowed with its own internal fire to Teclis's magesight.

They had found Sunfang and the last resting place of its bearer. Still he sensed something wrong here. All he needed to do was find it...

'Stop!' Teclis said. He said it loudly and with as much force as he could. But it was too late. The humans had seen the piles of gold objects strewn about the chamber. They had found the treasure they had searched for for so long. Nothing was going to stop them taking it. As a group they plunged forward into the room, ignoring Teclis's desperate shout. 'No! Wait! Don't!'

It was already too late. The air within the room shimmered

and ghostly, ghastly shapes began to take form. At first they were merely dancing sparkles of light but then the tiny shimmering motes raced together. They became outlines of creatures that looked like skinks. They hovered in the air above the corpses and then flowed into them, vanishing like poison gas breathed into the lungs of a victim.

The corpses shook as if the ground they lay upon was in the grip of an earthquake. One by one, the dead bodies pulled themselves upright. They lurched into motion like puppets on strings. More and more ghostly outlines shimmered in the air. They flowed towards alcoves in the walls and Teclis saw the mummified remains of other lizardmen lying in the darkness there. Once again, the motes of light vanished inside the bodies of the dead. Once again, the corpses began to move.

What had happened here? The slann were not famous for their knowledge of necromancy. They were said to have shunned it. Was this spell the product of some later degenerate cult? Or was it a product of the curdled magic he had sensed.

Teclis cursed. This was his fault. He should have given them more warning before he opened the door. He should have stressed the fact that no one was to enter much more strongly than he had.

It was too late for regrets now. The trap was sprung. All he could do was pray to the old gods and hope they were listening.

There were dozens of dead bodies within the tomb now, all animated. Their flesh had an odd dry quality and as they moved they made a strange wheezing sound as if the air being forced from whatever remained of their lungs was whistling out through gaps in their flesh. There was a stink of herbs and embalming fluid and the faintest hint of the sickly sweet odour of corruption.

The animated human corpses moved strangely, as if whatever was wearing them was confused as to how to make them walk. The first of the reanimated had reached Leiber's men now. They were just standing there, slack-jawed, paralysed by the sight of one horror too many.

Tyrion was already in motion, blade held ready to strike. He was obviously torn between obeying Teclis's injunction against entering the room and leaping into the fray. Teclis did not know what to tell him. The best plan might be to retreat in the face of this undead horde.

One of the humans went down. The walking corpses simply tore him limb from limb, painting themselves in his blood then using his torn-off arms as bludgeons with which to attack Teclis's companions. That forced the still living humans to react. They responded violently, hacking with their swords, lunging blades deep into unbeating hearts, slashing the throats of things that no longer needed to breathe. The living humans could not kill their foes with normal weapons. Teclis tried a spell, but it fizzled out as it passed into the air of the chamber. Powerful wards were still active in there, dampening and negating his magic.

Another of Leiber's men went down, screaming and struggling, as the wave of moving corpses passed over him. 'Tyrion!' Teclis shouted. 'Help him.'

Tyrion sprang to the doomed man's aid, blade lashing out with the force of a thunderbolt. The impact sent the animated corpses reeling backward. The blade took large chunks out of their dry flesh. They did not bleed. They felt no pain. It looked like the only way to stop them would be to chop them to pieces. Fire might work, but without being able to use his magic there was no way to make it.

Or was there?

'Tyrion! Get Sunfang. That will hurt them.' Teclis wished he was sure of that, but it seemed like their best chance of getting out of this hellish place alive.

Tyrion seemed to have worked this out for himself. He was already in motion towards Aenarion's time-lost blade.

CHAPTER SIX

TYRION LEAPT AT the walking dead man with the burning sword. He knocked aside the clumsy stroke of Sunfang and struck Argentes's corpse in the face with the pommel of his blade.

Argentes clutched Aenarion's sword in the unbreakable grip of his dead fingers. Tyrion grappled with him, determined to get his hands on the weapon he had sought for so long.

But the animated corpse was incredibly strong and his many companions surged towards Tyrion, keen to rend his flesh. The elf prince grasped Argentes's hand and broke his wrist with a twist. White bone jabbed out through dry flesh. Still Argentes would not let go of the sword. He grabbed Tyrion's throat with his good hand and squeezed. Tyrion made his neck muscles rigid to resist being choked but iron-hard nails bit into his flesh, drawing blood.

Tyrion twisted Argentes's sword hand, smashing the last of the bone and tearing the strip of flesh and the tendons that still attached it to the arm. Sunfang dropped free and he caught it.

It felt like a living thing in his hand. The blade burst into tiny flames. Tyrion could feel the blazing heat coming from the sword but the flames did not seem to do the metal any damage. It did not soften or become malleable.

He lashed out at Argentes with the sword he had carried for so long.

The smell of seared flesh filled Tyrion's nostrils when the blade bit home. A hideous shriek emerged from dry lips. A grey tongue flickered forth as if imitating the action of a serpent. In a moment the bone-dry corpse was in flames. It reeled away from Tyrion, tumbling backwards into the ranks of its own undead companions, setting the clothing of some of them alight as well.

'For Emeraldsea and the Phoenix King!' Tyrion shouted his battle cry and leapt among the attackers, striking right and left, setting fire to animated corpses, searing their flesh, burning their bones black as they fell. The magic of the blade made it much more deadly to these creatures than it would be to the living.

TECLIS SAW THE effectiveness of Tyrion's blade against the undead. He could work similar fiery magic, just not within the protected confines of the inner sanctum. He needed to lure the monsters outside their circle of protection before he could destroy them.

Inside the sanctum the humans had panicked and were fighting desperately, simply trying to stay alive. No one was paying very much attention to him. It was going to cost them their lives.

Why should he care? He could save himself and Tyrion. The others were only humans. He had no reason to care whether they lived or died.

By elven standards they were going to die soon anyway, so what difference would a few more years make? Chances were they would be carried off by disease or disaster within months if they made it back to their homelands anyway.

And yet he did care. He felt responsible for them. He had brought them here. They had followed him into this danger. And though their lives were short, they were the only lives they had, and if he did not do something they would be lost.

Most elves would not have given him a chance of living a few years when he had been but a sickly child. He found that he had a certain sympathy for humans that most other elves lacked. He could share their perspective. He could see himself in them. They were poorly made and despised by his kindred as well.

'Everybody out of the chamber,' Teclis shouted. 'Now!'

'They'll just follow us,' Tyrion responded.

'That's what I want!'

Tyrion shrugged. 'Come on, lads,' he bellowed in his best battle-ground voice. 'Get out of there. My brother has a plan.'

His voice carried effortlessly above the din of battle. More importantly it had that note in it that commanded obedience.

Leiber and the other humans almost jumped to obey. They raced and scrambled for the doorway, tearing themselves from the grip of ravening undead, twisting and writhing and scrambling over and through the moving corpses until they reached the exit.

Tyrion was behind them, pushing them on, encouraging them, helping them get free of their attackers, somehow never getting pinned down himself. The blade had given him the power to dominate this situation.

He pushed Leiber through the doorway and sent him sprawling. Another human ended up beside Teclis, terror and hope at war on his face. Teclis tried to smile reassuringly but it did not work. He lacked his brother's charisma. Tyrion was already fighting his way back across the chamber to get the rest of the men out.

Teclis breathed deeply, willing his heartbeat to stop racing and his mind to become calm. He reached out, twisting the winds of magic to his will, feeling them flow through him and around him, responding to his gestures and his voice and his attitude of mind. He thought of flame and tiny fires flickered into being around him, sending shadows skittering away into the gloom. He intensified his command and the fires grew hotter and brighter, blazing forth from his hands in sudden hellish eruptions.

The humans scrambled away from him, moving back down the

corridor away from the combat as fast as they could. Forces flowed around him, in great spiralling serpents of fiery energy. Now all he had to do was trigger them. He waited for Tyrion to get out of the chamber.

His brother slashed his way through more walking corpses over to where the human had fallen. With a sudden flurry of blows he cleared the area, lifted the man over his shoulders and made for the door again.

Burdened by the additional weight, unable to use his weapon, all he could do was run. Teclis wanted to shout for him to drop the human and get himself clear. His feelings of responsibility towards the man were as nothing to what he felt for his brother. Something made him keep his mouth shut though. Perhaps the belief that Tyrion could win free.

The undead clustered around his brother now, seeking to pull him down, clawing at his armour, scratching his face and exposed flesh. Tyrion kicked and butted and used his body weight to push assailants aside, but even he could not do anything against the enormous tide of desiccated flesh through which he was attempting to swim.

'Drop him!' Teclis shouted. 'Get yourself out. Don't be a bloody hero.'

Tyrion grinned and kept moving. Leiber surprised Teclis by springing back into the room to aid Tyrion. He said something that Teclis could not hear. Tyrion dropped his burden and started fighting again with the sword. Leiber dragged his companion through the archway and out into the corridor. Tyrion followed a moment later.

'Back!' Teclis bellowed. 'Get clear and don't come back!'

They took him at his word, rushing down the corridor. Teclis found himself facing the regiment of animated corpses. For a moment the sight of them almost froze his heart. He took a step backwards and they followed, leaving the chamber and its protections behind. Teclis kept back-pedalling. They kept following until the corridor was full of them.

Teclis spoke the final words of his spell.

A gigantic wall of flame sprang into being in front of him, hot as hell, with all the incandescent force of a blast furnace. Corpses shrivelled. Eyeballs popped. Skulls exploded as the brains within superheated. Blackened bones kept moving forward through the flames until even they were consumed.

Within moments it was all over. Tyrion looked at him with something like awe.

'That was impressive,' he said.

'If we are going to get the treasure we need to do so now,' said Teclis. 'We may not get another chance.'

Tyrion held up the blade. 'I've got what I came for,' he said.

Teclis gestured at the surviving humans. 'They haven't.'

'Go ahead,' said Tyrion to Leiber and the others. 'You have earned it.'

TECLIS STRODE BACK into the death chamber and studied the inscriptions on the walls. He knew enough about the ancient slann writings to know that he had stumbled across something important. There was something about the runic language that he recognised, something that niggled at his subconscious, and told him that he really needed to pay attention to what he was seeing.

He recognised one of the runes in particular. It could mean either the end of the world, or the end of an age or both. Another rune concerned the elves. A third concerned the coming of Chaos. A fourth represented a Keeper of Secrets. The way they were laid out hinted at a conjunction of all these things. They were all inter-related although he did not know how.

He understood only a few of the words, or rather the pictoglyphs, but those that he did understand filled him with dread. He knew that the ancient slann had been master diviners and that they had left writings predicting the future that had often come true.

He was not entirely sure that he believed in the efficacy of these visions as exact prophecies. He sometimes suspected that the slann had the means to predict the ebb and flow of magic. If you could do that, you could predict the coming of a new dark age simply because you would know when it was possible for daemons to enter the world.

This was something for the scholars back at the White Tower to unravel. Teclis began to copy out what he had seen, sketching the runes as best he could upon parchment, doing his best to memorise everything that he could not copy down.

Leiber and his fellows filled their backpacks with golden objects and Tyrion watched them all bemused. The humans had gone from being terrified to being ecstatic in the space of a few minutes. They picked up glittering strands of slann jewellery and inspected them and then stuffed them into their backpacks, only to take them out moments later when they had found a yet more attractive and possibly valuable example of the gold worker's art. They were laughing out loud and whooping with joy.

Leiber looked around like a man who has achieved a long-held dream and no longer has any idea of what he wants to do with his life. In that moment Teclis felt sorry for him. Finding the treasure chambers of Zultec had been more than simply a means of getting rich to him. It had been something that had given his life meaning.

Teclis thought about his father and the dragon armour of Aenarion. He wondered what would happen to Prince Arathion if he ever worked out how to remake that ancient, potent artefact. Would his life suddenly be without meaning and purpose? How would he motivate himself to go on?

Teclis looked at Leiber with some curiosity. The man was not diving into the ancient piles of gold and jewellery. He was watching his followers do that but was not helping himself to anything. One of the men came running up to him and offered him a necklace. He was shouting about the value of it, about how much it was worth and how they could use the money to buy a farm, a ship, an estate, if that was what they wanted. He was laughing and crying at the same time and telling Leiber that never again would they want for women, wine or food.

Leiber just stood there, uncomprehending. After a moment, he reached out and inspected the necklace, letting the links drip through his fingers, holding it up before his eyes as if he did not quite believe what he was seeing. He turned to Tyrion like a child wanting to show a parent a new toy and then he let the necklace fall to the ground as if it was worth nothing to him.

One of the humans came up to him and tried to stuff a small gold statue into his backpack.

'Take it! Take it!' He said. Teclis smiled at him and gently shook his head. He did not need the gold. He needed space in his backpack for the notes he was making. The human understood him at last and walked away pointing at his forehead and circling his finger to tell his companions that he thought that Teclis was mad. Teclis did not care. He knew that he operated on a different scale of values to the humans. It mattered to him not at all how they judged him.

'I wish I had some wine,' said Leiber. 'I could use a drink. That's for sure.'

He had walked over to Teclis, curious as to what the elf was doing. He looked at the runes Teclis was copying and nodded his head.

'It's some mighty spell isn't it?'

Teclis shook his head. 'Some lore of the slann.'

'I don't know what it is, but I think it could be very important.'

'I envy you your knowledge.'

'It is not knowledge yet, it's just a feeling I have that something here could be of the utmost significance.'

'I know what you mean,' said Leiber. 'I used to feel that way too.' He sounded almost melancholy.

CHAPTER SEVEN

GENERAL DORIAN SILVERBLADE, master of the army of the north, Lord of Halustur, by grace of Malekith, keeper of the iron key and lord high marshal of the realm of Naggaroth waited nervously in the antechamber of the Witch King's throne room.

Frantically he reviewed all of his words and deeds for the past few months to see if there was anything that could possibly have caused a fall from grace. As far as he could tell there was nothing. Not even his most ambitious subordinate could have found an action or a speech that could possibly have been construed as disloyal. If they had made something up, they would swiftly discover the folly of spreading lies to the Witch King. Malekith had his own sources, and he checked and double-checked everything.

No. Dorian had performed his duties in an exemplary, some would say superlative fashion. He had held the border against Chaos for decades and he had overseen the arrival of the new allies Morathi had recruited as well as it was possible to do. There had been a minimum of fuss and trouble with the followers of the

Dark Gods since their unexpected conversion to the cause of the rightful heir of Aenarion. If they planned treachery while within Naggaroth they would find themselves swiftly manoeuvred into a position where they could be destroyed by the druchii armies shadowing them.

Dorian knew that even the most diligent performance of one's duties did not always guarantee Malekith's favour, but it was unusual for the Witch King to take against those who served him well. Still, like every other dark elf he had skeletons in his closet that could be held against him. He supposed that there was always that business with his accursed half-brother Urian which ensured that the whole family would be forever tainted, and then there was his relationship with Cassandra, sorceress and follower of many secret paths, not all of them particularly favoured by Malekith.

He doubted that even those meant that much. If Malekith had been going to punish him for Urian's transgressions he would already have done so. He had made his displeasure with Poisonblade known in the most spectacular fashion possible. For a thousand years druchii would talk about his fate in fearful whispers.

Dorian shuddered when he thought of his last sight of his brother hanging half-flayed from hooks over that blood-filled cauldron. Leather-clad torturers had driven truesilver spikes through his empty eye-sockets into the pleasure centres of his brain, and then muttered spells which turned agony into ecstasy and pleasure into pain. They had done it randomly so that the most awful torture became orgasmic pleasure, and the most gentle painkillers turned into nerve-wracking toxins.

Of course, Urian had gone mad many times, but he had always been nursed back to health. His body had hung there for thirteen months in this antechamber, kept alive by food and water pumped into his stomach through leather tubes and transfusions of blood from dying slaves hooked up to vampiric engines. Then one day Urian was just gone. Never mentioned again in Malekith's hearing, his body tossed unmourned on some rubbish heap in Naggarond.

All because of one ill-considered joke. And he had been a favourite of Malekith's up to that moment. His skill as a pit fighter and his wit and scholarship had all contributed to making him so. Malekith had made an example of him though, and now few considered speculating on how the armoured Witch King entertained himself in the privacy of his personal chambers.

Dorian had never liked his younger brother but it was a waste. Urian had been perhaps the greatest swordsman Naggaroth had seen in twenty generations. He had been a scholar of peculiar lore, an expert on poisons who had delighted in demonstrating their uses in the pits in which he had fought and made his name. He was merry and terrifying and entirely too self-confident. Dorian did not mind admitting now that he had feared him in a manner in which it was not entirely seemly to fear a younger sibling.

And yet he found he still missed him sometimes. They had come from the same place, poor scions of an impoverished ancient line. They had chosen different paths to fame and fortune at the court of Naggaroth, Urian in the fighting pits and bedchambers, he on the battlefield. They had both achieved success. One of them had gone on to demonstrate how transitory that could be. Dorian hoped he was not about to do the same.

Had he said anything about this to Cassandra, he wondered, and had his sorceress lover betrayed him for it? She was loyal to Morathi, in the same way as he was loyal to Malekith, but that meant nothing. The mother and the son shared information about their minions even as they manoeuvred for advantage against each other. It had been that way in Naggaroth for millennia.

He wondered whether Cassandra could be the cause of this summons. Had he said anything outrageous to her when they were drunk on narcotic wine? He somehow doubted it. His tolerance for such things was better than his lover's. Of course, she was a sorceress, a follower of Morathi and that was automatically suspect, but Malekith knew about this. Dorian had reported the contact as soon as it happened. He was as much a spy on Cassandra as she was on him. It was the way the realm functioned.

There was always the chance he had missed something, or Malekith was going to bring up some long-forgotten, by Dorian anyway, indiscretion and punish him for it. It would not be the first time it had happened. He had known generals summoned to the royal presence who fully expected a promotion, only to have a centuries-old conversation repeated verbatim to them, and a treasonous slant put on it. His old commander, Hartelroy, had gone that way, which was a pity for he had been a good general and a decent enough druchii.

Dorian knew it was pointless looking through his past for acts of weakness or sins of treason. If Malekith wanted to find them, he would, no matter how blameless a life Dorian had led. And their entire system was set up so that no one could lead an entirely blameless life. If you did not criticise the king, you criticised his enemies in the Cult of Khaine, only to discover a decade later that those enemies were now trusted allies once more and your criticism of them could be construed as treason.

It was better to keep your mouth shut and say nothing at all, but what druchii could do that? There were so many parties, so many orgies, so many great public festivals at which drunkenness was not only expected, it was practically mandatory, as was narcotic indulgence.

And after all, if you were sober what was it you were trying to hide? And once you were drunk, tongues always wagged. In private gatherings, with friends, under the warming influence of the black grape, people suddenly felt compelled to speak things better left unsaid. And ears were always listening. No matter how small the group, how trusted the friends, there was always someone who saw some way of gaining some advantage from an indiscretion.

Dorian liked to think he could hold his drink, and with the

example of his brother constantly before him he had every reason to, but even he had sometimes said things, let words slip that might be used against him. Perhaps that time was at hand.

The massive stone door to the great throne room slid open. The chamberlain, sumptuously garbed in ermine and purple silk, emerged. 'His majesty will see you now, General Dorian,' he said. There was no clue in his manner whether Dorian was going to reward or execution. It was always the same.

Dorian entered the great audience chamber. It was cold. No fires burned. Malekith did not need them and it would have been in bad taste to remind him of the time he had attempted to pass through the Flame. Icicle stalactites clung to the ceiling. Dorian's breath came out in chilly clouds. He pulled his cloak tight about his shoulders and began the long slow march towards the throne. He kept his back straight, determined to be a soldier to the end.

The audience chamber was vast and empty and his metal shod footsteps echoed within it. He walked between lines of body-guards who might have been statues for all the movement they showed. Doubtless some of them were elves he had once known, who might even have served under his command in the old days, but none of them showed the slightest flicker of recognition, which was as it should be.

Even at this distance, Malekith dominated the chamber. He was huge, out of all proportion to his surroundings. His bodyguards looked like children. His massive armoured figure looked even more like a statue than his guards did. Only the cold flicker of his eyes showed there was something living in there, an intelligence that had outlasted the millennia.

It was not just by sheer physical size that the Witch King dominated the room. He had an aura about him such as a dragon had. He radiated power and a force of will that was terrifying. He was god-like in his way. You only had to get near him to realise it. There could be no doubt that you were in the presence of a king, and something more than a king.

Another figure flanked the throne, an elf woman of astonishing beauty. Chains hung from her limbs that contained powerful, binding magic. Dorian was surprised that he had never seen or heard of her before. Hers was the sort of loveliness of which poets would sing. She studied Dorian with languorous eyes, erotic interest all too visible. He did his best to ignore it. She was standing beside Malekith which would make any such encounter dangerous, no matter how exciting it might prove to be.

'General Dorian, it is good to see you' said Malekith. His still-beautiful voice boomed out. It was not exactly jovial. It was always going to be too cold and remote and impersonal for that, but at least there was no anger in it which was a good sign, unless the Witch King was playing with him as a cat toys with a mouse.

Dorian bowed. 'It is kind of you to say so, sire.'

'You have done a sterling job protecting our borders and your work supervising the arrival of our new allies has been exemplary.'

The terror started to lift from Dorian's mind. It was like a massive downward pressure on his whole body had been removed. Evidently he was still in the Witch King's favour.

'I live only to serve you, sire,' he said.

'If only more of my subjects felt that way,' said Malekith. Was he making a joke, Dorian wondered? It seemed very unlikely. Be careful, he told himself. He felt like he was moving onto very new, very uncertain, very dangerous ground.

'I am sure they are all as loyal as I, sire.'

'Spoken with true druchii ambiguity, Dorian,' said Malekith. 'But I can assure you that very few are, which is why you are standing in front of me now. I have new duties for you, more important than any you have been assigned in the past. If you carry them out to my satisfaction you will be rewarded as no elf has ever been rewarded before. If you fail in them you will be punished as no elf ever has been.'

It was typical of Malekith that he had to mention punishment, Dorian thought. He could have left it unsaid. They both would still have known it was the case anyway, but the Witch King liked to remind his subjects and himself who held all the power.

'I shall not fail you, sire,' said Dorian.

'See that you don't. Say nothing of what you hear today to anyone until I give you permission to do otherwise. Is that clear?'

Dorian knew he was expected to speak. He nodded and said, 'Yes, sire.'

'Very good, Dorian. Now I will satisfy your curiosity as to why you have been summoned.'

The Witch King spoke on then, and Dorian knew why he had been sworn to secrecy. His heart filled with wonder and terror as Malekith outlined his plan and Dorian's part in it. Truly nothing like this had been attempted in all the long years of history. By the time Malekith finished, Dorian was holding his breath. He also knew that the Witch King was not joking. If he succeeded in playing his part he could name his own reward. It was that important.

'Rest assured I shall not fail you, sire,' he said. 'And I would like to thank you for selecting me for this.'

'The only thanks I require will be your success,' said Malekith. 'In a few hours there will be a general staff meeting. You need not attend it. You will be selecting the troops you need and equipping them with the special amulets I have prepared.'

'As you wish, so shall it be, sire.'

MALEKITH STUDIED HIS assembled generals. They represented the most powerful elves in his kingdom. They were feared throughout the lands of Naggaroth. They were soldiers, sorcerers and skilful politicians without equal. Yet here, in his presence, they quivered with barely restrained terror.

He would have preferred it to be different. Yet he knew there was no way that it could be so. He was no longer like any other elf, if he ever had been. His armour saw to that. It did more than protect him. It was a barrier to any natural contact between him and any other member of his race. Sometimes that had its advantages. Sometimes he wished things were otherwise.

He dismissed these feelings of weakness when he saw that the daemon's eyes were upon him. N'Kari watched him intently as always, even when he appeared not to be doing so. Malekith did not need his own eyes to know this. He could sense the daemon's attention through the bond they shared, the bond that had been created by the binding.

He became aware of the fact that more than the daemon were looking at him. All of the dark elves present gazed upon him expectantly. They knew that something of great significance was planned. They knew that he was about to reveal some great scheme to them. Why else would he have called them all to this conference? Why else would there be so many powerful nobles in the one spot.

Malekith let his eyes scan the chamber. It was a vast war room containing maps of Ulthuan, the most detailed that could be put together by his spies and by use of magic. On it was marked every major fortress, city, town, waystone, garrison and wizard's tower. The mobile forces of the Phoenix King were indicated by small jewelled statuettes. As yet, none of his own forces glittered on the huge map that dominated the centre of the room.

Sometimes eyes strayed to the daemon. They did not know who it, or rather she in her present form, was. They were curious as to why she was present. The sorcerers among them would get some sense of the daemon's power and of the power of the restraints holding it, and that would give them pause for thought.

His mother would have known in a moment, of course, which was one of the reasons she was not here. He had sent her to oversee her barbarian army, letting her believe she was gaining a new lever to use against him while he changed the delicate balance of power within his kingdom forever.

He allowed himself a moment to savour the sensation of the fear and respect and wonder and then he strode forward, knowing that all eyes were completely focused on him though and all of those present were wondering exactly what he was going to do and say.

'We are going to Ulthuan,' Malekith said. 'All of you already know that. All of you know that I intend to reunite the kingdom under my righteous rule and crush the rebels who defied my father's will.'

Dark elves were not usually given to shows of emotion but a few of those present applauded and a brief mutter of excited chatter flowed around the room. Malekith smiled inwardly. By stating the obvious he had piqued their curiosity and got them wondering about what he was really going to say.

All of them knew that he had failed to conquer Ulthuan before and were wondering what was different this time, whether they would come out of the experience better than their forebears had. They all knew that invading the island continent was a titanic risk with commensurate rewards. They were wondering how to mini-mise the risk to themselves and maximise their potential gains.

They felt themselves to be standing at the centre of things, to be gaining an advantage just by being here. Being nobles, all of them felt that they were entitled to as much as they could grab and all of them felt that they were clever enough to exploit the situation. Malekith did not care. In fact he was counting on it.

'You will be the spearhead of a plan that has been centuries in the making,' said Malekith. He paused to let them consider that. 'I have been planning and forging weapons and binding supernatu-ral allies to aid us. The day that you have all long awaited is at hand. All of you will lead mighty forces to great victories and for the best of you, for those of you who serve me well, the rewards will be gigantic.'

He paused again for a few heartbeats to let them consider that. Some of them were licking their lips. They knew that he did not waste words and they knew that he did not make empty promises any more than he made empty threats.

'My mother, most blessed of matrons, has won us potent allies.

From the far northern Chaos Wastes, hundreds of thousands of the followers of the Dark Gods have come to enter our service – although they do not know that yet.'

His last remark was met with a storm of cruel laughter. All of them knew that the humans were mere spear fodder for their asur kindred. The humans would not share in the rewards, Malekith intended to see to that. He had a plan for dealing with them at the end of the campaign that would ensure that was the case. He had no intention of letting his mother keep that particular sword hanging over his neck.

'The force that will accompany us is only a small portion of the human strength. The vast majority of it already sails towards the northern coast of Ulthuan. Of course, it will be spotted by the patrols of the false Phoenix King. The rebels think that that is where the blow will fall and a large proportion of their strength is being diverted to meet that threat. It will be a long time before they realise what is truly happening.'

'I do not intend to rely upon humans to reclaim my rightful kingdom. The honour and duty of that falls upon you, my loyal subjects. You are the ones who will lead in my righteous conquest and reunite the kingdoms. You are the ones who will do the important fighting and you will claim the true rewards of victory. You are the ones upon whom failure will press most heavily.'

All mirth vanished as he spoke the last sentence. They had heard him promise rewards. They knew that he would punish failure as he always did. He had let them know who their master was. It was a task that needed to be performed on a regular basis given the nature of his subjects and their ruthless ambitions.

'Your forces are smaller in number but much greater in skill. You are the ones who will conquer cities and fortresses and claim them to your own.'

Once again he dangled the rewards in front of them and watched them salivate. He had specifically stated that they might claim what they conquered for their own. He could see them performing the calculations almost visibly. Here was a chance that would not come again in their lifetimes to extend their estates, increase their flocks of slaves, bolster their fortunes and surround their names with glory.

'Some of you will lead armies overland in pursuit of great strategic goals. Some of you will have other duties.'

They were wondering now what he meant by that. Did he mean to punish some of them by denying them the right of conquest and holding them back from the front line of the war? Or did he mean something else? He let them wonder for a few more moments while he let his eyes rest upon each of them in turn.

'All of you must know now that I have made great magical allies and summoned them from the realms beyond our world. All of you are wondering why I have done this when I can rely implicitly on your own warlike skills. The answer is very simple. One of the allies that I have summoned will give us the keys to victory, will let us overcome every enemy army, take every enemy fortress and reach the furthest extent of the rebel kingdom, before our foes even know that we are there.'

A look of concentration passed over every face now – they were all wondering exactly how he proposed to achieve this miraculous feat. It was something that had eluded the greatest of sorcerers through all of the ages and they were wondering whether their king had finally gone mad.

'All of you must know this. I, your king, have bound one of the greatest foes of our people into my service.'

He gestured and N'Kari's true form was revealed. The great four limbed monster towered over every living thing in the room. It flexed claws that could shear through the thickest armour. It roared and the very sound was thrilling and terrifying.

All of the druchii present, even the bravest, flinched. They wore the same expressions on their faces as they would have if he'd introduced a pack of starving lions into the room.

'Before you stands N'Kari, the Keeper of Secrets, the daemon defeated and banished by my father, who led the Rape of Ulthuan, who was once the greatest foe of all our people. I, Malekith the Great, son of Aenarion have bound this beast to my service. I have done this knowing full well that given the chance, this foul thing will betray us if it can and knowing that, I will not allow it to do so. I have bound this creature not because I need it to fight for us, although it will kill anyone I tell it to.'

Malekith paused for a beat to let them consider that piece of information. None of them wanted to be the victim of a greater daemon. None of them would go against him in any way while they thought that was a possibility. He wanted them to fully consider the consequences of any rebellion against him.

Particularly, given the fact that he had bound a daemon that was a sworn enemy of their people. He thought it best to get the information out there in the open and to use it for his own advantage.

'The reason I have taken this creature into my service is because it knows the secrets of how to pass swiftly, secretly and unstoppably through the island-continent of Ulthuan. It has done so before and it has taken an army with it. Cast your minds back over a century to the rumours that came out of Ulthuan then. I am in a position to tell you that those rumours were true and that what the merchants of the marketplace whispered is exactly what happened.'

He could see shocked looks passing around the room now. He was giving them a lot to think about in a very short space of time, but he knew they were capable of absorbing it. He also knew it was best to give it to them all at once on his own terms, rather than wait for it to come out piecemeal.

'Of course, my servant failed then because it did not have the force that we have, or the skill at warfare, or the knowledge of when and where it is appropriate to attack. We can succeed where N'Kari failed and we will do so because it is our destiny.

'With the service of this bound daemon we shall be able to move so swiftly that our enemies will not know where we are or how to stop us before it is too late. We will be able to amass our forces to overwhelm our enemies before they know what has hit them. This more than anything else will give us a victory. This time all of Ulthuan will be ours. This time we will succeed. This time victory is inevitable.'

Malekith allowed some of his own enthusiasm to show in his voice. He could see that it was being communicated to his followers by his words and his gestures. All of them had sufficient knowledge of matters military to understand what an enormous advantage N'Kari would give them. All of them were nervous about the presence of the daemon but all of them could see exactly why it was there. There was silence for many heartbeats and even Malekith felt the tension in the room.

After a silence of long moment, all of them cheered. After an initial hesitation all of them were as convinced as he was that victory was their destiny.

'On the table,' Malekith said, 'you will find your orders. These are sealed and you will communicate them to no one except where you are authorised to do so. All of you have a part to play in this great victory. All of you will share in the spoils of victory. All of you will be part of the great historical process of reuniting the kingdom. All of you will be remembered for as long as that kingdom exists and elves gather to talk about great military triumphs.'

The elven nobles present almost came to blows in their haste to reach the table. He knew then that he had them. Then he saw the smile on the face of the daemon and wondered why it looked so happy.

CHAPTER EIGHT

WEARY ALMOST BEYOND belief, Tyrion and his companions emerged from the swamp. The last few leagues had been the worst part. They had wandered from the jungle into the marshes surrounding Skeggi. The ground had become treacherous quicksand, mud and stagnant pools filled with the spores of the worst diseases.

All of them except Teclis were covered in filth. His magic had protected him from that. Yet, despite the weariness, despite the dirt, despite the loathsome nature of their surroundings, all of them were triumphant. They had made it all the way back from Zultec without losing anybody else. And the humans were filled with the knowledge that they were rich, while the elves knew that they were going to be even more famous very soon.

Ahead of them they could see the strange wooden longhalls that made up the bulk of the dwellings in Skeggi. They resembled the halls of the Norsemen back in the Old World, but in one important respect they were different – they stood upon stilts that raised them above the mud. Those buildings on the outskirts of the city needed them. Some of them sat in small algae-scummed lakes that resembled moats. The only way to get to them was either by small boat, rope-bridge or by jumping across the stumps of chopped down trees that made up a kind of stepping stone.

Right now the party was up to their waists in muddy water and starting to draw attention from the natives. They were very conspicuous – two tall elves and a small group of survivors from what had been a much larger party when it set out. Some of those present recognised Tyrion, some of them recognised Leiber. All of them were curious as to what the party had done and how they had survived.

Now came the tricky part. Skeggi was a dreadful place, lawless, ruled by feuding warlords and bandit gangs. It combined the worst aspects of Norse society and that of the theoretically more civilised Old World. Some of the people greeting them now might decide to rob them in a few moments, once a sufficiently large gang of allies had assembled.

They would make formidable foes too. Most of those present were tall, strapping warriors descended from the Norse. They were blond-haired with golden, tanned skins and broad-shouldered, muscular bodies. All of them were armed with heavy axes or sharp swords. After the rigours of the past few weeks Tyrion should not have been too bothered, but he knew the perils of over-confidence and he did not want to fall victim to a random robbery when he was so close to returning to Lothern in triumph.

'If we are attacked, burn as many as possible with the most spectacular magic you can summon,' he said to Teclis in elvish. 'If you should happen to set a few buildings alight in the process so much the better.'

'And what will you be doing while I commit these theatrical acts of arson?'

'I will be killing as many people as I can in the most disgustingly bloody fashion I can manage. If we make an example of enough of them, the rest will leave us alone.'

'It's nice to hear you being so cheerful now that we are so close to safety.'

'No one is safe in Skeggi,' Tyrion said. 'The priests of the goddess of mercy will pick your pocket while they stick a dagger in your back.'

'They are somewhat unorthodox in the way they practise their faith,' said Teclis. 'It's always the way. Heretical sects breed in these out of the way places.'

'Joke about it all you like but be ready...' Tyrion said.

In the distance, Tyrion could see the monstrous brutal structure of the fortress. It was the size of a small town and had been built by a dozen generations of raider lords on the site of the original keep of Losteriksson, the town's legendary founder. The only thing that came close to being as noticeable was the giant barrow that had grown over the spot where Losteriksson had first set foot on this land.

As they progressed deeper into town, more and more people swarmed around them. Some were menacing-looking Norse warriors, others were the sort of shipwrecked wharf rats from the Old World. A few tired looking prostitutes shouted half-hearted terms of endearment at the elves and their companions.

'Leiber, you made it back, I am surprised,' roared someone who obviously recognised their guide. 'You finally find all that lost gold you always raved about?'

It was a leading question if Tyrion had ever heard one, and it was the one most likely to trigger a bloodbath if the wrong answer was given. They had talked about this all the way back but there was no telling what the humans would do now that they were back among their own kind.

In a way Tyrion was glad they had only taken the sword and a few keepsakes. There was not very much for their companions to kill them over. The humans were more likely to get themselves into trouble than the two elves. Of course, that would not make very much difference if they got dragged into a needless fight.

'I got more than enough to buy your mother,' said Leiber. 'But then that only ever cost a couple of coppers anyway, and she would give change.'

It was a good answer. It told the listeners that it was none of their business what Leiber had found and that they could expect only insults if they asked. The question was whether it would be enough to ensure they were left alone.

THEY PUSHED THROUGH the teeming streets of the town, trying to ignore all of the people staring at them. The fortress loomed over them, bringing back memories of a previous visit that Tyrion would have preferred to forget. He had spent some time in chains in that horrible place and he was determined that it would never happen again.

As they walked on, a sense of ending came over him. He was soon going to have to say goodbye to the humans. Most likely he would never see any of them again. The people he had known on his previous visits to Skeggi were all dead or withered ancients. Human lives were so brief that once their paths separated he was unlikely to come across them again, or if he did they would be so changed as to be almost unrecognisable to him.

He was not sure why this troubled him. He felt a certain attachment to these men as he would to any comrades with whom he had shared dangers. It seemed that the humans felt the same way because one or two of them were staring at him sidelong.

He sensed that they were at once relieved and saddened by this parting of the ways. They had found what they were looking for. They were wealthy men. Perhaps they felt grateful to Tyrion and his brother for providing them with this wealth or perhaps it was something else entirely, he could not be sure. All he knew was that by the time they had reached a crossroads at the centre of the town, all of them knew that their quest together was over. They were walking more slowly, starting to look at each other in a vaguely embarrassed way.

Leiber was the first to speak. 'It looks like we will be going our separate roads. I just want to say that it was an honour and a privilege travelling with you. I hope one day that we might be able to do it again.'

If he did not sound entirely sincere, at least he was trying to be polite, Tyrion thought. He felt like he was being called upon to answer on behalf of himself and his brother so he said, 'We could not have asked for better travelling companions.'

The humans all nodded and Tyrion found himself shaking hands with his companions. A few moments later they had started to drift apart, most of the humans heading towards one of the low taverns which filled the streets of Skeggi. Tyrion looked at Teclis and smiled sourly, 'It will not take long before word of our discovery is common knowledge in this port.'

'What do you propose that we do about that, brother?'

'There is nothing we can do. We just need to hope that the local robbers don't decide to pay us a visit. It would not surprise me to find out that Leiber and the other lads were found in the gutter with their throats cut by this time tomorrow.'

'And you want us to avoid that fate?'

'It would seem sensible, wouldn't it? After all, it would be bitterly ironic if we survived all our adventures only to get ourselves killed in some back alley in this gods-forsaken place.'

'Then I think the first thing we should do is look for a ship out of here.'

'That might just be putting ourselves at the mercy of one of the local pirate captains. They are as much cutthroats as most of the people around here, probably more so.'

'Then perhaps we should look for a trading ship that will take us all the way back to Ulthuan.'

'I suppose that means that you're going to suggest we head down to the docks right now.'

'No time like the present!'

* * *

THE HARBOUR AT Skeggi was a makeshift place of rickety wooden piers flanked by the local longhouses. There were no great warehouses, only the fortified dwellings of the local chieftains. There was a white sand beach on which long ships were drawn up.

Looking as out of place in the harbour as a swan among a flock of ducks was an elven clipper bearing the arms of House Emeraldsea, a golden ship on a field of green. Tyrion was even more surprised by the fact he recognised the vessel. It was the *Eagle of Lothern*, on which he had voyaged during that long ago time when he and his brother had first been summoned back to Lothern.

It was the last thing he would have expected to see in this shabby human town. There was only one reason for one of the great trading vessels belonging to their mother's family to be here – it was seeking himself and his brother. Then he noticed something else. The vessel was flying a black flag.

Someone very important had died.

A sudden shock passed through him as he wondered who it could be? He hoped it was no one in his own house. He had not seen such a flag since his grandfather had died. He hoped it was not someone else that he loved – like Lady Malene.

Two other possibilities sprang immediately to mind – it might be the Phoenix King or the Everqueen. It seemed unlikely that Finubar was dead. He was still very young for an elf and it was unlikely that anything but violence could have killed him.

It was not unknown for a Phoenix King to be assassinated or to be killed in battle but, as far as Tyrion knew, the elves were not at war with anyone. At least they had not been when he and his brother had left Lothern. Had some major conflict blown up that he had missed? It galled him that he might have lost a chance to win glory for himself and his family.

He saw that someone on the crow's nest was waving at him. They had already been spotted through a spyglass and it looked like someone on the ship wanted to make contact with them.

Teclis came up beside him and spoke softly, 'This does not look good.'

'I fear you are right, brother. Let us find out what the bad news is.'

'CAPTAIN JOYELLE, IT is a pleasure to meet you once again,' Tyrion said as he pulled himself over the side of the ship. He could tell that the captain was pleased that he remembered her. He was quite famous now and he supposed that meant something.

'I wish it was under more pleasant circumstances,' she said. 'I bear terrible news.'

'What is it?' Teclis asked. He was being lifted up on a bosun's sling. He did not like to scamper up the web of ropes draped over the side of a ship unless he absolutely had to. 'Nothing has happened to Lady Malene, I hope?'

'No, Prince Teclis, the lady of the House is well and sends you her greetings. The bad tidings are that the Everqueen is dead.'

'The Everqueen?' Tyrion's mind reeled. He felt grief well up within his heart. She had been the spiritual leader of the elves for as long as he had been alive and considerably longer. Her blessing was invoked at the start of every major venture, every voyage, every season's crop planting.

'That is terrible news indeed,' Teclis said. 'It is a strange coincidence that you should be waiting here to give it to us.'

'It is no coincidence at all, Prince Teclis,' said the captain. 'I was dispatched to bring the news to your brother and to summon him home.'

Tyrion tilted his head to one side as he concentrated upon the captain. 'Why?'

'A new Everqueen will soon be crowned and a new Everqueen must have a new champion.'

'And what exactly has this to do with my brother?' Teclis asked. These days, he really had not the slightest sensitivity to any of the nuances of politics outside those of the Tower of Hoeth.

Tyrion understood at once. House Emeraldsea wished to have a candidate of their own be the champion of the Everqueen and he was the best possible candidate that they could put forward.

Even for one so comparatively young for an elf, he was already a famous warrior. He was good-looking, well spoken, intelligent, diplomatic and he knew all of these things about himself. As the Everqueen's champion he would be ideally placed to help influence her decisions and that would give him, and through him House Emeraldsea, considerable political influence. He understood at once exactly why he was being summoned home.

He was not sure how he felt about this himself. He had plans of his own. There were things he wanted to do with his life. The position would entail a great deal of responsibility and an enormous curtailment of his freedom.

Wherever the Everqueen went her bodyguard went. Her champion was always at her side, ready to protect and fight for her honour. The position had existed ever since the reign of the second Phoenix King. Prior to that no one had ever thought that the Everqueen needed a bodyguard. But the first Everqueen, Astarielle, had been slain by the followers of Chaos and ever since then the Everqueen had had a champion at her side.

'Our family wants me to enter the great tournament,' he said. Captain Joyelle nodded. Teclis's expression suddenly changed. He understood now. He smiled at Tyrion.

'It is a very great honour,' he said.

'I am fully aware of that fact,' said Tyrion. His sour expression must have told his listeners that he was less than thrilled by the honour implied. Teclis's eyes narrowed. Captain Joyelle looked slightly embarrassed.

'I was instructed to bring you this news and to take you home to Lothern. Lady Malene told me you would eventually find your way back to Skeggi.'

It was the only possible place they could get a ship out of this part of Lustria so it was a fair bet. Not that Lady Malene was incapable of locating them by magic if she wanted to. She was a mighty sorceress.

'Fortunately,' said Teclis. 'Our business in the jungles of Lustria is concluded and we have found what we came for.'

'You have found it?' Captain Joyelle asked.

Tyrion drew Sunfang with a theatrical flourish. Fires danced along the length of the blade. Captain Joyelle's eyes widened and her mouth fell open. All of her officers looked stunned. As well they might, thought Tyrion. They had just come face-to-face with one of the great legends of the first and mightiest kings of the elves.

'Is that...' asked Captain Joyelle.

'It is Sunfang,' said Teclis. He could not keep his satisfaction from showing in his voice. 'The sword of Aenarion, forged by Caledor Dragontamer himself at Vaul's Anvil in the dawn ages of the world.'

'I never thought that in my lifetime this blade would be recovered,' said Joyelle. 'You have brought us some happiness in this time of great distress, Prince Tyrion. May Isha bless you.'

Teclis's sour expression showed that he understood what was going on. He was used to the fact that his brother would get the credit for any of their joint ventures. Tyrion wondered if he really cared about it all that much. He supposed that it might get annoying, but there was nothing either of them could do about it. It seemed sometimes as if there was a conspiracy among the elves to ignore any of the achievements of his brother and heap praise upon him. There were times when Tyrion felt very guilty about that.

He did not have time to feel that way now. There were other things he needed to consider.

MORATHI STRODE INTO her son's audience chamber aware that all eyes were upon her. The courtiers stared. The assembled warlords of the great Houses looked at her with lust. She kept her face impassive, giving no clue to her inner turmoil.

When she had heard the stories she had left the Chaos horde and her own army and taken the fastest ship she could find back to Naggaroth. She needed to know whether the tales her spies had brought were true and one glance was enough to tell her that they were.

Morathi stared at the daemon that looked like a girl and found that it was as bad as she had feared. She could not quite believe what her son had done. She did not know whether to be proud or angry so she settled for both. Malekith had bound a Keeper of Secrets to his will. It was a feat of astonishing boldness. Such creatures were treacherous and powerful beyond belief and could turn on their summoners with fatal consequences in the space of a heartbeat.

And yet, he had done it.

The daemon was there and appeared to be under control, standing amid a crowd of dark elves who had no idea of how close death hovered.

The infernal thing was well bound by those strange alien shackles and yet Morathi still did not feel entirely secure. It was like being in the same room with a chained lion. The beast might not be able to get free, but you still would not want to put your hand into its mouth. Morathi glanced around at the elves present.

'Beloved son, I would have words with you in private.' All eyes moved from her to Malekith. She could see the druchii present were afraid and rightly so. None of them wished to offend her, but disobeying her son would be instantly fatal.

Malekith nodded. The elves began to filter out of the chamber, leaving mother, son and bound daemon alone. Morathi looked at the daemon and then at Malekith. She kept her anger under control, not a thing she would normally have any cause to do, but it was always counter-productive to rage at her son. He only became more icy and controlled.

'What have you done?' she asked eventually.

Malekith merely loomed over her. The armour gave him awesome presence. He seemed less like a living being than the daemon he had bound. He said nothing. It was obvious he was going to force her hand.

'You have bound a greater daemon of Slaanesh to your service. Do you know what that means?'

'It means I have found the key to unlock the defences of Ulthuan.'

'Maybe. It also means you have acquired the eternal enmity of an infernal being.'

Malekith surprised her by laughing. 'I had that anyway. This is the creature that had sworn to wipe out the line of Aenarion. That is what makes this so amusing.'

'You find this amusing?'

'N'Kari, Chosen of Slaanesh, meet my mother, Morathi, consort of Aenarion. The two of you should be friends. You have much in common.'

The daemon and the sorceress exchanged looks. Malekith's metallic laughter grew louder and colder. It was worse even than she had imagined. This was the creature that had led the Rape of Ulthuan, who had twice been beaten by Aenarion, who had every reason to hate her son and work his undoing.

'You will destroy us all,' said Morathi.

'I think, dearest mother, that is your plan, not mine.'

Morathi gave Malekith a searching look. How much did he really know? How much had he guessed? The fact that he had bound this abomination showed one thing. He had come a very long way as a wizard. He was to be numbered among the greatest mages, living or unliving, since these days one had to take into account certain undead abominations when making the calculation.

The daemon merely looked at them and smiled. She guessed that Malekith might be doing the same beneath his metal mask but she could not be certain.

'Oh yes, mother, I know of your schemes. I just wanted you to know that I will not allow them.'

William King

'You will not... allow them!' Her anger showed in her voice this time. At once she knew it was a mistake but she could not help herself. Her pride and her fear had both been aroused. Any other living thing in the world would have cowered before her unveiled wrath. The metal monster her son had become just stood there impassive as a statue. 'Who are you to forbid me to do anything?'

'I am your king. I think you forget that sometimes. I am the absolute and unchallenged ruler of Naggaroth and soon of the whole elven world.'

Morathi wanted to rage, but something about the confidence that gleamed in his voice gave her pause. 'And when did you propose to tell me how this will be accomplished,' she said.

'In good time, mother, although I am sure you can work it out for yourself given your undoubted knowledge and your gift of foresight. Or your spies will tell you. I just want to make sure there are no misunderstandings between us.'

'I am sure I do not know what you mean?'

'Let us say that if I find you have been disturbing the pattern of Caledor's work, I will give you to my pet here as a plaything. You would like that, wouldn't you, N'Kari?'

The bound daemon smiled and nodded.

'You will have to forgive her for not being more conversational,' Malekith said. 'I have forbidden her to speak until I am convinced she will be civil.'

Rage and fear warred within Morathi but she let neither show on her face. The fact that her son knew or had guessed her plans made no difference to her determination to carry them out. It would only make the process more difficult and the stakes higher. She smiled a genuine smile this time. This only made things more interesting.

'Return to your barbarian army, mother, and see that it carries out its duties well.'

'Of course, beloved son. How could I do otherwise?'

116

'Soon the invasion of Ulthuan begins. You will be queen once more in Ulthuan.'

And more than queen, my son, Morathi thought. The daemon smiled as if it understood what was going through her mind.

CHAPTER NINE

'So what now?' Teclis asked.

Tyrion stared off into the distance. The sea stretched as far as the horizon, black, oily, reflecting the moon and the night sky. Already Tyrion felt better for being out of the jungle. He was wearing clean clothes for the first time in months. He was not being eaten alive by mosquitoes as he slept. He had eaten shipboard rations and even though it was very basic by most standards, it was food that he liked. He could hear elvish being spoken all around him, and he was reassured to be once more surrounded by his own people.

For the first time in a very long time he felt like he could go to sleep securely, and not have to fear waking in some terrible peril. And of course, because this was the case, for the first time in months he was having difficulty sleeping.

It did not surprise him to find his brother upon the deck. Teclis was a night person. He liked to be awake and studying while others slept. It was a habit he had acquired in their youth when he had difficulty falling asleep because of his numerous illnesses. It had never left him, even now after he had used alchemy to acquire almost normal health.

He was glad that Teclis was awake. He felt the need to talk to someone about what troubled him and his brother was one of the few people that he could do that with, even though they were no longer as close as they had once been when they were children.

'I could not sleep,' said Tyrion.

'That is strange,' said Teclis. 'Normally by now you would be lying there snoring, keeping the rest of us awake. Do you miss the jungle? Is the alarming absence of danger getting on your nerves?'

'Something like that,' said Tyrion. 'I have been thinking about the future.'

'I know how thinking always disturbs you. I am not surprised that you cannot sleep. My advice to you is give up on that. Thinking is not something that suits you. Doing is more your style.' Normally Tyrion would not have minded his brother's teasing but right now he was not in the mood for it.

'I am serious,' he said. 'I am not sure that I like being summoned home in order to be put forward as a candidate in some political contest.'

He spoke softly so that no one might hear them. He did not want word of his doubts getting back to the ruler of House Emeraldsea, at least not until he was certain that he wanted them to.

'Would it be so bad being the champion of the Everqueen?' Teclis asked. 'It is a great honour. One of the greatest that any elf could ever aspire to.'

Tyrion considered his words carefully. He had rarely even hinted at his secret ambitions to anyone, even his brother, over the past century. He was not sure that he wanted to do so even now. His grandfather had been the only elf he ever really talked to about them, and Lord Emeraldsea had shared them. 'I know. It's just that I am not sure it is an honour I want. I have been thinking about other things.'

Teclis raised an eyebrow. 'Such as?'

'You remember when we were young, you dreamed of being a great wizard. I dreamed of being a great warrior. I wanted to be a hero.'

'You *are* a hero,' said Teclis. For once he sounded serious. There was no mockery in his voice. Tyrion was surprised and rather touched.

'That was the dream of a boy,' said Tyrion 'I have other dreams now. I want to lead armies. I want to do something to help our people in this world.'

'You want to write your name in the history books,' said Teclis.

'Not just that.'

'You have... political ambitions? You have set your sights on the Phoenix Throne?'

'What if I have?' Tyrion asked.

'I am not judging you, brother,' said Teclis. 'I thought you were happy to be a simple warrior. I had not dreamed that you aimed so high.'

'Neither did I, not really. And I'm not even sure about them myself. I would just like to keep my options open.'

'And you think that becoming the champion of the Everqueen would limit you in some way.'

'You know it would! The champion must be at the Everqueen's side. The only time he can ever leave it is when she dispatches him on a mission. Being the champion of the Everqueen is to be nothing more than a glorified lackey. That is not what I imagined my life would be like.'

'Then don't do it. You don't have to. You don't even have to enter the lists if you don't want to.'

'You're being very naive, brother. House Emeraldsea has made an investment in us. They want to see it repaid.'

'I am astonished to hear myself say this but I think you are being too cynical. You are an ornament to the House. You add a certain lustre to their name just by existing. You are a hero of the blood of Aenarion. Without you they would be known only as the wealthiest merchants in Lothern.'

For such a clever elf, Teclis could be astonishingly naive when it came to politics. 'Our beloved relatives are playing a very long and deep game. Like all the great Houses, they seek power not just prestige. You and I are counters in that game, pieces on a board. They want us where we will be most useful.'

Teclis steepled his fingers and smiled coldly. 'And you think you would not be useful as Phoenix King.'

'I have never said I want to be Phoenix King.'

'You have all the qualifications. You have the looks, the charisma, the intelligence, the reputation...'

'The gold? The political support?'

'So you *do* want to be Phoenix King.'

'What male elf does not?'

'I, for one.'

'You are a special case. You love nothing more than magic.'

'There are many other special cases.'

'Look, brother. I do not know whether I want to be Phoenix King, or whether I have what it takes to be one. I do know that in order to become Phoenix King, you need a lot of powerful political allies and a lot of money. A good deal of horse-trading goes into the making of our ruler. If I wanted to be Phoenix King, I would need the support of Emeraldsea, and a great deal more.'

'I understand.'

'I will never get that support if I alienate Lady Emeraldsea now.'

'I understand that also. What I don't understand is why you think she would not want you to be Phoenix King.'

'I don't think that. What I think is that Finubar is young and already a powerful ally of our kin. He is not likely to die any time soon. And in the meantime I think she would prefer to have a definite hold on the Everqueen than a warrior who might never become Phoenix King many centuries hence.'

Teclis nodded slightly, as if he was finally seeing the point. 'A bird in the hand beats a Phoenix in the future.'

'Yes.'

'It does not matter.'

'I can assure you it does.'

'Your life will be long, Tyrion. You can't predict how things will turn out.'

'I can predict that if I do not do what is asked of me now then Malene will never support me, nor will any of her successors.'

'Then do what she asks, go to the tournament and lose.' Tyrion looked at his brother in wonder. Was it possible that even after all these years Teclis did not understand him?

Teclis smiled again. 'No, you could not do that, could you? You have never liked to lose at anything. Is that what is really bothering you? The possibility that here is a competition you might not win.' The mockery had returned to his voice.

Tyrion shook his head. 'The thing that bothers me is the possibility that I might win.'

TECLIS LAY ON the deck and stared up at the stars. The gentle rise and fall of the ship helped him relax. He remembered how, long ago, he had been plagued by seasickness and what a torment that had been. Now, like most of the other ailments, it was just a memory. It was odd how things that had dominated his life for so long could just vanish, leaving behind only strange dream-like recollections.

Of course, yesterday he and his brother had been in the jungles of Lustria. Now they were aboard the *Eagle of Lothern* scudding across the ocean. The jungle was the dream now, the ocean the reality.

Strange thoughts raced through his head. What was time? How did it work? What is this process that keeps us moving inexorably into the future at the same rate every day? Is it true that gods and daemons live outside time and are aware of multiple selves, in all places, at all times? Is that how their prophets are sometimes given glimpses of the future?

He considered Tyrion. To most people his brother always seemed the very epitome of the devil-may-care warrior, living life to the fullest now, because tomorrow he might be dead. Teclis knew his twin was cleverer than that, and much more thoughtful.

Did Tyrion really aspire to the Phoenix Throne or was this about something different entirely? Was he simply afraid of being tied down, of assuming responsibility? Teclis doubted it was the latter. Tyrion had commanded troops in the field. He was not frightened by that sort of responsibility at all. Perhaps it was the loss of freedom of action that he feared, of being drawn into the web of social entanglements that all elves eventually found themselves ensnared in.

Both he and Tyrion owed House Emeraldsea a debt. Their kindred had aided them, supported them, paid for their education, given them their start in life. Lady Malene had seen to it that Teclis had gotten the best training at the White Tower. Both of them were aware that one day those debts would be called in and need to be repaid, his own as much as Tyrion's.

Teclis was not troubled by that. When the time came he would worry about it. Right now he had other things to think of. Perhaps that was Tyrion's problem. He could lose himself only in action, in doing. When he was not, he fretted. His was not a nature suited to being at rest. He craved action, distraction.

Perhaps his brother was not really suited to be Phoenix King because of that. The elves did not need another war-seeking ruler. The thought seemed disloyal but it haunted Teclis for the rest of the night.

'I WOULD LIKE to look at that sword,' Teclis said. He had entered his brother's cabin in the dawn light. Tyrion was already awake, lying on the bunk, staring at the ceiling.

Tyrion shrugged, unfastened the sword-belt and passed it over to him. He did not seem particularly self-conscious about disarming himself in the way most warriors would. Teclis supposed it was because his brother trusted him, and also because he had no doubts he could get the weapon back if it was needed.

Teclis pulled the blade from its scabbard. For a moment, it felt as heavy to him as it really was. He had managed to restore his health by the use of alchemy but he would never be strong. He could feel Sunfang straining his fingers and his wrist. Only for a moment though, then the blade glistened, glowing as if flames were trapped within the metal, and it felt light enough even for him. Teclis smiled with pleasure.

'So it works for you too,' said Tyrion.

'Of course,' Teclis replied. 'Very useful.'

'It takes some getting used to,' said Tyrion. 'The weight and balance seems to adjust as you wield it. It's like a living thing.'

Teclis swept the sword through the air. It left a glowing trail behind it, faintly visible even without use of his magesight. He smiled with pure pleasure.

'Careful,' said Tyrion. 'I don't want you taking my head off accidentally.'

'It might make you smarter,' said Teclis.

'Think of the pain it would cause the ladies of Ulthuan.'

Teclis would have responded but he was too busy concentrating on the sword. The enchantments designed to make it easy to wield were only one part of the complex web of magic pinned in place by the runes on the blade.

There were other spells present, fascinatingly complex ones which hinted at great power. Filled with curiosity, he extended his thoughts and activated one. A jet of flame blasted from the point of the blade. Only Tyrion's lightning reflexes kept him out of the way. He sprang to one side and the flame hit the porthole setting it to glowing.

Panicked, Teclis sought to bring it under control. The jet of flame set the bedding alight before he managed to douse the fire blazing from the point of the blade.

Tyrion threw the porthole open, picked the burning blankets up and cast them through the window. He blew on his slightly burned hands. His face was sooty, his jerkin singed.

'How much is House Silverbright paying you for my assassination?' Tyrion asked. 'Tell me, I will double it.'

It was a line from a melodrama popular in the theatres of Ulthuan when they had left. He was smiling as he said it.

Teclis was anything but amused. He was embarrassed and frightened by what he had done. He could easily have hurt his twin, possibly injuring him permanently. 'I am so sorry,' he said. 'I did not mean to do that.'

Tyrion grinned. 'If I thought you had, you would not be holding that blade. Nor would you be conscious.'

He did not say it as a threat, simply as a statement of fact. Teclis knew that it was exactly the case as well.

Tyrion spoke more softly now. 'Learn a lesson. I saw that look of concentration come over your face, the one you get when you are lost in the contemplation of the wonders of magic and I knew you were about to do something extremely stupid. When the point of the sword started glowing I was certain of it. Was that you or the sword that did the trick with the flame, by the way?'

'It was the sword. There is a spell woven into it. At the blade's heart, Caledor trapped one of the elemental spirits of the volcano. It burns in there, its life force powering the blade. You can unleash part of it by contacting the spirit.'

'Useful. Having a sword that lets you breathe fire like a dragon, I mean. Nice to know the trick is still possible. I had always thought the ancient tales exaggerated.'

'You would not want to do it too often. You might over-draw the life force of the elemental and unravel all the magic in the sword. If you use it, you need to give the sword time to regain its health. Using its magic in that way is like an elf losing a lot of blood. It takes time to recover.'

'You think I could learn to use it then.' Teclis knew his brother had noted away what he was saying but as always seemed concerned only with his own purposes. They were very alike in that way.

'Undoubtedly. It was intended for use by a warrior, not a wizard.'

'Excellent.' Tyrion sounded genuinely pleased. 'How do I do it?'

'I will endeavour to find out if you will allow me to concentrate.'

'Just don't concentrate too hard. I don't want you stumbling on some new way to accidentally kill me.'

Teclis nodded. It was not a mistake he was going to make again. 'If I do find a way to kill you, it won't be accidental,' he said. It came out more ominously than he meant it to. Tyrion just grinned his idiot grin, as if certain that nothing in this world could really harm him. Teclis sincerely hoped that really was the case.

He was embarrassed and angry at himself and displacing it onto his twin, which was not fair. 'I did not mean that,' he said.

'I know,' said Tyrion. 'Just find a way to let me use the sword. I will leave you to it. Try not to set fire to the ship. It's a long swim to Ulthuan.'

'I can't swim,' said Teclis.

'All the more reason for being careful then,' said Tyrion as he left the cabin.

URIAN STARED INTO the mirror and waited for contact to come. How many times had he stood here over the past few centuries, he wondered? How many times had he made the strange pilgrimage through the underground labyrinth beneath the Silvermount Palace to find this place? How many more times would he have to do so?

The answers did not come. At the moment, his master did not seem to want to put in an appearance either. Urian made himself look devoted and alert. He was never sure exactly how the magical mirror worked, whether Malekith could see him even when he could not see the Witch King. Knowing the way his master's mind worked it seemed entirely possible.

Suddenly the colours in the mirror swirled, Urian's sardonically smiling reflection vanished to be replaced by the monstrous armoured figure of his master. He lounged like a massive, animated statue on his gigantic metal throne.

Standing beyond and behind Malekith, held on chains like a hound on a leash, was the second most astonishingly beautiful elf woman Urian had ever seen. Only Morathi was more lovely and she was not there to be compared, so it was possible this one's beauty exceeded even hers. She looked much younger and much more innocent than Morathi, but that meant nothing. Urian was well aware of how deceptive appearances could be.

There was something about the chains on this one's limbs that worried him, a magic that dazzled the eye and tired the brain. He let his eyes linger on her, wondering who she was. From behind Malekith's back, she winked at him. So she could see him and was aware of who he was. That might prove to be a bad thing in the long run.

'You are to be congratulated, Urian.' Malekith's voice emerged from the mirror with perfect cold clarity. The Witch King sounded as pleased as Urian had ever heard him. 'The Everqueen is dead. Your reward will be extraordinary.'

'Serving you is reward enough, my liege.' Urian was proud that he managed to keep any trace of irony from his voice. There were times when he could get away with that in front of his master but instinct told him that now was not such a time.

'Please, Urian, let us not even pretend that is so,' said Malekith. 'I am your liege, and it is my duty and my pleasure to reward my favoured vassals.'

'In that case, I await your magnanimity with breathless anticipation, my lord.'

'You shall not have to wait too long. Within this year I will have vast new estates to disburse to my most loyal subjects.'

Despite the fact he had long awaited this moment, excitement stabbed at Urian's vitals. So it was finally going to happen then – the long awaited invasion of Ulthuan for which secret preparations had been going on for centuries. 'I am thrilled to hear it, my liege.'

'It pleases me that you managed to carry out your last task without being discovered. It means you will be in place to exceed yourself when our forces come to Lothern.'

'You have given the orders for the re-conquest of Ulthuan, sire?'

There was an eerie, evil joy in Malekith's voice that Urian had never heard before. 'I have. Hold yourself in readiness for further instructions. Within a moon, the world will be changed forever for the better. Perform your duties well and I will give you Lothern for your fief.'

It was astonishing generosity on Malekith's part. He would be satrap of the richest and most glamorous city in the world. The opportunities to become wealthy would be limitless and he was already intimately acquainted with the citizens. They would hate him of course, as a traitor and a turncoat, even more than they hated the Witch King. He wondered how long Malekith had planned this for. From the beginning was Urian's guess.

'What do you have to say, Urian?' It was clear that an answer was required.

'My apologies, liege. I was simply overwhelmed by your generosity. It rendered me speechless.'

'Then I have been generous indeed to achieve such a miracle,' said Malekith laughing. His good humour was even more terrifying than his wrath.

CHAPTER TEN

Tyrion strode into Lady Emeraldsea's audience chamber. It was his grandfather's old office and little had changed since that ancient elf had occupied it.

Malene looked up from the account book she had been reading as he entered, her amber eyes hidden behind copper-framed bifocals. She was as beautiful and severe-looking as ever but there was something different about her, something that made her seem older, even if she did not look it. She had been that way since her father died and she had taken over the running of the House. The responsibilities pressed down heavily on her.

'You wanted to see me as soon as possible and here I am, aunt,' Tyrion said. 'I have come straight from the ship. My brother has gone to our old house since you stated you wished to see me alone.'

Malene looked a little hurt. She had always preferred Teclis to him. 'Prince Tyrion, how good of you to join me. We have been wondering where you were.'

'We were in Lustria, aunt,' said Tyrion. 'As well you know.'

'And I trust you found whatever was so important as to take you there at this critical period in history.'

'Yes, my lady, we did. We found Sunfang, the sword of Aenarion, believed lost centuries ago.'

'Where is it?'

'Teclis has it. He wished to inspect it, to divine its mysteries. You know what he is like when it comes to new magic.'

'It has been a long time since anyone saw that blade,' said Malene. 'May it bring you more luck than it brought its previous bearers.'

'I was grieved to hear of the death of the Everqueen,' said Tyrion, wanting to get down to the true business of the evening.

'As were we all, Tyrion,' said Malene. 'We are all deeply grieved by the loss. However, life must go on. A new Everqueen has been crowned and her new champion must be chosen.'

'And you believe me to be a suitable candidate for that position,' said Tyrion.

'There is no one in our House better qualified. It is a great honour to be the champion of our new queen. Do you consider yourself worthy of it?'

Tyrion did not like Malene's tone. 'I should think that there is no honour in Ulthuan that a descendant of Aenarion is unworthy of.'

'It is good that you take such pride in your lineage. However, these are new times, and being of ancient blood is no longer sufficient qualification for any position in our realm. Merit counts for something as well.'

'I believe my deeds speak for themselves,' said Tyrion.

'I'm glad that you feel that way – you will soon have a chance to prove those words.' He felt inclined to rise to the challenge just so he could prove her wrong, but he fought down that urge. If he was going to do something, he was going to do it because he wanted to, not because someone had played on his emotions.

'I take it then that you wish me to enter the lists,' said Tyrion.

'You take it correctly,' said Malene. 'I don't think it would do you any harm to be settled down in a position of responsibility. You have developed a reputation for being something of a rake and a brawler recently and it reflects badly on both yourself and this House. And there is no greater responsibility in all of the realms than the safety of our queen.'

Tyrion was not pleased by her comment about his being a rake. It stung a little, not least because there was some truth to the accusation. He knew his relationship with the Lady Valeria had put one of his family's oldest and most precious alliances in peril. Of course, he was not the only party who had caused that particular crisis.

'But there is more to the position than merely being her bodyguard, isn't there?' Tyrion said.

His aunt gave him a wintry smile. 'I don't think you will find some of those duties particularly onerous. Many would consider them a pleasure, in fact. They say the new queen is very beautiful. But then they always do.'

'But that is not why you want me to seek this position, is it?'

'Of course not, Tyrion. If you become champion, you will spend a lot of time in the company of the Everqueen and your opinion will become of considerable importance to her. The new Everqueen is very young and very impressionable and you are a very impressive elf.'

'And I should make sure that her opinion of House Emeraldsea is a good one.'

'As ever, your understanding of the situation is swift and accurate. But there are other good reasons for wanting you to take this position.'

'And what would those be?'

To his surprise, Malene lowered her voice. A worried look flickered across her face. 'Something bad is happening, Tyrion. I can feel it. I don't know what it is yet but I want us to be ready when it comes.'

'What do you mean?'

'We insure a lot of ships. The number of ships lost on the northern routes is so low that we have made more money than at any other point in my lifetime even after reducing the premiums.'

'And you think this is a bad omen?'

'It is unnatural, Tyrion. We normally count on losing some ships to druchii piracy. We have lost nothing for years. Nothing at all.'

'They say the druchii are dying out.'

'I do not believe it. I think the Witch King is merely quiescent.'

'I hope you are wrong.'

'So do I but I am not. Something has changed in the world, something about the winds of magic. They blow stronger than they have during my lifetime and they are strangely tainted. I am not the only mage who has noticed this. Others are as troubled as I am.'

'This is more my brother's field than mine.'

'I fear it will disturb all our lives before long. I fear we must be prepared for the world taking a darker turn. That is why I want you with the Everqueen. She is young and she has much to learn and she may not have much time to get ready.'

'Ready for what?'

'I don't know but whatever it is, it will be bad. We have lived too long, too peacefully. We have grown lax. The cults of luxury are growing strong again. More of our young people than ever are joining them.'

Tyrion wondered whether Malene, all appearances to the contrary, was starting to succumb to the weaknesses of old age. Perhaps soon she would be explaining to him how much better things had been in her youth. He pushed these thoughts to one side. He knew his aunt better than that. There were other things he wanted to talk about.

'My grandfather always claimed, in private and to me at least, that he had ambitions for me,' Tyrion said.

'I know he did.'

'One day he wanted me to be seated on the Phoenix Throne.'

'That is not in the least surprising.'

'How do you feel about that?'

'I would be proud and happy if it happened.'

'I do not see how it can if I am to be a servant of the Everqueen.'

'So that is what is troubling you – I was wondering.'

'You must admit it would be difficult for me to go from being the champion of the Everqueen to the throne itself.'

'Difficult, yes. Impossible, no. Contrary to what you appear to think, Tyrion, you would not be her slave. Nor would your service to her be eternal.'

'Most champions serve until they or their queen dies.'

'Most do, it is true, but not all. You can resign the position.'

'That is not very honourable.'

'True but if you had duties to your family that required you to be present or if you were summoned to be a candidate for the throne…'

'I don't think it would be good for my reputation.'

'And you must always keep that in mind, mustn't you?'

'You know I must. If your father's dream is to be fulfilled.'

Malene laughed. 'And yours, of course.'

Tyrion tried to voice his frustration. 'I do not even know if I truly want to be Phoenix King but I would like to have the option open to me, if I decide in favour.' Tyrion wondered if he should mention the prophecy that had been made about him by the Priests at the Shrine of Asuryan when he had been tested long ago. He decided not to. He had never mentioned it to anyone but his brother.

'I understand, Tyrion. But Finubar is young and may reign for a thousand years. In the meantime, you can best serve your House by doing what I ask.'

'What if I don't want to?'

'All of us have to do things we don't want to, Tyrion. I would rather be studying the Art, or aiding Teclis with his inspection of the sword of Aenarion right now, but my father is dead, and someone must look after our interests. In a few centuries you will be better qualified to do that than I.'

'I am not sure I want that position either.'

'You may not have much choice if I am not here. Who else will look out for your brother's interests or your father's? Prince Arathion had burned through all of the money you left for him, buying materials to repair the dragon armour of Aenarion, performing more research into its history. So far I have covered his notes of hand, but I cannot keep doing so forever.'

And there was the stick, Tyrion thought. Someone was always going to have to look out for his father. Tyrion had left him enough money to keep a noble house in luxury for decades and already it was gone. He supposed he could have words with his father, but he knew how useless that was. His father would simply forget them as soon as Tyrion was out of sight.

'And what is my reward to be, if I am successful?'

'I should have thought that becoming the champion of the Everqueen was reward enough. But, in case that is not enough for you, my young horse trader, be assured that you will have our gratitude.'

Tyrion knew exactly what Malene meant. He was sure that the House would show its gratitude whenever he did something to its advantage. He was also beginning to become aware that the position was one that came with a measure of power attached to it. It was not the sort of power that he cared for or that he wanted to have, but he could see that it might be useful to him in the future. More to the point, it was a source of power completely independent of Malene and his kindred. It would be his and his alone.

'When do I leave?'

His aunt nodded, gratified.

'A ship is being prepared to take you to Avelorn. Anything that you require shall be provided for you. Clothing, gifts, horses – name it and you shall have it. We want you to make a good impression, after all.'

'I shall do my best, since it is so important.'

'And Tyrion…'

'Yes?'

'It might be best if you did not see Lady Valeria before you went.'

Tyrion grimaced. Something else was on his mind. 'How much would it take to cover my father's debts?'

Malene named the sum. 'Transfer it from my account to his. And add a further thousand in gold.'

'But Tyrion, that is almost all you have.'

'It is only money,' said Tyrion. 'I can always get more.'

She looked at him, and saw at once the point he was making. His aunt was a clever woman. He was letting her know he could only be pushed so far even by threats to his father.

'Not all elves are so lucky,' she said.

CARRYING SUNFANG, TECLIS entered the family home. Tyrion had already gone to the Emeraldsea mansion to talk with its mistress. Teclis was hurt that Malene had summoned Tyrion and not him.

He had always felt that she preferred him to Tyrion but since she had become the head of the House she had spent more time with his brother than with him. Of course, Tyrion showed a great deal more interest in the business of the House and spent a lot more time in Lothern than he did.

'Greetings, Prince Teclis,' said Rose. She curtseyed respectfully, as any retainer to a noble elven household was expected to. She was a human, an indentured servant, a slave by any other name. It was all the fashion in Lothern these days although still illegal in the rest of Ulthuan. She was pretty too… for a human. She looked at him in a way that no elf maid ever had. 'It is good to have you home.'

'It is good to be home,' Teclis lied. He was not glad to be back in Lothern, even after a week at sea. He was certainly not glad to be back in this place.

The walls of the old family house hemmed Teclis in. Childhood memories of sickness and pain came surging back. He had never liked this place and yet it was part of the fabric of his being. With the wealth Tyrion had acquired raiding and trading, they could afford to re-open it. They could afford to have retainers and indentured servants. Their father had moved in and shipped all of his research material back from the wild mountains of Cothique.

'Can I get you anything?' Rose asked.

'See that a fire is lit in my bedchamber and please notify Prince Arathion that I am home.'

'Your father is out, visiting Korhien Ironglaive I believe, sir.'

'Thank you. Perhaps you could have a light supper prepared and sent to the first floor living room.'

'At once, sir.' Teclis made his way into a richly appointed waiting room, laid Sunfang down on the table, poured some mildly narcotic wine into a golden goblet and stretched out in a comfortable leather-bound chair beside the fire.

It was all very different from the grinding poverty he remembered from early childhood. Here in Lothern he found all sorts of thoughts and resentments came crowding in.

It was funny that his brother had the gift of managing money so easily and so well. He and his father had always seen Tyrion as the least intelligent one of them, but the truth of the matter was that his brother was much cleverer than they were about many things. As with everything he set his mind to, he did it well. He had mastered the making of money as easily as he had mastered the use of weapons, perhaps because in this day and age, the two were so closely connected.

Tyrion had made a small fortune during the raids on Naggaroth and he had invested the proceeds in some spectacularly successful trading voyages and the purchase of land which had been leased at high rents to the new breed of human trader down in the port.

Tyrion was now part owner of a number of trading ships and shared the profits of all their voyages. Having re-established the foundations of prosperity for their branch of the family he seemed to have lost all interest in the subject, delegating the management to competent retainers recruited from House Emeraldsea.

Teclis liked to think that he could have done the same, but he found the process too dull to bother with. His interests were magic and scholarship. He was grateful that his brother was generous enough to share his wealth but he resented it. It was just one more way in which he was beholden to his twin. He sometimes felt there would be no end to his obligations. His brother was an expert in using his generosity to bind people to him. Even his kindness came with invisible strings attached.

By Isha, he was in a sour mood tonight. He took another sip of the wine. It tingled on his tongue. He knew he was simply a little depressed. The great Lustrian adventure was over and he was back in Lothern with work to do and all the tiny, encroaching obligations that entailed. He should start inspecting Sunfang but at this moment he struggled to find the energy.

It was a mental thing not a physical one. Drugs, diet, sorcery and a regime of exercise had done much to compensate for the weakness and physical handicaps the diseases of his youth had caused. None of these things could rid him of the mental lassitude he now felt, nor make him any less of an outsider in society. All of them still looked at him sidelong, with secret contempt. He was sure of it. They had done ever since he was young, and would do so until the day he died.

In Lustria, with Tyrion and the humans, he had felt at ease. His brother had never held him in contempt and to the humans he was just another elf, a blessed immortal. If anything, his magical talents had made him seem even more god-like than Tyrion to them.

Perhaps that was why his initial reaction on his return was to come back to this house and lock himself in. He wanted to keep himself from view. To be out of sight of other elves. He let out a long breath. He was back and he had work to do.

A sound in the doorway alerted him. He looked up to see his father standing there. Prince Arathion looked older and even more decrepit than Teclis remembered him. His cheeks were sunken and hollow and his eyes had a bright mad gleam to them.

'I heard you had returned, my son,' he said. The voice at least was the same as Teclis remembered it. Light, aristocratic, a little sad, with something of the fussy air of the life-long scholar. 'I came back as soon as the news reached me.'

'It is good to see you, father,' said Teclis. It was too. He had always been fond of his father, who was one of the few elves who never seemed to judge him, who, if anything, judged in his favour.

'Do you have it?' his father asked. The excitement was unmistakable in his voice. There was no need to ask what *it* was. Teclis nodded. He gestured to the table on which the blade rested.

His father crossed the distance in two strides and lifted Sunfang. He was getting weak in his old age, and needed the use of both hands to do so until the magic of the sword took over. He unsheathed the blade, and flames danced along its length. The brilliance of the illumination sent shadows skittering away to the far corner of the room. His father smiled and in that moment, Teclis found that all of the hardships of his long quest were repaid. A look of combined awe, wonder and pure unalloyed happiness passed across his father's face.

He twisted the blade back and forth in front of him, inspecting it from every angle. 'Astonishing,' he said, at last. 'Absolutely astonishing. I would not have thought it possible after all these years but you did it. You found it!'

'Indeed we did, father. There were times when I did not believe we could.'

Prince Arathion looked as if he wanted to jump for joy. He shifted his weight from one leg to the other as if he wanted to dance. 'It still functions,' he said, as if he could not quite believe it. 'The fires of Vaul's Anvil are still bound within it.'

There was something about his excitement that was contagious.

Teclis found himself nodding enthusiastically. His father sheathed the blade and placed it reverentially back on the table. He looked at the glass of wine in Teclis's hand, nodded and poured himself one. He drank it down in one long gulp, and the poured another glass which he just held in one trembling hand, as if he had suddenly forgotten all about it.

'I can't believe it,' he said again. He sounded as if he wanted to cry. He placed the glass down, walked across the room and ruffled Teclis's hair. Teclis recoiled, surprised and embarrassed by the physical contact. His father had never been the most demonstrative of elves and they were not the most demonstrative of families. 'I can't believe it.'

'Well, it's done and now the real work begins,' said Teclis.

His father did not seem to be paying him much attention. He walked back over to the table, put down the glass, picked up the sword, partially unsheathed it and then slammed it back. 'Just think, my son, once Aenarion held this blade in his hand. Aenarion! The first Phoenix King carried this sword through most of his early battles with the forces of Chaos.'

'I know, father,' said Teclis gently, now starting to get slightly worried by his father's excitement.

'I am holding in my hand the sword that Aenarion once held.'

'I am sure he probably held it a lot better,' said Teclis.

His father gave a small start and put the sword down once again as if he was frightened of breaking it. Silence filled the room for long moments until Rose brought in Teclis's meal. She put it down on the table beside the blade. It seemed somehow sacrilege to place something so banal beside something so sacred, but it restored a feeling of sanity to the proceedings.

Both Teclis and his father laughed, much to Rose's incomprehension. She had no idea of the significance of the sword, Teclis realised. Prince Arathion apologised for his rudeness. Teclis said nothing until the retainer had retired from the chamber.

'You have inspected it, of course,' said Prince Arathion.

'I have looked at it,' said Teclis 'but I needed to bring it here, to have the tools I need to analyse it in depth.'

'How long do we have it?'

'Until Tyrion departs. It will be going with him to Avelorn. It is his.'

'He claimed it, of course.' There was some resentment in Prince Arathion's voice. Teclis told him how Tyrion had taken up the blade. As he did so, it struck him that his father had never asked how it was found and was showing very little interest now. He was only half-listening, his eyes constantly drawn from Teclis's face to where the sword lay on the table. When Teclis finished he said, 'Very good. Just think. We have the only surviving functioning artefact of the Archmage Caledor here in our home.'

'There is the Vortex, father,' said Teclis, surprised to find that he was somewhat annoyed by his father's lack of interest in the hardships that he and Tyrion had endured.

'Of course, of course,' said Prince Arathion. 'I meant things created by his own hand, like this weapon, like the armour, like the amulets he is said to have made for the Everqueen's children.'

He paused for a moment and went over and picked up the sword again. He unsheathed the blade slowly, so that the flames gradually underlit his face with ever more brilliant radiance. It made him look somehow daemonic. 'It still works, even after all these millennia.' He was repeating himself but did not seem to care.

'Yes,' said Teclis. 'And now our task is to find out how!'

'We had better adjourn to the laboratory,' said his father.

'Indeed,' said Teclis. 'Let me mix myself another potion. It's going to be a long night.'

TYRION STRODE INTO the living room and smiled at his father and Teclis. In spite of his cordiality, Teclis could sense his twin was troubled and angry.

'Things went well with Lady Malene,' Teclis said, knowing full well that they most likely had not.

'Yes,' said Tyrion with his customary smoothness.

'That is good,' said their father, taking things, as always, at face value.

'You are going to Avelorn?' Teclis said.

'Indeed,' said Tyrion. He looked long and hard at their father, as if he wanted to say something. Their father never even noticed.

'Then your brother and I had better get started on Sunfang. You'll be wanting to take it with you, of course.' Father sounded hopeful that Tyrion would say no. Teclis already knew the answer.

'Of course,' said Tyrion. 'I wish you good luck with your researches. I am going to change and then I am going to visit the taverns.'

He swept out of the room. Their father smiled. 'Always the carefree one,' he said, almost fondly.

You just don't understand, Teclis thought. He said, 'Let us get down to the laboratory. We need to map the spells on the sword and get the notes down in record time.'

'Let's get started then,' his father said enthusiastically.

WITH HIS TWIN'S departure, Teclis set to the serious business of really examining the ancient blade. He and his father went down to the laboratory in the basement. He made sure that there was a plentiful supply of parchment and ink and then began.

He set the blade on the floor and inscribed a chalk circle around it. Swiftly he inscribed runes around the edges of the circle, making the signs of Isha and Hoeth and numerous minor deities of knowledge. He relaxed and began to chant. His heartbeat slowed, his breathing deepened, his spirit hung loosely within his body. He inspected the aura of the old sword.

And it was *old*, he realised, an artefact of the ancient time when mortal gods had walked the Earth. It had been made when magic flowed much more strongly through the world. He could tell from the brutal strength of the spells, so difficult to replicate in the modern era, that magic had been more abundant when this weapon had been made. The world had been fundamentally different.

Slowly, it seeped into him, the realisation that his father was right, Aenarion had held this blade. He had fought and killed with it. He had trusted his life to it. It was a weapon intended to be wielded by a hero, one touched by the power of the gods. He was not sure that his brother would ever be able to use its full power. He did not lack the heroism. He simply had not passed through the Flame of Asuryan as Aenarion had.

Teclis had touched the Flame, using his own magic, during the final battle with the Keeper of Secrets. He could sense resonances of it within the blade, most likely simply traces of the fact that Aenarion had handled it. There had been a direct link between the Phoenix King and this weapon. Echoes of Aenarion's blazing ferocity could be felt by someone sensitive enough.

Beneath that there were echoes of another personality, one of more interest to Teclis. The presence belonged to one infinitely sadder, wiser and far less bold, the first of the true Archmages, Caledor. He too had handled this blade and he had done so before Aenarion. The spellwork flowing through it was his.

Teclis looked at it, fascinated. It was as individual as handwriting. That was always the case. Two mages could cast the same spell and it would look and feel different to the knowledgeable observer. It would flow in a different way, be cast with different levels of energy, sometimes would get different results. Magic was always personal in that way.

What could he tell about Caledor from his work?

The elf had been meticulous– the runes on the blade had been inscribed with care, and the flows of fire magic through them were still bound as tightly today as they were the day the sword had been forged.

He had been strong-willed. No one could have bound one of the Elemental Spirits of Vaul without being so. He had not been at all artistic. The magic was utilitarian. There was none of the florid scribblings of trace energies that many mages used to leave their own mark on spells and artefacts. The elf that had made this sword had been grimly determined to create the most powerful weapon he could for his friend. He had not been concerned with imprinting his own personality on it.

And, of course, that single-minded determination had left the strongest mark possible. Now he had a sense of the wizard as if he had been standing in the same room with him, of the indomitable will, the desperate courage, the despair.

Caledor had not been a warrior. He had never wanted to fight. It was not in his nature. He had been driven to it. He had been a maker where Aenarion had been a destroyer. He had made even this sword with reluctance, but having been driven to it he had made it to the best of his ability. He had put all of his genius into the creation of something whose purpose he despised.

We live in the shadow of titans, Teclis thought. We live in the world that destiny-cursed pair created. This sword is like the whole history of our people. It bears the stamp of Aenarion and Caledor.

He thought about the Vortex, which, even to this day, protected and maintained Ulthuan, channelling its magical energies, keeping the continent above the waves, draining the fatal power of the winds of magic from the world. Caledor made our land, in the same way as Aenarion shaped our people. The whole continent was part of his vast geomantic design.

Teclis considered the scope of the mind that could do that – plan and execute the most powerful spell in the history of the world in the midst of fighting the greatest war ever. The same elf who had forged this blade had forged a continent. The world had been fundamentally different when Sunfang had been made, and Caledor had been the one who altered it when he created the Vortex.

Surely there was something to be learned from understanding this spell work. So thinking, Teclis threw himself once again into studying the weave and pattern of the magic and imprint of the elf that had made it so.

Hours later, grimly elated, exhausted and at the end of his strength, he felt that he had grasped the essential nature of the magic. He thought that perhaps one day he would be able to forge a weapon, if not as powerful as this one, at least of a similar level of sophistication.

'You have penetrated the blade's secrets?' his father asked. It was not really a question.

Teclis took up his pen. 'I have discovered a very great deal. Let's get it all down while it is fresh in my memory.'

TECLIS SLUMPED WEARILY into his armchair. He looked over at his father and saw that the old elf was transformed. His face had lit up with something approaching joy. He looked as if he was about to burst into dance. In his hands he held the scrolls containing the notes that Teclis had made during his examination of Sunfang. He kept running his gaze over the runes again and again, as if he could not quite believe what he was seeing.

'What is it, Father?' Teclis asked. His father looked as if he was about to burst into tears. He did not seem able to force the words out.

'I think we have found it, my son,' he said. 'I think we have found what I was looking for over all these centuries. I think we found the missing piece of the puzzle.'

Teclis found his father's excitement contagious. Weary as he was, he rose and limped over to where Prince Arathion stood. He looked over his father's shoulder at the complex mass of magical notation that he had left on the parchment.

For once, his father was ahead of him when it came to understanding magic. He simply could not see what it was that the older elf was so excited about. Then again, he told himself, he was tired and he did not have his father's long experience of studying this sort of spell. It was quite possible his father was the greatest expert on this sort of thing in the world. He had concentrated obsessively on it for centuries.

'I don't see it,' Teclis said.

'There,' his father said, his finger stabbing towards one section of the inscription. 'Do you see it now?'

'I'm afraid not.'

'I think this is the missing part of the weave, the thing that has prevented me from being able to reactivate the armour over all these centuries. I think this is the magic that will enable me to bind all of the complex spells together and make them work. It will be expensive and it will take time but I think I can do it.'

Teclis began to vaguely see what his father was getting at. It was not something that would have excited him, or even have got his attention had it not been pointed out to him. It was a relatively simple thing but once he looked closely at it he could see the cleverness of it.

It was a small, intricate piece of spellcraft, designed to link together a mesh of other spells, reinforcing them and letting them draw on each other's power. Anything inscribed with this particular rune would be much stronger and yet much easier to use. It was something that was difficult to spot because it was so embedded in the rest of the spells on the blade, but once you saw it…

'I see it now,' Teclis said.

'I knew you would – eventually,' said his father with a smile. 'It is quite brilliant and I can see how it has eluded me for so long. It will take quite a bit of work to recreate the links in the armour but once that is done, I should be able to bring it back to life. Of course, I won't be able to make the spell as strongly as Caledor did. There's less magic in the world now.'

When he said that his father looked troubled. 'Although that may be changing. The winds of magic have been blowing much stronger recently and there is an odd taint to them. You must have noticed that.'

'I have only just returned to Ulthuan, Father, and all of the spells I have worked have been in this shielded laboratory.'

'Of course, but you will see what I mean the first time you try to work magic outside.'

'I'll take your word for that but now I'm going to bed. It's been a very long night and I am very weary.'

His father did not look tired. He looked younger and more energetic than Teclis had seen him look in decades. He looked keen to begin working on his lifelong project once more. Suddenly and ominously Teclis was reminded of Leiber. What if his father did succeed? What if he lost his life's purpose? What would happen then?

He told himself it was just the tiredness speaking, that there was nothing to worry about, but he had a very strong foreboding that this discovery would prove bad for his father. He was a wizard and he respected his forebodings for they very often proved correct.

CHAPTER ELEVEN

'DRINK!' SAID ORYSIAN. He handed Tyrion a skin of wine. He was already quite drunk. Wine had spilled from the corners of his thick-lipped mouth and dribbled down his chin. A challenge glittered in his narrow eyes. It was obvious in his wine-thickened voice.

'Don't mind if I do,' said Tyrion, seizing the wineskin and tipping its contents down his throat in one long, theatrical swig. The rest of his companions laughed. All of them except the human slave who carried the lighted lantern seemed vastly amused.

Tyrion loved this, striding through the night-time streets of Lothern with his pack of friends, elves with whom he had spent many a night carousing down by the docks or in the taverns and brothels of the old city. Looking at them he understood his aunt's words about the bad reputation he was getting for himself.

They were all of about his age or younger and they were all heavily armed and ready for a fight with members of any other faction they might encounter in the streets of the city. Of late, such running street battles had become part and parcel of life in Lothern – what was worse, in various areas the humans seem to be getting involved, fighting proxy wars on behalf of their patrons.

Lothern had become a much more violent place in the last century than the relatively peaceful city-state Tyrion had known in his youth. He had to admit that he was part of that problem.

He was one of the elves who took the most joy in street-fighting. He had a reputation for it and he was seen as a champion of House Emeraldsea. His grandfather and his aunt had disapproved but they were of an older generation, born in a simpler time.

They did not really understand the new world bred of riches and foreign trade and the opening of Lothern to a tidal wave of new money and goods.

At this moment, with the wine burning in his belly like liquid fire, Tyrion did not really care what his aunt or anyone else thought. He swaggered along with his hands hitched into his sword belt, daring any passer-by to look at him the wrong way. Very few could look him in the eye. They were afraid and there was something intoxicating about their fear.

This was not his usual practice – he liked to think of himself as a peaceful elf except when provoked, but at this moment in time he would welcome some violence. His companions sensed that. They were going out of their way to be provocative to anyone who got in their way, knowing that when Tyrion was in one of these wild moods there were very few people in the city who could stand against them. Merchants hastened into their shops, passers-by scuttled across the streets.

Only the soldiers of the City Watch held their ground and even they looked nervous, for they were outnumbered by this mob of richly garbed young elves. They knew also that these wealthy trouble-makers had the influence to avoid the consequences of breaking the heads of a few poor guardsmen.

The sight of them gave Tyrion pause. The guard were just doing their jobs, trying to keep the streets safe. They were not the enemy.

They did not need trouble from the likes of him. They were the sort of elves he had led on battlefields. He had no quarrel with them.

There was something ugly about the faces of his companions, an expression of brutality and superiority that did not sit well on their fine features. Tyrion realised that exactly the same expression was on his face and he did not like that. He did not like to think he was simply part of the herd.

He forced himself to pause and smile and consider the reasons why he was doing this. He knew that it was not wise. No matter how tough an elf was it was still possible for anyone to be killed in the rough and tumble of a street brawl. He had lost a number of friends that way over the years.

It was wasteful and it was stupid. There were few enough elves as it was and with more humans appearing in the city every year it set a very bad precedent and example. The humans would see that the elves were fractious and divided and they would realise that it was a weakness. It was one that the elves really could not afford to display in a city where they were even now outnumbered by strangers.

He wrestled with his own anger, looking for the reasons and finding them easily enough. He did not like the way his aunt had spoken to him and he did not like being treated as if he were some sort of lackey – he was of the blood of Aenarion, after all. He smiled with genuine mirth; he certainly had the mad pride associated with that particular bloodline. It was coming out now. The wine had made sure of that.

His aunt had her own reasons for doing these things. Tyrion understood that. The trick was going to be to make sure that he did not do anything rash because of that. Knowing her motivations, he could put these to good use and manipulate his aunt for his own purposes, or at least he hoped so. It was never wise to assume such things with elves who were so much older and more experienced than he was. Although he was already very confident of his own gifts in that particular area.

He looked around at his friends. They were taking their cues from him. They seemed to sense the conflict in his mind. A few of them still looked angry and spoiling for a fight, a few of them looked as if they were waiting for him to say something funny, most of them just looked confused.

He grinned at all of them and spread his hands wide and said, 'Come, let us visit the Golden Lion and I will buy you all some fine wine – there is much to be celebrated. I have found the blade of Aenarion, a thing lost for many centuries. It is an omen of great things.'

Most of them laughed but Orysian said, 'I thought you wanted to blood it this evening. Our enemies have been casting aspersions on the bravery of House Emeraldsea in your absence. I thought you would have brought this fabled blade. We are all dying to get a look at it.'

Orysian was a brute, Tyrion thought. He wanted to be thought tough and he was. He wanted to be the centre of attention the way Tyrion was, but he could not be, because he lacked Tyrion's good looks and charm. Tyrion knew the other elf would have challenged him to a fight, if he had not been so certain he would lose. Instead he contented himself with sniping resentfully at Tyrion. Still these things made him easy enough to handle.

'It would be a very bad omen to blood the blade of Aenarion on asur,' said Tyrion. 'That is why I have left it with my brother this evening – so that I will not be tempted! Anyway, I have had enough fighting over the past few months to last me for at least an evening. While you were drinking in the taverns of Lothern, I was fighting lizardmen, carnosaurs and flesh-eating plants in the jungles of Lustria.'

A look of disappointment passed over Orysian's coarsely handsome features and he said, 'Doubtless you will bore us with all the details before this night is out.' Tyrion could see that Orysian was going to be the problem here, so he singled him out for attention.

'Don't worry, I will regale you with endless tales of my own heroism and bravery which you will, by the end of the evening, envy even more than my startling good looks and wit and charm.'

'I have heard it said that words can be just as deadly as swords and our friend Tyrion is about to prove that by boring us all to death,' said Orysian, rising to the bait.

'As ever, jealousy is an ugly thing,' said Tyrion. 'I have seen you bore a few of your enemies with the sword. The last time I saw you fight I thought it was your intention to watch your opponent die of old age... and let us never forget that they were elves.'

'It would still probably have been preferable for them than listening to your stories,' said Orysian.

'Then imagine what it would be like for them to listen to yours. Heroic tales of the number of courtesans you have kissed and bottles of wine you have drunk interspersed with stories of the cakes you have knifed to death.'

All of the others were laughing now. Even Orysian was amused and flattered to be singled out by the hero of the hour. Tyrion smiled at them all, having turned the mood to his own wishes. He kept it up all the way to the Golden Lion. He did not want to fight tonight. He had too much to think about.

LIKE A CONQUERING army, Tyrion and his companions burst through the doors of the tavern.

'Drink!' Orysian shouted.

The Golden Lion was crowded. Glittering elven courtesans glided from table to table. Glowstones shimmered in chandeliers illuminating everyone. Servants carried goblets of hallucinogenic wine to gold-inlaid tables, or hookahs of Arabyan kif to those elves who desired it.

It was a vast place, furnished with articles from every corner of the globe, carpets from Araby and clockwork automatons from the Worlds Edge Mountains. Hanging from the ceiling was the huge skeleton of some aquatic monster harpooned by the tavern's owner back when he was a simple sea captain, or so he claimed.

It lay on the edgy territory between the human quarter and the Great Dock. It had once been a warehouse as could be seen by its huge internal area, with an enormous ceiling and many landings looking down over the central pit. On these landings there were still the loading bay doors where hauliers had lifted cargoes into the warehouse.

Most of the serving wenches and staff were humans. That was increasingly the way with all menial labour in Lothern. Some of the great trading houses had even started using slaves as labourers in their warehouses, although technically it was still only permitted to sell slaves in Lothern for purposes of transhipment. There was no business in this world that could not be pursued in this greatest of port cities. The merchants of Lothern did not want to miss out on the slightest copper piece of potential profit.

Tyrion glanced around to see who else was present. The place had gone quiet for a moment when the patrons had noticed his entry. It pleased him that he was so well known here. The tavern's owner came to greet him.

'Prince Tyrion, I had heard you were back.'

'News travels fast, Garion,' said Tyrion.

'In Lothern, always.' The owner led them to a massive platform where they could stare down on the less wealthy and famous below. Drinks were brought. The most beautiful courtesans began to drift away from other tables towards their own.

Tyrion sipped his wine and studied his friends. They were a typical cross section of the young, outrageous and wealthy of Lothern at this moment in time; part of the new generation that had grown up over the past century as Lothern was transformed from a half-dreaming city into the hub of a global trading empire. They had the swaggering, piratical look of young merchants on the make. Many of them had captained ships to the far corners of the globe.

Here was Lucius, whose family had grown wealthy in spices and silks from Cathay and the Mystic East. He affected long flowing wizardly robes of the Cathayan upper echelons. It was intended as a joke, a parody of the self-importance of the mandarins but somehow it suited him.

Here was Kargan, who had made a fortune raiding the coasts of Naggaroth and the dark elf colonies. He was lean and scarred with a vulpine look to his features and two dark elf blades strapped to his sides. He hated the spawn of Naggaroth with a black passion that matched that of the druchii. He had lost a beloved sister to their slavers and was taking a lifelong revenge. Tyrion had made his first real gold shipping out with him and raiding the coasts of Naggaroth. Although he was very far from squeamish about these things himself, Tyrion found Kargan's bloodlust somewhat disturbing.

Here was Drielle, a she-elf who prided herself on being every bit as ruthless and tough as her male companions, who wielded a sword in battle with the same skill as they did, and who never refused a bet or a challenge. She was also reputed to be the best navigator in Ulthuan. Tyrion had funded several of her voyages and turned a huge profit on all of them.

There were others cut from the same cloth, spending freely, gambling unwisely, drinking all they could. They were all part of the same social group, all useful to each other. Tyrion had made small fortunes on the back of bits of gossip picked up from one or the other, and made sure to return the favours whenever he could.

These elves were not the powers in their Houses now, but they would be one day, and it did no harm to cultivate them. They could all be useful to him for as long as he was useful to them. In the future they would provide the spine of a very strong power base. One day these people would rule Lothern, and through Lothern the rest of the world.

Of course, they were not without rivals. There were other cliques and factions in the city, many of whom hated his friends or found it necessary to pose as if they did. In some cases, as with young Paladine Stormcastle over there, it was because they belonged to families who were hereditary enemies of the Emeraldsea. Tyrion suspected that under most circumstances he could have liked Paladine, but it looked as if they were doomed to be at each other's throats by an accident of history or birth. They were rivals in business, for the favours of courtesans and the notice of the Phoenix King. It could be no other way, and there was no sense in regretting it.

Paladine rose from his table and walked over to Tyrion's accompanied by a couple of his swaggering hangers-on. He had a new pet, Tyrion noticed, a small monkey dressed in the britches, tunic and exaggerated codpiece that the humans liked to wear. It even had a broad-brimmed feathered hat. It was a joke at the expense of the humans, an expression of contempt that Tyrion was not sure was at all wise in this new era. The monkey waddled over and bowed to Tyrion, as it had obviously been trained to do, then it began to scratch its private parts. All of the elves laughed except Tyrion.

'Prince Tyrion. I had heard you were back.'

'And if you had not heard, you could see it with your own eyes.'

'I hear you found the blade Sunfang,' said Paladine. Tyrion nodded and waited for the inevitable sneer. He did not have long to wait.

'Your crippled brother has a gift for sorcery and forgery, I have heard. It would not surprise me in the least to learn that the blade you bore was some sort of fake.'

A gang of other young elven blades was closing in. Tyrion did a swift head count. His own group would be outnumbered unless some of the others here came to his aid. Most of them were looking on, waiting to see what happened. There was an atmosphere of tension, of barely controlled violence about to explode. Tyrion shrugged and forgot about his good intentions from earlier. It looked like a brawl was inevitable. That being the case, he thought, he might as well enjoy it.

Tyrion yawned. 'I have been having some difficulty sleeping of late. I am glad you have come over to bore me. It is very relaxing.

And what have you been up to while I was in the jungles of Lustria? Bravely keeping your father's account books, wielding that razor-sharp pen of yours to good effect, terrorising the clerks in the counting house with the prospect of listening to your jokes.'

Paladine flushed and stepped forward. His monkey shrieked and capered, obviously disturbed by the anger in the voices around him. Out of somewhere a flagon of ale came flying, tumbling towards his head, soaking his clothes. Within seconds a brawl had erupted. Tables were smashed, punches were thrown.

'No blades, lords and ladies, no blades,' Garion shouted. Tyrion wondered if anyone would pay the slightest attention.

STANDING ON TOP of the moving mountain that was the Black Ark as it ploughed through the waves, Malekith studied the horizon. The sea was dark with ships. Every one of those ships contained troops loyal to him, or as loyal as elves and fickle Chaos worshippers were ever capable of being. It did not matter. They would serve his purposes in the end. He was not going to let anything spoil the mood of triumph this day.

He was returning home after all these years. That was what it felt like. He had dwelled in the cold northern lands for a much greater portion of his millennia-long life than he had spent in Ulthuan, but still it was so. He had brooded over the fate of the island-continent far more than he had over the lands he had seized so long ago.

His first memories were of the blue skies of Naggarythe. He still had vivid recollections of his first horse ride, the sight of dragons moving across an empty sky, the cloud-girt mountains, the emerald seas. He could remember talking with his father in their few quiet moments together when he was young.

Much had changed since then and he had been the one who changed it. By his actions he had sunk part of the ancient land. He now believed his mother had tricked him into that as part of her own secret plans. It was difficult to truly remember. It had all been so long ago.

This enormous sea-going vessel had once been part of a mountain citadel. Mighty magics kept it afloat. Without the power of the ancient sorcery that pulsed all around him, even now it would be on its way to the monster-haunted ocean bottom. It was not a ship. It was an enormous berg of hollowed-out stone, filled with warriors.

The sea seethed with the crude vessels, carrying the army of savages his mother had recruited in the Northern Wastes and bent to her will. Their guttural chanting and bestial bellowing drifted across the waves as they tried to placate their crude daemon gods. Sharks and smaller sea monsters swam in their wakes, devouring the offerings the barbarians made, still living members of their own tribes sent on as messengers to the afterlife they thought they were going to.

The joke was on them. Long ago, when he had been little more than a child, his mother had told him the truth. There was no paradise, no afterlife such as the priests spoke of. There was only the black horror of the realms of Chaos in which daemons devoured the souls of the dead, feasting on them, as they feasted on the strong emotions of the living. His father had hinted confirmation of this, and his father had seen more of the workings of the universe than any living being before or since when he passed unshielded through the Flame.

Malekith himself had caught no glimpses in the hazy, agonising time when he had attempted that feat himself. He had caught sight of the presence of Asuryan and the god had rejected him... That fact still burned as much as the pain of his wounds.

Behind him, emerging from the bowels of the Black Ark, he sensed the chained malevolence of the daemon he had bound to his will. N'Kari still wore the form of an astonishingly beautiful elf maiden, naked, but now forged from steel, tattooed with runes that parodied those on Malekith's own armour. Normally Malekith would have brooked no mockery, but there was little more he could do to punish the daemon than what he was already doing.

Let it have its little joke. In the end, it too would do his will. That was what was important.

Sometimes he let it shift to the form it was most at home in, that of a monstrous four-armed denizen of the deepest hells. At all times, the chains of cold iron and truesilver glittered on its limbs, the jewels on each of the alien bracelets pulsing with the power of the spells that bound the daemon to his service.

It was temporary, Malekith knew that. Not even his spells and that ancient alien artefact could hold the daemon enchained forever. He could feel its evil and its hatred where he stood. It was a palpable force, radiating outwards like heat, curdling the erotic, narcotic clouds of vapours that billowed always around N'Kari's form.

'Brooding, Malekith?' the daemon asked. Its voice was innocent and beautiful and completely at odds with its appearance, but then it could look and sound like anything it wanted. Malekith envied it that. There were times when he thought he would give anything to wear the body he had once possessed, to feel cool air on his skin, not to be entombed in iron. He pushed that weakness aside.

'Dwelling on the past?' the daemon asked.

Malekith did not ask how the daemon knew. In some ways it was preternaturally sensitive to the thoughts of others, in other ways completely blind. Also, it would never do to lose sight of the fact that the daemon was not of this world. It had gifts, in some ways like his mother's.

'That is my business, daemon.'

'For the moment, your business is my business,' said N'Kari. It brandished its chains. 'You have made this very clear to me.'

'This does not mean I have to discuss it with you. Do not make me sorry I granted you permission to speak once more.'

'Who else are you going to discuss it with, Witch King – those idiots out there on their pathetic ships?'

'I do not require to talk about it with anyone, least of all you, lackey.'

'Then you are most unusual among your kind. Always they need to talk, to boast, to vaunt their pride. They are worse than humans in their way.'

Malekith was inclined to agree, but he was not about to admit it to this creature. 'You were thinking about life and death and the gods,' said N'Kari.

Malekith wondered if the daemon had been reading his mind. He did not think that was possible. His helmet was inscribed with very potent runes to prevent exactly that sort of thing from happening and he had shielded his thoughts for millennia using magic.

No, he thought, the daemon was simply making an obvious insinuation and attempting to unsettle him, and that was not something he was going to allow.

'That shows no great gift of understanding,' said Malekith. 'It is what most elves would do, standing on these heights, and looking at this view.'

'While engaged in an exercise on this vast scale...' said N'Kari. 'It is what you mortals are like.'

'I am no mortal,' said Malekith.

'That remains to be proven,' said the daemon, allowing some of its malice to creep back into its voice.

'By you?' Malekith allowed his contempt to show in his voice. An elf or a human would have quailed.

The daemon merely smiled. 'My time will come.'

'If ever it does you will find me ready.'

'I did this once,' said N'Kari. The daemon sounded thoughtful. 'Invaded Ulthuan. In the time before ever your father arose to oppose me.'

Malekith laughed. The sound was iron, cold and biting as a blade. 'It seems mortals are not the only ones compelled to talk, to boast, to reminisce.'

'It is a weakness of being bound in this form in this world,' said N'Kari. 'Every day I become more like you. I live. I breathe. The realm of my birth becomes an ever fainter memory. But then you understand that too, don't you? We have some things in common you and I.'

'I very much doubt that.'

'You are attempting what I once did. I suspect your results will be much the same.'

'I will prevail. I do not seek to destroy the world and enslave my people. I am merely reclaiming what is mine by right of birth.'

'Are you certain of that?'

'Of what?'

'That you are Aenarion's son? Your mother was, to say the least, promiscuous. I lay with her myself many times in many different forms. More than even she is aware of.'

Malekith knew the daemon was merely trying to goad him. He would not let it.

'The Flame rejected you. It did not reject Aenarion.'

There was nothing Malekith could say to that, so he let it pass. He knew it was pointless debating these things with daemons.

'Why do you think that was?'

Malekith exercised his will. The bracelets that bound the daemon pulsed with energy. It stood frozen in place, unable to move or speak until he willed it. He returned to contemplating his fleet.

Soon, he thought, he would be home and there would be a reckoning: with this daemon, with the elves of Ulthuan and with their gods.

CHAPTER TWELVE

TECLIS WOKE FROM an unpleasant slumber. Strange dreams had haunted his sleep, filling his mind with images of destruction and slaughter. In every nightmare was the hideous image of Morrslieb, the Chaos moon, blazing brightly in the sky. Something had transformed it into an eye through which a daemonic god looked down on the world.

He washed, pulled on his robe, and went down to breakfast. He had barely sat down at the table when there was a knocking at the door. Moments later Rose entered and said, 'A messenger from the White Tower wishes to see you, sir.'

'Send them in,' said Teclis. He was surprised to see a Sword Master of Hoeth, a tall slender woman with a great two-handed blade strapped to her back. He recognised her at once. 'Izaraa,' he said. 'What brings you here this fine morning?'

'The High Loremaster has summoned a conclave at Hoeth. I was dispatched to give word to all associates of the White Tower. I heard you had returned so I brought you the message.'

'What business is so urgent that the High Loremaster would summon us all back to the tower?'

'I do not know, Prince Teclis. All I know is that it concerns the Chaos moon. Many dark portents have been observed and perhaps the realm is threatened.'

'Omens indeed abound. I dreamt of Morrslieb this very night and awoke from a vision of it just before you arrived.'

'Such things are not uncommon at the moment, prince.'

'I had not noticed them before I returned to Ulthuan.'

'Rumour has it you were in Lustria, far south of here.'

'Rumour for once speaks truth and you are right; perhaps I have only recently returned to the area wherein these baleful omens hold sway.'

'You will come to Hoeth, Prince Teclis?'

'Most assuredly. I was returning anyway to consult the library. This only makes the errand more urgent.'

'How will you get there?'

'My brother is due to sail north very shortly. I can arrange to travel with him.'

'Good, then I shall bid you farewell. I must travel on and summon others.'

'I UNDERSTAND YOU just came back from Avelorn,' said Tyrion to Prince Iltharis. His head hurt a little from all the wine he had drunk the previous evening. He had a few bruises from the brawl. He needed this sparring session to get rid of the grogginess and work the stiffness from his limbs. That was why he had come to the courtyard of the Emeraldsea mansion. Around the ancient fountains members of his family's faction practised their skill at arms.

Was it his imagination or did Prince Iltharis flinch at the mention of the forest realm? Tyrion continued to strip off his shirt and don his practice armour. Iltharis paused and looked at him and then said, 'Yes, I have. Why do you mention it?'

'My aunt wants me to go there and take part in the great tournament to become the champion of the new Everqueen.'

Prince Iltharis let out a long breath that sounded suspiciously like a sigh, 'Of course. Of course. I thought for a moment that you too had become overcome by morbid curiosity, like so many of my fellow citizens of Lothern.'

'Morbid curiosity?' Tyrion began strapping up the padded tunic. He looked directly at his friend as he did so. It was plain that the prince was a little upset, which was very unusual because he was normally the most self-possessed of elves.

'I was one of the last people to see her alive. I was talking with her about my latest history when she was taken ill.'

'I did not know,' said Tyrion. 'I was in Lustria when all of this was happening. I was summoned back because of the death.'

That certainly explained why Prince Iltharis found his question so upsetting, Tyrion thought. It could not have been pleasant to be there during the last moments of a woman so beloved by all. In some ways, witnessing the death of the Everqueen was like witnessing the death of a god.

Prince Iltharis continued to don his own training gear. 'So I have heard. In a way I am grateful for your return. The fact that you have come back bearing the sword of Aenarion has given all of the gossips something else to talk about.'

'I thought you liked to be talked about,' said Tyrion with a smile. Prince Iltharis spread his hands wide.

'What elf does not? But I prefer to be talked about for my good looks, my charm, my skill with a sword, the beauty of my prose. It is not really pleasant to be gawped at like a trained monkey simply because you were present at the last moments of a famous woman.'

'I have never seen you like this,' said Tyrion. 'I believe the death of the Everqueen has really upset you.'

It was not something that Tyrion would ever have suspected of Prince Iltharis. He was very good at giving the impression of caring for nothing.

'Now my dear Tyrion, please don't start accusing me of being sentimental. That would be just too much.'

'I suspect you do have a sentimental streak, Prince Iltharis.'

Iltharis picked up a wooden practice sword and began to limber up with it. 'I shall have to beat that suspicion out of you then, Prince Tyrion.'

'I wonder if you still have that in you, or whether old age is creeping up on you.' Tyrion began to perform a few exercises designed to loosen his own muscles. Prince Iltharis laughed.

'Ah, the cockiness of youth. To tell you the truth, I am glad that you have come back. I have missed the opportunity to put you in your place. Simply because you have won a few duels you overestimate your own skill and underestimate everybody else's.'

'I do not think it would be possible to overestimate your skill,' said Tyrion. It was true too; he had never encountered another elf as good with a blade as Prince Iltharis. Tyrion knew exactly how good he himself was with a sword. There were few people in Ulthuan capable of matching him with it, but Prince Iltharis was even better. He learned something new every time he faced off against the prince in one of these practice bouts. It was one of the reasons he still went in for them.

'Do not think this late showing of humility will save you from another thrashing,' said Prince Iltharis. 'Although, it is nice to be able to practise with someone other than Korhien who poses a bit of a challenge.'

'I see you have regained some spark of your customary insouciance,' said Tyrion. 'I was starting to think that you had entered a new and morbid phase of your decrepitude.'

'Decrepitude, is it? I'll give you decrepitude! Ready?'

'Ready.'

'Then defend yourself,' said Prince Iltharis. He lunged forward, fast as a striking serpent and Tyrion was hard put to parry. As always, when fighting the prince, he found himself constantly on the defensive, rarely able to take the initiative and mount an attack of his own.

Prince Iltharis was astonishingly swift and moved with a fluid ease that Tyrion envied. He seemed able to anticipate every one of Tyrion's counter-attacks and neutralise it easily. And he did all of this with the infuriating air of an elf who was not really trying, who could easily raise his performance to a much higher level if he wanted to.

Tyrion understood enough of the psychology of combat to know that this was as much a part of Prince Iltharis's arsenal as his superlative technique with a sword. It gave him a huge edge over his opponents, even ones as confident as Tyrion.

Tyrion was no longer the youth who had provided Prince Iltharis with such easy victories when they first met though. As his hangover cleared he unleashed the full fury of his sword arm, attacking with a combination of brute strength, lightning reflex and sheer skill that few could match. He forced Iltharis to take first one step back, then two. He struck at the blade and by sheer fluke managed to knock it from the prince's hand.

For a moment, triumph filled him. It looked like he was going to defeat the prince for the first time ever. That blow must have numbed his sword hand. Then Iltharis plucked the blade from the air with his left hand and returned to the attack. Tyrion could tell that his right hand was hurt, but it did not even slow him down. Within a few heartbeats, he found the wooden practice sword at his throat.

'You really are improving, Prince Tyrion,' said Prince Iltharis. 'I don't know what it was you were doing down there in Lustria, but I don't believe I have had such a good workout in the past two centuries.'

'I was still not good enough to beat you,' said Tyrion.

Prince Iltharis smiled. 'In another two centuries you will be much better and I really will be old. Maybe you will be able to beat me then.'

'That is not much comfort,' said Tyrion. He suspected it was not intended to be.

'You are good enough to become the Everqueen's champion though, at least when it comes to swordplay.'

'Not if you compete.'

'There is more to becoming champion than using a sword. You must be proficient with all weapons and fighting from horseback. You must be able to sing and dance and play the part of the dashing hero. Being champion is as much about looking good as it is about being able to fight and there you have the advantage, my young friend.'

'I am surprised to hear you admit it.'

'An ability to realistically assess one's own strengths and weaknesses is useful for every fighter,' said Iltharis in his most professorial mode. It was a manner he sometimes assumed with Tyrion, master speaking to pupil. Tyrion could not find it in himself to resent it.

'You seem less excited about taking part in this great contest than I would have expected,' said Iltharis. He sat down on a nearby bench and took a glass of wine from the tray a human servant was holding.

'I like the idea of competing. I am not sure I like the idea of the prize.'

'They say the new Everqueen is a beauty.'

'It is being her servant that I do not like.'

'Ah, the pride of the line of Aenarion...'

'Mock all you like, my friend, but I had become accustomed to the idea of being my own master.'

'We are none of us that, prince.'

'You are the last person I would expect to hear preaching sermons about duty. You spend your time doing exactly what you want.'

'Just because I deplore responsibility myself does not mean I cannot appreciate its benefit in others. Our society would fall apart if everyone was like me.'

Prince Iltharis seemed suddenly serious. 'Believe me, Tyrion, I have had my share of unpleasant duties in my time.'

Tyrion knew Iltharis had fought many duels on behalf of the political interests of his House. He talked about them flippantly, but being known as someone who was little better than a paid assassin must take its toll.

Tyrion laughed. 'I had not thought to find you so mournful.'

Iltharis gave a rueful grimace. 'I cannot help it. I look around me and see everything is in flux. The Everqueen is dead and it makes me uneasy. The world is changing, Tyrion, and I do not think it will be for the better for the people of Ulthuan. I cannot help but feel that my life and everybody else's will soon be very altered.'

'You are serious. The world *is* changed.'

Iltharis smiled. 'Indeed. I am filled with odd forebodings. If we do not meet again after you go to Lothern, remember that I wish you well.'

Tyrion wondered what had brought that on. 'And I you, Prince Iltharis.'

The prince gave him a strange sour smile. 'Come, let us leave this gloomy place and go and get something stronger to drink.'

He seemed his old self again. Tyrion wondered what was really bothering him.

AFTER HE LEFT Tyrion, Urian cursed himself. He was getting sloppy, weak and emotional. He had been startled when Tyrion asked about the Everqueen, had felt certain that his guilt must show on his face. It had taken him most of the practice duel to become accustomed to the thought that Prince Tyrion did not suspect him and did not need to be killed on the spot. He probably could have done it and made it look like an accident, but he liked Tyrion and he had not, so far, been ordered to kill him.

It was more than the shock and the guilt though. He realised that over the centuries he had been here, an agent in place, he had grown accustomed to his life in Ulthuan.

He liked it, found it pleasant and would have been grateful for it to continue indefinitely. Instead, he knew now for certain that it would be ending soon. Malekith's plans were close to fruition and, despite the fact he had no idea as to the specifics, he knew they could not bode well for the high elves.

His forebodings for the future were based on that knowledge. Many of the elves he knew here would be dead soon, or under the iron heel of the Witch King's rule. He would be revealed as a traitor in their midst and one of the new rulers. There had been a time when he had looked forward to that with great glee. He no longer did. He thought that when Ulthuan fell, something great would be lost and the world would be a poorer place for it.

He tried to steel his nerves by telling himself the high elves were foolish and degenerate, weak and easily deceived, but he could not even deceive himself about that. He had lived too long among them, had become more like an asur than his druchii kindred. He was an odd creature now, caught between both worlds, deceiving both as to where his sympathies lay.

He had not been lying to Tyrion, he realised. He really did feel a dark and terrible foreboding about the future. Everything *was* going to change for the worse. He told himself that he had better get used to the idea. Soon Malekith would rule this place, and he had no sympathy at all for those who were not utterly loyal. Urian had better be absolutely certain where his loyalties lay.

CHAPTER THIRTEEN

'GREETINGS, DOORKEEPER,' KORHIEN Ironglaive said. 'Welcome to my
humble chamber.'

Tyrion presented Korhien with some wine from his father's cellars and looked around. Korhien's chambers were simple by the
standards of the Phoenix King's palace, which meant they were
luxurious beyond belief even by the standards of Lothern. Carpets from Araby covered the floor. The hangings were ancient silk
tapestries. Paintings from the golden age of art during the reign of
Aethis hung on the walls. The crystal window had an astonishing
view of the harbour.

Tyrion took a seat on a divan and looked across at his father's
oldest friend. Korhien looked almost the same as the time when
they had first met over a century ago. He had a few more scars
but the agelessness that the vast majority of elves possessed until
extreme old age was still his. He was as tall, fit and muscular as a
youth, and moved with the easy grace of the very highest echelon
of warriors.

'I hear your quest to the world's far edges has been successful.'

'We found it, Korhien. We found the sword Aenarion carried in his youth.' For once Tyrion could allow all of his enthusiasm to show. He could not with his other friends, even Prince Iltharis.

Korhien raised an eyebrow.

'What?' Tyrion asked.

'Nothing,' Korhien said.

'Spit it out. There's never been any need for restraint between us, why start now?'

Korhien laughed. 'Very well, since candour is what you demand. I was thinking that I am not sure whether it's a good omen that you have found that sword.'

'Why?'

'Aenarion started with that blade. He moved on to another one.'

'You are not seriously suggesting that I am interested in drawing the Sword of Khaine?'

'What I am suggesting, doorkeeper, is that it would not matter whether you are or not. If it is your destiny to do those things you will, and you are very clearly someone marked by destiny.'

'I would never have believed you were so superstitious, Korhien.'

'Nor would I. But sometimes I look at you and I wonder into what pattern the stars are aligning behind your head. I wonder how much of it is deliberate, and how much of it is Fate, the gods, whatever you want to call it.'

He sounded unusually thoughtful. No, Tyrion thought. That was not fair. The White Lion had always been much more thoughtful than most elves ever gave him credit for being. It was just that his thoughts did not usually drift down such strange channels.

'You are serious, aren't you?'

Korhien nodded. 'A god reached out and touched your life once, Tyrion. It intervened to save you. How many elves has that ever happened to? I can count it on the fingers of one foot and contrary to the opinion of some I am not a Chaos mutant.'

'We were in the Shrine of Asuryan. The god was protecting his own.'

'Asuryan did not save any of the warriors with you, or any of the priests guarding his shrine. He lent his power to you and your brother. I would respectfully submit that he most likely did it for his own reasons. Now you return from the blighted edges of the world carrying a blade that was forged by Caledor and borne by Aenarion himself. I can almost feel the forces of destiny lining up behind you.'

'You are unusually full of forebodings this fine morning. And to think I only came over to offer you a cup of wine.'

'You are of the blood of Aenarion, doorkeeper. That means something.'

'It means I belong to a select group that has been prodded and tested and manipulated by its own people, hunted by daemons and secret cults, whispered about behind its back and accused of all manner of unspeakable crimes. I did not ask for any of this, Korhien.'

'Ah, but you did. No one forced you to go seeking that blade. And yet you did.'

'You think I have some ulterior motive?'

'Don't you?'

'What do you mean by that?'

'I think you are not without ambitions. I think you are interested in a career in politics and you, or the people behind you, are using your resemblance to Aenarion to build a legend around you.'

'The people around me? You mean my grandfather in his time or my aunt now?'

'And their faction, yes.'

'Are you talking for Finubar here? Does he think I threaten him?'

'No, doorkeeper. On both accounts. I am speaking for myself, based on my own observations. You are not a threat to Finubar, because he is the Phoenix King and only his death will change that. And you are not the sort to try your hand at assassination, nor is your aunt.'

Tyrion was annoyed but he did not let that show in his voice. 'I am glad you think so.'

'You asked me for honesty, doorkeeper. Would you prefer that I did not give it to you?'

Tyrion shook his head then smiled, seeing the absurdity of the situation. 'No. I prefer you as you are, Korhien, and I prefer you to say what you think. I am just surprised that you have such a low opinion of me.'

'That I do not. It is just that I sometimes look at you and wonder how it is all going to end. Your life is taking on a strange shape and so is that of your brother. I worry about you both.'

'It would be best not to mention that to him. He likes to think he can take care of himself.'

'You both can, but that does not stop me from worrying. Now tell me about your aunt. How is she these days?'

Korhien and Malene had been lovers once, but the decades and politics had pulled them apart. He still seemed interested in her though. Perhaps she was in him. They were still friends.

'She seemed a little worried when I last talked to her,' Tyrion began.

'IT IS GOOD to see you again, aunt,' said Teclis with what he felt was a little too much formality. He was unsure of his reception so he had fallen back on good manners. It was unusual for him.

Teclis looked at Lady Malene. Physically she did not look any different from the beautiful elf woman he had first seen the day before his sixteenth birthday over a century ago. She was still beautiful in a severe way and as ageless as any other elf. She looked somehow older though.

There was something to the set of her shoulders and the way her lips compressed. A slight frown was always present on her forehead. Responsibility had changed her. Just the way she sat hunched over her father's old desk made her look different.

Tyrion would have been able to tell him in exactly what ways and quite possibly explain why, but he had always lacked his brother's gift for reading people.

She looked up and smiled with a genuine warmth that always surprised him. He never really expected anyone but his father and his brother to look at him like that.

'Prince Teclis,' she said. 'This is a pleasure.'

'Not entirely an unexpected one, I hope.' Try as he might, he could not keep the hurt from his voice. He had always thought that she preferred him to Tyrion, the only person other than his father who had ever done so. It hurt him, more than he cared to admit, that she had summoned his brother first and in private.

'I knew you had returned along with your brother. I saw him yesterday evening.'

'I know.'

'It was business of the House,' she said, as if that explained everything, which he supposed it did. She took her duties as the new ruler of House Emeraldsea very seriously.

As she said it she rose from behind the desk, walked around it and hugged him. The intimacy of the gesture was startling. He was not used to any physical displays of affection. He returned the hug clumsily and backed away as quickly as he could, staring at her from arm's length.

'I understand you have become quite the adventurer,' she said, returning to her place behind the desk as if she understood his embarrassment. 'You have found the sword of Aenarion.'

'Not the blade everyone thinks of as Aenarion's sword,' said Teclis. 'But, yes, we found Sunfang.'

'Many said it was impossible,' she said. 'I knew you would succeed. You and your brother always do at anything you truly put your minds to.'

'I wish I shared your faith in my abilities. You are, of course, correct about Tyrion.'

'You always sound so sour these days when you talk about him,' she said. Teclis thought it certainly was so when he talked to her. He could not help himself. He did not wish to be displaced in her affections. He could never bring himself to say that openly though. He realised he was being unfair to Tyrion as well, which galled him, for he knew his brother would never behave so towards him. It was just one more way in which he was better.

'I do not mean to, but it is hard sometimes,' he admitted. 'I live on his charity, me and father both.'

Malene studied him. 'You do not live on his charity. He has given most of what he owns to you and your father. It is all yours now, not his. He told me to tell you that if the matter ever came up.'

'Why would he do that?'

'He knows your father needs the money and he was letting me know something as well.'

Somehow this did not make Teclis feel any better. 'He earned that money with his raiding and his trading. He did it while I was studying at Hoeth. I think sometimes he does these things to make me feel bad.'

'You think your brother gifts you with gold in order to make you feel bad?' Malene's smile was curious. 'Explain!' For a second, she was the old Malene, his tutor in magic and alchemy.

'Even Tyrion's generosity is a weapon. Or rather, a display of superiority. He is saying he is the one who is in a position of power. He is always the one who helps us, helps me. It is never the other way.'

Malene steepled her fingers. 'I am surprised it has taken such an intelligent elf so long to realise this,' she said.

Teclis smiled sourly. 'I have never been good with people.'

'Better than you think.'

'You agree with me then?'

'Of course. The question you really should ask yourself is why your brother behaves this way.'

'Because he likes to feel superior.'

'No. Because he still feels inferior.'

'Why should he do that? Everyone always praises him. He is probably the best-loved elf in Lothern.'

'It was not always so.'

'I do not remember it any other way.'

'I do.'

'Your memory is better than mine then, lady.'

'We both know it is not. But I can still remember a day that you seem to have forgotten.'

'What day is that?'

'The day I first saw the pair of you.' Malene smiled fondly, as if recalling something that was special to her.

'You saw a sickly child and a perfect elf boy.'

'I saw a father who doted on the sick son who resembled him and who shared his interests. I saw another boy who was excluded because he had no interest in or talent for the Art, only for things his father despised or considered of no consequence. It was a small house and there was only one parent.'

'You think Tyrion still remembers that?'

'Probably not, but it does not matter. It set his feet on a certain path and he probably cannot even remember now why he still walks it. What matters is that he does.'

Teclis turned this thought over and over in his mind. He had been so lost in his own bitterness that he had never even thought that Tyrion might have some of his own. He always seemed so happy and secure. 'I am not sure I believe that. He has never said anything to me.'

'He is even more self-contained than you are, though you may not believe that. And he has said something to you. He says it by his actions.'

'You are as wise as you are lovely, lady,' Teclis said eventually.

'And it is pleasant to discover you have acquired some elven graces over the years. Now I presume this is not purely a social call. You have something you wish to discuss with me.' It had been a social call really. He had just wanted to see her and reassure himself, but he could not say that out loud.

'Tyrion told me you were troubled about something before he

went to visit Prince Iltharis today. He said you told him that the winds of magic have changed. He did not know what it meant, but he said it sounded ominous. My father has been saying similar things. And I had a message from Hoeth this morning. It seems the High Loremaster shares your fears.'

'I am troubled, Teclis. More than I can say. There is something not right with the world, and not right with the flow of magic, although I cannot put my finger on exactly what.'

'Then I have something that may disquiet you more. In Lustria I found a slann prophecy. I feel it may be of grave importance. If I am not mistaken, it concerns the return of Chaos to our world, and if I understand the slann dating system, it is due to happen soon.' Teclis took out the drawings he had made and showed them to her.

'It does not strike me as chance that this sort of thing would fall into your hands right now,' said Malene. She looked thoughtful. 'I know very little of slann pictoglyphs, otherwise I would offer to help.'

She sounded wistful, almost as if she were looking for an excuse to get involved in some magical research again.

'I need to know who the best person to discuss the matter with would be,' Teclis said.

'High Loremaster Morelian is the greatest expert we have in the slann languages.'

'I suspected as much but it is nice to have that confirmed. Do you think he would help me?'

'He'll probably tear your arm off trying to get those out of your grip. A new and authentic slann text – it's the sort of thing he dreams about. I've known him since he was my tutor at the tower. The slann have always been an obsession with him.'

'I am familiar with the type,' said Teclis thinking of his father. Malene could obviously tell the way his thoughts were running.

'Do not confuse Morelian with Prince Arathion. You do not get to be High Loremaster without being perceptive, ambitious and politically minded.'

'I know him by sight, of course, but not that well.'

'He will know you too, but, of course, I will write. It can't do any harm.'

As the head of House Emeraldsea, his aunt was one of the richest and most influential women in Ulthuan, a personal friend of the Phoenix King. Since she was a mage, she was also a powerful ally of the White Tower at court. Again, almost as if she could read what he was thinking, she said, 'I see you are becoming quite political yourself.'

'I have a long way to go before I can match my brother.'

'You'll get there in the end.'

'I am not sure I want to.'

'You'll be High Loremaster one of these days. I am sure of it.'

'It is not an honour to which I aspire.'

'Now you really do sound like your brother,' Malene said. Teclis wondered what she meant by that.

THE SHORES OF Ulthuan glittered on the horizon. Malekith saw the shimmering haze in the air that he remembered so well. It was the glow of magic that hovered perpetually over the island continent and had done ever since the time of the Archmage Caledor. The whole mighty fleet cruised along the coast now, heading for their goal.

Beside him his generals looked grim or pleased or filled with anticipation according to their temperament. Some of them directed lustful bemused looks towards N'Kari, who now wore the form of a lustrously beautiful elf maiden. Her shackles in particular seemed to focus their attention. Malekith easily guessed which direction their thoughts were taking.

Slaves walked through the chamber bearing platters of food and drink, their eyes downcast submissively as they attempted to avoid drawing any attention to themselves. Today it worked. The assembled nobles paid them no more attention than they would any other piece of furniture.

There was a certain febrile festival atmosphere about the command chamber. All of those present knew that war was about to begin and that it was going to be hard, but all of them also believed they were going to win. None of them knew the full extent of his preparations but all of them knew him, and they knew he would not have launched this attack unless he was utterly certain of victory.

They sipped drugged wine and smiled and calculated spoils. A few of them discussed reclaiming ancestral estates that had been lost millennia ago.

Malekith deliberately said nothing to damp down the conversations about reward. He wanted to foster this atmosphere of feverish competition and greed. His lack of intervention was duly noted by those who had spent a lifetime watching him for the slightest clues as to his whims. He knew that eventually the message would spread to all present in the fleet.

Sometimes he noticed the sorcerers present turn their gazes on N'Kari for a moment. The most powerful present blanched and fell silent and that too was noted by the audience he had assembled. And that too was good. He was giving them all a demonstration, making a statement of how powerful he truly was. Word of that would get out too.

And in the inevitable druchii fashion it would filter its way down to every rank of the army. All of them would know that their lord and master had bound a greater daemon of Chaos to his will. They would wonder about what other allies he could command.

He felt something like happiness at this moment. His plans were under way and he was confident of eventual victory. So far everything had gone as anticipated. He was not foolish enough to think there would be no setbacks or that everything would go according to plan, but he had amassed a sufficient concentration of resources and power to counter any threat that might arise. It was only a matter of time before Ulthuan fell, and after that he would deal with his remaining enemies.

Not a few of those present were his mother's lovers and secretly sworn to her service. They thought him unaware of that fact and the time had not yet come to apprise them of their error. That day would dawn soon enough and Malekith was looking forward to it with relish.

One of the things he abhorred most was disloyalty.

CHAPTER FOURTEEN

'IT SEEMS LIKE you have become a person of some importance,' said Atharis. Tyrion looked at his old friend. They sat together in his office in the Emeraldsea palace. Physically, Atharis had not changed much from the young fighter Tyrion had met when he first came to the city all those years ago. His nose was still broken and he refused to have the healers use magic to set it properly. He was higher ranked in the House now and trusted with many secret duties.

'While you have steadily been working your way down in the world,' Tyrion said, smiling to take the sting out of his words. Atharis had made quite a name for himself among the brothels and stews of Lothern. He was also a very successful merchant, representing the family interests whenever their grandfather had chosen to send him.

'We cannot all be blessed with the blood of Aenarion,' said Atharis. 'Some of us have to get by using only our natural intelligence and charm.'

'That explains why you have been doing so badly then,' said Tyrion. Atharis punched him on the arm playfully.

'It is good to see you again,' he said. He sounded sincere. Once, long ago, they might have been considered rivals but Atharis no longer seemed to see things that way. Tyrion was glad.

'It's good to see you too,' said Tyrion. 'I understand that we are to be travelling together.'

'Your aunt could not allow you to travel to the court of the Everqueen unescorted. I am to be in charge of your retinue. I am responsible for seeing you don't disgrace House Emeraldsea.'

And doubtless you are also responsible for reporting my actions to my aunt, Tyrion thought.

'And how big is this retinue of mine going to be?'

'Well Lady Emeraldsea feels you need at least fifty warriors to protect you from the marauding deer of Avelorn. You also need servants in order to make sure that your clothes look sufficiently impressive and that your hair is properly combed. So, you're probably being accompanied by the crew of an entire fighting ship. Let's hope that your participation in this tournament proves worth it.'

'Let's hope,' Tyrion agreed sourly. 'So am I getting a ship to go with the crew?'

'Of course you are. Your aunt has rerouted one of our Inner Sea traders to make sure that you get there in time. We are even supposed to row you if the winds prove unfavourable.'

'That's good,' said Tyrion. 'Because you look like you could use the exercise.'

'I'm still capable of giving you a good run for your money with the sword.'

Tyrion laughed. 'I'm surprised my aunt isn't sending you then. You could represent our House just as well as I can.'

'Alas, Lady Malene does not see things that way. Otherwise I would gladly do so. Our new Everqueen is supposed to be quite the beauty.'

'I have never heard of one who wasn't,' said Tyrion. 'All of the poets always sing praises of their good looks and all of the books say how lovely they are.'

'And, of course, no poet ever lied and no scholar ever propagated a falsehood,' said Atharis. 'You know this as well as I do.'

'Is there anything else I should know?'

'The protection of your sacred person is not the only reason that you're being allocated so many fighters. You are bearing some coronation gifts for the new queen of the forest. Your aunt feels that she must be sufficiently impressed with the wealth and generosity of our House. Obviously the poor rustic girl is going to be swayed by our silks and gold and some pretty mirrors brought all the way from the dwarf lands.'

'I imagine that we will not be the only ones bringing gifts,' said Tyrion. 'Every noble family in Ulthuan will be taking this chance to demonstrate its loyalty and generosity.'

'Indeed. I often think it would be more profitable and sensible if we came to some arrangement with all of the other families not to do this sort of thing. Then we could keep the gold for ourselves.'

'But gold is only a means to an end. How would we prove ourselves to be richer and more generous than all of our rivals if we did not give such gifts.'

'Doubtless we would find a way. We are elves after all, famous for our ingenuity when it comes to proving our superiority.'

'In the meantime,' said Tyrion, 'I suppose we shall have to go about doing so the old-fashioned way. After all, if it worked for our ancestors it should work for us.'

'Indeed. We're leaving with the tide. Let us head down to the docks and watch some other people working. I always find work very stimulating when I am not the one who has to do it.'

TYRION WATCHED AS the crew loaded the ship. How often had he done this in the past, he wondered? There were times when he felt like half of his life had been spent aboard ships, going somewhere or returning to Lothern.

The vessel was anchored on the pier at Lothern's northern docks. The Inner Sea was a different sea from the wild outer ocean. It was superficially calmer and safer, bounded on all sides by the landmass of Ulthuan, surrounded in its entirety by lands. There was less trade here, so the docks were smaller and less busy, but still bustling. Goods were shipped out to the rest of Ulthuan from here, and the produce of Saphery and Chrace and other places found its way to the great port, and from there to the rest of the world.

The ships here were smaller and more homely-looking than the great ocean-going clippers.

He saw his brother riding down to the harbour. As ever, no one paid too much attention to him. He was just another tall slender elf mounted on a fine steed. He was a terrible rider for an elf but still stood out less than usual. His limp made him noticeable when he walked. His twin rode right up to the pier and paused for a moment to study the ship. He waved and Tyrion waved back.

'I see your brother has deigned to join us,' said Atharis.

'You don't like him, do you?' said Tyrion.

'He never gives anyone much of a chance to like him. If he were less caustic, he might have more friends.'

Tyrion could not deny the truth of that. 'His life has been hard. It is not easy to be less than perfect among elves.'

'None of us are perfect,' said Atharis. 'Not even you. We don't use it as an excuse to be rude to everyone else.'

'I think he got into the habit of getting his retaliation in first when he was young. People were often rude to him because of who and what he was.'

'I can tell you are going to go on making excuses for him,' said Atharis. 'He is no longer a sickly youth. He is a powerful mage and regarded as something of a hero among his kind.'

'His kind?'

'He is a wizard.'

'He is an elf.'

'It is possible to be both, my dear Tyrion.'

'Mages are not a breed apart.'

'You may want to explain that to them, my friend.' Teclis limped up the gangplank, leaving his horse in the care of one of House Emeraldsea's dockside factors. He saw Atharis and made a sour expression. Atharis responded in kind.

'A pleasure to see you,' said Teclis ironically.

'I am as pleased to see you as you are to see me,' Atharis responded. His smile was insincere, and obviously so.

Tyrion wondered at his brother's talent for making enemies. Atharis was not the least amiable elf in the world. It would not take an enormous effort to keep on the right side of him. Instead Teclis seemed to take pleasure in being disliked.

'You are ready to depart?' Tyrion asked his brother, to forestall any further sniping. 'You do not seem to have brought much gear with you.'

'It is already on board. The servants brought it this morning. How about you? Are you ready to woo the Everqueen?'

'If she is as beautiful as everyone says, yes. I am just not sure I am ready to be her champion.'

'There are others who may have a say in that, your fellow competitors for the great honour of being in her service.'

'You are in an unpleasant mood today, aren't you?' Tyrion wondered whether Teclis was being deliberately rude and abrasive because Atharis was present. He tended to adopt such a persona in public, even with his own brother. It was one of his less engaging habits.

'Forgive me,' he said. 'I have had a rather disturbing and sleepless night.' He shot Tyrion a warning glance so that his twin would know for certain that he did not want to discuss this further in public. 'Now if you will excuse me, I would like to go below. There is some reading I must catch up on.'

'Don't let us keep you from your books,' said Atharis. 'I am sure you have matters of earth-shattering importance to consider.'

'Oddly enough, I do,' said Teclis airily. 'I am sure you will hear of them soon enough.'

'I cannot wait,' Atharis said softly to the wizard's departing back. Once Teclis was gone, he said, 'It is hard to believe you are twins. You seem to have got all the good looks and charm in your generation of your family.'

'Possibly,' said Tyrion. 'But he got the brains and the magical talent.'

'I think you got the best of the deal.'

'That might be part of the problem,' said Tyrion.

'You are not as foolish as you look,' said Atharis.

'WHY DO YOU keep taunting Atharis?' Tyrion asked. He stepped into the small cabin as soon as Teclis opened the door.

'I don't like him and he does not like me,' his twin replied.

'Perhaps if you were more pleasant to him, he would be more amiable.'

Teclis laughed bitterly. 'Do you really think so?'

'You do this to everybody. Most elves just ignore it but some of them respond very badly.'

'And you think they might respond better if I was nicer to them?' A note of mockery entered Teclis's voice.

'There is that possibility.'

'There is no possibility,' said Teclis with flat certainty. 'Atharis does not like me because I make him uneasy. Most elves do not like me because I make them uneasy. I do not look right. I do not talk right. I am a cripple. I should have been exposed at birth. You know there is something to be said for the old ways.' By the end of his speech, Teclis's voice had become a high-pitched parody of the way most elves talked in polite conversation.

'You are not a child anymore,' Tyrion said. 'No one talks to you that way and you do not have to talk to them as if they did.'

'You really don't understand anything, do you?'

'Then make me,' Tyrion said.

'I am an outsider in my own country, Tyrion. I do not belong here and I never will. I am not beautiful. I am... flawed. I know it. Everyone else knows it. Elves do not like to be reminded they are less than perfect, that there is even the possibility of it.'

'You exaggerate.'

'Alas I do not. And you are in no position to tell me otherwise. They like *you*. You are what they think they themselves are. You are perfect.'

'No I am not.'

'Perhaps, but you look it, and this is a place where appearances are everything. You are a butterfly. I am a moth.'

'Now I really don't follow you.'

'People like butterflies. They are bright, vivacious, good-looking. They are creatures of the day. People hate and fear moths. They are dark, night-going. They do not like to feel a moth's wings on their face. Look closely at them and moths and butterflies are very similar creatures, but people feel very differently about them.'

Tyrion laughed. 'I am trying to talk to you about the way you treat other elves and you start talking about moths and butterflies. Do you realise how strange that makes you sound?'

'I am strange, Tyrion. I am an outsider. I am a magician.'

'You are sure you are not a moth now?'

'Don't play the fool, brother. It does not suit you. You know what I am talking about. It's cockroaches and ladybirds.'

'Go on...' Tyrion could not keep a certain amount of mockery from his voice.

'They are both insects. People think one looks sweet. They are repulsed by the other. Look at them closely and they are the same except for colour. My basic point is that appearances matter. They colour what people believe. You look one way and I look another. You could be as rude as I am to any elf, and you would still get away with it. I could be polite as a courtier at the court of the Everqueen and they would still hate me.'

'So you are using this as an excuse not to try?'

Teclis looked shocked. 'Don't you think I've tried? I tried so hard for so long that my face was frozen in a permanent grin. I might as well have had lockjaw. I tried as hard as I could and no one wanted to know. They still don't. Keep that in mind before you judge me and come down on the side of *your* friends.'

'I do not judge you and I never take anyone's side against you. Surely you know that?'

'I do not know that. You started this little conversation telling me not to be rude to your friend Atharis.'

'I merely suggested that you might try being politer to him, and you might get on better. I am trying to help you.'

'I will thank you not to.'

'As you wish,' Tyrion said. 'But I think you will find that if you give other elves the chance, they will give you one.'

'You never give up, do you?'

'That is my nature.' They looked at each other for a long moment, their expressions frozen in looks that were almost of hostility. Tyrion did not quite understand how, but his well-meant advice seemed to have pushed them to the brink of a serious disagreement. He realised that he had misjudged things and that he did not know his twin as well as he thought.

Another idea occurred to him. They had got on well enough when they were adventuring on their own. Since they had returned to Lothern, they were at odds.

It was the situation, not them. Now they had returned to the homeland of the elves, he was once again accepted and his brother was once again an outsider. The centre of power in their relationship had shifted and they were both responding to it.

He suddenly understood why Teclis was so much happier travelling and adventuring and why he spent so much time isolated. At least he partially understood. He doubted he could grasp all of the situation because he was not his brother.

Teclis smiled at him and the tension was broken. They both laughed, but both of them knew that things were different now

that they had come back to Ulthuan. Tyrion knew that it was
because he had returned home and Teclis never could.

'Since you have asked me, I will try and be civil to Atharis,' Teclis
said. 'Watch and see what happens.'

Tyrion said nothing. He felt that Teclis was right. Atharis would
not be his friend. He would go on being an outsider. Whether by
reason of his appearance or his manner, or because he now chose
to be. It was his brother's role in life.

He thought about what Korhien had said about destiny and he
was more troubled by it than he ever had been before.

AFTER DAYS AT sea, Tyrion was glad as the ship approached the
harbour at Cairn Auriel. The sun beat down on the deck. It was
not as warm as it had been in Lustria but it was still very warm. A
cool breeze blowing in off the sea gave some relief from the heat.
Tyrion stood in the shadow of the command deck and watched
the shore come closer.

Cairn Auriel was not a large port by the standards of Lothern
but it looked like a pleasant place, a natural harbour cut into the
high cliffs on the western coast of Saphery. A silver lighthouse
watched over it. Long marble piers protruded outwards from a
beach of golden sand. The town itself was a place of graceful
white towers tipped with golden domes. Dock workers helped
moor the ship and get the gangplanks into place so that Teclis
could get off.

Tyrion strode over to where he stood. He let his smile widen and
said, 'Once again, brother, we must say farewell.'

'We shall see each other again,' said Teclis. 'All that remains is for
me to wish you good luck in the upcoming tournament. See that
you do not disgrace our family too badly.'

'I shall do my best,' said Tyrion.

'Doubtless I shall hear how well you have done from passing
minstrels and other travellers,' said Teclis. 'You might even consider sending a messenger to let me know how things go.'

'I'm sure the wizards of the White Tower have ways of receiving news much more swiftly than letter,' said Tyrion. 'But I shall write.'

'It always comes as a pleasant surprise to find that you're capable of it,' said Teclis. The ship was tied up now and the gangplank was firmly in place.

Teclis's baggage had been carried down by sailors and lay on the white marble of the pier. The two brothers clasped hands. The wizard left the ship and strode off in search of horses.

Tyrion watched him go until he was out of sight. By that time, the crew had cast off the moorings and the ship was being washed back out to sea.

Tyrion was suddenly struck by the ominous foreboding that it might be a long time before he saw his brother again.

MORATHI STOOD ON the prow of the great wooden ship and watched as her followers raced ashore. Tens of thousands of the Chaos-worshipping barbarians leapt from their ships into the roaring surf and raced up the black sand beaches. Behind her, thousands more ships crowded the seas. Most of them carried humans and beastmen and less wholesome followers of the Dark Gods. Some of them were packed with her own followers, from the Cults of Khaine and the Cults of the Pleasure God. They were the druchii who would form her bodyguard amid the humans. Not that she needed one.

The chieftains of the great horde gazed upon her with worshipful eyes. They would do what she required of them in return for her approval and her caresses. They would fight with each other for her favours if she wanted. Perhaps she would have them do so at some point, but right now she needed them to co-operate.

There were elven fortresses nearby that needed to be taken, and elven cities that needed to be conquered and enslaved. Soon she would set this land ablaze from end to end and teach the people to fear and adore her as they had done in the past. In an odd way it felt good to be home.

Naked, she plunged into the sea and let the cool water flow over her. Like a goddess she emerged dripping from the surf, aware that all eyes were upon her. In the distance she could see a beacon fire had been lit. It looked as if the asur were aware of her presence.

And so it begins, she thought. She was curious as to how it would end.

CHAPTER FIFTEEN

TECLIS FOUND THE agent of the White Tower easily enough. The elf recognised him at once and knew what he needed. Swiftly he provided Teclis with a satchel of supplies, a saddle and two horses which he could use in relay.

Teclis rode up the pathway out of Cairn Auriel and followed the trail that he knew would eventually lead him to the Tower of Hoeth. It felt odd – for the first time in months he was on his own. Ever since he and Tyrion had set out on the quest to find Sunfang, he had been in company with his brother and quite often many others. He had not had time to think or to study or to brood or to plan. As he rode along, he found that he quite enjoyed the quiet of the woods and the respite from having to constantly deal with other people.

He felt better now that he was on his own. He enjoyed Tyrion's company but several months spent daily with his twin had proven tiresome in the end. It was simply too much for an elf as solitary as he was. He loved his brother but he did not want to spend every waking hour of every waking day in his company.

Now at last he had time to think. He was pleased with the way the adventure had turned out. After decades of searching they had finally found Sunfang. His brother now had a weapon that was worthy of him and had burnished his reputation as a hero of Ulthuan.

Teclis did not really care how this victory affected his own reputation among the general populace. It might redound to his credit amongst the wizards of the tower but only insofar as it reflected upon his scholarship. His theories as to the sword's whereabouts had been proven correct. He felt certain that many of his fellow wizards would be as interested in the slann text that he carried as the details of the search for the sword. Of course, he would leave a record of that at the library so that future generations would have access to the knowledge. That was part of his duty as a scholar.

At the moment it was the slann text that troubled him. There were people at the tower who knew far more about slann hieroglyphics then he did and he wanted their help translating it. He had understood enough of what was on the thing to know that its portent was ominous. More than that, since he had returned to Ulthuan, he had started to sense that time was running out. He was uneasy and he did not know why. He was a wizard, though, and he trusted to that strange sixth sense that had so often warned him of trouble in the past.

He was not the best of riders and he had to concentrate on following the trail through the woods. Occasionally, he paused to re-weave his protective spells. The forests of Saphery were not without their dangers.

There were subtle protective spells woven onto the milestones that marked this pathway. They would keep the most dangerous beasts away and ward off some of the strange magical dangers that were to be found in these forests. He did not want to stray too far from this trail though and he did not want to rely on its magic alone to protect him.

In some ways, he was pleased that Tyrion was not here. It meant that he would need to rely upon himself. His brother had a genius for organisation that would show up in even the littlest of things, such as making a camp or pitching a tent. While Tyrion was around there had been very little need for him to do anything and now he would need to do everything.

He was quite looking forward to that. He was not good at any of it but he enjoyed the practice. When he thought about how sick he had been in his youth and childhood, this was not an unexpected pleasure. He could never have foreseen that one day he would be riding alone through this distant, dangerous forest with nothing but his spells to protect him.

It was quite something. He meant to take advantage of every single moment of it while it lasted

TECLIS GATHERED UP some moss and twigs to make a fire. He came back to where he had staked out the horses with a bundle of kindling held in his robes. He opened his hands and let it fall to the ground and then started to arrange the sticks in the same way as he had seen Tyrion do, although not so neatly or so well. Tyrion would have used a flint to get the fire going but Teclis did not have to do that. He spoke a word and called upon the winds of magic and the moss and twigs burst into flame.

He sat down by the fire and opened the satchel of supplies that the agent had given him. Inside he found dried fruit and beef jerky along with a selection of waybread. He never had the greatest of appetites at the best of times, so he took the tiniest morsel of waybread and began to chew it. He had already filled his canteen from the nearby stream when he had chosen the campsite. As he ate, he pondered the odd thing he had sensed when he lit the fire. It made him even more uneasy than he had been all day.

The winds of magic were tainted even here. He was not sure that most wizards would have noticed this thing – few of them were as sensitive as he was. His skin tingled slightly when he worked a spell and he had felt a twinge, only the faintest of twinges, of nausea. He suspected that the alchemy he used to maintain his health made him more susceptible to such things.

What was happening, he wondered?

It was possible that there was something nearby, some trace of old Dark Magic from the first Chaos incursion that still tainted the area. That might explain why it was so weak. Such influences had been fading for a very long time. That was the best case he could think of. He did not like to think what else it might portend.

He lay on his back, with his hands behind his head, and stared up at the stars visible through the gaps in the branches overhead. The woods did not seem as quiet at night as they did during the day, but he knew that that was an illusion. It was simply that his hearing was keener because his sight was dimmer.

It was good to be beneath the familiar stars of Ulthuan again. He could see one of the constellations that his father had taught him to recognise when he was a boy. Aenarion's Sword Belt it was called. It glittered above him cheerily.

He could hear something moving off in the woods. Most likely a fox he thought, certainly nothing larger. Not that he was any expert on such things, he thought sourly. It could be a beastman attempting to creep up on him for all he knew. He sat upright and rummaged in his saddlebags until he found a small group of stones that he had etched with runes.

He placed them around his campfire and spoke the words of an old spell. The runes on the stones glowed and small rainbows of light arced from one to the other and then faded. The wards would protect him and alert him if anything passed between them, bringing him awake instantly if it was larger than a rat.

Of course, that would not protect him if it was an arrow or a spear. He told himself that he was being unnecessarily cautious but that was his nature. He arranged his saddlebags under the blankets and then spoke the words of another spell so that to any onlooker they would look like a sleeping elf.

He positioned himself a lot further from the fire and wrapped himself up in a blanket and wove an illusion that would make him blend into the landscape. He lay there in the darkness thinking if there was anything that he had missed, if there was something that he should do to increase the security but nothing came immediately to mind.

He began breathing exercises to enable himself to relax, to drift off into sleep. It was a long time before he could stop listening to the small noises of the forest and allow himself to slumber. Before he fell into sleep, he thought he felt again some taint to the magic around him. He hoped it would not affect the wards that he had placed on the other spells that he had worked for its protection.

He opened his eyes after what seemed like only a moment. The fire had burned down but he sensed a presence. It was odd because his wards had not woken him. He looked up and a shadow figure loomed out of the darkness, tall and slender, with a high forehead and a receding hairline unusual in an elf.

There was something immeasurably ancient and immeasurably sad about the stranger. He did not appear to be threatening. He was staring off into the distance, as if looking for something. When he turned to look at Teclis, it was a shock. He had no eyes. Where they should have been was only darkness, inside which something blazed.

Teclis felt as if he was falling into those eyes, and as he did so he could see that the lights formed a pattern, enormously large and astonishingly complex. It reminded him in some ways of the layout of Zultec. He could see that the pattern was flickering and unstable and starting to unravel in parts, and for some reason Teclis found this to be hugely threatening, as if his life depended on that not happening.

For a moment, everything appeared to be on the brink of dissolution, and he shouted for it to stop. He came awake with the echoes of the shout ringing through the forest. Panicking he glared around, seeking the tall stranger, but there was nothing there and his wards were undisturbed.

'Just a dream,' he told himself as he rose to see to his disturbed horses. He felt sure that was not all it had been.

AS HE RODE, Teclis could feel the magic all around him. It was subtle, sly, hidden from most people, even the most sensitive of elves, but it was there. The defences of the Tower of Hoeth were ancient, powerful and strange.

There were no walls. Daemonic guardians did not patrol the woods around the tower. Spectacular magic did not blast intruders from the cloudless sky. Instead, the ancient wizards who had built the tower had protected it in a manner befitting their cleverness.

If you were a threat to the tower, you simply would not find it. You would wander lost in the woods, sometimes catching a glimpse of the mighty structure but never arriving at it.

Teclis had often wondered how this effect had been achieved. He could understand some of the components of it. Obviously there was an enchantment of divination present. The spells that guarded the tower needed to be able to detect any evil intention in those who approached it. They needed to be able to reach into an enemy's mind, or perhaps even their very soul, to find this out.

And after that they needed to be able to twist that person's perceptions so that they could not find a way into the heart of the wood. The basic theory was simple enough.

Like many other scholars at Hoeth, he had pored over Bel-Korhadris's notes. He had caught glimpses of the workings of the Scholar-King's mind, but he had not been able to follow the whole process. No one had.

Bel-Korhadris had been the greatest geomancer since Caledor Dragontamer, with a gift amounting to genius when it came to the building of magical structures. When Teclis looked at his notes he was in the position of a peasant looking at a pile of bricks and an architect's plans for a mansion and then at the mansion itself.

He could see that the two things were connected, that they could somehow be used to create something magnificent. He just did not understand how.

Yet.

One day he would. Just as one day he would understand how Caledor had created the Vortex. If he lived long enough he would manage it. His thirst for knowledge was so great that it would not be denied.

Always when he studied the work of the great ancients, he felt this nagging sense that if only he worked harder, was just a little bit cleverer, understood just the tiniest amount more, he would gain the insight that he needed. So far it had not come, but he felt that one day it would.

He had heard some people claim that there were sophisticated teleportation spells involved in the tower's defences, but that seemed like nonsense to him. He knew that it was possible to warp time and space but it took an enormous amount of energy, which would be detectable by the most unsophisticated mage. Working on the minds of travellers would be far more efficient and far more difficult to detect. Of course, understanding the basic principles of how such a thing could work did not qualify him to be able to work the spell.

There were other things to be considered about it. The spells covered an area of leagues around the tower. They were always in effect and had been ever since the tower was built.

Something maintained them and there were no obvious runes or points of focus that he had ever found. Perhaps elementals or daemons had been bound into the spell. After all, something at some point was making a judgement as to whether the approaching traveller was hostile or not. One possibility was that the judgement was left up to the traveller themselves. After all, who would be in a better position to know?

In any case it was magic of enormous sophistication and power. In its way it was a feat that was quite the equal of the building of the Tower of Hoeth itself, or of the creation of the vast web of spells that covered the Eastern Sea approaches to Ulthuan. The fact that it had been woven so discreetly into the fabric of this normal-seeming forest made it all the more impressive.

He tried to avoid thinking about the magic and simply concentrate on enjoying the ride. The woods were beautiful in a quiet way. It was cool under the shadow of the trees and the air smelled fresh. Birds sang among the branches and the brilliant sunlight of Ulthuan poked its fingers through the canopy of leaves. It was all enormously different from the jungles of Lustria. It lacked the smell of rot and the overpowering heat and humidity against which the only protection had been his magic.

He found that he was humming an ancient tune to himself. In some ways he was nearing the closest thing that he had to a home in the world. The tower was a place where mages gathered to study together and work spells and use the ancient library, easily the best in the world. It was a community of kindred spirits all sharing goals and ideals. It was a place where everybody understood him in a way that was simply impossible for the non-magically adept to do. It was the one place in the world where he was not an outsider, and where his physical handicaps were not held against him, at least some of the time.

Nonetheless, he found himself ambivalent about the place sometimes. He had grown accustomed to being an outsider, even enjoyed it in a perverse sort of way. It was, to a certain extent, the core of his own identity, of his view of himself.

Of course, sometimes having other people around could be pleasant. He was going to enjoy the sensation caused by his announcement that he had found the sword of Aenarion. He was going to enjoy talking about his discovery of its enchantments with his colleagues. He was going to enjoy sharing with them the knowledge that he suspected was in the ancient slann inscriptions he had brought back with him, even if that was knowledge of the disaster. There was something about being the centre of attention that he sometimes enjoyed, and he knew that he did not really care how he became the centre of attention when he was in this sort of mood.

Whistling to himself, smiling happily even though he carried news of impending disaster, he approached the White Tower. For whatever reason, the defences did not turn him away.

TECLIS COULD REALLY see the White Tower now. It was an enormous ivory spear, aimed at the underbelly of the clouds, easily the tallest structure that he had ever seen, quite possibly the tallest building in the world. It stood astonishingly high, immensely thin, tipped with a pointed cupola from which the High Loremaster could look down upon the vast width of his domain.

It was an awe-inspiring sight, at once fragile-looking and monumentally impressive, the sort of thing that could only be created by magic of the highest order. Many claimed that this was the crowning achievement of architecture and Teclis was not inclined to disagree.

Ever since he had first seen this building, he had loved it. It symbolised to him everything that was good and worth preserving about his people. When people talked about being willing to die to save their country, Teclis had never understood it. He could understand talking that way about this place though.

The Tower of Hoeth was not just a tremendous feat of architecture. It was the centre of learning for the entire island-continent of Ulthuan, the greatest repository of knowledge that the elves had ever created, greater even than the fabled library of Caledor the Archmage back in the dawn of the world. Hundreds of the greatest sorcerers from all across the continent came here to consult the library and to talk with colleagues and to share their knowledge with the students, among whom Teclis had once been numbered.

He was no longer a student. He rather missed that. In some ways it had been the happiest time of his life. He had had nothing to do but to study ancient texts and scrolls, to learn magic under the tuition of its greatest practitioners. There had been a time when every day revealed a new wonder and every night had been given over to learning how to work the small miracles of magic.

It had been an innocent time when he had nothing more to think about than which area of study he wanted to dive into next. He had been flattered by the attention of great wizards who found it worth their time to school him. He had been overcome by the sheer scale of the library, whose shelves and corridors filled the entire bottom of the tower, and the huge labyrinth of tunnels and cellars beneath it. He had been even more impressed by the complex labyrinth of spells that made the experience of studying in the library different for every person who visited it.

He knew he had seen shelves that had not been visited since the library was built and he knew that other people had found their way to parts of the library that he never would. The library showed each scholar what they needed to find when they needed to find it. It was as if some guardian spirit presided over it and gave to each student what was required.

As he wound ever closer to the tower, he began to notice the other guardians. In the shadows of the trees and bushes the Sword Masters of Hoeth waited. Each of them was equipped with a huge two-handed sword and each of them knew exactly how to use that weapon. Tall helmets shaded their eyes and heavy leather armour covered their bodies. One or two of them waved to Teclis as he rode by but most of them ignored him, concentrating on watching the approaches to the tower, even though no threat had ever managed to penetrate this far.

If one should perchance manage to do so, they would find armed warriors waiting for them and that would not be the least of the defences that they would encounter.

Potent spells walled the tower, protection against supernatural intrusions and divinations. The Loremasters did not want anyone spying on them and it was within their power to see that that did not happen. The spells were almost unnoticeable when they were dormant save, perhaps, to a wizard as perceptive as he was, but they were there, omnipresent and ready to be activated at the slightest sign of an intrusion.

As he got closer and closer to the tower, he found himself moving through larger and larger clearings. In some of the clearings were the glasshouse farms which provided food and drink for the wizards. In others were the small villages where the retainers lived. Nearer to the tower, the open spaces held small groups of wizards. Some of them were scholars gathered together to discuss matters of research. Others consisted of a Loremaster and his students, engaged in the business of teaching and learning magic.

A few of them noticed him as he passed and pointed to him. He was well-known here, recognised as one of the most powerful of the new generation of wizards. His deeds were already discussed where mages gathered and he was sure that when word of his latest exploit got around, he would once again become the focus of all attention in the White Tower of Hoeth.

He waved at one or two of the academics that he knew and acknowledged others with a nod of his head. There were people here that he would need to talk to soon – scholars of ancient slann lore and wizards specialising in their odd means of divination.

He would also need to talk to artificers about what he had learned about the spells woven into the forging of Sunfang. He had an idea that he wanted to implement. He wanted to make his own blade using some of the techniques he had learned from the study of Caledor's work.

He did not want to copy that ancient masterpiece, though there were things that he could use, and possibly even improve on. He was being arrogant when he thought that, but a certain self-confidence was the mark of the true master wizard. After all, it was not enough to simply duplicate the work of the ancients, one had to engrave one's own signature on the work and leave one's own mark in the history of magical scholarship.

He dismounted from the steed and it was led away by a retainer, who seemingly had materialised there just for the purpose of doing so. He walked into the tower and made his way to the chambers that had been assigned to him. They were as he had left them, his books still strewn on the table, a scroll on which he had been penning magical formulae partially rolled up beside them.

He limped over to his bed, threw himself down upon it and looked up at the ceiling, knowing that above him the spire of the tower raced towards the sky. He was home. He had time to rest and gather his wits before he began to face the challenges awaiting him.

There was work to be done, and, for some strange reason, he did not feel like he had much time left to do it in.

MALEKITH STRODE UP to the waystone. Tens of thousands of eyes were upon him. Most of those present were confused, wondering why so great an army had come ashore at this remote spot. They had expected to be besieging a city like Lothern by now.

Let them wonder, he thought. They would find out what the plan was soon enough.

He surveyed the land, drinking in the landscape of Ulthuan from which he had been so long away. He had a fine view out to sea where his ships lay at anchor and the Black Ark of Naggaroth sat like a volcanic island newly emerged from the waters of the bay. He could see the local farmers his warriors had captured and crucified for entertainment.

He shook his head at the stupidity of it. What a waste! Those elves could have been sold as slaves or made servants, or even simply put to death if they had committed some crime against Malekith's laws. It was not the way with the druchii though; they had to outdo themselves in proclaiming their decadence and cruelty. He blamed the influence of his mother and the cults she had introduced so long ago for that. The time would soon be here when he would bring them to heel.

Let them have their sport, they would be fighting soon enough and under the iron discipline he expected from the soldiers. They could indulge themselves – for now.

He inspected the waystone, studying the ancient runes marked in its side. He could feel the power surging through it, tapping into the ancient spell Caledor had cast on the last day of his life.

He could only see a tiny part of the vast network of energy that radiated out from the spot but he understood how it worked and just how awesome the concept was. This was probably the greatest feat of magic ever achieved by elves. It was difficult to see how it could be surpassed, although that would not stop him trying.

Once he had reunited the elves he would need to find some great projects to unify them behind him. Wars against the rest of the world would do to begin with but after that, once the world was reconquered, he would need to find some other great works to keep his subjects busy and prevent them from plotting against him, as elves always would if given the time and the opportunity. There had to be a way to improve on what Caledor had done, to use it against the powers of Chaos. If there was, he would find it.

That was for the future though. Right now he had other things that he needed to be doing. He gestured for N'Kari to approach. 'This is what you need, isn't it?' he said.

The daemon nodded. 'From here I can do all you require.'

'Then I suggest you proceed,' Malekith said. 'The sooner you are done, the sooner you can have vengeance on those you hate.'

'Let it be as you say,' N'Kari said, a measure of irony showing in its tone.

The daemon set to work, weaving a very intricate spell around the waystone that somehow tapped into its energies and the energies of something beneath it. Malekith watched fascinated, trying to understand what was being done.

Even with his vast knowledge of magic it was not quite possible. He wondered how much of what the daemon was doing was true magic and how much of it was deception, purely for show. He did not doubt that some of it was a trap that would have fatal consequences for anyone who tried to emulate the spell exactly as it was being performed now. It was what he would have done under the circumstances. He could expect no less from a Keeper of Secrets.

Soon a shimmering gateway glittered in the air before them. The assembled ranks of dark elf warriors eyed it uneasily. They did not quite understand what was going on here, although they could see some powerful magic being cast. Only his generals were completely familiar with the plan and he suspected that even they had not really believed it was possible until they had witnessed it.

Malekith turned his cold gaze upon his army. He let them feel the power of his will. Not a single soldier present could hold his glance for more than a heartbeat and none of them dared even attempt it. All of them were thoroughly cowed. It pleased Malekith to note the result. It was possible for one being such as himself to intimidate tens of thousands. All it took was courage and iron will.

He raised his hand and gave the signal that the first phase of his great plan was about to begin.

His generals gave orders to the officers. His officers gave orders to their warriors. One by one, a unit at a time, the soldiers advanced into the gateway the daemon had opened and disappeared. Malekith turned his glance upon N'Kari. If the daemon planned treachery, this would be the time to attempt it. It would cause the maximum damage to Malekith's plans. Once again, he ran over all of the binding spells and oaths he had placed on the daemon, looking for a flaw, but he could not find one. It was too late now anyway if there was.

This was just the first portal of many that it would open. If the daemon planned treachery it would have many opportunities. Still, within days, if all went well, his army would be in position to make the greatest surprise attack in history.

Now the Great War had truly begun.

CHAPTER SIXTEEN

Tyrion smelled Avelorn before he saw it. Even over the salty tang of the Inner Sea, he caught the scent of pine and a hint of the fresh air of the forest that lay just over the horizon. And there was something else in the air, some kind of magic, faint yet tangible, that set his skin to tingling and made him feel more alive than he had in a very long time.

Soon, green was visible right across the horizon. Enormous trees overhung the water, packed so densely that it was difficult to see what was beneath their eaves. It was a forest, ancient and primordial, of the sort that had existed when the world was young, before the coming of Chaos changed everything. Perhaps some of those trees over there had existed during that dark time. It was possible that he was looking upon a thing that had existed when Aenarion was young.

The ship sailed on, leaving white foam in its wake. Gulls circled overhead. Atharis came up beside Tyrion and said, 'We shall be there soon. I hope you're prepared for your first look at the legendary Everqueen.'

'I'm sure she will be beautiful,' said Tyrion sardonically. 'Everybody tells me this.'

'Why do you sound so sour about it? Anybody would think that you did not want to be her champion.'

'Perhaps I just want to be different. Perhaps I just want to make up my mind for myself, not believe what everybody tells me.'

'You're starting to sound like your brother,' said Atharis.

'I am sorry if that disturbs you. It's just that everybody speaks about the Everqueen in the same tone of voice. Everyone who has ever met her sounds like they worship her except Prince Iltharis.'

'Yes, he only ever sounds like he worships himself.'

Tyrion laughed at that. 'You know him too well.'

'He was one of the last people to see the old Everqueen alive,' said Atharis. 'She probably wasn't very happy that one of the last faces she ever looked on was not one of her devotees.'

'I think even he was disturbed by that event.'

'You talked to him about it, did you?'

Tyrion nodded. 'It was the most upset I have ever seen him.'

'You're probably the only person who has ever seen him upset then,' said Atharis. 'He is the most cold-blooded elf I have ever met.'

'You don't like him?'

'I never said that,' Atharis said. 'He is amusing enough in his own way and I don't suppose he's any more self-centred than most of us. I just don't think he liked me all that much.'

'I don't think he likes anybody all that much.'

'He seems to like you well enough. Probably because you are one of the few people that he can spar with and still get a bit of exercise.'

In the distance a bay was visible, the mouth of a river merging into the sea. The forest around the estuary had been cleared a little and there was what passed for a port in this part of the world. 'It looks like we have arrived,' said Atharis.

Tyrion could see that there was a large number of ships in the harbour, a much greater number than there really ought to have been in a port this small. A large number of people had sailed here for the tournament, judging by the amount of ships that he could see riding at anchor.

'We shall need to head on upriver to find the tournament grounds,' said Atharis.

'It looks like we won't be the only ones,' said Tyrion.

'WE'LL BE READY to go soon,' said Atharis.

'Good,' Tyrion replied. 'We don't have much light left.'

It had taken most of the day for his party to unload their horses and gear from the ship. They had to go as close as possible to the shore and then lower the horses into the water with winches and cranes, which was always a tricky proposition at the best of times.

While they were doing, this Tyrion waded ashore and explored his surroundings. The small village was right by the waterside. It had no walls and was built from logs with wattle and daub roofs. It looked very primitive for elven building but it somehow fitted in with the landscape. Perhaps this was how elves lived in ancient times. This was one of the few permanent settlements to be found on the coast. Most of the elves that dwelled within Avelorn were nomadic or lived deep in the woods.

'You seem unusually thoughtful,' said Atharis.

'This place is making me so. It's all very different from what I imagined.'

It all seemed stranger and older and wilder than any place he had ever been. The trees were hoary and ancient. Panthers stalked beneath the canopies of leaves. Somewhere off in the distance he heard the growl of an even larger predator, a manticore or a griffon perhaps. This would be a great land for hunting, he thought. It would be something to come here with a bow and some trusty companions and live off the land.

'Mount up,' said Atharis. 'We have a long way to go.'

'The sooner we start the better then,' Tyrion said. At the head of a force of fifty warriors and an equal number of retainers, he took the trail into the heart of ancient Avelorn. He could tell from the tracks that they were not the first to take this route in recent times. The thought was to occur to him more than once in the days of riding ahead.

IN THE DISTANCE, Tyrion could just make out singing and the sounds of flutes, lutes and other traditional elven musical instruments ringing out through the forest. The sounds drifted on the wind, carrying the sad, sweet music of the elves to his ears.

Tyrion's company rode down into a clearing crowded with musicians and archers and groups of elves that were cooking, singing and dancing. It was as if a city had suddenly sprung into being under the eaves of the trees. The ancient woods were crowded with people. There were elves everywhere, under the boughs of the great oaks.

There were hundreds of tents visible and quite possibly thousands more hidden just out of sight among the trees and dells. They ranged from mighty pavilions, large enough to house companies of bowmen, to small lean-tos set up by poor elves with nowhere else to stay during this great festival.

The sound of musical instruments filled the air. A hundred songs mingled into one vast chorus. Thousands of voices sang the praises of the woods and the sun and the most beautiful queen who had ever lived.

There was an underlying note of sadness to the song that told the listener that the singers mourned the passing of someone who had been deeply loved, even as they celebrated the ascension of her cherished daughter.

Tyrion reined in his horse and paused to listen, drinking in the sound, surprisingly touched by what he was hearing. The rest of his party paused to listen as well, moved as much as he was.

As they stood there, a group of female elves armed with bows and dressed in leather armour came towards them. These were warriors of the Maiden Guard. They inspected Tyrion's party closely and their leader, a tall, stately beautiful elf said, 'You are here for the tournament?'

'Yes,' Tyrion said. 'I am Prince Tyrion and I have come from Lothern to take part in the competition.'

'You're very welcome here, Prince Tyrion,' the elf maiden said. 'We shall guide you to your campsite. You will want to be near the rest of the competitors.'

The Maiden Guard showed them to a place overlooking a stream. It was on a slight rise that gave them a good view of the vast open field on which the tournament would take place. Tyrion could see that there were many beautiful pavilions scattered around the area. Outside each of them stood a tall proud banner which told of the presence of a champion within.

Some of these little clusters of tents were the size of small villages. Some of those champions had a much larger retinue than he did. He wondered why they had brought small armies with them. Did they expect to be fighting a war for the favour of the Everqueen? Or was it all simply part of the great game of making a good impression, not just upon the new queen, but upon all rivals present?

He did not know and he did not really care. His own ego was not daunted by their presence, nor did he compare the size of his own retinue to those of his potential rivals and feel in the slightest intimidated.

He did however realise that the game had begun the moment he arrived, if not before. All of these things were moves on the board. He realised that his aunt had carefully calculated the size of his own retinue to be large enough to make an impression, but not so large as to seem ostentatious.

His followers went about their work under Atharis's careful eye. They were soon erecting his pavilion. Tyrion joined in. He always enjoyed using his hands and there was something about setting up these temporary structures that appealed to him. He helped drive the central post of his great silken tent into the dirt and then he aided his fellows to throw the fabric shell into place, pull the hawsers tight and then drive in the pegs. He could see that some of the watching nobles were appalled to observe him performing manual labour and rushed off to tell their friends the gossip. He did not care.

When his own small village of tents was in place, he took the Emeraldsea banner himself and drove it into the ground outside his pavilion, like an explorer claiming a new land in the name of the Phoenix King.

He was not sure this was entirely appropriate behaviour or an entirely appropriate image to have in mind as he did it, but it suited his mood and he was pleased to see the green ship on a gold background flutter in the breeze before him.

He felt like he had staked a claim to his own place in this vast temporary city.

'WHO IS THAT?' Tyrion asked Atharis as they sat together on the slope outside his tent.

He pointed towards a tall, noble-looking elf, garbed in glittering armour and riding upon a most impressive steed. The warrior was accompanied by a group of knights almost as stern looking and impressive as himself. He waved in a friendly fashion as he passed.

'I believe that is Arhalien of Yvresse, judging by the device on his shield. He is widely regarded as the most likely winner of this tournament.'

'Why?' Tyrion asked.

'He is a great warrior. He has slain hundreds of dark elves. He has never lost a tournament with lances. He rides like he is from Ellyrion and fights like a Shadow Warrior. He is brave, noble, of ancient lineage, a noted poet, a fine dancer, a bold war-leader. He is everything a hero should be – sickeningly dull.'

'You sound as if you have studied him.'

'I have been forced to learn the life stories of all of your likely opponents. Your grandfather was a believer in thorough preparation. Your aunt is keeping that proud family tradition alive.'

'He knew this day would come?'

'Of course he did. The old Everqueen had to die sometime and it was a fair bet that her champion would not wish to serve her successor. Your grandfather had plans for all contingencies and your aunt is his daughter. Although I must admit that neither of them expected this to happen so soon. They would not have allowed you to go gadding around the world with your brother otherwise.'

'Is he a better warrior than I am?' Tyrion asked.

'I don't know. I doubt anyone except Prince Iltharis is better with a sword than you are, but if anyone is it will be Arhalien, or perhaps Prince Perian of Valaste. In addition, Arhalien has had far more practice with a lance than you have, and far more experience of tournament fighting. It is something of a sport where he comes from.'

'That is not real fighting,' said Tyrion.

'Perhaps not,' said Atharis, 'but it is the sort of fighting that will be going on here. And don't underestimate how vicious these contests can be. Competitors have died before now and not always by accident.'

'You don't think that is possible here? In the tournament to decide who will be the Everqueen's champion? That would make a mockery of everything the tournament stands for.'

'My dear Tyrion, there are times when I wonder whether you are really an elf. The forms will, of course, be observed, but there is a great deal of power and prestige at stake here, and you know how elves can be over those. This is a deadly serious matter. Deadly serious. I suggest you treat it as such.'

'I will bear that in mind.'

'We have found a poet to compose verses for you. You will merely need to memorise the couplets he writes and recite them.'

'I will not do that,' said Tyrion. 'I am here to compete on my own merits.'

'I have never known you to court failure. You are no poet, my friend, whatever else you might be. Many of those warriors over there are almost as adept with a pen as they are with a blade. Those who are not will have their own pet minstrels to compose verses for them. Why should you be any different?'

'Because I am different. I will win this in my own way or not at all.'

'It may well prove to be the latter.'

'If that is the case, let it be so.'

'You do not seem at all determined to win.'

'Let us rather say that I am not determined to win at any cost.'

'Then you start at a grave disadvantage.'

'So be it. You mentioned Prince Perian of Valaste as being good with a sword.'

'He is. Very good indeed. He fancies himself a bit of a wit too. A thoroughly unpleasant character if you ask me.'

'I do ask you.'

'He's vain, arrogant, spoiled–'

'A typical elven noble then...'

'Wait until you meet him. He is a veritable paragon of elven flaws. If I wanted to pick one elf to exemplify all that is bad in our people, it would be him.'

'I am starting to suspect you don't like him.'

'And to think people call you slow of mind. Such perceptiveness, Prince Tyrion...'

'Most people assume that no one so beautiful could be so clever,' said Tyrion.

'I see you are ramping up your egotism to compete with Prince Perian,' said Atharis. 'A bold strategy.'

'I am going to have to, aren't I? It's going to be like rutting deer competing to see who leads the herd, isn't it?'

'Not the metaphor I would have chosen, but yes. We really should get our tame poet working on your verses.'

'Is there anyone else I should know about?' Tyrion asked.

'At least a dozen, if you can stand being bored with the details. And I am sure there will be those I have missed. There's always some dark horse who enters these tournaments.'

'You'd better get started then…'

TYRION AND ATHARIS sat inside his tent, lounging on pillows and sleeping mats and drinking fine old wine from filigreed silver goblets. Tyrion could smell food being cooked and hear his body-guard sitting around gossiping outside. They had spent most of the afternoon discussing Tyrion's potential opponents. There were no shortage of them.

'Well, we are here,' said Atharis, raising his goblet in a toast.

'Yes. Our epic quest has been accomplished,' said Tyrion. 'After many hardships we have finally reached our goal. I wonder how we managed to survive days of riding through these deadly forests. I think I saw some particularly savage-looking sheep at one point that filled my heart with dread.'

'There is no need to sound so satirical, my prince. We *are* a long way from civilisation now.'

'How will we endure life among these rustics? Missing Lothern already, Atharis?'

'I would not speak too loudly about the rustic charms of our present neighbourhood. Those Maiden Guard look as if they might carve you up for it. So do many of the yokels.'

Tyrion wondered whether his friend really felt that way, or whether he just felt out of his depth away from the city he knew and loved, and surrounded by the great woods and their inhabitants.

'This is a lovely place,' Tyrion said.

'It might be lovelier if it were not so crowded. I swear there are more people here than in the streets of the Foreigners' Quarter.'

'There are certainly more elves. So this is where our people have been hiding all this time. I was wondering.'

'This is probably the largest gathering these woods have seen in centuries. Warriors have come here from all over Ulthuan for the

tournament. There are probably many still here from the coronation. They just can't be bothered to set off home yet. The lazy
bastards.'

'I can understand that. There is something in the air here that
encourages lingering.'

'I trust you, too, are not going to go all rustic on us? I think that
would be just too much.'

'I meant it literally. I think there is some magic in the air here
that clouds people's minds. Can't you feel it? There is a pulse of
tranquillity about us.'

'I thought that was just all the dreamsmoke in the air. I wonder where I might get some. It may make our stay here more
endurable.'

'I shall leave you in charge of that. I am going to take a look
around.'

'Don't get lost, and try not to fall in with any of the local
enchantresses. You may find that you never want to leave.'

'I don't think there is much danger of that,' Tyrion said, rising to
his feet and striding towards the doorway.

'If you find any dreamsmoke vendors, bring me back some,' said
Atharis.

'Find your own,' said Tyrion.

TYRION WANDERED THROUGH the vast city of tents, feeling very much
a stranger. In some ways it reminded him of the jungles of Lustria.
All around were trees, some of the gigantic ancient things thousands of years old.

It did not feel as close or threatening as the jungle had and there
were no poisonous snakes or biting insects that he could detect.
Instead there were lots of elves. They had come from every corner
of Ulthuan to attend the court of the Everqueen.

He wondered how many of these people danced constant
attendance on the Everqueen and how many of them were here
for the tournament.

As always, people stared at him. He was used to that and he paid it no more mind than he would have in the streets of Lothern. He rather enjoyed it as a matter of fact, particularly when the onlookers were women. He smiled at anyone who caught his eye and did his best to look amiable.

Teclis would hate this place. His brother did not like being the centre of attention or being surrounded by crowds of people. He would doubtless have something sarcastic to say about all of these happy, thoughtless revellers. He wondered how much of what he was seeing was the product of magic. Teclis would've known, of course. He lacked his brother's sensitivity to the flows of the winds of magic.

Even he suspected that some spell was at work here. The people look too happy, too energetic, too thrilled, even for elves in the mood for merrymaking. An atmosphere of almost complacent contentment hovered over this place. Every single person that he saw really wanted to be here and was really happy with the fact that they were. He could not think of any other place he had ever been in his life where that was true. Over the city of Lothern, for all its thrilling commercial energy, a certain melancholy brooded, shadowing even the happiest festival days.

This place reminded him, in an odd elliptic sort of way, of the atmosphere in the Shrine of Asuryan. There was the same sense of some ancient power touching the world. A girl danced by, flowers in her hair and a smile upon her lips. She blew him a kiss as she passed and, smiling, he answered in kind. She skipped back over to him and looked at him closely, examining him frankly and with considerable appreciation. He looked back at her in the same way, unembarrassed. He had heard tales of the way people behaved at the court of the Everqueen and he was determined to fit in as well here as he did everywhere else.

'You're here for the tournament?' The girl asked.

'I am indeed,' Tyrion replied.

'You hope to become her champion?'

'I am unsure about that,' he replied.

She laughed. The sound was like the tinkling of silver bells. 'You're unsure? How is that possible?'

'It is a very long story,' Tyrion said.

'We are elves. If we do not have time for long stories, who does? My name is Lyla'

'Mine is Tyrion.'

'Like the hero of the Shrine of Asuryan?'

'Exactly the same.'

'I had heard he was as good looking as you.'

'That is quite possible.'

'You are he, are you not?'

'I was at the Shrine when it was attacked. I do not think I was all that heroic. I was hiding in it at the time the daemon came.'

'Do you have a twin brother who is a great sorcerer?'

'I have a twin who is studying at Hoeth. Although I am not sure he is all that great a sorcerer. He would probably tell you he was.'

'Let us drink wine. I am curious about you now.'

'Lead on,' said Tyrion. Ten minutes later they were naked in her tent. There was something to be said for the festival atmosphere of this place, he thought.

TYRION TOOK LEAVE of Lyla and continued on his way.

As he walked through the cool shadows of Avelorn, Tyrion studied the people around him in a more leisurely fashion. This was a place utterly unlike Lothern. It moved to a different rhythm. Its people had a different attitude to time. They seemed more relaxed.

He watched a circle of elves gathered round a poet declaiming the ancient epic of Caledor the Conqueror. They knew the words, mouthing them silently as the poet spoke.

Tyrion watched them watching the poet. He knew the work and knew the reciter had been about his business for hours and most likely would still be speaking at sunset. These people had the time and the interest to do this, to watch the performance while other elves, selected by lot or from the family retainers, brought them food and wine. It was the sort of reading that you only saw in abbreviated form among the busy money-making elves of Lothern. It was like stepping back into the past, into the golden age of the first Everqueen, and he knew it was deliberately so.

He looked for notes of falseness and because he was looking, he found some. Here and there, some of the audience were asleep. Others paid no attention and inspected their nails, but this had probably been so during the golden age as well. Perhaps this was part of a different golden age, but a golden age nonetheless. These elves were keeping the old ways alive. They saw themselves as guardians of a certain sort of elfness, and he did not doubt that they were correct to do so.

Lothern was the future, if the elves were to have a future. It was commercial, home of an outward looking, sophisticated, mercantile Phoenix King. It was a city of trade, a hybrid cosmopolitan place where the elves mingled with other peoples and learned from them and adapted to the new and altered world.

In Avelorn, the elves were behaving as they had before the age of Aenarion. It was beautiful and moving and rather sad. Sad because all of this took an effort to maintain and it was dying away. It was an enclave frozen in amber.

No, he told himself. That was not fair. This place still lived. It was the beating heart of asur society. It was where artists and poets and dancers came, to compete, to find an appreciative audience, to seek fame and a certain kind of glory. It was not the sort of glory that he himself was interested in, but he could understand why some elves were.

He moved into another glade. Elves in green raiment practised archery, drawing and firing at targets hundreds of paces away. These were not competitors in the tournament he realised. These were just ordinary citizens of Avelorn, training with their weapons as was their right and duty. The practice made them the finest archers in the world, and the backbone of the elven citizen-armies.

He inspected them, as a general might inspect his troops. Each of them was an elf in his or her prime. All of them must have handled bows for decades, if not centuries. All of them were hale and hearty and would remain so for hundreds of years.

No other troops would or could have their skill or their discipline or their experience. Simply by virtue of still being alive for so long, they would have fought in dozens of skirmishes and battles. They would have survived encounters with numerous foes.

Like the poets he had just witnessed, they too were part of an older Ulthuan, one that dated from the age of Morvael, of the first great citizen-soldier levies. They were part of the culture. They too moved to a different beat than the elves of Lothern.

It came to Tyrion that elves like these could be found all over the island-continent. In aggregate, they must far outnumber the elves of Lothern although they had no single town or city that was even a fraction of the size of the city-state. Probably they were much more representative of the people as a whole. And they looked at least as much to the Everqueen as to the Phoenix King for leadership.

Perhaps for the first time in his life, in this place, he started to get a sense of what his own people were like, all of the folk beyond the city in which he lived and the mountains he had called home from his earliest youth.

For these people here, the folk of Lothern were something new and strange. The people here were the ones who represented the mainstream of life. Looking at them, he saw the majority of the elves as they wanted to see themselves and he realised that he was not at all like them.

He passed on, entering a vast clearing in the forest filled with silk pavilions and corrals for proud elven steeds. The symbol of the Everqueen was on everything and he realised that this must be the place in which she currently dwelled. Maiden Guards strolled everywhere, but no one looked at him suspiciously. It was inconceivable that anyone would want to harm the ruler of Avelorn.

Magic shimmered in the air, the sort of powerful conspicuous magic his brother could work. Beneath it he sensed the presence of another type of magic. The air was thick with it, a constant stream of something living, beneficial, potent. He remembered again the atmosphere of the Shrine of Asuryan, and the feeling here was of the same kind, although not produced by the same being.

In Asuryan's Shrine the being had been of fire, powerful, destructive, mercurial, somewhat akin to Chaos. Here, whatever was present was slower, more placid, enduring, fertile. It was a spirit of earth and forest, and its locus of power was in this place. Or perhaps in the person of the Everqueen.

A thought struck him. Perhaps Lothern was a place of water. If the old magical schemata of the elemental universe was to be believed, then there must be a place of air as well. He wondered where that could be, and it struck him that perhaps the place was in the north, a place of cold and storm winds, perhaps where Malekith was.

He amused himself with such idle fantasies as he passed through the shadow of pavilions and onto the grounds where scores of elven artisans were at work creating the tournament fields.

A pulse of excitement started to beat in him. There was going to be a great contest here and he was going to take part in it. It was a ritual that had been enacted only a dozen times during the course of history, and it was one that had a significance that was embedded deeply in the nature of his people.

He understood that perhaps he was seeing things at an unusual time, during a change in reigns. The old queen was dead. The new queen was just that – new. The tone of her reign had yet to be set. Her likes and dislikes were as yet unknown. There were those who had known her as a child, and who thought they knew her as a woman, but they could not know what she was going to be like as the Everqueen. She was a butterfly newly emerged from that particular chrysalis and she might be changed as utterly as her relationships with those around her were going to be.

If he won the tournament he really would have a chance to influence the tone of this new age. He would have his chance to be part of her court, to sway her choices. It was not the sort of power he wanted, or the sort of role he craved. He was a warrior, not a courtier.

And yet, he had to admit to himself, despite his reluctance to do so, there was something here that appealed to him. This felt like the setting of one of those tales of heroism and chivalry he had so loved as a child. It was glamorous and full of intrigue. It was beautiful. There was pageantry and magic. He could picture himself as a knight at the court of the fairest of elf queens. It was the sort of role he had delighted in imagining as a boy. It still had its appeal even now, although he could see the folly of it.

In spite of all his reservations, like all those others, he was happy to be here.

CHAPTER SEVENTEEN

IN THE MORNING sunlight, Tyrion watched the gathering of heroes. More and more warriors arrived on the tournament grounds, great champions shorn of their retinues, single fighters who had come alone, perhaps following a dream, perhaps merely to test themselves against the best the island-continent could provide.

He stood on the field itself, where today only contestants and representatives of the Everqueen were allowed. Atharis and his retainers watched from the surrounding hillocks along with the followers of all the other champions present. He saw Arhalien of Yvresse turn and bow to his followers before he passed through the arch and onto the tournament field. His retainers cheered him but could go no further.

Tyrion saw proud armoured riders from Ellyrion mounted on their matchless, prancing steeds. He saw a lovely woman warrior from Tiranoc, staring around with fierce wary eyes. There were grim-faced soldiers from Yvresse, and tall, hard-faced elves from the Shadowlands, as harsh and craggy as the land that bore them.

They looked at him as much as he looked at them, and there was a challenge in their stare. They knew instinctively that he too was here to compete and that he would be a rival, and they could tell just from the look of him that he would be a worthy one.

In some glances there was hostility but in most of them was an odd form of comradeship. They were all here for the same reason, and by the nature of the contest, they were set apart from the mass of other elves. It was something that they shared, a kinship of spirit born of rivalry, yet forging a bond. That was the way he felt it at least, and he suspected that for those he saw it would be the same.

He looked at his potential rivals and wondered about them. What were their stories? What sights had they seen on the way here? What drove them to compete? What was it they sought?

He felt like simply going over and asking. He was endlessly curious about these things. He could not do so though, not out of shyness, but because he knew that it would be misconstrued. Perhaps they would see him as only seeking an advantage, as attempting to uncover weaknesses, and perhaps he would be.

There would be time enough to get to know a small fraction of these warriors. There would be drinking bouts and dances and all manner of merry meetings. It was something he could wait for with anticipation, part of the pleasure of being here.

He could tell by the way some of them looked at him that his reputation had preceded him. They had heard of the battles he had fought and the way he had survived an encounter with a Keeper of Secrets while still only a callow youth. They knew he had crossed blades with a monster that had fought against Aenarion himself, and that he was of Aenarion's blood.

That thought cast a shadow over his happiness. One day the monster would be back and it would come looking for him, and it occurred to him that it would come looking for the new Everqueen as well. Like every Everqueen before her, she was descended from Aenarion's lost daughter, Yvraine. She too would be a target when N'Kari returned to pursue his infernal vengeance quest.

Tyrion tried telling himself that he might live his entire life without ever encountering the daemon. There was over six thousand years between its last two appearances in history. He could live and die and his descendants unto the tenth generation might do the same, before the daemon reappeared.

He doubted that things would be that way. He had a feeling that he and N'Kari were destined to meet again, that their paths were due to collide during his lifetime and, if that happened, he would need to find some way to banish the daemon forever, not just for his own safety but for the safety of his children and their children beyond them. He needed to find a way if he could. He let his hand rest on Sunfang. Perhaps the great blade held the secret. He prayed that it was so.

Horns announced the coming of the Everqueen. Surrounded by her Maiden Guard, she made her way into the massive stand that had been erected overlooking the tournament field. At this distance it was hard to see anything but a tall, stately golden haired figure, graceful of movement, wealthy of dress, carrying a mystical staff in her hand. There was something about her though, a sense of power, deeply hidden, that commanded attention.

Tyrion was not the only one watching her arrival. Every eye on the field was drawn to the stand and its new occupant. It was understandable. She was after all the reason they were here. He glanced around and saw something odd. Everyone present was looking at the Everqueen with an expression that combined awe, religious reverence and love. He had not realised they all felt quite that way, and then it dawned on him that they probably could not help themselves. What he was seeing was most likely the result of a very powerful spell.

He wished Teclis were here to advise him about this. He was genuinely curious now.

* * *

HORNS SOUNDED AGAIN. This time the sequence of notes was different, a summons to battle, a challenge, a demand for attention.

The herald of the Everqueen took up his position on the great dais in front of the stand. All eyes were upon him now. He spread his arms wide with a flourish. Then he paused, dramatically, in order to focus attention before he launched into his speech.

The herald was a tall elf with silver hair. His features were very fine. He carried himself with great dignity. And yet beneath this, there was something else, a suggestion of the mountebank, of the need to please and the need to be at the centre of attention that was somewhat at odds with his majestic air.

'Friends, fellow elves, subjects of our beloved Everqueen,' he said, turning with a flourish to the stand. His voice carried over the murmur of the great crowd. He gave the impression of speaking in a conversational tone, but there was some magic at work that carried his voice to every corner of the field.

'We are gathered here at the start of the reign of a new Everqueen to select her champion. Unto that champion will fall the duty of guarding our kingdom's greatest treasure. Into his hands will be placed the life of the Everqueen. He will be called upon to defend her from all threats and all challenges and to protect her from harm, even if it costs his own life. The victor of this great tournament will be participating in a grand tradition that stretches from the earliest days of our realm.'

Tyrion thought the herald very self-satisfied and pleased with the sound of his own voice, but the words resonated anyway. He realised that up till now he had been thinking about this tournament simply from the point of view of his own needs and desires.

He had known about the responsibilities the position of champion entailed but he had never really thought about them and about the place implied in history and culture. Now he was forced to.

If he did win, he would be subordinating his own life to that of the Everqueen. He would be expected to give up his own life to save hers if need be. Was he really up to that challenge?

The answer was fairly simple given his personality. If the duties of champion fell to him, they would be performed to the best of his ability.

He had risked his life before on behalf of the kingdoms and for lesser reasons. He was certain that he was capable of doing so in the service of something much more important.

While he was thinking this, the herald spoke on, invoking the names of famous champions of the past and recounting their deeds and their sacrifices.

Tyrion was stirred, as were the people round about him. There was magic in the air again and he knew that the herald was using it. There was something about the elf's voice indeed. It was not just a spell, although there was an element of that. It was simply that the way that the elf spoke touched something deep within the soul. It went beyond his choice of words and the beauty of his speaking voice. There was something in Tyrion and in the others present that responded to it on a level deeper than thought.

It was a talent worth possessing, Tyrion thought. To be able to address troops in this manner would be a gift indeed. One of the most important things for a leader was being able to motivate the warriors who followed you and this type of magical speaking would be invaluable for that.

The herald continued, 'Today, friends, mighty and worthy warriors have come together from every corner of Ulthuan to compete in a contest to find a worthy heir to those mighty champions of the past. By the time this full moon has passed, a new champion will have been selected to guard the peerless treasure of our realm.'

The herald gazed upon the assembled competitors and smiled. 'Looking out at all of your faces, I can see there only the noblest of intentions…'

That beautiful voice carried no note of irony and yet it was there. Tyrion sensed it.

'Selflessly you seek to enter the service of our great queen. Selflessly you are putting aside personal ambition in order to take up a duty. It tells me something about the greatness and nobility of the spirit of our people and our kingdom that so many of you have come together here with no other desire than to serve.

'I can see that all of you are worthy. It saddens me that only one of you will, at the end of the contest, be able to take up the role of champion. However, the elf to whom this great honour falls will know that he has faced and bested worthy opponents indeed. You represent the best of the people, their great spirit, their great desire for self-sacrifice, their great love for their queen. I am proud to stand here before you and tell you what you need to know to participate in this contest.'

The herald was really milking the moment here. And why not? It was the sort that only came once in most elves' lifetimes. How often was a new Everqueen crowned? How often was a new champion chosen? This might be the only time this contest would take place in Tyrion's lifetime or the herald's. The winner in the next few days would be remembered for as long as there were elves in the world.

He realised that this was important to him. Glory was important to him. More than wealth, he craved renown. He wanted to prove himself worthy. The question was – was he willing to pay the price?

'Today we begin with the tournament. The first round will decide who continues into the next rounds. Today every participant will prove his worthiness with a blade and shield. These are the most basic weapons of the warrior.'

Tyrion thought that the bow was actually the most basic weapon of the warrior, but he could see why the stress would be laid upon using sword and shield. These were the sort of weapon that a bodyguard was much more likely to be called upon to use.

The herald held up a small brooch. It was in the shape of a leaf and the bronze suggested the colours of autumn. 'Each of you will be issued with a bronze leaf and each of you will be matched against a worthy foe. The winner of the contest will be awarded his opponent's leaf. He should return it to the heralds and progress to the next round of combat. The winner of that contest will be awarded his foes brooch to return to our watchers and progress to the next round. This will go on until there is only one winner and only one brooch. And it will set the pattern for all of the other contests that will take place. Once the horns sound, you will go from here and collect your brooches and proceed to the fields of trial, where you will be assigned your opponents.'

Everyone seemed light-hearted now and ready to begin and he felt the same way. After all these days of waiting, he was about to step forward into the contest. He found that his heart lifted at the prospect of a fight. Whatever happened, he was determined to enjoy himself today.

Smiling, he walked off towards the trestle tables at which lesser heralds were waiting to distribute the tokens of the contest. He collected his and pinned it to his breast. All the other warriors present were doing the same.

TYRION ENTERED THE roped off area in which the first round of the tournament was to take place. He walked across to the sergeant-at-arms and was issued with a blunted sword, armour and a shield. He swiftly donned the armour. It was heavier than the very fine mail that he was used to, but it was adequate and he did not doubt for a moment that it was capable of resisting the blunted edge of the weapon he was carrying.

Of course, that did not mean that injury was impossible. The weight of a blade swung in combat practice could still break an arm or a rib. It was not unknown for elves to be killed during such trials. He knew that he would need to be cautious, because any sort of broken bone would disbar him from the championship and immediately end all hopes of winning.

Next he tried the blade and found it reasonably well-balanced. It did not harmonise with his movements with the supernatural grace of Sunfang. It was not even as close to being as good as the sword he'd carried most of his life, which had been a gift from Korhien. But it would do. Given a few moments he could habituate himself to its use. The shield was the fairly large kind commonly used by infantry. He strapped it on to his left arm. He had worn this kind of shield many times over the course of many battles. It felt like donning an old familiar pair of boots.

Once all of these preparations were completed he began running through a few practice exercises of the kind he had performed almost every day of his life. As he did so he was aware that he was being watched by a number of the warriors around him.

A few of them made favourable comments on his technique, a few of them looked jealous, most of them simply watched as if hoping to gain some advantage from studying their rival. He considered pretending to be slower and clumsier than he was but decided against it. He knew that some of his foes would be intimidated by witnessing his performance and that would give him an advantage of a different sort.

The sun had risen quite high in the sky before the last competitor had given his name to the heralds and been announced. At last, though, everyone was armed and equipped for the first stage of the great contest. An atmosphere of excitement began to palpably form over the assembled host of warriors.

Thousands of spectators had gathered on the hillsides surrounding the competition glade; their presence as much as the presence of the Everqueen gave the tournament an excitement all of its own. It was very different from the atmosphere that he had experienced before a battle. Then the only audience consisted of your comrades and your enemies and the former were too concerned with their own survival to pay much attention, while the latter were only interested in killing you.

The onlookers gave this contest a very different tone. They made it special in a very different way. This audience was interested in every competitor and were here as much to be entertained as to witness the outcome of the tournament for the favour of the Everqueen.

Tyrion was very aware that eyes were on him. He knew that he was a striking figure and easy to pick out from the crowd of other contestants, and he had absolutely no doubt that his own name would be known among those who had come to watch.

This contest was open to all. There was no selection process other than volunteering. The role of the Everqueen's champion was one that many legends were attached to. Commoners and freeholders had held it, at least according to song and story.

Tyrion wondered about that. In practice the sort of weapons and gear that a champion was required to be capable with required gold and lots of it, and the qualifications concerning poetry, music, dance and courtliness were ones that the wealthy would have a much greater chance of acquiring than the less well off.

Looking around, he could see that there were many dreamers here today. Some of them perhaps believed they had a chance at being the hero of a storyteller's tale. Others were most likely only here because they wanted to take part, to have a place in a legendary elven festival. Long-lived as elves were, there would not be that many opportunities to do so for anyone.

The horns sounded again to announce the contest had begun. At this stage there would be multiple competitions at once. There were too many involved to allow the luxury of single combats taking place one at a time before the crowd. Heralds paired competitors off against each other.

Tyrion was drawn against some peasant swordsman from Chrace. He made short work of the contest, beating his first opponent in the initial swaggering of blades. After the combat was over, he bowed to his beaten foe and accepted the beautifully worked copper brooch, then walked around to watch the other competitors. The losers went out to swell the crowd.

The second round took place between those who still wore copper leaves. Tyrion found this just as easy as the first round and took his opponent's brooch from him at the conclusion of the fight.

233

As the day wore on he acquired more and more brooches. By late afternoon, the contest was down to the last four. Tyrion found himself facing against Arhalien. It was something that had to occur sooner or later and he welcomed it.

The Yvressian lord was standing at the barrier chatting with his retainers. A herald came forward to introduce them and witness the fight. Arhalien looked just as interested in Tyrion as Tyrion was in him. His manner was aloof but polite and not unfriendly. He was the very model of a warrior lord.

'Prince Tyrion. I have heard a lot about your prowess with a blade,' he said.

'Poets everywhere sing of your skill,' said Tyrion determined not to be outdone in politeness.

'I have heard you are but recently returned from Lustria, where you have added another glittering chapter to the tale of your deeds. Rumour has it that you have found the sword of Aenarion.'

'That is the case.'

'It is a pity that you are not allowed to use it in the tournament,' said one of Arhalien's retainers with a sneer. Arhalien looked at him as if appalled by his bad breeding.

'I do not need a blade like Sunfang for a tournament like this,' said Tyrion.

'The very fact that Prince Tyrion is standing here is testimony to his skill,' said Arhalien with a warning look at his follower. 'Boriane meant no disrespect,' he added to Tyrion.

'I am sure of that,' said Tyrion.

'I must say I am looking forward to this contest,' said Arhalien. 'It will be fine sport to encounter so worthy an opponent.'

'Your reputation as a duellist precedes you,' said Boriane. The sneer was better hidden this time, but it was still there. Beyond Lothern, duelling to the death was a thing that was very much frowned upon. It was regarded as more of a tool of assassination than a contest of honour.

Tyrion could understand why. It was a formalised way of

removing political enemies that resulted in the fewest comebacks against its practitioners. On Lord Emeraldsea's instructions he had provoked fights with almost a score of political enemies. He himself had been challenged dozens of times. He enjoyed the fighting, the killing and the victories, but he did not like being a political instrument. He was not sure why. He had been a soldier often enough and had killed under orders in that context. What had made it so different when he duelled?

The answer was simple. As a soldier he was killing the enemies of the realm. As a duellist he had killed other elves who were citizens of Ulthuan and subjects of the Phoenix King and Everqueen.

'You look thoughtful, Prince Tyrion,' Arhalien said.

'I was remembering the last duel I fought,' said Tyrion.

'Now is a time to fight, not reminisce,' said the herald. 'Are you both ready to begin?'

'Yes,' said Arhalien. Tyrion nodded. Tyrion raised his blade in salute to Arhalien. His opponent did the same then closed his eyes in a brief prayer to the gods.

The fight was not a long one. Prince Arhalien was indeed very good with a sword, but Tyrion was better. Arhalien did not seem to take his defeat badly.

'I shall just have to do better with my lance,' he said. Tyrion found that he rather admired the lord of Yvresse. He felt sure the Everqueen would not find a better champion.

'I look forward to meeting you again,' said Tyrion.

'And I you. We will have the opportunity soon,' said Arhalien. 'Our position in this contest gives us both the honour of sitting at the Everqueen's table this evening.'

IT WAS THE last fight of the opening day. The sun was low in the sky. All eyes in the huge crowd were focused on Tyrion and Prince Perian. All of them were expectant. They knew two masters of the blade were fighting here.

After the first passage of blades, Tyrion knew Prince Perian was the best swordsman he had faced since he sparred with Prince Iltharis. The elf had a natural gift for the blade and many centuries of practice. He knew how to use the heavy shield of the elven warrior. He was fast and he was very strong and he had a great deal of experience on the field of battle.

Looking at his proud face, Tyrion wondered whether he really should be fighting against this elf. Prince Perian would make a much better champion for the Everqueen. He was a believer. He was dedicated to the woman and he truly, truly wanted to be her champion.

His heart was in it in a way that Tyrion's was not. It might be best for all concerned just to let him win. He could return home having done his duty as far as his family was concerned. No one except himself would ever know what had happened.

It would take a warrior as skilled as Iltharis, and one who knew him as well as Korhien, to know exactly what he had done and even they could never be sure. So much of combat was a matter of luck when it got to this level of skill. The slightest misjudgement, the slightest lapse of concentration could see the contest go either way.

For a moment he considered it. Then he heard the crowd chant his name and sensed the adulation of the women. Part of him wanted to win, and worse than that, part of him was not sure that he could. Prince Perian was a great swordsman. They really were in the same class when it came to the use of their weapons. Prince Perian might even be better. Perhaps his sneering look was justified.

Something in Tyrion resisted that notion with every fibre of its being. He was not prepared to let anyone beat him while there was still breath in his body. If he was going to lose this fight then he would need to be defeated fair and square. His opponent would win because he was the better warrior, not for any other reason.

The crowd roared as Tyrion went on to the offensive. He smashed aside Prince Perian's shield with his own, stepped inside his guard and stabbed. Prince Perian parried desperately, padding backwards, obviously taken off guard by the change of pace and tactics.

Tyrion pressed home his advantage, sensing that he was never going to get a better opportunity to go in for the kill. He closed the distance, striking out at Prince Perian's shoulder, numbing a nerve and causing the blade to drop from his hand.

It was over. Tyrion had won. He was the victor on the first day of the great tournament. The crowd chanted his name. It was more intoxicating than wine.

As he was taking the applause the herald beckoned him over. 'Join the other contestants. The winners on today's field are to be presented to the Everqueen.'

THE EVERQUEEN AND her entourage entered the field. The face of every elf present changed immediately, taking on a glow of love and worship. They stared as if a goddess had just manifested herself in their midst.

Alarielle was beautiful, Tyrion did not deny that for a moment – she was tall, fair and possessed the most striking green eyes that he had ever seen – but he could see nothing to justify the adoration in which she basked. Powerful magic indeed was at work here. Was he the only one unaffected by it?

Even as the thought crossed his mind, their gazes met. A shock passed between them. She turned and looked away first. She seemed to have picked his face out of the entire crowd, possibly because it was the only one not wearing an expression of undying love, he thought sourly.

One by one, all of the final candidates for champion stepped forward to be introduced to her. She accepted their greetings graciously and as if it was her due. Tyrion found himself resenting this more and more as the ritual progressed. He tried to control his emotions, a thing he was normally very good at.

He struggled to make his expression bland and place a smile

upon his lips but it felt unnatural and stilted. Whatever sorcery was being worked on the crowd was having the opposite effect on him.

He was not used to feeling such emotions. He was normally amiable. It was not because he was self-conscious around women that he felt this way either; there were few elf males who were less so. He greatly enjoyed female company. There was magic at work, he felt sure of that. And that in itself was unusual, for he was normally the least sensitive of elves as far as magic was concerned.

As she came ever closer, he began to get some idea of what he thought might be happening. There was an aura about Alarielle and it did seem to command love and respect. He suspected that whatever sorcery was present affected him differently. For some reason, something in him resisted it, and perhaps this anger was part of that process of resistance.

Suddenly they were face to face. Tyrion was a head taller and he bowed to her, not fully and formally as was expected but in the social manner in which one greeted an equal or near equal. He could hear gasps of outrage from the crowd and he suspected that if he was not careful he might get lynched.

The Everqueen did not seem to mind though. She seemed more intrigued than outraged, although that might simply have been good manners and self-control. Members of the Maiden Guard glared at him. They looked as if they would like to knock him to his knees with the butts of their spears. That was not something that you could do to a freeborn elf though. The Everqueen placed her hand on the arm of the captain of the guard to emphasise it, he thought.

A chamberlain leaned forward between them, stared coldly at Tyrion then made the formal introduction as politely as ritual demanded.

'So you are the Prince Tyrion we have heard so much about,' said the Everqueen. Her voice was low and pleasant but it irritated Tyrion, as did her condescending manner.

'I am afraid I do not know what you have heard about me, your serenity,' he said.

'I confess I was expecting someone a little more polished,' she said with a trace of acid in her voice.

'I am sorry to disappoint,' he said. Out of the corner of his eye, he caught sight of Prince Perian smirking and he realised that he was not doing his own chances of becoming champion any good here and that was giving his rivals cause for amusement.

He liked that even less. He was getting off to a bad start. Perhaps he was sabotaging his own chances of winning because he did not want the prize.

Already the Everqueen was moving along the line, and he noticed that Prince Perian was following through the ritual with polished aplomb. He noticed also that the captain of the Everqueen's guard was staring at him coldly as if memorising his face.

He suspected that he had made an enemy there by his disrespect for her mistress. He smiled cheerfully at her in a way that he could not have managed with Alarielle and which was, as he knew, very provoking under the circumstances. The captain turned her head away quickly as if to hide her anger, but he saw that there was a red flush on her cheeks.

Very good, Tyrion thought to himself, very suave. He did not think he could have done worse in this situation if he had tried. In fact, he suspected that he would probably have done better. He told himself that he did not care, that he did not want to be part of this herd of worshippers, that he was quite happy that he was immune to whatever magic surrounded the Everqueen. He suspected however that he was not really immune, but rather it simply affected him differently.

Some of his fellow candidates looked as if they wanted to challenge him to a duel there and then. Some of them looked satisfied that a potential rival had eliminated himself from the competition so early, and some of them simply looked confused as if they could not understand his behaviour. They looked at him pityingly and that made him even angrier.

Tyrion knew that he needed to get a grip on himself. If he was going to be eliminated from this competition he wanted it to be because he was beaten by his opponents, not because he had beaten himself.

He resolved himself to do better. If he was going to lose here, he was going to lose openly and fairly after he had done his best. There were still tournaments to be entered and fights to be won and he had no intention of losing any of those, even if he could win nothing else. This was his chance to prove that he was among the best warriors in elvendom, if not the best.

Tomorrow he would find out.

CHAPTER EIGHTEEN

N'KARI COULD TELL the druchii troops were nervous. He could tell
they hated him. He rather enjoyed the sensation. He wore a form
appropriate for the situation, an armoured female parody of Malekith, which amused and served him in multiple ways.

It mocked the Witch King while at the same time reminding his
followers from whom ultimate authority flowed. It pained N'Kari
to admit that he needed that. The spells binding him prevented
him from bringing his full powers to bear. Without Malekith's
permission, he could not unleash them.

Fortunately, the dark elves were in the habit of obeying their
king. Malekith had ensured that it could not be otherwise, at least
when his eye or the eye of his direct representative was on them.

A delicious aroma of fear rose from the assembled soldiery and
their leaders. None of them wished to invite, or even give the
excuse for, punitive action. There were many ways that could be
turned to amusing advantage N'Kari thought. If he wished.

At the moment, he did not really want to. Malekith had

calculated things very finely. N'Kari did not want to interfere with his plans to ravage Ulthuan. He wanted very badly to see that happen and he had made up his mind to do everything in his power to help in this one area.

He wanted to kill high elves and the best way of doing that was to see that their savage kindred were in a position to do as much damage as possible. That was why he had spent the past few days in the ultimately tedious business of shipping the Witch King's troops to various points around Ulthuan.

He paused for a moment, wondering where this sudden complacency had come from. He examined the nature of the spells binding him for what felt like the millionth time. There was indeed an element of subtle compulsion woven into them, guiding his thoughts into these paths. That increased his anger but even that was channelled. He laughed and allowed himself to enjoy the mind-altering sensation. All that was happening here was that certain aspects of his mood and personality were being amplified. It was strangely enjoyable, a thing which was also a component of the spell.

In his deepest secret heart, N'Kari understood the insult and resented it. One locked-off chamber of his mind plotted vengeance and began to muster its resources. Other chambers of his mind entered into the spirit of things and plotted how it could aid in this new Rape of Ulthuan. He gave his attention back to the dark elves.

He let his stern gaze rest on every watching druchii in turn. They kept their faces impassive but inwardly they quailed under the gaze of one who so resembled their much-feared leader and at the same time was rumoured to be a daemon straight from hell.

All of them, except perhaps General Dorian, were wondering exactly why they were here and exactly what was going to happen. Being what and who they were, they must be half-expecting a trap. They must be asking themselves whether Malekith had resolved to dispose of them in some new and horrific way. They were the last of the original force that had landed in Ulthuan. All of the rest of the soldiers had been deployed near their objectives. They were the only ones who had been issued with special amulets. Most of them had no idea of the purpose of those charms save perhaps the sorceresses and their commander.

Being who they were, all of them in their secret hearts knew they were guilty of some treason and N'Kari gave them time to dwell on their own particular variations on that theme. Once the fear and anticipation had reached a crescendo, he opened the portal in the flashiest and most terrifying way he could. The basic composition of the gateway was unchangeable but he could use his magic to add little touches of his own to the spell.

The air chilled, thunder rumbled and the stink of ozone drifted into every nostril as the gateway appeared illuminated by crackling lightning. The area within shimmered with multi-coloured light. There was no way they could see through it and know their ultimate destination. They could be going across Ulthuan as they were told, or to the deepest hell. They would not know until they passed through and their well-controlled terror was delicious.

General Dorian gave the order to move. In lockstep, the first of the units began to march through the gateway he had opened in the fabric of reality. Even N'Kari had to admit that their discipline was impressive.

DORIAN STUDIED HIS bodyguard as they marched with him into the portal. They were the elite of his force, a fine selection of druchii heavy infantry, disciplined and capable. They would stand and fight while others died or fled because they were proud of themselves, their heritage and their bloodlines. It was this pride that made them the finest heavy infantry in the world. It was what allowed them to march through the gateway under the daemon's terrifying gaze without any apparent show of fear.

He understood them because he was like them. From birth, he had been brought up to see himself as one of the born rulers of the world. He had trained alongside his brothers for hours with sword and spear and shield and crossbow. He had learned to fight and to compete. His brothers had been both comrades and rivals. He wanted to outshine them and he had, with the possible exception of Urian, but that very rivalry had provided him with the motivation to excel. The same thing applied through the entire vast army on a very different scale.

Each soldier attempted to outshine every other soldier in his company. Every company tried to surpass every other company in the regiment. Every regiment tried to outclass every other in the army. And the army must prove itself against every foe.

Glory was both personal and communal. The Witch King looked down on all and distributed his rewards. He was feared and hated, but his favour was sought out as the ultimate source of power. It was not a pleasant system, Dorian thought, but it worked. And it worked because at the end of the day Malekith was fair.

He was proof of that. He had started off as a common soldier, or as common as any soldier ever was in his elite unit. His family had provided him with his weapons and his basic training. He had learned the hard craft of raiding and slaving along the coasts of the Old World for himself.

He had earned his rewards and the respect of his warriors. When the warhorns summoned the dark elves to battle against the hordes of Chaos, his retinue had proven themselves against the tattooed marauders with whose distant descendants they were currently allied. He had distinguished himself in raids on the slann lands of Lustria, and acquired much gold as part of the plunder.

On the greater battlefields he had come under the eye of Malekith himself and by a combination of ferocity, fearlessness and fighting skill he had attracted the Witch King's attention. He had risen eventually to become an honoured general in the armies of Naggaroth, being rewarded with the lands of fallen rivals, building his wealth on his share of the plunder.

Yes, Dorian thought, he had done well under the Witch King.

But he was not sure about this invasion at all. Oh, there was nothing wrong with seeking to reclaim the lost lands of Ulthuan. The spoils would be immense, ancient estates would be restituted, new ones earned. Many slaves would be taken and the most hated enemies of the druchii would be humbled. He had no problem with any of this. In truth, he looked forward to it.

It was not that he resented the vast use of magic instead of force of arms either. Sorcery was an integral part of the way the dark elves fought their wars, part of the strength of their nation, one of those things that made them superior to all other races. He appreciated both the tactical and strategic uses of wizardry and he knew that both Malekith and his divine mother were masters of it.

It was this business of relying on Malekith's bound daemon and travelling through the mystical gates it summoned that troubled him. There was something about these pathways that made his elven senses scream at the peril. He sensed the presence of daemonic things very close by.

What if something went wrong?

He glanced across at Cassandra. His sorceress lover looked calm, but he knew her well enough to spot the small signs of nervousness: the way she kept toying with the rune-inscribed ring on her left hand, for example. She claimed they were passing through the realms of Chaos when they went through these portals and, if that was the case, terrifying, ancient horrors were close, separated from them by a barrier thinner than the skin of a bubble. Even more than their lives, their souls were at risk.

And that was not the only disturbing thing about this business. Cassandra had whispered other things in his ear at night as they lay in their sleeping silks, spent from their wild lovemaking.

She claimed that the Witch King's new pet was a creature whose strength might conceivably be greater than Malekith's and which might break free at any moment. Of course, Cassandra was Morathi's creature, and he suspected that at this moment the Hag Queen was not best pleased with her son, but that did not mean she was wrong. If N'Kari truly was what Malekith claimed, it was one of the greatest enemies of his people in history, if not the greatest.

It made him fear that after all these long millennia, the Witch King's sanity had finally cracked, that this expedition might be doomed by that alone. Worse was the thought that such a powerful, malign and barely controllable being was the one opening these gates and leading them through these hellish realms. The possibilities for disaster were enormous. The lives of all his troops were in the hands of a creature that could and would, if given the opportunity, snuff them out on a whim.

But what could he do? Rebellion against the Witch King was near unthinkable at the best of times, and this was a time of war, when any disaffection in the army could be disastrous. And there were other things to be considered.

Malekith *had* bound the daemon. It *was* serving them, and the strategic advantages of being able to move huge forces across Ulthuan so swiftly and unknown by their enemy were enormous. The task he had been set was proof of this.

It was a gigantic risk but it could so easily pay off, and if it did... This would be a victory still talked about in ten thousand years. The spoils that would go to the victors would be fantastic.

Dorian knew too that this was a campaign that had been centuries in the planning. The Witch King must know what he was doing. Their foes would be taken utterly and completely off guard and in a war like this, the advantage of surprise would be worth legions of warriors.

For the moment then, Dorian was determined to follow, but if things went wrong, then it would be time to consider the possibility of a new ruler of Naggaroth and exactly how that might be arranged.

N'KARI LOOKED AROUND. His magical senses told him that they were in Avelorn. Not much had changed in these forests since he had rampaged across Ulthuan all those millennia ago. It would have given him as much pleasure as ever to watch them burn, but he could not make it happen. He was constrained by this accursed chain and the Witch King's spells not to invoke his power, even in self-defence. If he were attacked now, he would have to rely on the natural resilience of his daemonic incarnation to save him, nothing else would.

The winds of magic brought something else to his spiritual senses than the scent of the forest's old magic. He could tell that somewhere relatively close at hand were at least two descendants of Aenarion. Their psychic stench was quite unmistakable. One of them was even familiar, although it had been over a century since N'Kari had last smelled it.

It belonged to Tyrion who had helped in his ignominious undoing at the Shrine of Asuryan. Just the faintest hint of that spiritual aroma set N'Kari to flexing his hands like claws. He salivated at the thought of tearing that particular prey apart. This time he would not toy with his victim until after he was certain it could not escape doom.

Of course, right now there was nothing he could do. He was constrained to pass back through the portal he had opened and return to Malekith's side. He would need to do something to ensure that this situation did not last indefinitely.

His thirst for revenge on the whole line of Aenarion burned stronger than ever.

As soon as N'Kari vanished, a weight lifted from Dorian's shoulders even though the portal remained where the daemon had opened it, glowing in the air. He took a deep sniff of the pine-scented air. It was fresh and pure and smelled of living things. It was quite unlike the chill air of Naggaroth and yet there was something about its purity that reminded him of his homeland. He looked around and he could not help but smile.

It was said that long ago the first elves had been born in the forests during the long golden reign of the first Everqueen. It was still thought by many that the forests were the true home of his people and at this moment he could believe it.

This was indeed a magical place. He could feel it in the air. Powerful sorcery surrounded him. For a moment that made him fearful, but only for a moment. This was not the sort of magic that was intended to harm. It was the magic of growing things, of life, of this most ancient forest. Potent though it was, it had nothing to do with warfare or death or killing.

He looked around at his warriors and could see that their faces were similarly transformed. Just for a moment they had all returned to childhood. There was something about this place that would do that to even the most cynical dark elf. Druchii who hated each other and been rivals for decades exchanged smiles and then looked away from each other as if embarrassed, not quite understanding what was happening to them.

Perhaps he was wrong, Dorian thought. Perhaps this place did have the means to protect itself. Perhaps they were coming under its influence right now. If that was the case, he would soon put a stop to it. He bellowed instructions to his soldiers, telling them to form up in ranks, to set up a defensive perimeter, to be ready to protect themselves from any high elf who might stumble upon them.

Dorian looked at Cassandra. He could see from her look that she understood what had happened here. She understood how close they were to victory. They had established a beachhead in the most sacred heart of elvendom. They could use the daemon's portal to bring in an army and seize this land and its ruler.

Already scouts were fanning out from the point of arrival. If they encountered any rangers in the woods, they would capture or kill them. It would not do for word of their arrival to leak out before they were ready and the full force of the dark elf army had arrived.

No matter, Dorian thought. He knew that they were going to be blessed with success. The most difficult part had been achieved.

He was walking were no druchii had walked in a thousand years and he knew that they were within striking distance of the Everqueen herself, if she was at the tournament ground as Malekith predicted she would be.

The Witch King had got it right. His plan was going to work and Dorian felt satisfied that he had been chosen to lead the force that was to execute this part of the great work. He knew that he was going to cover himself in glory and the rewards for his success would be immense.

He could see that Cassandra looked at him in a different way now. There was more than simple calculation in her eyes. She realised what he was going to be and what she herself might achieve by helping him. The two of them were going to become immensely rich and powerful.

There and then Dorian committed himself to Malekith once more. He would do his absolute best to see that this succeeded and nothing had better stand in his way. He walked around the perimeter of the camp that was coming into being. Cassandra and her fellow sorceresses were moving over to where the sacrificial slaves waited. They would need to expend a great number of lives to keep the daemon's portal open, but that was a small price to pay for their inevitable victory.

Screams rose above the camp. The portal flickered and shone. Every now and again its surface shimmered and rippled and a new force of dark elf infantry arrived. With ordered precision, they took up their places in the vast armed camp that Dorian was building right in the heart of this most sacred forest. It was astonishing to think that such a feat could be achieved without anyone noticing it. And yet it was happening, he told himself. Nothing could stop them.

More and more dark elf soldiery arrived. Units of cavalry mounted on huge lizard-like Cold Ones emerged from the portal. The great beasts looked strangely dormant and docile for a few minutes after they arrived, obviously disorientated by their passage through the pathways the daemon had opened. After that, as if in compensation for their docility, they became even more savage than normal and their riders had to apply discipline with sharp prods and metal implements.

Dorian smiled. Victory, promotion, wealth and riches were all within his grasp. All he had to do was reach out and take them.

CHAPTER NINETEEN

'I HEARD YOU had returned,' said High Loremaster Morelian. 'I trust you were successful in your quest.'

Teclis studied the older elf. Morelian was very ancient looking. He was tall and stooped and very, very slender, with skin as coarse as a human's and hair so silver it appeared positively metallic. He had a small forked beard of a type very unusual among elves who were normally clean shaven. He gave the impression of great wisdom and knowledge, but there was a twinkle in his eye and a cheerful smile quirked his lips.

His chamber was austere. There was a large desk and many scroll racks around the walls containing a selection of ancient lore. Books lay in a pile upon his table along with blank parchment, uncut quill pens made from the finest goose feathers and a jar containing black ink. The High Loremaster had been making notes about the books open on the table before him, that much was clear from even the most cursory inspection.

'My brother and I found Sunfang but that was not all we found,' said Teclis. Morelian raised an eyebrow.

'You say that as if you found something even more important than Sunfang,' he said. Teclis opened his pack and placed the slann inscriptions on the table in front of him.

'Perhaps we did,' he said. The High Loremaster looked at the scrolls with something like awe.

'Is this what I think it is?'

'I'm not a fortune teller so I don't know,' Teclis said. 'I can decipher enough to see that it contains knowledge that might be important. That is why I have brought it to you. I know of your interest in these things.'

An expression of wonder passed over the High Loremaster's face. It reminded Teclis of the expression he had seen in his father's when the old prince had looked at Sunfang. Instantly he began to flip through the copies Teclis had made.

'You know what it is?' Teclis asked after a few minutes had passed.

'It is astronomical and astrological,' said the High Loremaster. 'It is written in a very compressed form of their hieroglyphic script. You were right to bring this to me. I think that your suspicions about its importance are correct. It is, among other things, an astrological calculation of the orbits of certain planets and moons and the way they are connected to the fluctuations in the cycles of the polar warp gates.'

Teclis was amazed that Morelian had been able to divine so much from such a cursory examination. Of course, this was his specialist field of knowledge. It galled Teclis to think that there was so much he did not know. This just reminded him of that fact. 'Is that all it says?'

'That is as much as I can make out in this short period of time,' the High Loremaster said. 'And I may not be correct about that. I am guessing as to the interpretation of quite a lot of the things inscribed. If you leave this with me I can probably have it translated fully in a few hours. There is something hidden here, I feel sure of it, something of great mystical significance.'

Teclis felt a reluctance to let the scrolls out of his sight, particularly if there was a mystical secret connected with them. He did not like the idea that someone other than himself would discover this hidden truth. He was fighting with his own personal daemons here, he knew. There was nothing he could do with the texts himself unless he was prepared to spend several decades improving his mastery of the slann language, and he did not have time for that.

'Of course, you may have them,' Teclis said. 'I am grateful for any help you can give me in this matter. I have been both troubled and puzzled by the little I have been able to deduce about what they contain.'

'It may be of the greatest importance to all of us,' said the High Loremaster. 'I suspect it concerns the times we now live in. I also suspect that the fact that you found it at this time is no coincidence. All things are connected, and mystical objects are more connected than anything else.'

Teclis had heard such things said before but he was not entirely sure that he believed them. Wizards tended to enjoy the benefits of exceptional hindsight, and pointing out the connections between things and events afterwards was much easier than spotting them at any given time.

'I'm not sure I know what you're talking about,' Teclis said.

'You should go and speak to Belthania,' the High Loremaster said. 'I know she wants to talk to you and she will be able to tell you more about what is going on than I can.'

Teclis felt certain that this was not the case, but he could also see that the High Loremaster was like a child with a new toy. He was desperate to get to work at once and Teclis understood the benefits of being able to harness that enthusiasm.

'I shall see to it at once,' he said.

'That would probably be for the best,' said the High Loremaster. He was already focused on the scrolls in front of him and hurriedly scribbling down notes about its contents. Teclis knew that he had already been dismissed from the master of his order's mind.

* * *

TECLIS ENTERED THE chambers of Belthania. Warriors in the livery of the archmage guarded a doorway that was carved from a sliver of the ivory fang of some great sea monster.

Why had she summoned him? They had met many times at social functions in Lothern and when he was studying at the tower, but he would not have said they were close. Perhaps there was some research she wanted to discuss with him.

A servant in black and gold showed him into a glasshouse protruding from the side of the tower, where it could catch the sun. It sat high in the tower with a magnificent view out over the forest. The floor was translucent crystal and he could see the grounds a long way below. The view made him nervous. The heat in the place reminded him of the jungles he had just vacated. Belthania was garbed in thin flowing robes of greenish silk that clung to the curves of her body. She smiled grimly as he entered. She had a faintly drugged, somnolent air to her, as always.

'Prince Teclis,' she said. 'It is good to see you again.'

She did not sound as if it was. The words were purely spoken from politeness.

He decided to match the tone. 'The High Loremaster suggested I pay you a visit. He said you wanted to talk with me.'

'Word has it you have recently returned from the jungles of Lustria, from the slann city of Zultec, and that you brought with you the sword of Aenarion.'

'My brother has it. He goes to offer it to the service of the Everqueen.'

'He may have need of it soon.'

'Why do you say this?'

'I have been studying the skies and performing other divinatory rites and the signs have not been good.'

'How so?' Teclis was curious. Divination was a famously imprecise school of magic. Its practitioners were regarded as little more than charlatans by serious scholars. Except Morathi. Her gifts had been proven again and again.

'The winds of magic are becoming increasingly contaminated by the powers of Chaos. You can feel it if you try any of the greater spells.'

'I have sensed something even when working minor spells of the Art.'

'You are certainly more sensitive than most to such things.'

Teclis wondered if she was sneering at him, but he saw none of the usual signs of contempt. 'Why am I here?'

'You saw no signs of anything similar in Lustria?'

'I noticed nothing of the sort.'

'Good, then perhaps things have not progressed too far then.'

'Too far for what?'

'I believe we may be entering a new age of catastrophe, Prince Teclis. The polar warp gates have long been dormant but they have started to erupt once more. The signs are all there if you know how to look.'

Teclis nodded to encourage her to keep talking. 'This is dire news if true.'

'It is true enough, I fear. Ships sailing off the northern coasts of the Old World have reported great drifts of tribes down from the Northern Wastes. They were accompanied by daemons and all manner of monsters. Agents have reported rumours that the Hag Queen herself was sighted there mere months ago.

'The Vortex has become progressively more unstable. The ghosts of Caledor and his companions have been sighted at many places close to the waystones. The land trembles. The mountains begin to burn.

'The winds of darkness blow hard again. The Everqueen is dead. A new Everqueen is not yet steady on her throne. I do not think this is all simply coincidence.

'The dreams of the Wise have been troubled. I wished to ask you if yours had been.'

So that was what this was about. Teclis mentioned his own vision in the forest en route to the tower. Belthania nodded as if she had expected to hear something like this. 'Did you have any such dreams before that?' she asked.

'No. But I have been far from Ulthuan in recent months. Have you done anything about these signs? Surely the Phoenix King should be warned.'

'We have sent messengers apprising him of this.'

'What has Finubar done?'

'Nothing as far as we can tell. But then what can he do until there is some definite threat?'

'From what you are saying, one of those will not be long in coming.'

'I would love to be proved wrong but I fear I will not be. I also feel that you have an important role to play in all of this.'

'What makes you say that?'

'It is a feeling I have. Things have been strange ever since the Keeper of Secrets returned.'

'N'Kari?'

'Yes. I fear he was a harbinger of a new age of terrors for the elves. He almost destroyed us once.'

'He certainly almost destroyed me once,' said Teclis, thinking back to the brief terrifying time over a century ago when he had faced the daemon.

'And yet you are still here. Perhaps that is why I think you and your brother are important. How many elves have ever survived an encounter with one of the greater daemons of Chaos?'

'I am not sure I could survive another. It was Asuryan who protected me then. If ever I meet N'Kari again, I doubt he will be foolish enough to attack me in the Shrine of the Phoenix God.'

'No doubt you are correct.'

'You think N'Kari may be behind all of this then?'

'I don't know. I do know that it is well past the time when he could have incarnated a new avatar and come back to seek his vengeance on you.'

It was a chilling thought, and most likely the real reason she had wanted to talk with him. 'I have suspected as much myself,' said Teclis.

'Be on your guard, Prince Teclis.'

'I shall be. I go now to perform some divinations of my own.'

TECLIS GLANCED AROUND his chamber and wished there was something more he could do. He had performed every simple divination he knew and the results had always been bad.

The hexagrams of the *Book of Change* had given a trigram indicating catastrophe. In the cards, the Plague Lord had appeared over the Changer of Ways, the worst possible conjunction it could display. The blood spray patterns of the White Bird ritual had been particularly ominous. Something terrible was going to happen, perhaps was even happening now.

He would find out soon enough what was destined to be. They all would. The sense of foreboding nagged at his mind. If he only had the slightest hint of what was going to happen, he could perhaps prepare for it, let those around him know. In any dangerous situation, even the smallest possible advantage could prove useful.

He felt like a prisoner awaiting execution for some unspecified crime on some unspecified date. The prospect hung over his head, colouring all his feelings, darkening his days. After performing the divinations, he found it very hard to return to his studies.

'IT IS VERY bad,' said High Loremaster Morelian. He looked very worried indeed, which given his normally cheerful nature was quite dispiriting. Teclis just stared at him unsure of what to say next. The High Loremaster looked at his notes and then back at Teclis. He steepled his fingers and then ran them through his hair.

'What did you find out?' Teclis asked.

'You were right to bring this to me. And you are right to be disturbed by it. I had not realised you were such a good scholar of the slann language.'

'I know only the very basics,' said Teclis.

'Even that is impressive,' said the High Loremaster. 'It normally takes decades for an elf to achieve that. The ancient slann language is not like ours. It is the tongue of a race so alien as to be almost incomprehensible. The hieroglyphs change meaning depending on their position with relation to each other. They imply shadows of meaning projected beyond and above themselves, an entire alien system of logic that it is very difficult to grasp even for one trained in the mysteries of magic. Their runes are language and mathematical and magical notation all rolled into one.'

'It surprises me that the primitive lizardmen that Tyrion and I encountered in the jungle could grasp such a thing.'

'I very much doubt that they can. They are warriors and labour-ers. It is the priestly caste that are literate, and more than literate by our standards. They and their masters, the ancient toad-gods of the race, are the only ones who could comprehend this fully. It is impossible for an elf or a human, or a dwarf for that matter, to grasp their thoughts. Even now I am only guessing some of the content. The only one who ever even came close was Caledor and I suspect that this was one of the reasons he became the supreme mage that he was.'

These words hit Teclis with the force of a blow. He suddenly realised that if it took him a lifetime he was going to need to master this language and he was going to need to begin to study it soon. It seemed like it was the key to understanding so much and might even allow him to surpass those ancient masters of magic who had done so much to shape the modern world. All of this was for the future. Right now he was more curious about what the inscription actually said. The High Loremaster seemed to sense this.

'As far as I can tell this text deals with our present time. Certain astrological references contained in it allow me to date the predic-tion with reference to the current position of the stars and planets. It is often the way with slann writing.'

He indicated the position of certain hieroglyphics. They were arranged within multiple etched circles which intersected in different places. Teclis knew that certain of the runes, under certain circumstances, indicated the names of planets and quite possibly the gods or daemons who ruled the movements of those planets.

The High Loremaster continued to speak, 'These runes indicate catastrophe of the worst sort. They refer to the polar warp gates and the gods of Chaos and the connection between them. I believe that the gates will open the same way now as they did during the first Chaos incursion and I don't think I need to tell you that that bodes no good for any of us.'

'Belthania says the same thing,' Teclis said. 'She has different reasons for thinking so, but she has come to much the same conclusions.'

'She is not the only one. The winds of magic blow strangely. Certain ominous portents have been observed by wizards as far apart as Cothique and Lothern. I have even been getting reports of such things from as far away as the Citadel of the Dawn.'

'What can we do about this?' Teclis asked.

The High Loremaster shrugged.

'I have written to the Phoenix King suggesting that we send an expedition into the Northern Wastes to discover exactly what is going on there.'

Teclis nodded. This certainly made sense. It was all very well talking about corruption in the winds of magic and strange signs in the stars, but the easiest way to confirm the truth would be to send observers to the place where actual events were happening.

'And what did he say?'

'I am awaiting his response.'

'Let us hope he comes to a decision soon. Otherwise it may be too late.'

CHAPTER TWENTY

TECLIS AND THE High Loremaster walked through the vaults of the Tower of Hoeth in silence. They had spent the past half hour discussing Morelian's researches on the slann inscription and seemed to have said all that was needful. He carried the High Loremaster's partial translation with him.

They passed cases full of wondrous artefacts dating to an earlier age. Teclis loved this place. It always calmed him. He tried to spend some time there every day when he was at the White Tower.

He passed the Staff of Kaladreon, once borne by the white herald of Bel-Hathor, wound round with spells that generated an aura of calm and peace. It was a beautiful thing, but not much use for it had been found in the modern world. He admired the spell-work as much as the intricate carving of the winged goddess of mercy woven into it.

He glanced at the Oracle of Mammakis, a statue in the shape of a lion which was said to come to life once every ten centuries and answer any question asked of it truthfully although not always to the liking of the hearer. The inscription said it would be another two hundred and twenty years before it spoke again.

Teclis stopped to look upon the War Crown of Saphery. It was beautiful in a way that very few objects were, and it was potent, worked around with mighty enchantments to aid its wearer when casting powerful spells. It was one of the most powerful artefacts possessed by the Loremasters of the White Tower. Whoever wore it would be able to achieve wondrous feats.

His hands itched to pick it up and place it on his head. There was something about it that almost compelled him to do so. He had rarely felt so drawn to any object. It felt as if it belonged to him and had done all his life and always would.

The High Loremaster saw the expression on his face. 'What is it?'

Teclis wondered whether he should confess his desire to own this object. He hesitated only for a moment and then said, 'I feel drawn to the Crown. I feel as if it belongs to me.'

'It is one of the most powerful artefacts in our vaults,' said the High Loremaster. 'It was intended for use in battle by a war mage. It helps the wearer concentrate and manipulate the winds of magic, and it protects him from some of the worst side effects of miscasting a spell. It has other powers as well. It is said to amplify the senses and shield the mind from the temptations of Chaos.'

The High Loremaster looked at Teclis oddly. Teclis felt almost embarrassed by his scrutiny. It was as if the High Loremaster suspected him of wanting to steal the helmet. 'Sometimes,' he said, 'one has a feel for certain objects that are involved with one's destiny. This may be the case with you and the Crown.'

'It is a beautiful thing but I hope I never have any use for it,' said Teclis. 'It is something for a warrior not for a wizard like myself. I do not see myself going to war at any time in the near future.'

'You can never predict what your fate might be,' said the High Loremaster. 'It is not something that even the greatest of wizards has any control over.'

Teclis doubted this, but he did not want to get into an argument with the head of his order.

'What do you plan to do now?' the High Loremaster asked.

'All this talk of the alignment of moons and stars and Chaos gates has made me curious. I wish to do some research of my own in the library.'

'That is a dark and serious subject. In theory, you need the permission of the High Loremaster to pursue it.'

'Do I have it?' Teclis asked.

'I think it is safe to say that you do.'

'I thank you for the work you have done on the slann text.'

'I should thank you, Prince Teclis. It is not often I have had such a fascinating subject to study.'

TECLIS WALKED DOWN the steps into the Great Library. Over the arched doorway was the symbol of the moon, the same symbol that appeared on the War Crown of Saphery and was the mark of the ancient princely realm. Sword Masters guarded the entrance.

Within this place were treasures uncounted: ancient books and scrolls, tablets of forbidden knowledge, palimpsests and metal etchings. It was one of the greatest treasure houses of knowledge in existence.

Of course, the guards were symbolic because it was very unlikely that any thief would even find his way into the tower. Not impossible though, Teclis thought, or else the Sword Masters would be deployed elsewhere. Or perhaps they were there to report on the mages studying within. It was not unknown for them to seek forbidden lore.

He nodded to the guardians as he limped past. They acknowledged his presence and a clerk wrote down his name in the register. If he checked that huge leather bound book he would find the names of the greatest magicians that Ulthuan had ever produced. Out of curiosity he had done just that in the past. It thrilled him to think that he was walking now where once those legends had walked.

He entered the main hall of the library. It was gigantic, eight stories high, with books running all the way to the ceiling. On each level was a balcony that ran around the entire chamber. Steps led up to these balconies. In the centre of the room were many tables at which wizards and scholars sat studying ancient volumes of lore.

At the far end of the chamber was another exit which led to a room very similar to the first. He progressed through a dozen such chambers until at last he came to a room with a much lower ceiling and several exits.

This was where things started to get tricky. In the main chambers of the library, which he had just passed through, nothing ever went astray. It was easy to navigate them and no one ever got lost. Once you passed through this area you were into something else entirely. Soon he would be in the Maze of Books.

From here there was a labyrinth of corridors and tunnels walled with volumes of lore which seemed to stretch off in every direction. He had walked through this place on many different occasions and had come to the conclusion that this part of the library was several times greater than the area of the tower which contained it, impossible as that was.

He knew that some sort of magic was at work but, as with all of the magic connected with the tower, it was infinitely subtle and very hard to detect even if you were looking for it. Occasionally he felt the flicker of some spark of power when he passed from one room to another but he never quite worked out what was happening, which annoyed him, for he was very proud of his skill as a wizard.

When he entered these corridors, he was entering a realm where the normal laws of the world did not apply. He had known other mages to claim that they were in the same room as he had been in at the same time as he was there, but he had never seen them and they had never seen him, even though they had been studying books that were barely a few strides apart on the shelves.

He knew that the Master Librarian of Hoeth kept a catalogue which purported to show the location of every book on every shelf, but that catalogue could not be copied and it appeared different to everyone who studied it. Teclis himself had made notes and drawn sketches but they had never agreed with the notes and sketches of other scholars. Nonetheless, anyone who followed the guidance of the catalogue could find the books he was looking for.

Once, as an experiment, he and a fellow mage had sought the same book using different directions and had walked into the same corridors at the same time. Somehow, without ever realising how it had happened, they had become separated. Teclis could very distinctly remember looking back over his shoulder and discovering that the person he had been talking to just a few heartbeats before was not there.

And yet, when he had arrived at the book he was seeking, his fellow scholar was also there. It was the sort of thing that new students to the tower were always doing out of curiosity and probably always would do until the end of time.

He was looking for knowledge concerning the coming of Chaos, which meant searching all the way back to the time of Caledor. This was located in the deepest section of the Maze. He passed through numerous galleries, in which students of magic studied and library servitors went about their business, and then he entered an area in which fewer living presences were visible. The corridors were dustier, and cobwebs hung in corners even though there were no signs of spiders anywhere. It was as if they were spun by his imagination. Sometimes, out of the corner of his eye he even seemed to see them take form.

He went down a flight of stairs he could not recall ever seeing before, and turned a corner and went down another. He was far beneath the tower now, in its very foundations. The place felt old. There was an air of antiquity about it, and the books that surrounded him. The niches in the walls contained small statuettes in an archaic style, depicting elves in garb that had gone out of fashion millennia ago.

He kept walking, feeling that he was getting ever further from his goal. The walls of books seemed to be closing in around him. For the first time in his life, he felt menaced by their presence, and by the library itself. He tried to turn back to retrace his steps, but when he followed the path backwards he could not find the stairs he had entered by, and after what felt like hours he thought he had passed the same statuettes of the goddess of wisdom several times.

What was going on here? Had the library turned against him? Had it decided that he was a threat or had become one for some reason since his return? Was this some variant of the spells that caused people to become lost forever in the woods around the tower. He breathed more deeply and fought against mounting panic. He guessed it was possible to be lost down here forever, if whatever power ruled over the Maze wished it.

He took another turning trying to retrace his steps and he found himself in a chamber he had not been in before. Had he taken a wrong turning, become disorientated, or was something else going on here?

He noticed that the room was lit by a small lantern and contained a table on which were several books. One was a volume of ancient poetry concerning the life of Aenarion and Caledor. The other was a history of Saphery. The last appeared to be a book of spells. It was this he reached for first. Also on the table was a game board that looked as if the squares were inscribed with slann runes. The pieces had already been moved, as if the players had only just left the room and intended to come back.

Weary and seeing nothing else better to do, Teclis sat down at the table. He placed the copy of the High Loremaster's translation of the slann tablet on the table. He opened the spell book. It contained a number of incantations written in old script. The hand was very fine. There was something familiar about it. Even though he was certain he'd never actually seen this writing before, there was something about it that reminded him of someone.

He turned to the opening page of the volume where he saw a famous mark. It was one that he recognised from the inscriptions on Sunfang, the rune that identified the sword's maker. This was a volume written in the hand of the Archmage Caledor. It contained spells that he had personally inscribed.

Excitement filled Teclis. This was a treasure he had never hoped to find. He felt sure somehow that no one except himself had ever seen this particular book. He was the one who was meant to find it, even though he was not sure why.

He continued to leaf through the volume, until his eyes came to rest on one particular spell. He could not say why exactly he was compelled to look at it. He was sure that it was not magic that made him do so. He would have felt that. He would have been able to resist the compulsion to read it as well. It was as if this particular spell was somehow intended to appeal directly to him. It was written in slann runes and yet he somehow understood them.

Something about the words embedded them in his mind immediately and set his lips forming them and his hands moving through the gestures of casting before he could even stop himself.

Even as he did so, he felt his eyes grow heavier and his voice grow throatier. His words became slurred and he started to mumble in a way that he had never done when casting a spell before.

Fear filled him. This whole episode was too strange. He felt as if he was caught in some vast intricate trap. This was not supposed to happen. It should not be able to happen. The Tower of Hoeth was supposed to be a safe haven for wizards.

Had he stumbled onto something strange and deadly? Had this happened before to other wizards? Would he simply be the last in a long line of people who had disappeared and were not

remembered? He supposed it was possible. After all, the magic of
the tower warped the minds of all who came into contact with it.

Even as these thoughts occurred to him, a wave of dizziness
overcame him and he slumped forward over the books.

TECLIS OPENED HIS eyes and wondered where he was.

The chamber was not like anything he had ever seen before. It
looked as if it had been furnished by elves, but not any of the
sort of elves he knew. The workmanship was crude, although still
beautiful and still the product of a fine sensibility. Everything
looked hastily made, as if the craftspeople had not taken the time
to give it the requisite level of polish.

Scroll racks and bookcases covered the walls of the chamber.
On a table in front of him was a game board inscribed with slann
runes similar to the one back in the library, but this was the most
fantastically complicated game board he had ever seen. Pieces that
looked like elves and daemons, and dragons and monsters were
strewn across it. One of the pieces even looked like him.

In the centre of the chamber stood a tall, stooped elf. He was
almost skeletally thin, with receding hair and an oddly-shaped
head. A woven carpet covered in a pattern that looked strangely
familiar lay on the floor beneath his feet. He turned to face Teclis
and there was nothing in his eyes except flaming light.

'You should not be here,' said the figure. Its voice was gentle and
soft and very sad. 'I should not be here either.'

'And yet we are,' Teclis said. 'A strange meeting.'

The stranger's flesh seemed almost translucent. Tendons and
sinews moved visibly beneath it. His face was a mask of strain
and his expression was that of someone constantly in pain. Teclis
recognised that expression only too well. He had often seen it in
the mirror.

'Stranger than you think and later than you think,' said the elf.
He limped over to the table and slumped down in a chair. He
contemplated the game as if he was about to make a move, then

he tipped his head to one side and studied Teclis for a moment. 'You look like him, you know.'

'Like who?'

'Aenarion. You are one of his blood, aren't you?'

Teclis nodded. 'How can you tell?'

'Your face and your manner and something else, something about your aura, gives it away. You are a wizard too, aren't you?'

'And so are you,' Teclis said. He knew who this was now and he had a suspicion that he knew where they were. 'Your name is Caledor.'

'It was. At least I think it was. I sometimes forget. I sometimes forget everything except the task, and there are dangerous moments when I forget even that. Even now I am neglecting it. My fellows must take up the slack and carry my burden for me. We do not have long here you and I. I must return to my duty. It is all there is for me now.'

The conversation had a strange logic that reminded him of something.

'This is a dream, isn't it?'

'I have difficulty telling dream from reality,' said Caledor. The muscles on his face twitched a little. Teclis wondered if he was quite sane.

'I read something. I cast a spell written in slann runes. It was written in your hand,' Teclis said.

'That sounds about right. I found the secret of the Vortex written in slann runes. I found it in the burned-out rubble of one of their ancient cities. I saw the pattern of it and I saw the way it tapped into the magical structures that lie beneath the surface of reality. I saw how it could be used to save the world and that is what I tried to do. How long has it been... since I died?'

'Over six thousand years,' said Teclis.

'So long,' said Caledor, his soft voice sounded wistful. 'If I'd known...'

Teclis did not dare ask him what he meant. He suspected he

already knew the answer. Caledor and his fellow wizards had given their lives to create the Vortex. Would they have done so if they had known what was waiting for them?

What must it be like to spend six thousand sleepless years weaving a spell that was constantly trying to unravel itself, to have to protect it from the forces that would destroy it?

'We have met for a reason,' Teclis said. 'At least, I would like to believe that this has not happened by chance.'

'It is hard to say what happens by chance and what does not,' said the first Archmage. 'Once I thought there was a pattern to everything, that it all made sense somehow and that I could understand it and it would be wonderful. I'm not sure any more. I am not sure of anything.'

'You've spent millennia maintaining a pattern, preserving the order of things.'

'I think that is what has changed me. If we were not here, if we did not constantly keep re-weaving our spell, there would be only Chaos now. And that is perhaps one of the reasons why you have been called here.'

'What do you mean?'

'The pattern is starting to unravel. It is sliding out of our control. The power of Chaos is growing stronger. The Vortex is becoming tainted by its energy and there are those out there who seek to accelerate the unravelling.'

'That is madness,' said Teclis. 'What possible benefit could be had from doing that? It would destroy Ulthuan and eventually the world.'

'It is good that you understand this,' said Caledor. 'But there are those who do not see things as you do. There are those who see the unmaking of the Vortex as an opportunity. They think that they can control the power of Chaos and remake the world as they want it to be.'

'Is it possible?' Teclis asked. It seemed that someone desired to transcend their own mortality, to have power like unto a god.

'In theory. In practice, I doubt that things would work out the way that Morathi expects.'

'So it is the Hag Queen that we are talking about.'

'Yes, and possibly her son, Aenarion's child, Malekith.'

The scale of the ambition revealed by Caledor's statement was breathtaking.

'How would they do it?'

'Tempted?'

'Who would not be?'

Caledor's smile was strange and sour. The complexity of the emotions in it made Teclis feel ashamed. The old wizard spread his hands wide and shrugged. 'Indeed. Who would not be?'

'What do you think they are planning?'

'If the pattern of the Vortex is destroyed, Chaos will overflow into your world. Eventually, matter itself will become mutable, the very structure of reality will become fluid as the powers of Chaos exert themselves. Once that happens, a mage of sufficient power and skill would be able, in theory, to remake the world in an image created by themselves.'

'Is that really possible?'

'Truthfully, I doubt it. We are talking about magic on a scale that only gods or daemon princes could work. Nonetheless, possible or not, I think that is what Morathi intends. I think it is what she always intended, even before she met Aenarion.'

'She must be stopped,' said Teclis.

'Indeed she must. You are here because we need a weapon against those who would swallow the world. You will be our sword.'

'Me?' Teclis felt suddenly very vulnerable. It was all very well saying that someone had to stop the most powerful sorceress of all time. It was an entirely different matter when you yourself might be the one chosen to do it.

Caledor's expression was bleak. 'We all feel that way when destiny taps us on the shoulder. I never thought that one day...'

He looked away and shook his head. The walls of the chamber seemed to fade, and Teclis looked out onto the vast, glittering space beyond. As far as the horizon an enormous pattern of light blazed. At its centre a cancerous darkness was eating away at it. Around that darkness blazing figures, elf-like but sky-tall, worked spells to keep it contained. Even as they did so, the darkness threatened to erupt in a different part of the pattern.

The walls returned. The chamber coalesced around them. Caledor, who had seemed for a moment to be one of those distant gigantic figures, was once more his stooped self, small and infinitely sad. 'We cannot do it. We are trapped here. We have screamed warnings in the dreams of the Wise. We have woven spells to summon aid to us. You are what we have been sent.'

'So she must be stopped,' Teclis said softly. 'What must I do?'

'You must return and tell the wizards of Hoeth to prepare for war. And you must prepare for war yourself.'

'Me? I am not a fighter.'

'You are of the blood of Aenarion. I doubt you will have a problem with killing.'

'It's the being killed I have a problem with.'

'Everything that lives has that problem.'

You do not, Teclis wanted to say. It was almost as if the old wizard could read his mind. 'I am no longer alive,' he said.

'I am sorry,' said Teclis.

'That makes two of us,' said Caledor. He tilted his head to one side, as if listening to something or someone very far away.

'Our time here is over.'

He rose from his chair with very great reluctance and walked as slowly as a prisoner going to his own execution towards the door. Every step seemed to take him a prodigious effort of will. He turned when he reached the door, his hand trembling on the handle.

'Farewell, Teclis, son of Arathion. Make sure your brother stays alive. If he falls, you fall and our world falls with you.'

Teclis did not know what to say. Caledor opened the door. The blazing inferno of the Vortex sprang into being behind him. Blast furnace heat washed across the room. Caledor stepped through the doorway and walked out onto the pattern, every step agonisingly slow. His body started to shrivel and burn as it had burned for over six thousand years. He raised his arms as if to cast a spell, a blazing figure crucified against the light, a weary ghost returning to hell to perform its final duties, of its own free will.

Watching him, Teclis knew he could not ever do that.

CHAPTER TWENTY-ONE

THE SCOUTS REPORTED back early in the evening. Dorian greeted them in his command tent. They were the best of their kind, males, trained from early childhood when they were abducted from their kindred on Death Night. They had proven early their gift for survival by living through being tossed into a cauldron of boiling blood. That had been the start of a lifetime of hardships that had made them among the best killers in a nation famed for its murderousness. Assassins of the Cult of Khaine.

'We have found the tournament ground, general,' said the assassin. 'It is where the king said it would be.'

'Did you ever doubt it?' Dorian asked, not because he thought the assassin ever had, but because he disliked him and his entire breed. They made him too nervous. They belonged to the Cult, body and soul, and it belonged to Morathi. It formed part of an extensive and alternative system of government to Malekith's. Rumour had it that the cults of pleasure performed the same function albeit in secret.

'Never,' said the assassin blandly.

'And they did not spot you or your brothers?'

'No, though we were close enough to the sentries to reach out and pluck hairs from their head.'

'I trust you engaged in no such frolics.'

'You seem determined to wilfully misconstrue everything I say, general. Do we have a problem, you and I?'

There was an obvious threat in the assassin's voice. Dorian would have had any one of his soldiers who spoke to him like that given over to the torturers but he could not do it to this elf and both of them knew it. Dorian felt compelled to let the assassin know he was not afraid of him either. 'If we did you would not now be standing here.'

The assassin inclined his head. 'That is the truth.'

He let his posture and his expression show that he believed that the reason for that would be that Dorian was dead, but the ambiguity of the response left honour satisfied on both sides. Dorian smiled to show that he understood that too.

'What did you find?'

'It is a vast tent city, full of armed elves but disorganised, more like a country fair in Bretonnia than an armed camp.'

'That is because it is a fair,' said Dorian. 'They do not expect an attack here of all places. Let us see to it that it remains so.'

'Quite,' said the assassin. 'My brothers scouted through it under cover of shadows. We have located the Pavilion Palace of the Everqueen.'

'It is guarded.' It was not a question.

'Yes, general, subtly and well. And even as we speak there is a great feast in which the Everqueen is surrounded by the pick of her potential champions.'

'Individually they will be formidable, but they are not a military force.

'True. There are a number of smaller forces, armed bodyguards of nobles and such. It amounts to a small army of warriors but it is not organised as an army. It is a collection of retinues.'

'Nonetheless, they will be able to fight.'

'And fight well, I do not doubt. But they should not be able to stand against a competently led attack.'

Dorian smiled, knowing the assassin had said that to cover his own back. He would have his own reports to make, to his own masters, and ultimately his mistress. Blame would need to be apportioned in case of failure and the assassin would see to it that it would not fall on him.

'You need not worry about that,' said Dorian, letting irony show in his own voice. 'I will see to it that everything goes according to plan.'

'I never for a moment doubt that, general,' said the assassin. 'Khaine's blessing on your blade.'

'And yours, and all your brethren. Tomorrow we will reap many souls for your master.'

'I look forward to making the offerings,' said the assassin. His smile was disquieting.

ALL OF THE elves competing in the tournament gathered in the great Pavilion of the Everqueen. It was a massive tent made of spider-silk and spiralborne thread, large as a palace and big enough inside to hold a full grown tree. Only magic made a structure of such enormous size possible.

Beneath the branches of the great oak, in the glow of magical floating lanterns, hundreds of trestle tables were set. They groaned under the weight of food and drink. Minstrels moved everywhere, singing the old songs and playing the old tunes. Over everything an air of almost feverish festivity hung.

Tyrion sat at the high table with the Everqueen, the captain of her guard and a number of her highest advisers, along with those candidates for the post of champion who had performed best in today's contest.

This was part of the test. They were under observation to see how they fitted in. They were being judged by the Everqueen and her advisers for their suitability in the role of companion and defender.

All of the elves were on their best behaviour, showing off their most polished manners, making their wittiest quips, eating and drinking sparingly and watching their rivals like hungry hawks.

It was fascinating for Tyrion to watch. Seemingly polite conversation was filled with traps designed to give one elf a chance to show off his knowledge and display the ignorance of his rivals.

One after the other, a number of conversational set pieces took place, each wittier than the next and each showing a dazzling knowledge of history and culture on the part of the person who inaugurated it.

It was like watching a sword fight. All of the competitors were very good at this sort of thing, Prince Perian perhaps most of all. He had a sly wit that reminded Tyrion of Prince Iltharis and he used it expertly to needle his fellow competitors before despatching them with an effortless quip.

Only Prince Arhalien seemed able to match Prince Perian and he did it politely, persuasively and without giving offence. Somehow he always seemed to be able to extricate himself from the most cunning conversational snares and all the while managed to maintain his image of good grace and good breeding.

Perhaps he came across as being a little stiff but that was no bad thing under the circumstances, Tyrion thought. He did not seem determined to put down his rivals and that made him seem refreshingly different and perhaps more diplomatic. If it was a strategy, it was a very good one.

Eventually, as he knew it must, the conversation settled on him. Prince Perian looked over at him and said, 'You're very quiet, Prince Tyrion.'

Tyrion felt all eyes upon him. He was very aware that the Everqueen was looking at him, as was the captain of her guard. Normally he did not feel particularly self-conscious. He was used to being the focus of attention but there was something about the gaze of the Everqueen that rankled him.

'I do not have very much to say,' Tyrion said.

'Prince Tyrion prefers to let his deeds speak for him,' said Prince Arhalien.

'I have never heard that being a great warrior was incompatible with being able to speak,' said Prince Perian.

'Certainly being able to speak is not incompatible with being a great warrior, as you have proven,' said Prince Arhalien.

'Surely, Prince Tyrion wishes to take part in the general conversation. We have not yet seen any examples of his scholarship.'

'Save with a blade,' said Arhalien.

'I cannot claim to be a great scholar,' said Tyrion. 'In my family that such honour belongs to my brother.'

'And why has your twin not chosen to enter the competition?' said Prince Perian. There was a sly smile on his lips. He had obviously heard about Teclis's infirmity.

'My brother is studying at the White Tower of Hoeth,' said Tyrion.

'I have heard he has good reason to hide away there,' said Prince Perian.

'I did not know he was hiding there,' said Tyrion. 'He certainly wasn't hiding when he went with me to Lustria and reclaimed the sword of Aenarion.'

'You reclaimed the sword of Aenarion. That's an interesting way of putting it,' said Prince Perian. 'Do you claim it is yours by right?'

Tyrion saw the trap waiting for him. To make any claim to the mantle of Aenarion would be boorish in the extreme, not to mention foolish. None could compare to the first Phoenix King. 'I claim it is mine because I found it and all those with any other legal claim are dead.'

'A scavenger's claim,' said Prince Perian. 'It is said your father has the dragon armour of Aenarion, you have his sword. It is a pity that the first Phoenix King never left a crutch. Your brother might have had it...'

It was a cruel joke and had obviously been long prepared. Tyrion merely smiled. 'You think Sunfang would have been better left in the hands of the lizardmen?'

Clearly it was not the response Prince Perian was expecting. He remained silent. Tyrion continued to speak.

'Or perhaps you think it ought to have been found by someone more suitable, such as yourself. If that is the case, all you had to do was spend ten years looking for it and venture into the jungles of Lustria. As my brother did.'

'I see you are determined to tell us the tale of your adventure,' said Prince Perian. 'You have picked a roundabout way of introducing the subject but nonetheless...'

'You talked about my brother needing a crutch,' said Tyrion. 'It seems to me that he has, perhaps, done more than you have, while enjoying far less of the benefits of good health.'

Prince Perian looked flushed. He obviously did not enjoy being told that a cripple was more heroic than he was, particularly since he was the one who had brought the subject up.

Tyrion looked around the table. It was hard to tell whether he had won or lost this particular sally. He suspected that neither he nor Prince Perian had come out of it looking particularly good.

It was going to be that sort of evening, he thought.

STILL GLAZED IN sweat from their furious lovemaking, Dorian leaned on one elbow and contemplated Cassandra's naked form. The sorceress was as beautiful as ever. He reached over from the silken bedroll and picked up some grapes and fed them into her mouth one at a time.

'Black grapes from the vineyards of Har Ganeth,' Cassandra said. 'And on campaign no less. I never expected to encounter such luxury in the field.' Her voice was low and husky, out of keeping with her slender form. As ever he found it strangely thrilling. Like her, he was sleeping with the enemy. That too was arousing in its way.

'My slaves packed them in a metal container full of ice from

Mount Ebonfang. They stored it in the ice-caves in the hull of the Black Ark to keep them cool. It has only been a few days since we left it.'

'And yet here we are,' she said. 'More than halfway across Ulthuan in a place I never thought we would see.'

Was she testing him, Dorian wondered, trying to draw out some sort of half-treasonous response so she could report it back to her superiors? She ought to know him better than that by now.

'I never doubted our king,' Dorian said.

'Never in public anyway,' she said with a smile. 'And never out loud. Nor will you ever. I said I did and I meant it.'

'Such words could be construed on as defeatism,' he said. 'Treason in time of war.'

'Will you report me?' Another test, he thought. Was she exchanging a confidence so that he would do the same? It was a time-honoured technique and he was too old to fall for it.

'I would if I thought you meant it.'

She smiled at his response. She looked a little sad tonight, he thought, which troubled him more than he cared to admit.

'Tell me, Dorian, do you ever tire of the ambiguity of our lives?'

He studied her face. He knew it very well. He had known it for a century. They had been on and off lovers for much of that time. There was an expression there he had never seen before. 'I am not even sure what you mean, Cassandra.'

'We fence. We lay traps for each other. We do not trust each other. We fear we will report each other to our masters. We watch every word we say, even here in a makeshift bed in an armed camp in an enemy land, and even though we may die tomorrow night.'

Her words hung in the air. He sensed they held more depth of meaning than usual, that their relationship was at some kind of junction, that something was in the air tonight that had never been there before. Or maybe that was just what she wanted him to think.

'Of course we do,' he said, choosing to make a joke of the thing. 'We are druchii. What else would we do?'

Her answering smile was brilliant and shallow. Her face had become a mask in the half-light, one he could not read at all. It was odd, like looking in the mirror and seeing the features of a stranger. A single bright jewel glittered on her cheek. Surely, it could not be a tear.

'I don't know. We live in the shadow of ancient terrors, you and I. We have spent our lives there. We trust no one because anyone could be the spy who undoes us – our sisters, our brothers, our parents, our lovers, our friends.'

'A druchii has no friends,' said Dorian. It was the punch line of an old joke which, like most jokes, had a core of uncomfortable truth to it.

'There are spies everywhere. The worst thing is that our system turns all of us into spies on each other. And even when we are not, we behave as if we were. That is very sad,' she said.

'You are in a strange mood tonight, Cass,' he said. He surprised himself by sounding almost sincere. 'What has brought this on?'

'I am frightened,' she said.

'There is nothing to be frightened of. Tomorrow we will win.'

'Tomorrow we go against a god. A very old god.'

'A very old god in a very new body which will not yet have learned to focus its power, and whose power is not warlike anyway.'

'And which nonetheless has survived since before the time of Aenarion. The Everqueen was sacred to our people once as well, Dorian.'

'Perhaps once, a long time ago, but we follow other gods now, stronger gods.' It was strange to find himself arguing the religious line with her. She knew so much more about these things than he. Which perhaps was why she was so upset, assuming this was not just another one of the endless loyalty tests.

'Yes, I know,' she said, very softly, before burying her face in the pillow. He reached out to stroke her hair. The gesture was oddly tentative, with a tenderness he had never really felt before. 'Do you ever wish we did not?'

He chose his words with care. 'It is pointless. We are who we are. We do what we must. We follow the gods of our people because they are the gods of our people.'

She laughed then and turned to look at him, her eyes shining wetly in the light. 'Loyal as ever, Dorian,' she said. He knew he had passed a test, but not one she had set him. He had failed that.

Perhaps the next time he spoke with the Witch King he would report her. Perhaps.

IN THE MORNING sunlight, Tyrion cantered over to the lists. Only twenty-four competitors remained today, those who had done best in the swordplay. He forced himself to relax and hold his lance in the upright position, pennon fluttering in the wind.

Each of the fighters drew lots to see who would face off against each other. Tyrion was pleasantly surprised to find out that he was drawn against Prince Perian. Seeing the draw, Perian smirked at Tyrion. He was obviously confident in his own prowess with a lance. All of the competitors then rode to the edges of the jousting area.

The first few bouts got under way with Prince Arhalien winning his easily. Tyrion had never seen another warrior use a lance so well. Prince Arhalien carried the lance as if it were an extension of his own body. He easily knocked aside his opponent's shield and then unhorsed the elf as part of the same flowing motion.

Tyrion had to admit that he was not nearly so good. When he was much younger, he had practised with a lance. It was part of his image of being a knight. As his career as a warrior had progressed, he had gradually stopped practising in favour of using weapons that would stand him in better stead on the sort of battlefields he was fighting on.

He had simply allowed himself to be good enough, by his own admittedly high standards, but he could see that he was little better than average with a lance compared to his fellow competitors. It was an odd sensation for him to be forced to admit to the possibility of losing even before he started.

He concentrated very hard on the technique of the other riders as the jousting progressed. One of his many gifts was that, when it came to combat, he was able to see things that would have taken other elves a lifetime to notice with just a glance.

It did not take long to pick up the finer points of using a lance from studying these experts. He was even fairly sure that he would be able to duplicate their use of technique when his own turn came.

Some people in the crowd were shouting his name. He was a favourite with a large section of the crowd. A lot of the women present seemed to like him. Only the number of Prince Arhalien's supporters seemed comparable. It was becoming obvious to Tyrion that on many levels and in many ways, Prince Arhalien was his true rival, no matter what Prince Perian thought.

After what seemed like an age, he and Prince Perian were called to face off against each other. Tyrion rode to one end of the jousting area and Prince Perian rode to the other. Tyrion waved at the crowd and was rewarded with cheers. Prince Perian did the same but his support was sparser.

The horns sounded. Tyrion applied his heels to the flanks of his horse and set it moving forward at a slow canter. It swiftly gained speed. The posts of the barrier blurred past.

Hoofbeats sounded like thunder in his ears. He was aware of the flow of muscles beneath him as his horse raced forward. The sun glittered on Prince Perian's helmet and the wind pushed back its crest. Tyrion leaned forward in the saddle to make himself a smaller target.

Prince Perian and his horse grew in Tyrion's field of vision. Tyrion dropped his lance into the attack position at the same time as his opponent. He angled his shield to deflect the blow that he fully expected to impact upon it.

This was as much about steadiness of nerve as it was about technique and skill. Now was the time when he would take the full measure of Prince Perian's ability.

Just before the moment when the point of Prince Perian's lance would impact upon his shield, Tyrion leaned slightly to one side and the lance skimmed past. Tyrion made no such mistake. His lance impacted squarely upon Prince Perian's shield and sent him tumbling out of the saddle and sprawling into the hoof-churned mud.

The crowd roared. Tyrion was through into the next round.

TYRION FACED PRINCE Arhalien. It was the worst possible draw. Arhalien was much better on horseback than he was and much better with a lance. Still, there was nothing he could do about that, other than his best.

He did not feel full of confidence as he rode up to the lists. Realistically, his chances of winning were very small, although he knew that there was always a chance that luck or a mistake by his opponent would turn things his way.

Things were not over yet. He would do his best. It was all he had ever done. It was all he would ever do.

The crowd were silent as the two warriors rode into position. They sensed that this was an important fight, that these two contestants were the most likely candidates to become the next champion.

Tyrion had already proved his mastery with the sword. Prince Arhalien had proved his mastery with a lance. If Tyrion won this contest then he would establish that he was the victor in combat, the best warrior among all of the contestants.

If Prince Arhalien won then the two of them would be equally matched and it would come down to the choice of the Everqueen and her advisers as to who would become champion. Tyrion suspected that in that case he would not be the victor.

He needed to win here if he was going to win the tournament

outright, and all of his previous ambivalence returned. He was not even sure that he wanted to win even now. He told himself that that was just an excuse that he was making to himself as a cover for potential defeat.

He took up his position at his end of the lists. He raised his lance into the classic position and, knowing all eyes were upon him, he made his steed rear and prance. Some of the crowd applauded, some of them waved, some of them cheered.

Prince Arhalien stood quietly at the far end of the tournament ground, waiting for the horns to sound with a quiet dignity that Tyrion envied. It was an unusual feeling for him.

At that moment in time, he realised that he had come to a crossroads in his life. Suddenly it was just there. The outcome of this contest was going to be very important for his future. All of his competitive instincts were engaged. He was going to win this.

The horns sounded. The horses thundered forward. The two warriors crashed together like comets colliding. For a brief, ecstatic moment Tyrion thought that he had his opponent, but at the last second Prince Arhalien raised a shield and deflected the tip of Tyrion's lance.

Tyrion found himself flying through the air, twisting to avoid a bad landing. The wind went out of him as he hit the ground. The crowd roared and stamped and cheered and he realised that they were not roaring and stamping and cheering for him. They were chanting Prince Arhalien's name.

Tyrion lay on the ground and looked at the sky. So this was what defeat felt like, he thought. Clouds drifted across his field of vision. He felt strangely relaxed and depressed and not a little angry with himself. Nonetheless, he forced himself to get to his feet and walk over to where Prince Arhalien waited and salute him with good grace. Prince Arhalien responded in kind and Tyrion resisted the urge to curse him.

Spectators ran onto the field to congratulate Prince Arhalien.

They paid no attention to Tyrion as he limped away, pained and weary. For the rest of the long afternoon, he watched from the stands.

He had lost.

CHAPTER TWENTY-TWO

BY THE LIGHT of the full moon, Dorian watched the long columns of troops filter through the forest. The woods were dark and spectral, the trees huge and ancient. The druchii went without lights, relying on moonlight to illuminate their way. They moved mostly silently save for the occasional hissing of a Cold One. The great reptiles had been muzzled to stop them from bellowing.

Up ahead the assassins would be killing the sentries guarding the tournament grounds. Dorian looked over at Cassandra. Whatever doubts she might have had last night, there were none showing on her face. She looked calm and poised. Power glowed within her. She was ready to unleash deadly magic at the first sign of trouble.

Dorian felt unease in the pit of his stomach. He had to work hard to conceal it. If anything was going to go wrong, it would go wrong now. All it would take would be for one assassin to make a mistake, for one sentry to give the alarm...

And then what, he asked himself? What did it matter? This army was a huge force, disciplined and well-trained. Even if the alarm was given, what could the asur do against them? Individually they might be great warriors, but this was not going to be single combat.

Dorian knew that on the field of battle individual bravery counted for little if the tactics and formations were wrong. Even the greatest of warriors could be surrounded and cut down, or be shot from a distance or immobilised with spells or poisoned crossbow bolts. His force was well-equipped with all of those.

Perhaps the Everqueen would work some strange sorcery, or the enchantments that were said to surround her would overcome his troops. Dorian discounted that possibility. That was why Malekith had equipped them with those protective amulets.

The greatest danger was that some warning might reach the Everqueen and her bodyguard might spirit her away out of reach. If that happened Dorian had better fall on his sword, for the vengeance of Malekith would be swift and terrible. The Witch King rewarded failure with painful death.

Again and again, he went over things in his mind. He had prepared for every contingency he could think of. At least six companies would converge on the Pavilion Palace of the Everqueen. More warriors waited in the woods to scoop up anyone who fled.

The worst thing that was likely to happen was that the snatch would be bungled and the Everqueen would be shot down while trying to escape. He doubted Malekith would be overjoyed with that eventuality. Still, it would be preferable to letting Alarielle escape.

Be calm, he told himself. Nothing can possibly go wrong.

THE NIGHT SEEMED astonishingly quiet after the clamour within the Everqueen's Pavilion. Tyrion strolled through the darkness towards his tent. He felt odd after his defeat by Prince Arhalien. He was not used to being beaten, and beaten in such a public way.

He had been subdued at the feasting and had not even risen to Prince Perian's taunting. Fortunately the other elf did not seem to have much heart for it either. His defeat by Tyrion had put him well out of the running. His sneers did not have their usual confident edge.

All around, the elves were still revelling. A group of dancers skipped by, flowers wound into their hair, male and female intertwined. They had wineskins in their hands. One of them carried a lute. They begged Tyrion to accompany them but he turned them down as gracefully as he could. Tyrion wondered if he should seek out Lyla and distraction, but he was not in the mood. He wanted to return to his own tent and simply sleep.

Tomorrow, he would feel better. He looked up at the great moon that filled the sky. It seemed brighter here in Avelorn than it did elsewhere in Ulthuan. This place was so peaceful, he thought, so different from the hustle and bustle of Lothern. There were aspects of that he liked, that calmed his mind in a way that he had never felt it needed to be calmed before. It occurred to him that he would miss this place when he went away.

Atharis raised a goblet to him as he approached the tent. He lay there on a rug with the other members of Tyrion's retinue, drowning his sorrows with narcotic wine. Tyrion smiled at them all and walked past. He was not in the mood for company.

He entered his tent and threw himself down on his sleeping mat. He pulled a blanket across him and lay there listening to the sounds of the night. After the events of the day sleep would not come.

Being within the silken walls of the tent did something to him. By restricting his field of vision it made his other senses more keen. He lay there in the dark, thinking about his life and what he was going to do with it after this.

If the Everqueen preferred Prince Arhalien, and it seemed only logical that she would, then he would return to Lothern and take up trading once more. He needed to rebuild his fortunes and some raiding of the coasts of Naggaroth seemed like a good way of doing that.

Druchii were on his mind, as he drifted off the edge of sleep's precipice.

DORIAN'S FORCE EXPLODED into the tournament camp. Many of the high elves were asleep alone, in pairs or in groups. Others were revelling still, drunk on wine and laughter. Most of them had no idea what was happening even as they witnessed it.

All they saw were warriors who looked like them coming out of the forest. No alarm had been given so they could not be a threat. But why then did the newcomers have naked blades in their hands...

The scene repeated itself a hundred times on Dorian's way to the Pavilion Palace. Asur looked up surprised, dazed, a little confused. Sometimes they would smile as if they were witnessing a joke or a hallucination. Only a few looked frightened. Even fewer reached for weapons. Why should they? They were safe at the Everqueen's court. No enemy could possibly reach them, and certainly not in such force.

Dorian had seen similar things countless times in the past on slave raids along the coasts of the Old World. It took time to adjust to bad news and no one wants to believe that terrible things can happen, even as the event unfolds before their very eyes.

The difference was that this time it was elves being taken off guard, knowing fear and surprise. It did not really make all that much difference. Taken off guard, most living things behave like sheep.

He led his guard company towards the great Pavilion, ignoring those who scrambled to get out of his way, knowing that the companies following him would deal with those.

Beside him, Cassandra's face was calm. A slight smile played on her lips. Like him, she could see that this was going to work, that everything was going to be all right. Her hand still played with the amulet that Malekith had given them though.

He pushed on towards the tent, proud of the way his warriors marched in lockstep, spearing those asur who got too close, but otherwise concentrating on the objective and trusting in their comrades behind them to watch their backs. It was a very fine display of druchii discipline.

Somewhere off to the right someone screamed. There was a smell of burning on the wind. Things were starting to get out of control, he realised. People were starting to emerge from the tents to see what was happening. Many of them gawped. A few were cut down by crossbow bolts slashing out of the darkness. None of them seemed to have quite grasped what was going on yet.

The great Pavilion rose out of the darkness ahead of him. By Khaine, it was immense, the sort of thing Malekith might have taken into the field with him if he wanted to banquet his whole court. It was not a practical structure, not military, but it was beautiful. He could appreciate that as he looked upon it. The thing had been created with magic and with love to contain the living goddess of the asur.

A cruel smile twisted his lips. After tonight they would mourn the loss of their deity. She would be a slave of Malekith, bound to obey the Witch King's every whim. Dorian wondered what it would be like to have a goddess as his slave. Perhaps he would find out for himself, if only for a short time.

Female warriors guarded the entrance of the Pavilion. They looked up as they saw Dorian's force approach. Even at this distance he could see their eyes widen and read the expression on their faces. They were not quite sure what they were seeing, but they at least were on guard and they knew their duty. They raised warning horns to their lips to give the alarm. Crossbow bolts cut them down before they could sound it.

Dorian strode on, heading towards the entrance, pausing only to let his own guard precede him. As he did so, Cassandra gestured for him to halt, and cast a spell. The air glowed then she gestured for him to proceed. He was not sure what had happened but he had seen enough examples of her work in the past to know she did nothing without reason.

As they passed within, she said, 'No deadly wards, only alarms. The Everqueen is too kind-hearted to risk the chance of any harm accidentally befalling her subjects.'

Dorian nodded to show he understood. The same could certainly not be said of their own rulers. He wondered what it must be like to live in a world where the kings and queens did not fear violent death at the hands of their subjects. He guessed he would never know.

After this campaign Malekith would rule the world and his word would be law everywhere.

TYRION AWOKE FROM a troubled sleep, wondering what was happening. He could hear screams coming from all around him. He could smell burning, which seemed somehow obscene in this part of the sacred woods. Then he heard something else, something that chilled his blood, something he had heard in other parts of the world but that he had never thought to hear here – the war cries of dark elves.

His first thought was that it was some sort of joke. It did not seem possible that the sons of Naggaroth could've been able to penetrate so far into Ulthuan without any warning being given. In fact, it *was* impossible. Unless an entire army had been cloaked by some sort of invisibility spell, it could not be done. Even then he was fairly sure that magic on that scale would have been detected by the wizards of Ulthuan.

He shrugged. It was all very well telling himself that what he was hearing was impossible, but he was still hearing it. He had known warriors to die from simply standing around trying to decide how to react during a surprise attack. He was not going to be one of those.

Having come to a decision, the rest was easy. He buckled on the armour that was within his reach, unsheathed Sunfang and stepped out into the burning darkness. Corpses lay everywhere. Two of his companions lay with spear wounds in their sides. Atharis stared at the sky. He looked as if he might have been drunk, but there was a huge gash in his throat from which blood poured.

Shadowy figures erupted from the bushes around him. Bloody blades stabbed out at him. A warrior less quick of reflex would have died in that moment. Tyrion sprang lithely to one side, twisting to avoid a blow that should have gutted him.

Sunfang lashed out in response, leaving a blazing trail through the darkness. It crashed into the helmet of one dark elf warrior, cleaving it in two and splitting the skull beneath. Blood and brains flew everywhere, splattering against Tyrion's chest and arm.

He did not let it slow him down. He kept moving, shifting his position to confuse his enemies, sending his blade flickering across their fields of vision, knowing that its light would ruin their night-sight and give him some slight advantage in the ensuing melee.

He was certain that his foes were dark elves now. They spoke with the accents of Naggaroth and their wargear bore its unmistakable stamp. They fought with the disciplined organisation so typical of the inhabitants of their dreary northern land.

These were hardened veterans. They responded to his actions quickly and well, not in the least taken aback to find themselves facing an opponent of his skill. The fury of his onslaught did not dismay them. They fell back before him, not panicking despite the fact that he slaughtered another two of them as they did so.

Lesser troops would have fled under the circumstances, to have the table so suddenly turned on them in the darkness, but these warriors held their ground as best they could and fought back with the fury of maddened panthers.

The foes he faced were only one small part of the attacking army.

All around him he could hear the sounds of butchery taking place in the darkness and he could tell from the screams of the victims that most of those people dying were his own folk.

How many dark elves were there out there? Far more than there should have been, of that he was certain. Once again the thought returned to him that this was impossible, that these ruthless foemen could not be here and yet they were.

Even as he killed and killed again, the sheer impossibility of it bothered him. An army could not move in secrecy the way this one had done. Not unless sorcery was involved and sorcery on a scale that had rarely been seen in this world since the time of Aenarion.

There was something about the situation that nagged at him though, something familiar and yet strange that he felt he should be able to remember, and that he might possibly be able to do so if he were not fighting for his life.

Mere heartbeats had passed since he heard the first screams. It seemed much longer, in the way that it always did when he was in combat. Time always seemed to dilate under the circumstances. He struck down another dark elf and tried to work out what was going on.

Why were the druchii attacking here and now? Forget about the impossibility of it – that was obviously an illusion. They were here for a reason and in that moment it struck him what that reason was.

They were after the Everqueen. It was the only possible reason why they would attack here and now. Their intelligence gathering must have been extraordinarily effective, he thought, to know her whereabouts and be able to dispatch such a force to find her.

Once again, that was irrelevant. All that mattered was that he prevent them from achieving their goal, no matter what the cost. If the Everqueen fell into the hands of the dark elves, it would be the most terrible blow to afflict his people since the time of Aenarion.

Nothing quite so dreadful had ever happened before. If the

Everqueen was to die it would wreak havoc with the morale of the high elves. If she was to become a prisoner of the Witch King it would be even worse. With her as his hostage, he would be able to dictate terms in any subsequent peace that would be enormously to his advantage. That was if there was a peace and he was not seeking an outright victory and the total annihilation of the forces of Ulthuan.

Tyrion knew that whatever happened, he must find Alarielle and save her. His personal feelings counted for nothing under the circumstances. He must do his duty to his people. He must save the Everqueen.

DORIAN BURST INTO the inner chamber of the great Pavilion. Dead elf maidens lay sprawled on the floor, their swords close at hands. They had died like warriors, he thought approvingly, their wounds to the front. He hoped when his own time came he would be able to do the same.

At bay in the centre of the room, back to the great central pole, standing on a great carpet woven with scenes of grace and beauty, was the single most beautiful woman Dorian had ever seen, perhaps excepting Morathi. Even through the wards of the amulets protecting him, he felt the tug of reverence and even love.

He knew he was committing a sacrilege by being here and he wanted to beg her pardon and ask her forgiveness. He realised how clever his master had been launching the attack now. If this was how it felt before the new Everqueen possessed her full power, even through the protective spells of his amulet, what would it be like to enter her presence once she had her full strength?

Ruthlessly Dorian quashed his feelings of awe. 'Good evening, your majesty,' he said in his coldest parade ground voice. 'I bring you greetings from my master, Malekith the Great, true king of all the elves.'

The realisation of her predicament flashed across that beautiful face. In that moment, and just for that moment, she was no longer a living goddess but a frightened young elf woman realising that she was in peril, alone and surrounded by enemies who could not but mean her harm.

He did not feel sorry for her. He felt only contempt for one whose pampered existence had not prepared her for even the possibility of an experience like this.

The confusion and fear was only there for a moment before command reasserted itself. For an instant something infinitely old and wise looked out of her eyes. She opened her mouth to say something, perhaps speak a spell. At that moment, two of his guards grasped her, immobilising her arms. Another placed his hands over her mouth. Cassandra swiftly gagged her. She was cast down on her sleeping silks, limbs bound with whipcord.

Dorian and Cassandra exchanged triumphant looks. For both of them this was the supreme moment of their lives. They had captured the Everqueen. Malekith would reward them with kingdoms. His mouth felt dry. His heart raced. His dark druchii nature asserted itself. He wanted to howl with exultation. Instead he clenched his fist and placed his foot on the recumbent form of the bound goddess. Part of him wanted to kick her until she was a bloody corpse, but that would not fulfil the terms of his orders.

Outside, screams filled the night. Smoke drifted on the air. There was the sound of weapons clashing. The massacre had truly begun. It would not end till morning.

TYRION RAN TOWARDS the Everqueen's Pavilion. He could see that the dark elf troops were densest around about it. The bodies of the Maiden Guard lay sprawled everywhere, staring at the sky with sightless eyes. Tyrion had no time for regrets, to feel sorry for the dead. His business was with the living, assuming that the Everqueen was still alive. He believed that she would be, for that was what would make more strategic sense.

Charging into a horde of armed soldiers would not serve either Alarielle or himself. All that was likely to happen is that he would die a quick death and that the Everqueen would remain in captivity, assuming that was what had happened.

He needed a plan and he needed to come up with one quickly if he was to avert disaster. Mighty warrior though he might be, potent magical blade that Sunfang was, they were no match for an army. What was needed here was intelligence, not a strong arm.

He doubled back, moving away from the vast body of dark elf troops. He remembered the bodies of the warriors he had slain. They were wearing the armour of his enemies and that was something he could put to good use.

Swiftly he chose the armour belonging to the corpse whose head he had split and stripped it off. It was bloody, but on a night like this that would not matter. It would simply add to the authenticity of his disguise. He took the helmet from another dark elf corpse and put that on.

He wished he had a mirror so that he could check how he looked, but that was like wishing for an army of high elves to come out of the forest and save him – it was not going to happen. He was going to have to trust in the darkness and confusion all around him and hope that he was not cut down by any surviving high elves who might mistake him for one of the enemy.

He took a deep breath, stepped out of the shadows and began to move confidently towards the Pavilion as if he had every right to be among the attackers. He kept his shoulders pulled back and did his best to imitate the marching stride of one of the sons of Naggaroth.

In the howling confusion no one questioned him. No one paid the slightest attention to him being there. The fighting was all but over. The dark elves were triumphant. They grinned at each other like warriors who know they are in possession of the field. There was an exultant look in their eyes and cold smiles on their lips. That more than anything chilled Tyrion's heart. He knew those expressions from his own career as a soldier. He'd worn similar ones when he was victorious in battle and noticed them on the faces of his comrades.

If ever he had had any hope that the situation might be salvaged, it vanished then. He was on his own. If he wanted to, he could probably escape now, using his disguise to get clear of the dark elf force and vanish into the woods.

He considered it for a heartbeat, but knew that he could not do so if there was even the slightest chance that Alarielle was being held captive. He could not abandon this place without finding that out. It was the least he could do.

All around him, discipline was starting to break down even among the hardened druchii. The certainty of victory affected even the cold-hearted children of the uttermost north. Soldiers were starting to collect loot and slaves. He could hear the screams of prisoners being tortured and raped.

Tyrion hardened his heart. Even if he could rescue those who were in pain, he could not do that now. He had a mission of the utmost importance and he could allow nothing to distract him from that. But he swore in his heart that the dark elves would pay with interest for every scream they extracted from the lips of one of his own people.

Much to his surprise, the Pavilion was still upright. It was surrounded by druchii warriors who still looked alert and disciplined. They had the aura of elite troops, ones who might be entrusted with a mission of the gravest importance. Not for a moment did Tyrion doubt that he was in the right place. The question was how he was going to get inside.

One of the soldiers stared at him. It would be suspicious of him to back away now and he might be remembered if he returned in the future, so he squared his shoulders and strode confidently forward, as if he had every business being there, was on a mission of some importance.

He must have looked the part because no one questioned him as he strode within and made his way to the central chamber of the tent. There were several high officers, he recognised their rank from their garb. He had fought against that type before on many battlefields. In the centre, lying prostrate with her arms bound behind her back, and a gag on her mouth, was Alarielle. She stared at him with hate-filled eyes as he came in. She did not recognise him.

One of the high staff officers turned to look at him. Tyrion strode forward.

'What do you want?' the officer asked. 'What are you doing here, sergeant?'

'I bring a message from the commander,' said Tyrion. He was almost within striking distance now.

'What?'

'It is of the utmost importance,' said Tyrion.

'It had better be or I will have you flayed alive,' the officer said.

'I do not doubt it.'

'Then spit it out,' the officer said.

'It concerns the Everqueen. There's been a change of plans.'

'Impossible!'

'No,' said Tyrion. He drew Sunfang and decapitated the officer. With two more quick strokes he chopped down his companions. In a flurry of blows, he struck down the remaining dark elves within reach. Most of them died clawing for their weapons, desperately trying to react to the sudden fury of his onslaught.

DORIAN WONDERED WHAT was happening. A burning blade chopped down Captain Aeris and slashed off half of Captain Manion's face. The stench of seared flesh suddenly filled the Pavilion. Had one of the druchii gone mad, he wondered, or was this some kind of sorcery? Were the Everqueen's powers still at work?

Even as that thought occurred to him, Alarielle rolled away from beneath his feet, sending him tumbling backwards. That action probably saved his life, unintentionally, for he fell out of the way of that blazing sword. He felt the red heat of it mere fingers' breadths from his face. He saw the warrior wielding the blade leap among his guard, slashing left and right as he went.

Maniac or not, the newcomer was eye-blurringly swift. He made the hardened veterans of Dorian's guard seem like children. They could do nothing to stop him. They did not even seem to be trying. They had been taken completely off guard by the sudden, stunning savagery of the stranger's attack. He recalled his own thoughts about how people responded to surprise attacks earlier. It seemed his own troops were no more immune to it than anyone else. Sheep, he thought.

Cassandra raised her hand as she attempted to cast a spell. Somehow the stranger was aware of it before she even half began. He pounced like a great cat springing. The brilliantly glowing blade slashed downwards. The protective spells surrounding Cass overloaded, burning out in a blaze of power. The sword smashed into her, snapping bones like twigs, cauterising flesh as it passed through.

'No,' Dorian shouted, rising to his feet. This could not be happening, he thought. Life and victory could not be snatched away from them so quickly. He remembered Cass's forebodings of the previous night. It seemed they had come true, since Alarielle had summoned this daemonic warrior to her aid.

He ripped his sword from its scabbard and just managed to parry as the stranger was upon him. Dorian was gifted with a blade, and he knew it. He was considered among the best in the entire druchii army.

Somehow though, he instantly found himself on the defensive. It was all he could do to parry the newcomer's weapon. The light from it dazzled his eyes in the gloom.

The fury of the stranger's attack was astonishing. He struck with the speed and power of a lightning bolt. Dorian's arm was numb just from maintaining his increasingly desperate parries. He would have liked to have gone on the offensive. He would have liked to have avenged Cass but there was no chance of it. He could barely find the time or the energy to shout for help. It took all of his concentration merely to stay alive.

There was something about the newcomer's style that reminded Dorian of his brother Urian. It had the same fluidity, and the same tricky manner of placing a feint within a feint, so that you never knew where the true attack was going to come from. It was almost as if this newcomer had been a pupil of his brother. Was it possible that this was some incredible feat of treachery?

Even as the question entered Dorian's mind, the stranger's sword found its way past his guard. Volcanic agony erupted in Dorian's side and he fell forward into darkness.

So this was death at last, he thought, come when he least expected it.

'QUICKLY! STOP HIM! He's getting away,' Tyrion shouted, to send the guards outside sniffing down the wrong trail. He strode over to the Everqueen, tore off the gag, and slashed her bonds. She stared at him for a moment then her eyes widened and he saw the flash of recognition. 'Prince Tyrion!' she said.

'None other.' He strode to the opposite side of the Pavilion and slashed it with his sword. 'Come with me,' he said. 'We are getting out of here.'

She nodded, and dived through the gap he had created. He followed her out into the night.

'This way,' Tyrion said. He grabbed her by the hand and began to drag her through the undergrowth.

'We need to keep low and not be seen. If we are lucky they won't pick up our trail for a while. I can't imagine they brought hounds with them and there's been so much chaos around here, it will be difficult to pick up our tracks.'

'Sorcery,' she said. 'They will have wizards.'

'I was rather hoping you could do something about that.'

She stared and he saw the black hopelessness in her eyes. 'Why? What chance have we got of getting out of here, Prince Tyrion? The dark elves are already in Avelorn. They have killed my guard, my friends, my people. I have already failed in my trust.'

Tyrion shook her. 'You are alive. And while you are alive there is hope. What chance do we have? I don't know. I do know we will have no chance at all if we give up.'

She nodded but she did not seem to understand. Tyrion had seen the same look and same reaction written on the faces of young warriors after their first battle in which they had lost friends and comrades.

It must be worse for her. She was the Everqueen. She had grown up in luxury. She had never expected to see war or its aftermath.

'Listen to me,' he said. 'You are our queen. You were chosen by the gods. You are the heart of our realm. If you give up, we may as well all just surrender to Malekith. He will become king after all these millennia of waiting. Is that what you want?'

Slowly understanding came back into her eyes. He saw a powerful will begin to reassert itself. The moment of weakness and panic had passed. She was herself again.

'There is no need to clutch me so tightly, Prince Tyrion. You have made your point.' He let go of her arm. He could see he had grabbed her so tightly that he had left his the print of his hand on the flesh of her arm. 'You have a plan?' she asked.

Tyrion shrugged. 'I never thought beyond making sure you were alive and getting you out.'

'I have heard people say you had a gift for strategy,' she said. 'That you are a war leader of great cunning.'

'I did get you out,' he said.

She seemed to come to a decision.

'Where did you get that armour?'

'I stripped it from a corpse.'

'We need another set.'

Tyrion nodded. He understood what she was thinking.

'They might take us for deserters.'

'It will be enough if it gets us clear of this awful place. And I would feel somewhat less vulnerable.'

'Have you ever worn armour before?'

'I can learn.'

Tyrion knew how easy it would be to allow themselves to stand here discussing things until they were captured. It was a natural reaction. They had found a small island of safety. Their instincts told them to cling to its shores. Tyrion knew how easily such instincts could betray them.

'Wait here!' he told her. 'I'll be back.'

'What?'

'If someone sees me, I am just another dark elf soldier. If they see you...'

He did not need to explain any more. Behind him he could hear the sound of one voice rising over the babble. It seemed like someone was taking charge of the situation. It would not be long before the hunt began in earnest.

DORIAN ROLLED OVER. His side hurt immensely. When he touched it, it was wet but with a clear pus instead of blood. The burning blade had cauterised the wound even as it made it.

He had no idea whether he would live or how much internal damage there really was. Looking around the chamber he could see he was lucky to be alive. Every other druchii that had been present was dead, including Cassandra. She lay on her back, eyes open, but glazed as if she was staring in wonder at the tent ceiling. Her face looked normal but her body was ruined.

Dorian crawled over to where she lay and took her hand. It was cold. Soldiers flooded into the room, glaring around at the scene of carnage.

'What happened, general?' one of them asked. Dorian struggled to answer them.

'An elf with a burning sword,' he said. 'He killed us all and took the Everqueen.'

His soldiers looked at him as if he were raving, but they could not see any other explanation. 'Find him,' Dorian ordered. 'Find him or you are all for Malekith's torturers.'

He was already for that himself, he realised. The stranger had done him no favours letting him live. He lay there on the ground, holding Cassandra's cold hand, and found that he did not care all that much.

'PUT THOSE ON,' Tyrion said.

He pointed to the body of the dead elf soldier he had dragged into the undergrowth. Alarielle looked at the corpse in distaste but she began to strip it of the wargear.

'Did you kill her?' she asked.

'I cut her throat,' said Tyrion. She looked at him with distaste.

'That was not very chivalrous,' she said. He understood why she was saying it. She understood the necessity of what he had done but she was still shocked by it. She felt the need to vent her feelings, to do something to relieve her tension and fear. If that meant she despised him, so be it. He could live with that.

'This is not a tournament,' he said. 'This is war. People will die. You will send them to their deaths and you will smile while you do it.'

'I already caused a death, didn't I?' She indicated the dead warrior with her foot. 'I killed her when I sent you to get me a disguise.'

'Get used to it,' he said, knowing he was being brutal, but knowing also that he needed to make her understand the reality of the situation. 'It will be the first of many.'

'You enjoy this, don't you, Prince Tyrion?'

The answer was too complex to be gone into here so he just said, 'Yes. It is what I was born for.'

'Blood of Aenarion,' she said softly. He was surprised to hear pity in her voice. She stripped and put on the soldier's undergarments then her leather tunic and then her armour. Tyrion stood close and helped her do it. She had no experience with this sort of gear, so much was obvious. As he helped lace up the jerkin, they were close as lovers. He was suddenly very aware of her presence.

They stepped apart. 'We need to go,' he said. 'They will be looking for us now.'

* * *

WHAT HAD BEEN a place of pleasure had become a place of terror. Corpses were strewn everywhere, cut down in flight, in combat, while they had slept, while they had been drunk. The dark elves had spared no one. They had killed like maniacs, as senselessly as a wolverine in a henhouse.

Tyrion felt his heart become colder. A great rage was building up in him. This was not how a war should be fought. His expression became as cold and grim as a true son of Naggaroth. The Everqueen looked upon his face and shuddered. He did not care and he did not want to explain to her how he was feeling.

'This was not war,' she said. Tyrion agreed with her. This had gone far beyond war. It was a murderous venting of long suppressed rage.

'It is now,' he said. 'This is what war looks like now.'

She shot him a sidelong glance. 'Do they really hate us so?'

'Apparently.'

They followed a path deeper into the woods. Tyrion had no idea where they were going. He was not familiar with this place. He was merely trying to get as far away from pursuit as possible. 'Do you know where we are?' he asked.

She nodded. 'We are on the old game trail to the Glade of Promises.'

'Beyond that?'

'What do you mean?'

'We must find refuge for you. A place where you will be safe.'

She looked as if she wanted to cry. 'Avelorn was safe. If I was not safe in the heart of my own realm where will I be?'

'I don't know,' Tyrion said. 'But we will need to find somewhere.'

'You sound very angry, Prince Tyrion.'

'And you are not?'

'I have not had time to feel very much of anything, except afraid.'

'It is our enemies who will be afraid by the time we are finished,' Tyrion said. He knew he sounded petulant, like a small boy telling his friends that one day he would get even with a bully, but he meant it. One day there would be a reckoning for the carnage here. He would make the Witch King and all his minions pay.

'How could this have happened?' Alarielle asked.

'We were too confident,' Tyrion said. 'We thought the threat of Naggaroth had ended. It had not. There is only one way it ever will be. When the Witch King and all who follow him are dead.'

'I meant how did they find me? How did they get such a force into the heart of Avelorn? It should have not been possible. Our scouts should have seen them. The Eagles would have spotted them from afar.'

'Magic would be my guess, but what sort I do not know. It is a subject I know very little about. My brother would know more.'

'Chaos has returned to the world,' Alarielle said. 'I feel it. It is always there now, far in the distance, a great cancer eating away at the heart of the world. The winds of magic are tainted. Shadows lengthen, even here in Avelorn.'

'You think this has something to do with the invasion?'

'All things are connected. There is more power and more evil in the air than there has been for a very long time.'

How would you know? Tyrion wanted to ask. You are younger than me and I am not old as elves measure time. He kept his mouth shut. He would have sounded foolish anyway, for the Everqueen inherited more than a title when she was crowned. Who knew what hidden knowledge was available to her? Who knew what magical powers?

'Can you help us? Can you use your magic to shield us?' he asked.

'I will do what I can,' she said. 'My powers were not intended for warfare.'

'Anything you could do would help. We are on our own here.'

She seemed to realise the pressure that was on him. 'You have done your best for me, Prince Tyrion, and I will be forever grateful.'

'My best may not be good enough. There is an army out there

and they are hunting for you. Who knows what they will do when they find you?'

'Let us pray I never find out,' she said.

'Who shall we pray to?' Tyrion asked. 'Our gods seem to have deserted us.'

'One of your gods is still with you,' she said.

'Let us make sure it stays that way,' he said. They set off deeper into the dark woods. Behind them Avelorn burned.

ABOUT THE AUTHOR

The first of **William King**'s sixteen novels for the Black Library, *Trollslayer*, was published in 1999. He is the creator of the much-loved Gotrek & Felix series and the Space Wolf novels starring Ragnar Blackmane. William King's much anticipated return to the worlds of Warhammer has brought to life a new trilogy, the Tyrion & Teclis series, for which the first novel, *Blood of Aenarion*, was shortlisted for the *David Gemmell Legend* award. His novel *Angel of Fire* features the legendary Warhammer 40,000 hero, Lord Solar Macharius.

COMING DECEMBER 2013

WILLIAM KING

WARHAMMER

BANE OF MALEKITH

A TYRION & TECLIS NOVEL

THE THIRD BOOK IN THE TYRION & TECLIS TRILOGY

An *extract from* Bane of Malekith
by William King

On sale December 2013

TYRION LOOKED OUT of their rocky hiding place and studied their
enemies. Alarielle had chosen it because it would be impossible
for their foes to track them over this ground. She had gone off and
left a false trail beyond it and circled back to him. He had not liked
letting her out of his sight, but he had no choice. She knew about
these matters and he did not.

They had been running for most of the day and no matter how
they tried, it seemed impossible to outdistance the pursuit. Always,
the woods were full of the sounds of horns and druchii battle-calls,
as the various components of the army kept in touch. Gradually,
some of the noises had faded into the distance, but others had
managed to keep up, no matter how quickly he and Alarielle ran.

Looking back now, he could see why. These were not standard
infantry. They were lightly armed and armoured and moved with

the easy authority of the highest echelons of combat troops.

Their very appearance here was shocking. The dark elves moved confidently along the trail. They gave every impression of being at home, of having utter confidence in their right to be there in the heart of the most sacred place in elvendom. There was no fear in the way they walked. They were the hunters, not the hunted.

The cockiness in their manner almost compelled Tyrion to leap out and slay them. An insane anger burned deep in him, filling him with the urge to rend and slay. He wanted to wipe the confident smile off the smug face of the dark elf sergeant giving orders to his troops. He wanted to see fear blossom in the eyes of the two druchii warriors sharing a joke, doubtless at asur expense. His hand tightened on the hilt of Sunfang.

A hand gripped his. He turned and glared angrily at Alarielle. She shook her head. *I can kill them all,* he wanted to say. There were only a score of them. With the advantage of surprise, and the power of Sunfang, it was possible he could do it too, even with the Everqueen clinging to his arm.

He let out a long breath, realising how mad the thoughts cascading through his brain had suddenly become. Attacking a score of armed veterans was not a sensible thing to do. The chances were that he could not kill them all, and even if he could he might be wounded or slain in the process. It was a mad risk and there was nothing to be gained from it, save the satisfaction of a bloodlust that he had never even suspected he possessed.

Was this the Curse of Aenarion finally coming on him in full force? Or was it something else? Had the wound from the witch elf's blade infected him with something else, a taste of their reckless madness perhaps? He stayed frozen in place, waiting tensely to see if the dark elves discovered their trail.

One of them bent down and said something to the others. Had he spotted a track? Tyrion readied himself to spring into action if that was the case. It looked like his bloodlust might be slaked after all. Part of him would have welcomed it.

He could feel Alarielle tense beside him. If the dark elves overcame him, she might end up their prisoner once more. If that happened she would eventually end up within Malekith's iron-gauntleted grasp.

After a long moment, he felt her exhale. The dark elves moved on, still scanning the woods around them, hunters seeking prey. It seemed like a very long time before they were out of sight.

Tyrion and Alarielle lay in the undergrowth, slumped out of sight, close as lovers. Eventually they smiled at each other. It seemed that danger had passed them by for a while. Some buried instinct urged him to stay here, but he knew it was foolish. The horns in the distance were coming closer. It was only a matter of time before the larger force of druchii overhauled them and they would have the numbers to search thoroughly. They needed to get moving by another path than the ones the pursuing scouts had taken.

Reluctantly, he rose from the hard ground. He felt a small sharp pain in his side, where the witch elf had wounded him. It seemed to be getting worse.

ALARIELLE STOPPED WALKING, raised her head and looked around. 'What was that?' she asked. Her jawline was set tight and every muscle was tense. Tyrion reached out to touch her shoulder and he could feel the tightness of the muscles beneath. She shrugged off his touch and glanced around, wary as a deer that has caught the scent of a hunter.

He understood why. There was a sudden tension in the air that had not been there before. Fewer birds sang. Fewer small creatures moved through the undergrowth. He realised how tightly wound the Everqueen must be to spot this before he did. Normally he was the person most aware of his surroundings. She gestured for him to take cover and threw herself under a nearby bush. Tyrion burrowed into the undergrowth, not a moment too soon.

A group of druchii emerged into the clearing, moving carefully and calmly. They carried small hand crossbows and had wicked looking blades at their sides. Their movement was stealthy. There was something shadowy about them. They looked like creatures of the night, feral, predatory and deadly.

Their leader studied the ground where Tyrion and Alarielle had been standing. He made a gesture using hand signals that could have meant anything but which Tyrion suspected meant 'they are close, be careful'. He looked around the clearing and seemed to pick up their tracks. Tyrion knew the game was up and that he could only hope that there were not too many other druchii nearby. Alarielle clearly recognised what was happening. She stood up with her bow aimed directly at the scout leader. All of them turned to face her.

'It seems we have found our prey,' the leader said. His voice was as cold as the winds of the North. He sounded like a true son of his harsh land.

'I will put an arrow through the first one of you who moves,' Alarielle said.

'Perhaps,' said the druchii. 'And then you will be pin-cushioned by the rest of us.'

'It will be better than the fate that awaits me at your hands.'

'Our king wishes you delivered to him unharmed.' The dark elf's tone was reasonable.

'That was the fate to which I was referring,' Alarielle said.

'Shoot one of us and the rest will shoot to wound you,' the leader said. Tyrion knew his words were aimed at his followers. He did not want them making any mistakes in this tricky situation. He was obviously a careful elf. He glanced around the clearing again, puzzled, and Tyrion knew that he was thinking about the second person who might be there.

He had no recourse but to act. He leapt from the bushes, driving Sunfang into the back of one of the scouts. He heard a scream from nearby and, turning, saw that Alarielle had put an arrow through the eye of the leader. The remaining pair of druchii were distracted for a moment, unsure who to shoot at, the sight of a warrior in their own armour bearing a blazing sword confusing them for a crucial second.

Tyrion covered the distance between him and the closest in three strides. The immediate threat made the druchii swing his crossbow towards Tyrion. Sunfang swept down and cleaved it in two. Tyrion dropped the dark elf with his second cut and turned in time to see the last scout's crossbow pointed directly at him. There was no way he could close fast enough to avoid being shot. The dark elf's finger squeezed the trigger. An arrow flashed through the air and took him in the side of the neck, sending him falling to one side, spoiling his aim. The crossbow bolt flashed past Tyrion's ear, so close that he felt the wind of its passing.

Tyrion sprang forwards and beheaded the scout before turning to face Alarielle. 'Thank you,' he said. 'You saved my life.'

She was not looking at him and she did not respond. Her face was very pale and Tyrion turned to see what she was looking at. In the shadows beneath the trees hundreds of druchii marched, an army on the move, and he did not doubt for a moment that it was seeking them.

Already crossbow bolts were starting to flash towards them. Fortunately the bushes, the shadows and the low branches interfered with their flight but it was only a matter of time before they got the range.

'Run!' shouted the Everqueen. She did not have to tell Tyrion twice. They sprinted away through the trees with what must have been the better part of a regiment of druchii in pursuit.

TYRION AND ALARIELLE sprinted through the woods. Now and then they could hear the sound of the druchii screaming. The enemy had caught sight of their prey and felt it within their grasp. The woods echoed with the shouts and war cries of the dark elves. Tyrion's heart pounded within his chest. Alarielle looked back at him over her shoulder. She could run like a gazelle when frightened, and she was frightened now.

Despair filled Tyrion's heart. He could not see how they were going to escape the jaws of the enormous trap that were snapping shut all around them. From all around now he could hear druchii voices. It seemed like an entire army filled the wood, stretched out in a vast crescent, like beaters driving pheasants before them on a hunt. Tyrion began to understand what it must feel like to be hunted in that way.

He stretched his legs and began to overtake Alarielle. He was already breathing hard, much more so than he ought to be for this amount of exercise. It seemed that the wound in his side was beginning to drain his strength, and he did not like that in the slightest. Just when he needed it most he was losing his fitness. He cursed the witch elf once again, hoping that her wicked soul rotted deep in hell.

A few crossbow bolts fell around him. They had come a great distance and lost much of their power. A bolt clattered off a tree in front of him. He could hear the whoosh of arrows behind him. He had heard the sound before on the field of battle but he had never known so many missiles to be directed at only two people. It seemed only a matter of time before one of them hit home and either he or the Everqueen was impaled. That would be the end of the chase.

He began to zigzag, moving from side to side to confuse the archers but he realised that this was not such a clever plan. The people chasing him would be able to run directly after him and thus gain ground. Alarielle was pushing on and with great woodcraft was simply weaving in and out of the trees, moving in a straight line as possible while gaining as much cover as she could. Tyrion decided to do the same.

He heard another terrifying sound now. It was one that he had heard before in the cold northern lands of Naggaroth. It was a high-pitched noise somewhere between a scream and a roar. He ran abreast of Alarielle.

He risked a glance backwards and saw some of the great lizards striding forwards through the massed ranks of the druchii troops. Cold ones were bipedal wingless dragons and they carried armoured knights upon their back. Their movements were oddly slow and bouncing but they covered the ground very swiftly with their enormous strides.

It was only a matter of minutes before the cold ones reached them, if that. He heard running water up ahead. Just from the sound of it he could tell it was a mighty river. It seemed as if they were trapped. Tyrion prepared to turn around and fight. Even a battle against hopeless odds seemed preferable to being captured.

'What are you doing, idiot?' Alarielle asked. 'That is the River Everflow. We have a chance to escape if we are swift.'

'They will shoot us while we try to swim across.'

'There is another way.'

'Lead on,' Tyrion said. 'I hope you know what you're doing.'